PRAISE FOR *ORBITAL DECAY* BY ALLEN STEELE

"READS LIKE GOLDEN AGE HEINLEIN!"
—Gregory Benford, author of *Tides of Light*

"A DAMNED GOOD BOOK; LIGHTNING ON THE HIGH FRONTIER. I got a sense throughout that this was how it would really be."
—Jack McDevitt, author of *A Talent for War*

"BRINGS THE THRILL BACK TO REALISTIC SPACE EXPLORATION. It reads like a mainstream novel written i...

...of Science Fiction*

"A... EL OF WORKING-
S...

"AN AMBITIOUS SCIENCE FICTION THRILLER . . . skillfully plotted and written with gusto!"
—*Publishers Weekly*

"DEFINITELY HUGO/NEBULA MATERIAL . . . A MASTERFUL BLEND . . . Adventure, suspense, humor, drama, tragedy, politics, and so on."
—*Texas SF Inquirer*

"AN IMPRESSIVE DEBUT . . . exciting . . . Steele is certainly an author to watch!"
—*Aboriginal SF*

"STEELE GIVES US A GUIDED TOUR OF TOMORROW—and the future suddenly looks human, and real."
—Roger MacBride Allen
author of *Orphan of Creation*

"READERS WON'T BE DISAPPOINTED. This is the kind of hard, gritty SF they haven't been getting enough of!"
—*Rave Reviews*

Ace Books by Allen Steele

ORBITAL DECAY
CLARKE COUNTY, SPACE

CLARKE COUNTY, SPACE

ALLEN STEELE

ACE BOOKS, NEW YORK

CLARKE COUNTY, SPACE

An Ace Book/published by arrangement with
the author

PRINTING HISTORY
Ace edition/December 1990

For Damaris, Genevieve, Rachel and Lilli—
a capricious quartet of siblings,
And for Arthur, Elvis, and Bobby Zimmerman—
an unholy quorum of influences

Acknowledgments

The author wishes to thank:

Gerard K. O'Neill, author of *The High Frontier*, which initiated the O'Neill space colony concept, and the Space Studies Institute, which has continued research of the concept; Stewart Brand, who promoted the idea in *Space Colonies*, which inspired this novel; T.A. Heppenheimer, who refined things further in *Colonies in Space* and *Toward Distant Suns;* and Richard Erdoes and Alfonso Ortiz, whose *American Indian Myths and Legends* suggested the character of Coyote (as freely extrapolated here). All these books were invaluable references and are recommended as further reading.

Further appreciation is due to Michael Warshaw, Steve Jones-D'Agostino, Koji Mukai, Doug Long, Bob Liddil, Terry Kepner, Frank and Joyce Jacobs, and Robert Mendel for various favors rendered. My wife, Linda, listened to my ideas, fetched beer and pizza, and refused to let me discard this book when I thought about writing something else. Many thanks, also, to Ginjer Buchanan, Susan Allison, and Martha Millard.

In particular, I wish to thank the residents of Lukachukai, Arizona, in the Navajo reservation. Among them, I am especially grateful to the Reverend Fred Harvey of the Native American Church, and his family. Ten years ago, long before this book was ever conceived, I spent several days as a house guest of the Harvey family and as a visitor to Lukachukai. My observations of the Navajo way of life went into a journal; I dug it out of a file cabinet and used it as a primary reference in the research of this work. I never heard from Fred again, but that experience has been pivotal to this work. Any mistakes that I may have made concerning the Navajo people and culture are my own; anything I got right was because Fred, his family, and friends were good hosts and teachers.

—Rindge, New Hampshire;
January, 1988 - April, 1989

". . . I see the main use of space colonies as religious. They should be built, not as industrial enterprise, but in the spirit of the old cathedrals, like Canterbury. We should take it all very slow and build in meaningful earth-stories and myths. Clearly space colonies have more to do with myth than science or industry. I want the connection between the Indian Coyote stories and the space colonies to be very direct and clean. I want the building of the colonies to encourage folk life and country music and old time religion, not discourage it. I want the colonies to have a lot of winos and ne'er-do-wells hanging around the computer consoles, singing and praying and spitting and telling lies. . . . In my head I'm against all this space stuff. But in my heart, if they're goin' to build 'em, I want to be on one. I want to go to heaven, by hook or crook. I'd feel a whole lot better about it, though, if that guy hadn't hit that golf ball on the moon. I sure do dread being locked up in outer space with ten thousand golfers."

—*Gurney Norman*

Two years later, I found myself sitting on a wooden bench on Canaveral Pier, just outside the little bar that's located at the end of the boardwalk. The bar has a name, but even after having lived in Cocoa Beach for more than twenty years, I can never recall it. I doubt, in fact, that any of the residents know what the bar is called. One local says to another, "I'll meet you at the bar on the pier," and both people know which bar it is. It's sort of like Clarke County. If someone mentions Clarke County, it is seldom asked where it's located.

Canaveral Pier, along with the nameless bar, had been rebuilt by the town in 2018, after the original pier had been destroyed by Hurricane Judy two years earlier. It was just as well that Judy obliterated the original pier, considering that it had been slowly crumbling into the ocean at the time, a victim of the relentless battering of the Atlantic surf and its own decrepitude. The hurricane only saved the local taxpayers the expense of having it razed anyway.

The new pier was stronger, its timber reinforced with concrete and lunar aluminum donated by Skycorp and shipped from the Moon, yet it was a near-exact duplicate of the original pier, with arcade booths and food kiosks lining the boardwalk. The town could have just as easily replaced the pier with an artificial island similar to Disney SeaWorld, farther up the coast in Daytona Beach, but the residents and the Brevard County Chamber of Commerce, in their wisdom, opted for a replacement pier instead. The new pier retained the old-style, no-tech flavor of the twentieth century: weathered, whitewashed wood planks that burned the soles of your feet in summertime; ice cream that melted into gooey rivulets running down your knuckles and tasted slightly like salt, games that relied on keen eyes and a good throwing arm rather than biocybe implants at the base of your skull.

One of the small pleasures of the nameless bar on the pier were the old coin-operated telescopes on the deck outside the bar. You used to see a lot of them in the last century, on the overlook above Niagara Falls or on the observation deck of the Empire State Building, but they're mostly gone now. The telescopes had crashed into the surf when Judy had totaled Canaveral Pier, but they had been salvaged from the wreckage and lovingly restored to the new pier. The telescopes—big round steel objects mounted on thick posts, a quarter for five minutes—were obsolete, of course. Even a cheap pair of fiber-optic binoculars had many times their magnification, and only one of the two telescopes worked at all.

But I loved the telescopes. They were reminders of the first time I had visited the bar, back in 1985 when I was a much younger man: in my twenties, a novice reporter for a midwestern newspaper, who had lucked into covering the launch of Space Shuttle Mission 51-D. That was the one in which a U.S. Senator, Jake Garn, had been sent up on a junket, doing little more than getting spacesick for the dubious benefit of science. A moment in history. The night before the launch a Canadian photojournalist and I had sat out on the deck, getting ripped on tequila and beer chasers, cracking awful jokes about Barfin' Jake while an endless string of Jimmy Buffett songs had rolled out of the jukebox inside.

Those were the good old days, the pioneer years of the Space Age. Back then, when you dropped a quarter into one of the telescopes, you could view the old Titan and Atlas gantries along the Eastern Test Range on Merritt Island, south of the larger shuttle launch facilities at the Kennedy Space Center—Pads 39A and 39B and the original Vehicle Assembly Building, looming like a monstrous white block above the flat marshland. Next to the VIP stands and the Press Mound in the KSC, the bar deck was the best place from which to watch launches. It still is, even though the press has long since relinquished the Mound to the tourists.

Reporters rarely turn up for the Cape launches any more and the tourists would rather go to Disneyland. Finally, space travel became routine. The Titan and Atlas gantries are ancient history, replaced by pads for Big Dummy HLVS and various one-shot satellite carriers and the rugged old Mark II shuttles that lift off each day. NASA is still the landlord, but it's the private companies—Skycorp, Galileo International, Uchu-Hiko Kabushiki-Gaisha, Cheap Thrills Inc.—which haul most of the freight and people to orbit.

They always said the day would come when seeing a space launch would be as exciting as observing trucks leaving from a loading dock, and eventually they were right. Now only the geriatric farts like me show up to watch when the rockets go. This is an impatient age. If medical science hadn't kept me alive this long, I would be tempted to say that progress sucks.

And so . . . well-preserved at the age of ninety-three, one of the last of the original spacehounds sat on a wooden bench in the meager warmth of the afternoon sun on an early spring day. Retired from chasing deadlines, I wrote an occasional, redundant history of spaceflight, or sometimes banged out a science-fiction novel for the hell of it. Mostly I relished old memories, sometimes flew up to the University of Missouri for alumni reunions and to deliver lectures to bored undergraduates at the journalism school. As a venerable veteran journalist and self-acknowledged geezer, I never expected to get another tip on a hot scoop in my life.

For my past sins, though, God gave me one. A phone call placed to me by a name without a face had brought me to the bar without a name, and now a stranger pushed open the glass slide-door and walked out onto the veranda. He stepped in front of me and asked if I was who he thought I was.

"If I'm not," I replied, "then I owe Social Security a lot of money." It was a favorite line, calculated to make young turks respectful of my seniority. He smiled benignly. This one seemed reverent enough, so I decided to give the cranky-senior-citizen bit a rest. "I take it you're Simon McCoy," I added, returning his smile.

"Yes, sir. Thanks for taking the time to see me." McCoy stepped forward, with hand extended. Half-rising from the bench to shake his hand, I took a closer look. Tall, slender, longish but well-groomed blond hair, wearing a white cotton sports coat, baggy plaid trousers and a blue bow tie, carrying a shapeless white Panama hat in his hand. Faint British accent, like an Englishman who'd immigrated to the States as a child. Athletic grace, which made me slightly envious: he could still climb a flight of stairs without effort, or turn a young woman's head.

He sat down on the bench next to me. One of the bar robots—a concession to modern times, albeit not as charming as a waitress—rolled out onto the deck. McCoy ordered a Coke and I asked for a Dos Equis. The hell with my doctor's admonition to stay away from alcohol; if you can't drink beer in retirement, then what good are your so-called golden years? After McCoy had slipped in his credit card with instructions to run a tab, the robot disappeared back through the sliding door. He gazed at the stumpy little machine as it exited. "If it still existed I would have asked you to meet me at Diamondback Jack's."

I shook my head. "Jack's hasn't been around for twenty years. It burned down in . . ."

Then I stopped. Diamondback Jack's had been a beer joint on Route 3 on Merritt Island, a dive for pro spacers which only the locals had known about. How could someone this young know Jack's? It was hardly the kind of place where someone would put up a historical marker. "How do you know about Diamondback Jack's?" I asked.

McCoy shrugged nonchalantly. "I'm something of a history buff. When I visit a place I like to snoop around. Find out some local history, that sort of thing." He waved his hand towards the distant launch pads up the coast. "I guess we'll have to settle for this."

"No loss," I replied. "If we sit here long enough we'll probably see a launch. The weather's good, and Uchu-Hiko usually sends up a cargo vessel on Wednesdays. It beats looking at pictures of dead men in a broken-down bar."

McCoy laughed, absently fondling his Panama hat in his hands. "I'm surprised. One would think, as long as you've been here, writing about space, you would be too jaded to watch rocket launches."

I was about to reply, when the robot rolled back out onto the deck, its tray loaded with our drinks. McCoy picked up his Coke and raised it to me. "To your health."

"Such as it is," I grumbled, tapping my bottle against his glass. Time to end the small talk. "When you called me you said you knew something which might interest me. Mr. McCoy, I hope you're not a writer and this isn't a ploy for an interview. I stopped giving 'last of the breed' interviews years ago."

He shook his head. "Nothing of the kind. Please, call me Simon."

"Okay then, Simon, what's on your mind?"

"I understand you're writing a new book," he said casually. "About the Clarke County incident a couple years ago. The Church of Elvis, Icarus Five, the evacuation and all that."

I was taking a sip when he said this. His words made me choke and sputter; beer sprayed over the knees of my trousers. "Goddammit!" I snarled.

"Oh! Terribly sorry." Instantly apologetic, he pulled a handkerchief out of his coat pocket and hurriedly began sopping at my pants. " I didn't mean to get that kind of . . ."

I knocked his hand away. "Who told you about my book?" I demanded.

It was a serious matter. If McCoy had said I was fooling around with someone else's wife, it was something I could have denied. If he had simply inquired about my new book, I would have told him that I was cranking out another SF potboiler. Neither inquiry would have upset me. But there were only a few people, supposedly, who knew that I was doing an investigative work about the events of 2049 in Clarke County. My editor and my agent knew better than to blab, and my wife was always sworn to secrecy. As for my sources . . . well, journalistic sources always have their own interests at heart, and the sources for this story were already treading on thin ice by aiding me in the first place. Nobody should have told a complete stranger what I was researching.

Unfortunately, McCoy had already caught me by surprise. There was no use in pleading the First and Fifth Amendments now. To his credit, he didn't look smug. "Never mind how I know," he said. "There's things you should know about the incident. That's why I called you."

I almost laughed. It sounded like the same shtick every working reporter experiences: the mysterious source who suddenly calls on the phone, claiming to know in whose closet the skeletons reside. Sometimes it's disgruntled employees or nosy neighbors with an axe to grind. There's rarely anything they know which can be verified. On occasion it's a wacko, like the woman who bugged me constantly when I worked the city beat on a paper in Massachusetts, with her claim that the mayor and the entire city council were involved in a prostitution ring. You learn to hang up when they start babbling about conspiracies, or at least before they start outlining their plans to run for President.

"I doubt there's anything you know that's new to me," I said. "But thanks for the beer."

To my surprise, McCoy didn't get annoyed. He sighed and gazed out at the ocean. "I was afraid it was going to be like this. You're supposed to have an arrogant streak."

"Who's being arrogant?" I said. "I'm being realistic."

He looked back at me. "I suppose you think I'm another nut case."

"Oh, no. Not at all."

"The fact of the matter is," he continued, "you know little more now about the incident than what you could have gleaned from news accounts of the time. Your book will be nothing more than a rehash of the standard story. No new facts. Not only that, but you'll be dead wrong on most of it."

"Uh-huh," I said. "And you know better, of course."

"Yes, I know better."

"And what's the source of your information?" I was willing to play along for a while. He had bought me a beer; it would have been rude to leave right away.

"I was in Clarke County at the time."

I nodded and shrugged. "So were about eight thousand other people. Most of them didn't know what was going on even when the colony was being evacuated. It's like saying you were in San Francisco when the quake hit. That doesn't make you a seismologist."

"That's true. Being there doesn't give me any special insights. Yet there's more than that."

I smiled politely. "I'm all ears."

He paused, looking down at the beach. There was a pretty little girl in a swimsuit on the edge of the surf, feeding scraps of bread to a cawing gang of sea gulls circling around her. She looked fascinated and frightened at the same time. "I hope she doesn't get pecked by one of those filthy birds," he commented. "If I told you how I know . . ."

McCoy hesitated again. "You've probably heard this line before, but . . . well, if I told you right away, you'd probably think I was crazy. So I don't want to tell you, at least not now."

I reluctantly took my eyes away from the child. At my age, it's difficult not to envy youth. "You're getting warm. You sound a little more reasonable than most insane people I've talked to, though. So give me one good reason why I shouldn't just get up and leave."

"Does getting the story straight for your book count?"

"Everyone uses that excuse. Especially the ones who are crazy. Try again."

He smiled. "All right, try this. You're a storyteller, when it comes right down to it. You like hearing a good tale, and you like telling one even better."

I had to grin. He had me there. "So far, so good. Keep going."

"So here's the deal," McCoy continued. "I'm going to tell you a long and rather detailed story, and all you have to do is listen. You can take notes and ask questions, and when I'm done, you can decide whether it makes sense for you to incorporate my story into your book."

McCoy hesitated again, then added, "If you'll hear me out until the end, I'll tell you how I know these things, although I doubt you'll believe me. So all I want from you is an afternoon of your time."

"When you're my age," I said, "an afternoon is a great thing to ask for."

"It'll be worth it."

I thought it over. I had already written off this afternoon. I hadn't been planning to return home before dark, and who knew? Perhaps McCoy was on the level, and even if he was a crank, maybe this would be fun. Indeed, in my news-room years, I had sometimes amused myself by listening to crank calls from the UFO abductees and conspiracy mavens. "I suppose, of course, that you want to be mentioned in my book as a source."

McCoy didn't bite. He shook his head. "Not at all. In fact, I insist that I *not* be mentioned. My aim isn't cheap fame. I only want to make sure you get the story straight."

He paused, then added, "For the sake of future generations."

"Future generations," I repeated. "That sounds rather grandiose, don't you think?"

McCoy didn't reply. "Okay," I said. "If you'll buy me another beer, I'll listen. Tell me a story."

"Well, then . . ." Simon McCoy leaned back against the bench and stretched out his legs, balancing his Coke on his stomach. "Once upon a time there was a very frightened young woman named Macy . . ."

1

Departure
(Wednesday: 11:15 P.M.)

She had anticipated that the main passenger terminal would be crowded, and she was correct. The long Memorial Day weekend was approaching, and despite the late hour people were scurrying along the concourses and walkways of the vast airport, on their way to catch flights to all the usual vacation spots: Bermuda, Hong Kong, San Francisco, Sydney, St. Thomas, New York, Ho Chi Minh City. A group of little Japanese kids crowded against a railing, staring at a replica of *The Spirit of St. Louis* suspended from the ceiling, while beneath the antique airplane the holographic ghost of Charles Lindbergh, dressed in flying leathers and jodhpurs, delivered a prerecorded lecture on his flight.

Today, thanks to suborbital travel, you can fly to Paris in less than an hour, the young pilot commented as a baggage autocart rolled heedlessly through his body, *but in 1927 my solo flight took almost thirty-four hours and was considered the most dangerous flight yet. . . .* Yeah, Chuck, Macy thought as she turned away. Tell me about dangerous flights.

At least the vast numbers of men, women, and children swarming around would make it hard for her to be spotted, if indeed she was being followed. Even if one of Tony's goons found her here, a quiet abduction would be difficult. If someone grabbed her, Macy could scream rape, draw attention to herself, perhaps spook whoever it was into retreating. Above all else, Tony always wanted family business to be done quietly.

She hurried down the concourse towards Gate 27, passing through the security smartgate, which automatically scanned her face, verified her identity and the presence of the passenger tag on her ticket, and probed her body and the contents of her nylon shoulder bag, Macy's single piece of luggage. She glanced at a status screen as she walked by: 11:17 P.M. Tony was supposed to have picked her up at the compound at ten o'clock when he came back from "business." Even if he was his usual tardy self, she had little doubt that her absence from the Salvatore mansion was already known.

At this minute they would be searching for her. Macy had done her best to cover her trail, prepurchasing her ticket on the Amex card bearing her Mary Boston pseudonym, and bribing the cab driver who had picked her up in Ladue to forget her face. Yet she knew that Tony would quickly run through all the possibilities; undoubtedly, someone would already be on the way to Lambert Field, to see if Tony's woman was trying to catch a plane. Maybe that someone was getting out of a car even now, out on the sidewalk in front of the terminal, striding in through the automatic doors she herself had passed only fifteen minutes ago. . . .

Cut it out, she told herself. *Don't panic now. Just get on the shuttle down to Texas and you're home-free. You'll be out of St. Louis. Then in another couple of hours you'll be on Matagorda Island, and an hour after that, you'll be off the planet. . . .*

She harbored no illusions that putting 200,000 miles of outer space between her and St. Louis would be enough to keep her from Tony Salvatore and his goon squad. It would stall him, but not stop him. Yet all she needed was time and a little distance. Then she could get revenge, erase Tony from her life once and for all. The contents of her shoulder bag would see to that, once she delivered it into the right hands. So she hoped.

She found Gate 27, the United Airlines flight to Dallas-Fort Worth. The waiting area was crowded, but while there were still a few seats vacant, she did not sit down. She had to keep her face hidden a few minutes longer. Instead, Macy turned her back to the concourse and faced the wall, fixing her eyes on an ad screen.

By coincidence, it was displaying an animated holo of Clarke County. It rotated gracefully in space, the gentle silver-gray orb of the Moon gliding past in the background as the TexSpace logo shimmered into existence in front of the colony. Macy stared at it, and smiled for the first time since she had climbed over the wall surrounding Tony's mansion. Three days and she would be there.

The screen went blank, and in the moment before a chorus

line of Las Vegas showgirls began goose-stepping across the screen, she glimpsed in the black panel a reflection of the scene behind her. About twenty feet away, standing next to the gate entrance, was a man in a suit, perfectly ordinary—except for the fact that he was watching her. Not with the eyes of a casual stranger sizing up a beautiful woman who happened to be by herself, but with the gaze of a person who was discreetly keeping track of her movements.

A chill electric wave coursed from the nape of her neck to the bottom of her spine. Macy slowly turned away from the screen, forcing herself to stare out the windows overlooking the apron where the airliner nuzzled against the passenger walkway. In the reflection of the window she could see herself, and further away, the man in the suit was still watching.

She began to turn in his direction, and a fat man with a bawling kid in tow lurched into her. He stopped and excused himself before pushing past, and the kid trampled across the toes of her boots. When they were gone and she dared to look back again, the man in the suit had disappeared.

Macy Westmoreland would have panicked at that moment—absolutely flipped, lost her cool, bolted for the ladies' room or the nearest security guard or even, God forbid, to a phone to call Tony to say that she was sorry, she was coming home now, please don't have anyone kill her, or whatever opportunity came first—when the gate agent picked up her mike and announced that United Airlines Flight 724 nonstop from St. Louis to Dallas-Fort Worth was ready for boarding. Even before the agent had done the bit about carry-on bags and persons needing assistance, Macy was pushing her way towards the ramp.

FBI Special Agent Milo Suzuki watched as the woman shoved and squirmed her way to the front of the mob of passengers, almost falling over an old man in a wheelchair as she thrust her ticket into the hand of the ticket agent. He could hear the protests of the other passengers and caught the sour look on the agent's face. There was a brief exchange between the agent and the woman, then the agent reluctantly ran her optical scanner over the ticket and allowed the woman to be the first person aboard the aircraft.

Suzuki shook his head. "And away she goes," he whispered to himself. When it came to shaking off a tail, the woman was an utter amateur.

He walked away from the gate to the nearest phone booth, in

an alcove just off the concourse. Shutting himself inside and picking up the receiver, he pulled out his datapad and, after connecting the interface to the phone, dialed the number to the St. Louis field office's computer. Once he was logged in, he typed on the pad's miniature keyboard: WESTMORELAND, MACY— CROSS-REF. SALVATORE.

Within a few moments, the computer downloaded the file into Suzuki's datapad. A head-and-shoulders photo of the woman who had just boarded the airliner appeared on the screen. There was more information, of course, but this was all that Suzuki needed to confirm that it was, indeed, Tony Salvatore's mistress who had boarded a jet to Texas.

He opened a window on the screen and dialed into United Airlines' passenger reservations computer. At first, the AI system would not permit him access to the passenger list, until Suzuki typed in his federal authorization code—in effect, showing the computer his badge. Once in, he typed in Macy's name again. No record of Macy Westmoreland was entered in the United Airlines passenger manifest. Suzuki pursed his lips, then studied Westmoreland's dossier again. Bingo: she had a couple of aliases, chief among them ''Mary Boston.''

REQ. ITIN. 5/29/49: BOSTON, MARY, he typed. This name the computer recognized; it immediately printed out Mary Boston's travel itinerary, gathered from the flight reservations she had made through the airline. Milo studied the schedule, tracing it with his forefinger, frowned and then smiled.

How interesting. Macy Westmoreland had used her ''Mary Boston'' Amex card to purchase bookings all the way to Clarke County. United 724 would get her to Dallas-Fort Worth, where she would catch the special TexSpace commuter helicopter to the Matagorda Island Spaceport. From there, she was scheduled to catch the TexSpace SSTO *Lone Star Clipper* to Clarke County, traveling in First Class. In fact, she already had a room reserved at the LaGrange Hotel in the colony.

''So why are you running away from Tony, babe?'' Milo Suzuki muttered to himself. He saved the information he had gathered within the datapad's memory bubble, then logged off and disconnected the pad from the phone. Well, it didn't matter to him. He had followed Macy from the Salvatore compound, where he had seen her climb over the wall from his stakeout point up the street, and now he knew where she was going. All he had to do was contact the Dallas field office and have her picked up when United 724 landed there. There had to be some usefulness in the fact that Tony Salvatore's bimbo was apparently going AWOL.

He had just tucked the datapad into his pocket and had pulled his phonecard out of his wallet, when the door to the phone booth suddenly slid open and a man shoved himself into the booth. Milo Suzuki had just enough time to clumsily bring up his hands and open his mouth before the squat barrel of an over-sized pistol was pressed into his sternum.

Suzuki looked up into the impassive face of the intruder. "Golem . . ." he said.

Without a word, the intruder slapped the gun's barrel into the palm of Suzuki's upraised right hand and squeezed the trigger. There was a soft *whufff!* as a tiny sliver was fired into the FBI agent's hand.

"Yow!" Suzuki jerked back from the sudden sting. It was the last thing he ever said.

Two cc's of sea wasp venom—the secretion of a jellyfish found only in the Indian Ocean off the Australian coast, the rarest and most lethal natural poison known to man—was already coursing through his bloodstream. Within seconds it entered his heart. Suzuki's eyes widened as his heart began to beat wildly out of control. Gasping, he clutched at his chest and sagged against the back wall of the phone booth until, half a minute after the dart had been fired into his hand, he collapsed and died.

The intruder caught Suzuki with his gloved hands and carefully settled his corpse onto the booth's seat. He looked over his shoulder to make sure he had not been seen, then he quickly and artfully positioned the dead man's arms, legs, and head so that it appeared as if Suzuki was just another exhausted commuter catching a few quick winks in a phone booth. When the FBI agent's body was eventually discovered and examined, it would seem as if Suzuki had suffered a fatal cardiac arrest. The dart itself would dissolve within ten minutes; only a thorough autopsy would reveal the tiny puncture mark in his right hand.

The Golem pocketed his hospital-issue sedative gun; made of plastics and protected with a computer-fouling stealth chip in its handle, it had passed through the smartgate without raising any alarms. He then reached into Suzuki's coat pocket and retrieved the agent's datapad. He tucked it into the inside pocket of his own jacket, and stripped off his gloves and carefully backed out of the phone booth.

He shut the door of the booth, then strolled down the concourse without looking back. The United Airlines jet was taxiing away from Gate 27 as the killer reached the main terminal; by the time Suzuki's body was discovered by someone impatient to use the phone, the Golem would be long gone from St. Louis International Airport.

The Golem knew that Macy Westmoreland was aboard the plane, unreachable by him. But the G-man had found something and put it into his datapad; that information would make it easy for the organization to track down the boss's girl. She'd got a small headstart, but nothing more.

The Golem was a soldier who only carried out orders. This time, though, he hoped he was the one who got tapped for the inevitable wet job.

He had to admit it to himself. He enjoyed his line of work.

2

The Coyote Dream
(Friday: 6:59 P.M.)

In an elliptical orbit that varies between 100,000 and 200,000 miles from Earth, Clarke County glides through the darkness of cislunar space like an enormous, elaborate child's top. From a distance, it's nearly impossible to appreciate the size of the artificial world, for there is nothing else nearby to which one can compare it. Closer, though, with tiny OTVs and zero g ''freeflier'' factories parked in orbit around it, the vastness of the space colony becomes overwhelmingly apparent. With an overall length of 5,250 feet—just shy of a statute mile—and the broadest width, the circumference of its bowl-like central primary mirror, of 2,937 feet, the colony is dwarfed only by the solar power satellites in geosynchronous orbits closer to Earth.

Even so, Space Colony LH-101US is more staggering than the thirteen-mile-long SPS satellites. The powersats, after all, are unmanned solar collectors, while the first true space colony is home to thousands of people. Essentially a Bernal sphere, surrounded at each end by torus clusters arrayed along axial shafts, solar vanes and giant mirrors, Clarke County is the largest space station ever successfully built. The Great Pyramids of Egypt could be constructed within the biosphere, and the largest skyscrapers on Earth would all be diminished in stature if Clarke County were to be brought home.

Yet engineering feats are one matter and the human condition is quite another. People have lived together in communities for thousands of years, but no one has yet built a successful Utopia. You can transform sterile, cold lunar rock into air and water, living soil and comfortable houses, a new sky and a new home, but you can't so easily change human beings. In every town there are as many stories as there are the people who make up the community: some good, some bad, some absurd, and some that are best left untold.

Technology changes, and each age develops its own miracles. People, however, are as noble, ornery, vile, and downright weird as they always were.

Same as it ever was . . .

John Bigthorn sat on the front steps of the Big Sky town hall and waited for the sun to go down. It was the end of his duty shift; he had left one of his deputies, Lou Bellevedere, in charge of the cop shop, with a warning not to try to call him with any problems, because he was taking off his beltphone. It was dinner time and the town square was nearly vacant. Across the square, Ginny DeMille was closing the doors of Ginny's Café. She spotted the sheriff through the window of her little restaurant and waved to him, and Bigthorn was waving back when the alarm on his watch beeped.

Bigthorn mentally counted back from five, and at the exact instant his countdown reached zero, night fell on Clarke County. As the colony's halo orbit brought it once again behind Earth's shadow, a wave of darkness started on the eastern hemisphere of the biosphere, above his head, and quickly raced down the walls of the world as a solid terminator line. As nightfall moved across the habitat, it left behind sparks and ovals of light as photosensitive timers switched on house and street lights. Finally the terminator line reached Big Sky, and as it raced across the square the street lamps turned on as the bell in the meeting hall steeple chimed seven times. From the far-off livestock sector in the Southwest quad, on the opposite side of the biosphere, he could dimly hear the roosters crowing. Directly above his head, from the promenade outside the LaGrange Hotel, the *touristas* attending the daily Sundown Cocktail cheered and clapped their hands. In space, there's no such thing as a tequila sunset. Without a twilight time, night had come to Clarke County.

Bigthorn rose from the steps, pulled his dayback over his left shoulder, and began walking out of Settler's Square, passing a statue cast from a solid hunk of lunar aluminum. "The Final Shift," the statue was named: an exhausted-looking beamjack in space armor, helmet dangling from his right hand, staring upwards in perpetual awe at the artificial sky of the world he had helped build. A plaque at the base of the statue was etched with the names of the forty-seven men and women who had died—so far—during the construction of the colony. Every few weeks the sun rose to find that someone had climbed up on the statue during the night to place a pair of sunglasses on its face, crazily changing the Lost Beamjack's lonesome courage into blissed-out goshwow.

As Bigthorn left the square behind and walked down Western Avenue to cross the Heinlein Bridge above the New Tennessee River, a New Ark member driving a fertilizer cart stopped to offer him a lift. Bigthorn climbed into the passenger seat and the electric cart whirred the rest of the way off the bridge, down the sand-paved road into the relative darkness of the South hemisphere. Here, the only illumination came from the ankle-high lights lining the road. About halfway to South Station, where the farmer was destined to park his cart for the night at the agricultural center, Bigthorn got the longhaired man to let him off on the side of the road. The New Ark farmer didn't ask questions as he braked the cart, only wished him a good evening. People knew about Bigthorn's occasional retreats to his hogan on Rindge Hill.

The hill was a hill in name only—little more than an ornamental mound that rose a couple of hundred feet above the serried rows of double-planted corn and potatoes, covered with a small glade of maple and elm trees. Once he had carefully made his way through the croplands, Bigthorn climbed the hill in the darkness, disdaining the use of the flashlight hooked to his uniform belt, until he reached the hogan.

It was a low, six-sided cabin with a single door through which he had to bend almost double to enter. There was a round hole in the ceiling and no windows; its design was identical to the traditional Navajo hogan. It differed only in that it was not built of logs. Cut timber was too costly to be shipped from Earth, and the biosphere's transplanted trees were too few and too valuable to be used as lumberstock. Instead, like almost every other house-sized building in the colony, the hogan was built of bamboo.

It had taken a lot of quibbling with the County Zoning Board to get them to allow the sheriff to build his hogan in the farm section. The three-member board, for a while, insisted that he place it in the postage-stamp backyard behind his house in Big Sky, or in Challenger Green, the small public park in LaGrange. The problem with both sites, which the board myopically couldn't see, was that they afforded little privacy. Especially Challenger Green, where he would have been pestered and photographed by tourists. Bigthorn had no desire to make a weekly appearance as a sideshow attraction. Come see Chief Runnamuck perform his sacred peyote ceremony; free admission, no camera-flashes allowed, postcards available at the souvenir stand.

Fortunately the New Ark, which was in charge of the colony's agricultural project, recognized that as a Native American he needed a place for spiritual retreat. They had taken his side against the Board, and finally a compromise was reached: Bigthorn was given a small plot of land on Rindge Hill, on the condition that it not be permanently inhabited.

Thus the hogan was completely bare except for a small firepit in the middle of the packed-earth floor, a little pile of cedar twigs in the corner, and the fire extinguisher which was kept there in compliance with the usual safety codes. Bigthorn closed the door, gathered some of the twigs and racked them together in the pit, lighted them with a match, then unzipped his dayback. After unrolling a small wool blanket next to the pit, he began to undress in the flickering light of the fire.

John Bigthorn was impressive when fully dressed. Naked, he was almost breathtaking, six and a half feet of solid muscle under dark red skin, an apparition of the fierce nomadic raiders who had been the forerunners of the agrarian Navajo nation. No one was there to admire him, and if there had been any visitors, he would have used his authority to shoo them away. A Navajo sweat-bath is not meant to be seen by Anglo eyes.

However, his hogan was sometimes used for purposes other than his sweats. Teen-agers, for instance, occasionally appropriated the hut for their own rites of passage; more than once he had found empty wine bottles and used condoms on the floor. He didn't really mind, since a hogan is only a windowless shack when not being used by one of the *Dineh*, the People. No used rubbers were on the floor this time, so either Big Sky's kids were getting less adventurous or they were once again sowing their wild oats down on the Strip. Bigthorn made a mental note to pay a visit to the Chateau L'Amour. If the whorehouse was admitting underage tricks again, he'd have to suspend Bonnie's brothel license. . . .

Bigthorn shut his eyes and settled cross-legged on the blanket. Time to stop thinking like a cop. He breathed in the fragrance of the cedar smoke, felt the rising heat begin to open his pores, heard the fire gently snapping in front of him. He sat with his back stiffly erect for a long time, long trails of cool sweat oozing off his face and chest. He let his mind empty and his body relax, and after a while he decided that he was ready to dream.

Out of the pack came a leather flask of water and a sealed plastic bag. He took a sip from the water, then unsealed the bag. Inside was a small, pale yellow peyote button, broken off the stem this morning from the potted rows of peyote cacti he secretly cultivated in his house.

The first time he had taken peyote he had been eighteen years old and living in Lukachukai, his hometown on the reservation. On his eighteenth birthday his grandfather had escorted him to the lodge in the rocky hills above his hometown, where elders of the town's Native American Church had gathered that night to celebrate his passage into manhood. Such is the difference between the Dineh and the Anglos. The white man makes his rite of passage by screwing a cheerleader in the parking lot, the red man by eating peyote and walking tall with the spirits.

"This isn't meant for gringo hippies," Grandfather Abe had told him inside the lodge, pressing the fleshy button into his hand. "The Great Spirit gave the peyote to the Dineh so that they could have the means to walk with him before they died, to see beyond this world. It's not dope to be taken for kicks, Johnny. It is a holy sacrament, just as the white man drinks wine and eats bread in his church. The only good thing that bastard, Richard Nixon, ever did was to make peyote legal for us so the DEA wouldn't bust our heads."

"Who's Richard Nixon?" he had asked.

"Shut up and eat your peyote," Grandfather Abe had replied.

Fifteen years later, John Bigthorn took another peyote button and crammed it into his mouth, chewing thoughtfully on its foul-tasting tenderness. He swallowed the pulp and washed it down with another swig of water. Then he sat and stared into the low flames, letting the sweat drip off his forehead into the fire.

He had fasted all day in preparation for his sweat, but as usual the peyote made him sick. Nauseous, he managed to crawl out of the hogan before puking next to a tree. It was cold outside the hogan, so he crawled on hands and knees back into the hut, forgetting to close the door behind him. He was weak now. A dim electric current buzzed behind his eyeballs. Guts cramped, unable to sit upright, he sprawled on the blanket and stared up at the ceiling, watching the smoke from the fire as it drifted up through the chimney hole, wafting out into the darkness.

Presently, he rose with the smoke and soared upwards, through the hole, out of the hogan, into the fishbowl world of Clarke

County. Rising on a thin thermal like an eagle, his eyes swept over the dark centrifugal countryside. Below him, beyond the dark curving band of the river, lay the lighted streets and houses of Big Sky, spread out like a neon sand painting.

He continued to rise, nearing the axial center of the biosphere, passing the taut cables of the Gold Line axis tram, and his eyes followed the New Tennessee River as it traveled upwards along the equator to the East hemisphere above his head. Up there—now below him—lay the brighter lights of LaGrange, where rich *touristas* like the ones who used to bargain with Grandmother Sally for her blankets and silverwork prowled the overpriced shops surrounding O'Neill Square or sipped expensive drinks on the hotel promenade.

Now he was in the center of the world. Physical laws dictated that he should have remained there, suspended in gravitational equilibrium, but he was no longer part of the physical plane. Instead, he passed through the axis and continued to soar towards LaGrange, his arms and legs outstretched. He could see, under the street lights, tiny figures walking, riding bicycles, sitting on their porches. He wondered why those who happened to look up could not see him, a naked Indian flying through the sky. The thought was hysterically funny and he laughed aloud. His laughter echoed around the world, unheard as much as he was unseen. *I fly, I am invisible. Get as drunk as you can, wealthy white people, but you'll still never be able to do this. . . .*

Then he felt his attention being drawn, almost involuntarily, away from LaGrange towards the farm zones in the South hemisphere. His flight was taking him away from people into the dark emptiness above the livestock area. Looking down, he saw movement on Eastern Avenue in the Southwest quad. An animal was on the road, visible in the lights, and he wondered if one of the goats or pigs had managed once again to escape from the grazing lands. As he swept closer, quickly descending, he realized that the animal was neither a pig nor a goat.

It was Coyote.

Coyote sat on his haunches and waited until Bigthorn dropped lightly to his feet on the road a few yards away. *You're the guy who keeps the law, right?* Coyote asked.

''Yes, I am,'' Bigthorn replied.

Hmm. White man's law. Coyote absently scratched behind his ear with his right hind leg. *Can't even keep the fleas out of this place. Well, listen, there's danger on its way here. You'd better come with me. I need to show you what's going on before it's too late.*

Coyote stood up and began to walk away, heading south up the road. Bigthorn hesitated. Coyote was the great trickster. One could never trust him completely. He had managed to deceive the frog people out of their water, after all, and he had seduced Spider Man's wife. But Coyote seldom lied outright, or at least not to one of the Dineh. If he said there was some sort of danger, there was probably a grain of truth in his words.

Bigthorn followed Coyote until they reached South Window, the broad band of thick lunar-glass panes that stretched entirely around the southern half of the biosphere. They stepped over the rail and walked together out onto the window—in the back of his mind Bigthorn knew that Henrietta's Heroes, the window-cleaning crew, would be pissed off when they found his footprints on the glass—until Coyote stopped.

Okay, Coyote said, *look down there.*

He looked down. Through the window, reflected in the polish of the South secondary mirror, the stars wheeled past, planets and constellations and distant galaxies moving in parade as Clarke County rotated on its axis. Coyote sat back a few feet, watching him expectantly.

It was beautiful, but it was nothing Bigthorn hadn't seen before. "What am I supposed to be looking for?" he asked.

Numb nuts, Coyote replied. *Give 'em eyes, tell 'em there's a big problem, show 'em where it's at, and they're still too stupid to see for themselves.* Remarkably, Coyote spoke with the voice of Bigthorn's grandfather. He raised a paw and jabbed it at the window. *Look for a star that's moving differently from the others, you stupid turd.*

Bigthorn peered carefully at the turning starscape. Yes, there *was* a star moving on a different track from the rest. It gained brilliance as it grew closer, began to evolve in a more angular shape. He realized that it was an approaching spacecraft.

"I see a ship," Bigthorn said. "Is the danger aboard the ship? Which one is it?"

Coyote smiled a canine smile, the grin of a god. *Watch carefully, keeper of the gringo law.*

Bigthorn looked back at the ship. Suddenly, it exploded, transforming itself into a white sphere of nuclear energy that pulsed outwards with terrifying speed and force. He heard Coyote laugh—his grandfather's laugh—and when he looked up, Coyote had vanished. The darkness of night was swept away in the sudden, horrible glare.

Bigthorn only had time to realize that Coyote had tricked him, too, before the shockwave ripped through the window, glass exploding around him, slicing through him, in the first moment of the destruction of Clarke County. . . .

He was out cold for a long time.

When he awakened, Bigthorn found himself curled against the wall on the floor of his hogan. Every joint in his body ached. His mouth was cotton-dry and he was hungry. Sunlight streamed in through the smokehole and the open door. The fire in the pit had long since burned out, leaving a small, cold heap of ashes. And he was no longer by himself.

Jenny Schorr was sitting on her knees a few feet away, smiling. As he twisted around on his back, painfully, she held out his clothes to him; she had folded them neatly. Her eyes drifted down his body, hovering for a moment over his crotch, and she let out a low, coy whistle.

"Hoy hoy," she dryly commented. "Injun brave have heap good body."

"Thanks. Go to hell." Bigthorn closed his eyes for a second, then took the clothes and, sitting up, placed them in his lap. His head felt as if someone had hammered a rail spike through his skull. "What time is it?" he rasped through his dry throat.

"Nine o'clock . . . Saturday morning," she said.

"Oh, great." He lay his head against the wall. He should have been on duty an hour ago. "Did Wade send you out here?"

"He was worried, but he didn't know where to find you." Jenny's smile grew wider. "I had stopped by to : . . never mind, but he checked the message board when your home phone didn't answer. Blind Boy Grunt knew where you were."

Bigthorn squinted at her. "He did?"

She shrugged. "No kidding. Right there on the screen." He stared at her and she continued. " 'Bigthorn—Rindge Hill. Howling with the coyotes.' That was it. So I came up here to check it out, and looky what I found." She nodded her head. "For this kind of show, I'm glad I did."

"Whoopee." Bigthorn bent forward and snagged the leather flask he had brought with him, unstoppered the cork and took a long, soothing drink. Looking back at Jenny, he saw that she was still admiring his body. "C'mon, what's the matter? Never seen a naked man before?"

"None like this."

"*Gnngh.*" He was embarrassed. "If and when I find out who Blind Boy Grunt is, I'm going to twist his goddamn neck."

Jenny nodded her head. She was still transfixed by his groin, and it was making him distinctly uncomfortable. "You know," he said, "a Navajo hogan is a sacred place during a sweat."

"Really now?" A wicked smile spread across her face. "If you want sweat, I'll be happy to oblige."

He frowned, not catching her drift. "Hmm? I don't understand."

"Let me try to be a little more clear, then." She shook back her long blond hair and began to unbutton her white cotton blouse. "Maybe if I take off my clothes and lie on top of you," she said softly, "we could work up a little more sweat, hey?"

Bigthorn stared at her speechlessly as she removed her shirt, untucking it from her jeans. Her breasts were lovely. He would have loved to touch them. In the back of his mind, he had always wondered what Jenny Schorr looked like in the nude. Yet now that he was about to find out, he didn't want to know.

"Only if your husband says it's okay," he murmured.

"Neil?" Jenny shrugged. "Oz the great and powerful lost interest in this sort of thing a long time ago." She lay her shirt aside and reached for the top button of her jeans. "Saving the world takes a lot out of a man, y'know."

The sheriff forced himself to look away. Like it or not, he was beginning to get hard. The temptation was there . . . but he couldn't bring himself to follow his urges. "Please, Jenny . . . please stop."

She stopped. The seductive smile escaped from her face. "Is it because of Neil?" she whispered.

"Not necessarily," he replied. "It's just . . . well, on principle, I don't go around fucking married women. Don't take it personally."

She raised her eyebrows. "Considering the circumstances, what other way am I supposed to take it?"

"Well, you can put your clothes back on, for starters." He tried not to stare at her. He didn't even want to consider how long it had been since the last time he had gotten his ashes hauled, or the fact that Jenny was exactly the kind of woman who could make him want to die and go to heaven. Hell, man, who's going to know . . . ?

No one except you, bub. Bigthorn looked away again. "Sorry, but it ain't me, babe. Please . . ."

Jenny stopped unbuttoning her jeans. She looked at him sulkily, then picked up her shirt and began to dress. She even turned her back as he began to pull on his own clothes. For a couple of minutes neither of them said anything, until finally Bigthorn cleared his throat to break the nervous silence.

"I better get down to the cop shop," he said as he zipped up his trousers and reached for his uniform shirt. "Don't want anyone to get the idea that I've gone off on a bender."

Jenny didn't smile or meet his eyes. "No, you don't," she said neutrally as she buttoned her shirt. "Of course everyone knows you don't drink." She cast a glance at him over her shoulder. "Come to think of it, have you ever gotten drunk?"

"Yeah, but I didn't enjoy the experience." Suddenly, Bigthorn recalled his vision from the night before, what Coyote had told him. "By the way," he added, "you haven't seen the inbound flight schedule, have you?"

"Uh-huh. The *Lone Star Clipper*'s due in at eleven hundred." Jenny stood up and shoved her shirttails back into her pants. "Why do you ask?"

"Hmm . . . no particular reason."

"Right. Well . . ." She quickly slapped the dust off her knees. "Time to go be Neil Schorr's wife again." Jenny turned and bent over to pass through the low door, but then she stopped. "John . . . ?"

"Yeah?"

"What happened here . . . that's strictly between you and me, isn't it?" She glanced down at the cold fire-pit. "Believe me when I tell you that I still love him. You have to know that. But I have my needs, and he isn't doing anything about that." She hesitated. "Maybe being horny doesn't count compared to feeding a million starving children in Africa but . . . sometimes you start to think about doing stuff that you normally . . ."

Bigthorn held up his hand. "I understand, Jenny. Don't sweat it. It's just between you and me."

Jenny closed her eyes and nodded gratefully. Then she smiled again. "But if you should ever change your mind . . ."

Without waiting for an answer, she swept forward and planted a soft, wet kiss on his mouth. Then, with a parting wink, she ducked through the door of the hogan, leaving Bigthorn half-dressed on the floor. He could hear her whistling an old Beatles tune as she walked down the hillside.

"Great," he murmured to himself. "What a wonderful development."

3

Her Declaration of Independence
(Saturday: 9:23 A.M.)

Jenny Schorr walked down the hillside path from the sheriff's hogan, stepping over the irrigation canals that crisscrossed the agricultural zone, absently looking for the rare weeds that invaded the croplands. As she brushed through the early summer corn, Jenny found herself wondering if she was living at the end of a broken-down hippie dream.

Married ten years, reasonably happy with her marriage, and still she was throwing herself at the first naked man she saw. Jenny considered herself to be monogamous. If asked, she would have said that she was a faithful wife. So what was she doing, making an overt pass at someone who was little more than a cordial friend?

God, what got into me? The thought kept repeating itself like a mantra as Jenny hiked back towards Western Avenue, where she had left her tricycle. *Okay, so it's been months since Neil has paid any attention to me. But I can't be that horny that I'd start strip-teasing for the first naked man I run into. . . .*

Even if he is hung like a stallion, she thought. *Cut it, Jenny!*

She must have made a fool out of herself. Worse, she probably gave John the impression that she was some sort of slut. Jenny's face reddened at the thought. In a decade of marriage she never slept with anyone except Neil. She had always stood fast by her wedding vows.

On the other hand, she didn't believe that Neil had been entirely faithful to her. As the founder and spiritual leader of the New Ark, Neil always had women around who seemed ready and eager to ball their avatar. Jenny had seen plenty of lovely young ladies throw themselves on their guru—the ''Mary Magdalene complex'' some pop psychologist had termed it—and Jenny had not always been around to fend them off.

Nor had Neil always seemed morally compelled to hold them at arm's length. There was the time when she had gone for six weeks to Guatemala to oversee an earthquake rescue project, while Neil had stayed behind to supervise the spring planting at the Ark. When she had come home, Kate Watanabe was gone from the commune. She was pregnant when she left, and there were idle rumors that she had been sleeping with Neil. Neil, when confronted, had denied everything, but not long afterwards he began to lose interest in sex altogether.

Okay, maybe Neil's slept around. That doesn't excuse your own conduct, Jenny reminded herself. Worse than betraying Neil, it could wreck the Ark itself, or a least derail the High Grange Project.

She and Neil were the spiritual leaders of the New Ark Community; she had to keep that foremost in her mind. They had asked over 2,000 people, out of the Ark's 8,000 members worldwide, to relocate to a space colony thousands of miles away from everything familiar to them. Most had come from the Ark's original communal farm in Ashby, Massachusetts; they had sold the property itself, the former site of Fort Devens, in order to raise the money to bring everyone to Clarke County. Others who were not members of the Ashby farm had given up their homes. There was even one couple who had been forced to put their four-month-old child up for adoption, when doctors told them the infant's health would be endangered by the launch and flight.

So much had been sacrificed and risked, she remembered, all for the chance to prove that space could be settled by a spiritual community. It had taken years of negotiation between the Clarke County Corporation and the New Ark before the consortium's leaders were persuaded to turn over the space-ag industry to the Ark, to support the High Grange Project as a non-profit business. Too many people were depending upon their leadership for either one of them to get involved in a tawdry little affair.

Okay, Neil's gotten himself into a messiah complex, she thought. *He wants to feed the world from Clarke County. Fine and dandy. If he's the messiah of the poor and the downtrodden, then you're Mrs. Messiah. You don't have the liberty to be a normal woman with a normal sexual appetite.*

Right. But that doesn't mean I'm not goddamned sick of it. . . .

As she reached the edge of the field and stepped onto the road, the telephone on her belt chirped. Jenny unsnapped the phone and held it to her face. "Hi, this is Jenny," she said.

It's Neil, her husband's voice said, as if she couldn't recognize him. Perhaps this was another sign of their growing apart. *Where are you?*

"Ummm . . . Southwest quad, checking the irrigation canals. We have the weekly Ark meeting coming up, don't we?"

It's been postponed. We'll probably cover the items scheduled at the town meeting on Sunday. They're on the docket anyway. Listen, I'm at Colony Control right now. The selectmen's exec session, remember?

Jenny winced. The executive session of the county Board of Selectmen, usually held on Monday mornings, had been moved up to Saturday because of Memorial Day. "Sorry, I forgot," she replied. "Umm . . . why don't you guys go ahead without me?"

It's important, Jenny. We're discussing the Ark's troubles with LaGrange. Neil was insistent. *Please, can you come on over?*

Of course she could come on over. It wasn't a question, no matter how Neil phrased it. Even though she wasn't a member of the Board of Selectmen, she was one-half of the unit known as Neil and Jenny Schorr, and was expected to be present whenever the interests of the Ark were being discussed. Not that the continuous friction between the Clarke County Corporation and the New Ark wasn't of concern to her. It was only that she wished, for once, Neil would handle this stuff all by himself.

"Okay," she said. "I'll be there, in five. Colony Control, main board room. Right?"

Right. See you in five.

Jenny clipped the phone back on her belt and walked over to the large red tricycle parked on the roadside. Two plastic gallon jugs of drinking water were in the rear basket. She pulled them out and left them on the ground for the field workers, then she straddled the trike, settled herself on the seat, and began pumping the pedals with her sneakered feet.

It was a quick, easy ride to South Station. Although it appeared as if she were going uphill, she was actually heading closer to the colony's axis, coasting down the gravity-grade. By the time she crossed the footbridge over South Window, out of the farm sector and into the forest land surrounding the biosphere's South pole, she was peddling barely more than was necessary to defeat inertia. Jenny was gliding when she pulled into South Station, the round mooncrete parapet surrounding the Pole.

She nestled the front wheel of the trike into the community

bike stand and carefully climbed off. While gravity was Earth-normal at the biosphere's equator, here near the axis it was slightly less than one-quarter normal. The tourists waiting in queues to ride the Gold Line, the aerial cable car that traversed the empty line of axis between South Station and North Station, were trying to readapt to the fact that every move they made was exaggerated in one-quarter gravity. Often with disastrous results; many of the tourist injuries treated at Clarke County General were sprains and bruises suffered by overeager visitors who misinterpreted the phrase ''reduced gravity'' as ''anything goes.''

Jenny passed the tourists, doing the short-step heel-to-toe shuffle which inhabitants learn to adopt in reduced gravity areas, and headed for the Red Line tram, which was loading passengers for another trip down to the South tori. She waved her ID at the sensor and managed to scuttle inside the little monorail cab before the doors shut.

Colony Control was the name for Torus S2, located at the farthest end of the eleven tori that comprised Clarke County's South Section. Although the torus was huge, in terms of square-footage, it was also one of the colony's self-contained ''closed'' tori. Unlike the landscaped terrains of the agricultural and habitat tori and the Strip, where fields, plazas, and buildings lay under greenhouse-like ''skies,'' Torus S2 was composed of enclosed decks. Here were the colony's control rooms, computer centers, the field offices of the Corporation's member companies, and meeting rooms.

Colony Control thus felt more like the interior of a metropolitan office building than a suburban neighborhood. As large as the torus was, there clung to it a cavernous, yet still somehow claustrophobic atmosphere that was absent in most other areas of the colony. The potted ferns in the corridors were a weak substitute for the wide farm fields of the biosphere, and although the light fixtures in the ceilings automatically dimmed during the colony's twelve-hour night, it was hardly the same as seeing nightfall, even through the lunar-glass ceilings of ''open'' tori.

Jenny paused in the corridor at the observation window overlooking Main Operations, the vast central control room for the colony. The floor of Main-Ops was tiered with semicircular carrels, its walls lined with giant holo screens and computer displays. Just below the observation window, Jenny could see the shift-supervisor's station, raised slightly above the rest of the carrels.

Main-Ops was a striking sight. Most of the people who worked there were not quite so impressive. They were the reason why Main-Ops was sometimes called Wanker Central. Nervous young techies were crouched over and slumped behind their work stations, muttering (or yelling) into their headset mikes, eating freeze-dried crap (ham and cheese po'boys was the favorite entrée), staring at the giant images on the wall holoscreens, scribbling notes with light-pens, and forever snarling stupid insults at each other. Even on a routine day, the wankers always acted as if an asteroid was about to collide with the colony. Nerds in space.

Jenny grinned and continued down the corridor to the board room, where the meeting was being held. The smartdoor was locked, but it recognized her palm-print and allowed her to enter. The three people seated around the conference table looked up as she walked in, and Robert Morse studied her as she found a seat next to her husband.

"Something funny?" he asked politely.

Jenny shook her head, trying to get the smile off her face. Neil, stoical as always, give her a cold, businesslike look. Obviously they had started the meeting without her, and Neil did not appreciate the fact that she was late. But Rebecca Hotchner did not seem perturbed, although she would probably remain unruffled if an asteroid *did* collide with the colony.

They were still watching her. "Nothing really," she repeated as she quickly searched for something inconsequential to say. "Who's at the resort this weekend, Bob? Anybody interesting?"

The mayor of LaGrange smiled grimly. "Is that what's funny?" he asked.

"I'd heard something," Jenny bluffed.

"Oh, no," Rebecca Hotchner said, closing her eyes. "You would have to bring them up, wouldn't you, dear?"

Neil, confused, glanced around the table. "Who are you talking about?"

Morse cleared his throat. "We've got a group registered at the hotel this weekend. The, uh . . . Church of Elvis."

Hotchner shook her head and covered her eyes with her hand in dismay. Neil looked at the liaison for the Clarke County Corporation. "Church of Elvis? You mean, like an Elvis Presley club?" He gave a little shrug. "So what's the problem? They should get along."

"That's not the question . . ." Hotchner began.

Jenny had a sneaking respect for Rebecca Hotchner, which came from the knowledge of both her real and subliminal roles in this meeting. Although Neil Schorr and Robert Morse were obstensibly the leaders of the colony, acting as the elected mayors of Big Sky and LaGrange respectively, it was Hotchner who performed as the representative for the consortium which held the purse strings of Clarke County: Skycorp, Uchu-Hiko, TexSpace, Galileo International, Trump, Lloyd's, and the galaxy of lesser investors. Of the six-person Board of Selectmen, Schorr, Morse, and Hotchner represented the Executive Board . . . and Becky Hotchner was the only non-elected member.

Hotchner performed her duties quietly, remaining aloof, seldom pulling rank, always seeming to fade into the background at the town meeting. That was her public face. Yet in executive sessions like this, she was the unofficial arbitrator to whom everyone deferred, although Bob Morse officially wielded the gavel as the Board's chairman. True to the unwritten code, when Morse cleared his throat again, it was with a subtle batting of her eyelashes that Hotchner granted the floor to him.

"The Church of Elvis," Morse explained, "is not your typical fan club." A well-groomed gentleman who probably slept in a three-piece business suit, he obviously felt uncomfortable dealing with the unpredictable and the unusual. "It's a cult which believes that Elvis Presley was a divine emissary of God. They've only booked about seventy rooms, but in addition the Church has also leased Bird Stadium for a revival on Monday night."

He paused and sighed. "It's going to be televised on Earth. Live from here." He tapped the tabletop with his index finger for emphasis. "Umm . . . I think the main program is that they're going to bring Elvis back from the dead."

Jenny's eyes went wide open. "AAAAAHHHHHHHHHH!" she shrieked.

"Jenny!" Neil snapped, glaring at her.

"I know," Morse said, shaking his head. "I had the same reaction when I found out."

Everyone was laughing now except for Neil, who was forcing a vague smile so as not to be completely left out. "Oh, God!" Jenny gasped once she had recovered her poise. "Bob, how could you let these guys into LaGrange?"

The laughter quickly died away. Morse and Hotchner stopped smiling. Rebecca reached for the mug of coffee on the table in front of her. "That's why I wished you hadn't brought the subject up," she murmured.

"But it does get to the heart of the matter, doesn't it?" Neil said. "We've been discussing how to control the tourist population from impacting the High Grange Project. This business with the . . . um, Church of Elvis is typical of the problems the Ark is now facing.''

Bob Morse shifted in his seat. ''That's kind of a far reach, isn't it, Neil?''

''If you're not crazy about having an Elvis cult here, why were they allowed to come?'' Schorr replied, gently stroking his long, wispy beard. ''As LaGrange's mayor you've got the authority to regulate tourism just as I have authority to regulate the Ark's population. You delegated that authority to someone else, but it's still your job. I repeat, if you don't want an Elvis cult to hold a revival in Clarke County, then why let them come here?''

''If I had known what they were planning, I would have canceled it,'' Morse explained, ''but someone at the Convention Bureau approved the arrangements and signed the contract, so . . .''

''Don't you have to approve everything yourself?'' Neil blinked. ''Don't you have any guidelines?''

''It's not quite as simple as . . .'' Rebecca started.

Morse held up his hand. ''My situation is not the same as yours, Neil. I can deny an individual or a group the permission to visit LaGrange only if I have reason to believe that they threaten the colony as a whole. That's the law. I can't turn down a bunch of Elvis kooks just because I don't share their beliefs, no more than a town or a state back in the U.S. can stop a particular religion from being practiced or a group from taking up residency. Sure, these people are weird, but they're essentially harmless, like most of the visitors we have here.''

''That's not quite true, Bob,'' Jenny spoke up. ''That's where we've been having our disagreement. Maybe you're used to cleaning up after the tourists every day in LaGrange, but neither Big Sky nor the farm areas were intended to be an amusement park.''

''Nobody ever said that Big Sky was an amusement park,'' Hotchner said, brushing back her iron-gray hair with her hands, ''but most of the tourist action occurs in LaGrange and the Strip, except for the daily guided tours. The South tori are inaccessible without resident keycards, and the elevators will only take visitors to the Strip, the hospital, and lifeboat station or North Dock when a shuttle is boarding. So I don't see how the impact is happening.''

''Let me show you then,'' Neil said. ''Computer. Neil Schorr logon, Timeshare Two.''

A disembodied AI voice came from nowhere in particular. *Neil Schorr logged on Timeshare Two. How may I help you, Mr. Schorr?*

"Please display cross section of the colony, with geographic detail of the habitat sphere," Neil replied.

Affirmative. I'll budget you twenty minutes for this activity.

A wide column of space between the ceiling and the top of the conference table coruscated into a holographic display of Clarke County. For an instant the colony appeared as an opaque, solid model. Then the outer surfaces disappeared and the colony became transparent. The torus sections now appeared as hollow glassine tubes, while the biosphere resembled a large fishbowl. Major geographic features within the biosphere were etched in lines of blue, gold, and magenta. The entire display slowly revolved on an imaginary axis of latitude.

"Outline Broadway in the biosphere, please," Neil said. Broadway, the continuous roadway that linked Big Sky and LaGrange, became a silver band around the inside of the fishbowl. He pointed to the road. "I don't have to remind you that Broadway is the only roadway which directly connects the East and West. . . ."

"Unless you count the river," Jenny interrupted impulsively. Neil paused and everyone else looked at her. She swallowed and motioned to the map. "But, ah, I don't think anyone from LaGrange is going to swim down to Big Sky."

Rebecca hid her chuckle behind a cough into her hand. Robert stared at the map, and Neil glared at his wife for a moment before continuing. "The main problem is that tourists from LaGrange find it easy to rent a trike or take a short walk from the resort into Big Sky."

"Wait a minute," Morse said. "You can't tell us that's a problem, Neil. Clarke County has been marketed as a vacation destination, not just LaGrange. People pay money for the experience of living in the colony for a week. You can't just rope off Big Sky and the ag section, put them off-limits."

"Why not?"

"I see what you're getting at, Neil, but it's unworkable," Hotchner said. "You've got to remember that it's only a half-mile walk down Broadway from LaGrange to Big Sky. We encourage that. People can wander around the colony, to explore the place. You can't confine them to LaGrange and the Strip. If they wanted just that, what's to keep them from going to Vegas instead?"

"The fact of the matter is that the mission of Clarke County is to build and maintain a self-sufficient colony," Neil insisted.

"That's right," Morse interjected. "And part of that self-sufficiency is maintaining a stable economy of our own. Tourism helps pay the freight. You know that.''

''But the agricultural program also pays the freight,'' Schorr argued, ''and it's being disrupted by the tourist traffic. We're seeing the same recurring problems. Maybe *you* haven't seen it, but we've got big trouble in the South hemisphere. Tourists are finding, to start with, that they can eat more cheaply in Big Sky than in La-Grange, so they come over. They head for the residential swimming area when the beach in LaGrange gets too crowded. . . .''

''Those hardly sound like major problems,'' Hotchner said.

''They interrupt a daily pattern of . . .''

''You're right,'' Jenny broke in. ''Those things are just a nuisance, like the vandalism we've experienced. The main difficulties are with tourists going into the farm areas. They've been stomping into the fields, and that destroys crops. Their kids get into the livestock areas and harass the animals. You've even got TV ads running which show children chasing goats, like it's something you get with your TexSpace reservation. What's the line they use . . . 'Welcome back to Paradise'? Meanwhile, Mom and Dad are raiding the crops for ears of corn to smuggle back home in their luggage. A little souvenir of their trip to outer space . . .''

''That's not . . .'' Morse began.

''Yes it is,'' Neil said, ''and it's getting worse all the time. A few weeks ago someone broke into the chicken coop during the night cycle. Next day we found five hens with their necks broken. Someone having fun. Each of those birds cost three hundred dollars to import, Bob.''

''Well, I agree that's inexcusable,'' Morse said, ''but seventy-five percent of the farm program is being carried out in the South tori. The greenhouse sections are inaccessible to tourists without a guide.''

He held out his hands. ''Neil, I am not trying to say that the Ark's losses are acceptable, but you've got to remember that the farm areas in the biosphere are a showplace. Statistically speaking . . .'' Morse shrugged. ''Well, the losses there hardly endanger the interests of either the Ark or the Corporation.''

Neil shook his head. ''You're wrong there. The farming that's done in South Section has the higher yield because it's done through hydroponics, but as far as long-term goals are concerned, the biosphere's farm zones are more valuable. Hydroponics is a mature technology. We've been using it in space for more than a half-century. There's nothing really new there. What we're doing in the sphere is experimental and it could ultimately affect the whole course of space colonization. We need to know how agriculture works in O'Neill-type colonies if more are ever going to be built.''

Morse sighed. "As if we haven't enough trouble paying for the first one.''

"Not only orbital colonies, either,'' Neil insisted. "What about the plan to terraform Mars? That may be way off on the horizon, but with the High Grange Project we're collecting information on open-space farming which could be applied to the Green Mars program."

"Yet, but . . .'' Bob Morse began.

"Furthermore . . .'' Neil drove on.

Sitting back in her chair, watching her husband and Morse tangle in verbal wrestling, Jenny realized in a moment of *déjà vu* that she had heard every word of this discussion before, among these same people in this same room.

Neil would make the point that the Ark was not only growing food for Clarke County, Descartes Station on the Moon, and Arsia Station on Mars, but also that one-tenth of the produce was being shipped back to Earth to feed the starving masses in the Third World. So each bean a tourist trampled meant somebody was going to go hungry. And then Morse would argue that since profits from Clarke County's tourist industry alone were more than halfway to paying for the construction costs of the colony, the tourists were literally paying for Clarke County. Then Neil would counterattack with the claim that because the corporation had invited the New Ark to oversee the agricultural program, the Ark had the right to autonomous control over every factor that influenced the farms, including the tourists. Then Morse would dig in his heels and say, point-blank, that the Ark could move back to Massachusetts if it didn't like the way things were being done around here.

Then Neil would either get mad and stalk out of the room— leaving nothing resolved—or he would back down and Morse would toss him a bone by saying that a compromise could be reached, that the tourists could be asked upon arrival to please not trespass within the farm areas. Of course, this was a promise which had been made before. . . .

Jenny found herself gazing across the table at Rebecca Hotchner, and realized that Rebecca was silently gazing straight back at her. While the two men yammered away at each other, the two women silently held their own discussion. Jenny didn't believe in telepathy, but in that moment of clarity she could read the older woman's mind, the thoughts that were going on behind those cool blue eyes.

These men only believe themselves to be in control, Rebecca told her wordlessly, *but the fact of the matter, my dear Jenny, is that you and I are the powers-that-be, the decision-makers, the hidden matriarchy. Yet the difference between us is that my status is officially recognized, with a title that even appears on a letterhead, while you are simply Neil Schorr's wife. In the final analysis, I'm in control. I represent the consortium and the consortium owns Clarke County, and there really isn't such a thing as democracy here. For that reason, this discussion is pointless.*

"I don't have to point out to you, on an acre-for-acre basis . . ." Neil was saying.

"Nonetheless, the costs of this colony are being underwritten by . . ." Bob interrupted.

Rebecca continued to stare at Jenny. *Nothing is going to change,* her eyes said. *This is a company town. We control the purse strings, and you would be wise not to forget that.*

Hotchner's head tilted back a little. *So? Are you going to try to challenge that, dear?*

"Maybe I will," Jenny found herself saying aloud.

Hotchner blinked.

The two men, hearing Jenny's words, suddenly turned their attention towards her. The silence was a moment pulled out of time. Absolute stasis.

"What did you say?" Neil asked.

Jenny took a deep breath. "This is getting us nowhere," she said flatly. "It's like . . ."

She shrugged. "*Déjà vu.* I've been in this meeting before. The Ark has its interests and the Corporation has theirs, and the two are not one and the same. We want to successfully establish a colony in space, and you guys want . . . I dunno, Spaceland, Las Vegas in orbit, Six Flags Over Earth. A quick buck, when it comes right down to it."

"Jenny," Morse said gently, "that's not quite fair. We all want . . ."

"No, Bob," she insisted angrily, "we *don't* want the same thing, and you"—she found herself directly addressing Hotchner now—"don't want a compromise."

Hotchner closed her eyes. "That may well be," she replied evenly. Then she reopened her eyes to stare straight back at Jenny. "But it's the Clarke County Corporation which built the colony, and it's the Clarke County Corporation which says who stays and who goes. Without a radical change in that structure, Jenny . . .''

She allowed herself a victorious little smile. "Maybe it's the New Ark which goes."

There was a sudden, bottomless silence in the board room.

"So that leaves us with only one alternative," Jenny said.

"Jenny . . ." Neil started. There was a wrathful tone to his voice.

Jenny ignored him. "There's no other choice," she continued. "We'll have to recommend at Sunday's town meeting that Clarke County secede from the United States and make itself an independent, self-governing body."

She stopped. *Did I really just say that?* The words had just . . . come out. As if they had a life of their own.

There was a disbelieving silence until Bob Morse stammered, "What . . . how . . . what are you saying?"

Jenny kept her eyes locked on Rebecca's face. "This colony—this community—will not be bought-and-paid-for by a bunch of corporate greed-heads who want to turn us into a tourist trap. It doesn't matter who paid for Clarke County. Legally, it's a territory of the United States. Therefore, we can secede from the Union."

She felt a pulse beating in her temples. She took another breath. "And we shall."

Okay, so she had made her point. She had gotten their attention. Her instincts towards etiquette told her to shut up, or to say it was just a joke. Yet, at the same time, Jenny knew that she had just fired the shot heard round the Bernal sphere. There was no backing off from this one.

"We will make our own destiny," she added, clearly enunciating every syllable.

Then, because the power was flowing in her veins so fast and hard that she felt as if her head were going to shoot straight off her neck, Jenny Schorr stood up and walked away from the table.

Neil reached out to touch her arm. Was this the action of a partner turning to congratulate his spouse's courage? Or a husband trying to control his crazy wife? She didn't know, and she didn't care. She walked out of Neil's grasp to the door, pulled it open, and strode out into the corridor.

Every nerve in her body was numb until she reached the end of the corridor. At the Red Line tram station Jenny pressed the touchplate to summon the tram. She was alone in the station. She half-expected Neil to be following her, but when she looked around, no one was there.

What she had done, she had done all by herself. It had started, and ended, in a closed executive session. No one else would ever know.

"The shortest revolution in history," Jenny whispered to herself. She closed her eyes for a second and collapsed against a stanchion, trying to catch her breath. "Way to go, girl. That's twice in one morning you've made an ass of yourself."

Yet when she reopened her eyes, she saw something truly weird.

There was a video terminal mounted on the wall next to the slide-doors leading to the tramway tunnel. There were thousands like it all over Clarke County, electronic bulletin boards that routinely reminded inhabitants of schedules and public service announcements, continuously scrolling down the screen.

Now, however, the screen was displaying a computer-generated image of an Independence Day fireworks show: rockets lifting off from an imaginary horizon to explode in coronas of red, white, and blue.

In the middle of the screen was written:

AN IMPORTANT PUBLIC SERVICE ANNOUNCEMENT FROM BLIND BOY GRUNT.

Then, one line at a time, familiar words began to scroll up the screen:

"WHEN IN THE COURSE OF HUMAN EVENTS IT BECOMES NECESSARY FOR ONE PEOPLE TO DISSOLVE THE POLITICAL BANDS WHICH HAVE CONNECTED THEM WITH ANOTHER, AND TO ASSUME AMONG THE POWERS OF THE EARTH, THE SEPARATE AND EQUAL STATION TO WHICH THE LAWS OF NATURE AND OF NATURE'S GOD ENTITLES THEM, A DECENT RESPECT TO THE OPINIONS OF MANKIND REQUIRES THAT THEY SHOULD DECLARE THE CAUSES WHICH IMPEL THEM TO THE SEPARATION.

"WE HOLD THESE TRUTHS TO BE SELF-EVIDENT . . ."

How could Blind Boy Grunt have known what had been said in the meeting? It hardly mattered. Now it was all over Clarke County.

"Oh my God," Jenny whispered, closing her eyes again. "What have I done?"

4

Final Approach
(Saturday: 10:17 A.M.)

TexSpace SSTO shuttle *Lone Star Clipper* was a few minutes from initiating the OMS burn which would brake the spaceliner for its primary approach to Clarke County, when the bridge crew received a priority transmission, relayed by TDRS comsats, from Washington D.C. The co-pilot, listening to the message through his headset while he studied the checklist strapped to his knee, looked up from his work with an amused smile. "We've got another one, Rog," he said. "Washington, Six-Ten Priority."

"Hmm? What's that?" Captain Roger Bach, examining the holo of his ship's trajectory into Clarke County's navigational grid, didn't look up from his computer screen. "Six-Ten? Is that the FBI again?"

"Aye, sir. They want us to check the passenger list and confirm if we have someone aboard named . . . ah, Macy West-moreland." Pjotr Kulejan listened for a few more moments. "She may be traveling under an alias, so we've got a description. Female, obviously. Age, twenty-four. Five feet ten inches, one hundred and twenty pounds. Hair, brown; eyes, brown. No distinguishing marks. American citizen. Possible aliases are Macy Salvatore, Mary Boston, Sheila Shannon, Dorothy Taylor."

"Sounds like a woman with something to hide." Bach looked over his shoulder at the executive officer's station. "Naomi, would you run a check on those names, please? What do they want her for, Pete?"

Kulejan shook his head. "They will not say. They only wish to know if she's aboard. They're holding on for a reply."

Bach frowned. This was a little puzzling—a break from the

standard operating procedure. FBI inquiries to passenger vessels making runs to Clarke County or other orbital destinations were becoming almost commonplace. Since Clarke County, in particular, had been built, fugitives who had once fled to Mexico, Cuba, or Libya were now heading for space. Because Clarke County was U.S. territory, it was perceived as a particularly easy escape; it was not necessary for American citizens to obtain passports or visas to visit the colony, so all one needed was the money to buy a ticket and the ability to pass the routine prelaunch medical and agricultural inspections.

At least, this was the way it seemed to those fleeing from parole officers, the IRS, credit bureaus, divorce lawyers, or various law enforcement agencies. But the arm of the law was long enough to reach across even 200,000 miles of space. What was generally unknown was that space law had evolved to foresee situations in which a person fled from Earth itself. A federal judge could now issue a bench warrant which extended the FBI's jurisdiction into infinity and empowered the feds to temporarily deputize the Clarke County Sheriff's Department to make a collar, if necessary.

Transmissions relayed from FBI headquarters in Washington D.C. to commercial space carriers like the *Lone Star Clipper* were usually the next step. If it was confirmed that the fugitive in question was aboard a certain ship, the FBI then contacted Clarke County. Frequently, passengers floating through the transfer tunnel into the colony's docking area found two Clarke County cops—now registered as U.S. marshals—waiting to bust them; usually they were escorted right back into the ship for the long ride home. It had become hardly more difficult to extradite someone from space than it was from Guam.

However, Bach reflected, the FBI normally informed spacecraft crews of the charges on which the fugitive was being sought. It was a routine precaution, if not common courtesy. Most of the time these people were only running from tax fraud indictments or minor felony convictions, but it was conceivable that a true desperado could panic and pose a genuine threat to the ship and its passengers. Thus the feds generally let the crew know what was going on so that they could keep an eye on the suspect until the ship had docked.

This time, though, the G-men were being unusually tight-lipped. *That's strange*, Bach thought uneasily. *I hope we're not in trouble here.*

Naomi Wada, in the meantime, had punched up the *Lone Star*'s passenger list on her terminal and had scanned the ninety-seven names on the mainfest. "We've got a 'Mary Boston' aboard, Captain," she said.

"Let's have a look at her," Bach replied.

The executive officer interfaced her console to the display screen between Bach's and Kulejan's stations. The head-and-shoulders mug shot of a lovely young woman, taken at the passenger terminal on Matagorda Island as part of the preboarding routine, appeared on the screen. The photo resembled the description given to Kulejan by the FBI. Bach noticed that the woman looked a little distraught in the photo. Of course, a lot of passengers about to make their first orbital flight looked that way just before launch.

"Mary Boston came into Matagorda on a TexSpace helishuttle from Dallas-Fort Worth a few hours before boarding time," Naomi said, checking her passenger file. "She paid for her reservation with an Amex Platinum Card. . . ."

Kulejan grunted. "Beauty and bucks," he said. "A woman after my own heart."

"Don't ask for a date," Bach muttered. "Where is she, Naomi?"

"First Class, Cabin Eight. She's traveling alone. Don't get any ideas, Pjotr."

Kulejan laughed as Bach patched himself into the comlink. "Special Six-Ten, this is Captain Roger Bach. We confirm that we have your suspect aboard, traveling under the name of Mary Boston. Do you wish us to take any action? Over."

A cool female voice came over the link. *We copy that, Captain. Please be advised that Mary Boston, ay-kay-ay Macy Westmoreland, does not, repeat, does not represent any danger to your ship. Please do not make any effort to detain or interfere with her. Over.*

"We understand," Bach replied. "Will she be picked up upon our arrival? Over."

There was a short pause. *We cannot confirm or deny, TexSpace Three-two-one. Repeat, do not interfere with the subject. This is a priority request. Over.*

The three flight-deck officers glanced at each other. Bach shrugged. "That's affirmative," he said. "Glad to be of service. Over."

Confirmed, TexSpace Three-two-one. Thanks for your cooperation, Captain. Special Six-Ten over and out.

The comlink with Washington was cut. "Well, now," Bach

said. "The feds are interested in Ms. Boston, but it's going to be hands-off all the way. Curious, huh?"

Pjotr Kulejan sighed and turned his attention back to his clipboard. "Not my worry. I don't think the sheriff's going to understand this stuff, either."

Bach laughed dryly. Looking up, he could see through the wide, curving windows above his station a bright, spindly star gliding slowly into view. "Yeah, Bigthorn likes things quiet on his reservation."

"Well, he's going to get heap big noise this week," Wada remarked. "Remember? The Elvis geeks we've got down in the zombie tanks?"

Bach shrugged again and turned back to his console. "Not my problem either. Okay, people, let's look sharp for that burn. APU main bus, check . . . ?"

Clipper-class SSTO shuttles were as far removed from the first-generation NASA space shuttles as Boeing 747s were from Douglas DC-3s. *Columbia*-class shuttles were 180 feet in height, including their external tanks and SRB boosters, and had a gross launch-weight of 4.4 million pounds; they were capable of carrying ten persons, if they were close friends, to a low-orbit ceiling of 300 nautical miles. By contrast, the fourth-generation shuttles were luxury liners. Lifting off horizontally from runways with the aid of scramjets and reaching space with liquid-fuel rockets, the spaceplanes were 384 feet long, had a gross launch-weight of 68.7 million pounds, and could transport a hundred persons to a LaGrangian halo orbit 200,000 miles from Earth.

Despite the SSTO clipper's size and power, though, the journey from Earth to Clarke County still took nearly three days to complete. Yet while all men are created equal—to paraphrase George Orwell—some men are created more equal than others. Thus there were three classes of accommodations for passengers.

Most preferred the cheapest standard, the Third Class "sleeper" fare: artificial hibernation induced by psychoactive drugs, so that one slept through the trip in a life-sustaining "zombie tank," the spacefaring equivalent of steerage. Not only was this the least expensive ticket, for some it was the easiest, since they did not have to adapt to zero g during the journey—an unpleasant prospect for many. However, the major drawback of Third Class was the horrible, listless hangover the zombie drugs induced for a few hours after revival.

Second Class was available for those who wanted to experience the adventure of spaceflight. Yet, except for a small exercise gym and an equally diminutive passenger lounge, Second-Class accommodations aboard the clippers were scarcely larger or better furnished than the cabins of conventional airliners. Passengers spent most of the trip strapped into a couch, watching one in-flight video after another and becoming increasingly stir-crazy. Second Class, therefore, was usually the fare of choice for the adventuresome, or a least those who foolishly considered themselves to be adventurers.

First-Class passage was the most expensive—tickets averaged $100 per pound plus surcharge, as opposed to an average of $20 per pound for Third Class—but it was arguably worth the cost: a private cabin (albeit about the size of a walk-in closet) located on an exclusive deck, access to a larger passenger lounge, hot-water showers (as opposed to one lukewarm sponge bath for Second Class), and gourmet dining on Lobster Newburg and continental breakfasts (food-paste tubes and peanut M&Ms for Second Class, glucose on IV lines for Third Class).

One of the original NASA astronauts had lived long enough to ride on the *Lone Star Clipper* during its maiden flight. The old man's comparisons between his cramped couch in an Apollo command module and his silk-sheeted sleepbag in his First-Class cabin had helped fuel TexSpace's advertising campaign that popularized space tourism among the masses. It didn't matter that the average tourist rode to Clarke County comatose in a zombie tank in Third Class or dry-heaving into a vomit bag in Second Class. The image that had been indelibly printed upon the mind's-eye of the general public was of genteel, serene, Pullman-car comfort during three days of romance and adventure.

Macy Westmoreland had not been interested in romance or adventure when she had reserved a First-Class cabin aboard the *Lone Star*. Nor was she impressed with the dubious glories of spaceflight; she experienced during her first day in flight what the powersat space workers used to call ''Star Whoops.'' The only reason why she had opted for First Class was because she needed a private cabin. Privacy was necessary for her escape.

For the last sixty hours, Macy had isolated herself in Cabin 8. She had not visited the First-Class lounge, and she was beginning to smell decidedly rank because of her refusal to leave her cabin to use the shower stall down the corridor. When she was finally capable of digesting food again, she had requested that her meals be brought to her cabin, yet she was so nervous that she barely touched them. The only times she was disturbed was when the steward knocked on her door to announce meals or to check on her condition, and each time that happened she instantly flashed upon the handsome, cruel face of Tony Salvatore. Most of the time she told the polite young man to go away.

Macy lay—or rather, hung—in her sleepbag, wrapped like an insect suspended in a spider's cocoon, against the wall of her cabin, distantly watching the window-like viewscreen as Clarke County grew increasingly closer. The shuttle was making a fly-by of the colony and the screen was displaying a close-up view of Clarke County as seen from the side. To Macy, it looked like one of the gimmicky electric corkscrews which Tony's business associates persisted in giving the *capo* every Christmas.

The captain's voice was coming over the intercom. *Welcome to Clarke County,* he said. *As you can see, we're making our primary approach at an angle perpendicular to the colony's axis as we match our course with the rotation of the North docking sphere. We're now firing our orbital maneuvering system in preparation for final approach and docking. . . .*

A sudden tremble ran through the length of the clipper. Macy felt the shudder and sighed thankfully. Soon she would be inside the colony. She had no idea what she would do once she was there—as a tourist, she was limited to a one-week stay, and she needed far more time than that—but for a little while, at least, she was out of Tony's reach.

She hoped, at least. Macy never really believed in God, despite her Roman Catholic upbringing, but now she prayed, and not for the first time during her long journey. Please, God, don't let the bastard find me. Please, dear God, don't let him send the Golem after me. . . .

Although the colony appears to be rotating as it spins on its axis two point eighty-five times per minute, this motion will seem to slow down and cease as we match rotation with North Dock. Also, from here you can see the construction work which is still being done on the colony's North end, the four tori which are still being built. If you look closely, you can see the work crews. . . .

Once again, Macy's eyes wandered across the padded walls of her cabin, the stylish NeoVictorian fixtures—brass handrails, leather foot restraints, fluorescent lights camouflaged as gas lamps, the framed print of an English hunting scene next to the viewscreen—to the sliding fake-oak panel of her closet door. Inside was her single piece of luggage, the nylon shoulder bag. A little black bag with her only hope for a future hidden inside.

She had no idea how much money was in there. There had not been enough time to count it. When she had cleaned out Tony's bedroom safe, she had hastily shoveled the bundled $100- and $500-bills into the bag. Tony's petty cash fund: At least a few hundred thousand dollars, maybe half a million in cash. Hardly a major dent in Tony's gross assets—the real money remained in laundered bank accounts scattered across four continents—but it was Salvatore money nonetheless.

But the money wasn't what would save her. At the bottom of the bag rested a small bundle of diskettes she had unexpectedly found in the safe and had impulsively scooped into the bag. Macy had not been given the time or opportunity over the last few days to boot up any of the plastic wafers—each unmarked except for a single digit, numbered 1 through 7—but in hindsight she had little doubt what the diskettes contained, the only thing which Tony would logically want to keep in a private safe within sight of his bed.

The Salvatore family spreadsheets. Not the doctored and fumigated books which were given to the IRS during one of their audits. The real books, the ones which showed where all the bodies were buried (literally and figuratively, hah hah). The records which could send Tony Salvatore and his whole goddamned operation straight down the toilet where they belonged.

Thank you for traveling TexSpace, and we hope that you will enjoy your stay in Clarke County. . . .

Tony Salvatore might be able to let his mistress go. Tony Salvatore might be able to write off hundreds of thousands in petty cash. Tony could, and probably would, find another woman, and five hundred grand probably represented the profit margin from only a few weeks of the family's operations. But, Macy instinctively knew, Tony Salvatore would not—could not—let go of seven diskettes that could land him in prison, or even on Death Row if the right inferences were made. Many times, she regretted stealing the diskettes. She should have stolen only the money. Money and sex were tangential matters to someone like Tony, who prized power above all else.

On the other hand, those seven little plastic cards could give her the only things in the world that she truly desired. Freedom and revenge.

Especially revenge.

Revenge for all the things he had done to her. Seducing a confused, screwed-up young woman from Boston who was all too willing to sleep with someone who could keep her in the fast lane. Degrading her into the drug-addled whore of a sleek, smiling monster. Slapping her around the bedroom when he had not gotten his ya-ya's out of sex. Making her take the other names—Mary Boston, Sheila Shannon, or the most denigrating of all, Macy Salvatore—when they had gone to parties together, while she posed in designer gowns and clung to his side as a silent, painted bimbo while Tony laughed and shook hands with the elegant, loathsome creatures he called his ''business associates,'' all the time wanting to slash his throat with the broken stem of a champagne glass. . . .

The voice of the steward who had looked after her during the voyage came over the intercom: *The captain has informed us that we are cleared for docking with Clarke County. Please check your seat harnesses to make certain that they are securely fastened, and please do not leave your seats until you've been cleared by the flight attendants. United States and Canadian citizens may leave through Hatch One at the right side of the forward section of the Second-Class deck. Foreign passengers, please leave through Hatch Two, where you will be escorted to passport control. If you have traveling companions in the Third-Class section, please follow the signs to the Green Line tram, which will take you to the Third-Class reception area in Torus Nine. On behalf of TexSpace, we thank you for . . .*

Her eyes were shut again. She missed watching the viewscreen as the bright rectangular slot of the North Dock's SSTO bay grew closer. Please, dear God, she prayed, protect me and let me destroy Tony Salvatore.

Because I can't count on you to do what you haven't done already. And if you're thinking about it now, please, let me get revenge first.

Amen.

5

Elvis Has Risen From The Grave
(Saturday: 11:05 A.M.)

As the pressurized passenger tunnels locked against the *Lone Star Clipper*'s airlock hatches, Sheriff Bigthorn watched North Dock's control center overlooking the enormous SSTO bay. He held onto the coffee squeezebulb he had cadged from the dockworker lounge and watched as spacesuited hangar techs swarmed over the shuttle's sleek white hull, attaching power and fuel lines, checking the fuselage for signs of atmospheric erosion or micrometeorite pits, opening service ports to tinker with the spaceliner's complex innards.

Four TexSpace and Skycorp dock supervisors were at their stations in the control center, hunched over their consoles and screens, monitoring the post-arrival processing of the shuttle. It was a routine procedure, carried out a couple of times a week, and someone had slipped an old twentieth century rock tape into the jury-rigged cassette deck on top of the console, which was plastered with a sticker reading "Welcome to Clarke County—Now Go Home." The old Kingsmen number "Louie, Louie," rasped from the deck, providing a funky aural backdrop for the technochatter muttered into headset mikes by the dock supes.

"Ah, yeah, we roger that, Rhonda, pressure oh-point-oh-five on the starboard main tank. Can you get a snake in there to drain that stuff, please, Phil?"

"Gornick's boys are on the port LOX tank now. They'll get it as soon as they're finished there. . . . How's that, Pauline? Oh, right, yeah, I gotta positive reading on that, it's pegging the meter. . . ."

"Jesus, what's with that Number Two hatch? I've gotta positive feed on your external electrical. . . . Oh, waitamminit, the goddamn safety hasn't been set, lemme . . . okay, there we go, try it . . . okay, so it was my fault, gimme a fucking break. . . ."

"Foreward OMS safed, yup . . . aft OMS safed, gotcha . . ."

"Tell your IBM to blow it out its serial port, bud, my board says the central-six trunk bus is copacetic and I say it's copacetic. . . . Look, don't gimme no shit, it's wrong. . . ."

"Okay, we've got a good seal on the starboard hatch, go ahead and pop it open. . . ."

The dock crew, Bigthorn decided, were a strange bunch of guys. The sort of people found doing the hard-core, nuts-and-bolts work of the frontier: pragmatic, persnickety, downright rude stiffs who seldom used deodorant and had lousy table manners, but who nonetheless got the job done.

He scalded his mouth with another sip from his squeezebulb—they couldn't make decent coffee, either—and tried to concentrate his attention on the disembarking passengers, seen thirty feet away through the Plexiglas walls of the ramps as they were herded and helped off the shuttle by the flight attendants. Coyote had told him something evil was aboard this ship. Coyote had scorched his brain with a horrible vision. Coyote was a trickster, but at the heart of his lies was always a little truth, and Bigthorn had learned to trust his encounters with the ancient demigod.

The sheriff tried to reach out with his instincts to figure out which of these passengers posed a potential danger to the colony. They were the same instincts—the sixth sense every good cop acquires—which allowed him to zero in on shoplifters in O'Neill Square's tourist shops or on an unlicensed dope dealer on the Strip. Yet last night's peyote session had left him fatigued, his head feeling as if it had been stuffed with cotton.

I need sleep, Bigthorn thought. He sucked on his squeezebulb, watching the tourist parade. *I should put Wade in charge of the office. Clock out, go home, get a shower and a few hours of sleep. Hell, I'm wearing yesterday's clothes, haven't brushed my teeth or shaved or . . .*

He noticed a pair of cargo loaders clamping a ramp against a large hatch on the port underside of the shuttle. If that hatch led only to a cargo hold, they would not be bothering to attach a pressurized sleeve to it before jacking it open. He tapped one of the supervisors on the shoulder. "Hey, Skip, where's that hatch lead to?" he asked, pointing towards the bay.

Skip, the most obnoxious of the control supes, barely acknowledged his question. "Third Class," he muttered. "The zombie tanks." He immediately returned his attention to his job.

"Hey, lookit, Maurice, we don't got all day here, so just get a snake on that tank and drain it before I get pissed, okay . . . ?"

Bigthorn watched as the first stainless-steel sarcophagus emerged on a conveyor belt from the hold. Of course. Half of the passengers were in suspended animation. Perhaps the person he was seeking was in a zombie tank. Bigthorn was looking around the cupola for a vacant data terminal, when the phone on his belt chirped. He unclipped it and held it to his ear. "Station Twelve," he murmured.

Hey, John. Wade Hoffman, his deputy sheriff, was nauseatingly cheerful this morning. *Where are you at, big guy?*

"Down at North Dock. What's the story?"

I got a call from Robyn Abbey at the livestock area. She says a couple of the goats managed to get loose. They pawed off their restraint collars and now they're eating their way through the soybean fields in the Southeast quad. She wants you to . . .

"I know," he said disgustedly. "Damn, Wade, what do I look like, an animal-control officer? Can't Robyn get some of the Ark people to get her goats? She's getting mine with petty bullshit like this."

Hey, you're funny today. . . .

"Have you heard me laughing?"

She says she tried, but the goats don't like the idea much. One of them butted Dale Cussler in the stomach and he had to be taken to the clinic. She wants you because you're so good with animals.

"Right. Okay, I'll come down and shoot the critter." Bigthorn sighed and kneaded his eyelids with his fingertips. "No, don't tell her I said that, she'll just get pissed off. Tell her I'll be right over. Listen, I want you to get in touch with the Tex-Space office and get them to send us the passenger list for TexSpace Three twelve, the flight that just came in. I want it in our system by the time I get back from the Southeast quad. Got it?"

That's affirmative. I'll . . . oh shit, I almost forgot!

"What?"

I just remembered. We just received a priority message from FBI headquarters in Washington regarding one of the passengers on that flight, but it's not a bench warrant. They want you to contact them ASAP. Wade paused, then added guiltily, *I was about to call you when Robyn called and started honking about her goats.*

Well, now. This was an interesting coincidence. "Did the feds say who the passenger was or what this is about?" he asked.

Nope. You're just supposed to call a number and talk to someone named Sherman Brooks in the Organized Crime Division. Apparently it involves some sort of ongoing investigation.

"Okay, I'm coming straight back to the office, then."

What about the goats?

"Is D'Angelo on duty? Send him over to deal with the goats. Tell him I don't care if he's from Brooklyn and has never seen one before."

There was a short pause. *Danny says that not only is he from Brooklyn and has never seen a goat before, but he wouldn't know what to do if he met one.*

"Tell that rookie son of a . . . never mind, just put him on."

In a few seconds Daniel D'Angelo, another Sheriff's Department officer, came on. *Danny here, chief.*

"Listen, Danny, there's an old Navajo trick for dealing with goats. Just stand in front of it, point your finger between its eyes, and say in a stern voice, 'Goat, lie down.' I guarantee it'll work. Now get going, that's an order."

There was another pause, then Hoffman's voice came back on the line. *He got it, Chief. He's going right now to see if it'll work for him.*

"Great. I'll remember to try it sometime myself if it does. I'm on my way back to the office. And get me that passenger list from TexSpace."

You got it. Anything else?

"Yeah, make me some coffee." Then he added, in his best Perry White imitation, "And stop calling me Chief. Station Twelve out."

He clicked off, hung the phone back on his belt, and stuffed the remainder of his squeezebulb down a recycle chute before grabbing a handrail and pulling himself hand-over-hand out of the control center. "Later, boys," he threw over his shoulder as he exited. "Have fun." None of the controllers responded.

The TexSpace Third-Class resuscitation area was a "lounge" only insofar as it was decorated and furnished in the Neo-Victorian manner, with plush leather chairs, gold-filigree wallpaper, and ornamental spittoons arranged between the brass-frame beds on which the passengers lay until they awakened. In fact, the lounge was more like an outpatient wing, located on the medical deck which took up most of Torus N-9. Once the

Third-Class passengers were removed from the zombie tanks and administered the counteractive drugs that brought them out of biostasis, they were wheeled into the lounge and laid out on the beds, where they could gradually regain consciousness in a less technophiliac environment.

Biostasis for space travel had been achieved not by cryogenics—dozens of people from the twentieth century were still paying for that mistake—but through psychoactive drugs, clinical derivatives of *dioden hystrix*, the fungus that Haitian *houngan* had used for centuries to fake the deaths of men and women, then later revive them and enslave them as *zombis*, the so-called living dead of modern myth. The derived "zombie dope" had the desired effect of slowing down the physical metabolism and mental processes to a state resembling natural hibernation, making short-term human biostasis possible. First used by NASA and Japan's NASDA for deep-space missions to Mars and the outer planets, the "zombie tanks" were perfected and eventually approved by the U.S. Food and Drug Administration for commercial use by TexSpace and other space lines. As much as fourth-generation space shuttles, zombie-tech had opened the way for low-cost space tourism.

The undesirable side effect of biostasis (besides the rare incidence of a passenger lapsing into a permanent coma) was the godawful hangover one experienced upon awakening. It was a cerebral numbness which left a person in a highly suggestible, near-hypnotic state for as long as an hour after gaining consciousness. This was the effect for which the houngan had prized their crude creation, and pharmacologists had never quite ironed the side effect out of the biostasis spinoff. For this reason, Third-Class passengers were kept in an undisturbed, comfortable area until they were ready not to accept a casual insult like "drop dead" as a literal command.

Most of the time, the strategy worked.

Zombie tanks provided, as an incidental development, a low-profile means of getting into space for those who didn't wish to be noticed. This was how Henry Ostrow, known in some circles as the Golem, found himself awakening in the Third-Class lounge, feeling as if he had spent the night with Johnnie Walker, José Cuervo, and Jack Daniels.

Henry Ostrow lay for a long while on the bed, staring up at the ceiling, performing little mental exercises—like running through multiplication tables and silently reciting Poe's *The Raven*—which he had long ago learned to keep himself alert during moments of woolgathering while, say, waiting for a target to emerge from a long lunch at a restaurant. At the age of fifty-one, Ostrow retained the cold discipline of a professional bad-ass, although under his present alias as Cecil Jacobson he was a St. Louis real estate agent on vacation.

Finally, Ostrow sat up slowly and swung his legs over the side of the bed. At the peak of physical condition, he had recovered from the zombie dope a little more quickly than the other Third-Class passengers, most of whom were still unconscious in their beds around him, their eyelids fluttering in time with the canned music—"Promises, Promises," now seguing into "Classical Gas"—wafting from hidden speakers in the rococo ceiling. Henry Ostrow was a man who could lift a teacup with an out-stretched pinky, and the next second drop the teacup and grab for a semiauto submachine gun, but at this moment he was not quite prepared to meet Elvis Presley.

Elvis was dressed in a skintight black leather outfit with silver studs running down the legs and more zippers than considered practical running along the wrists and pockets of his jacket, which was open to his naval, exposing several gold chains and a crucifix. Elvis groaned as he sat up clumsily in his own bed next to Ostrow's, ran a hand encrusted with huge gold rings through his pompadour, and gazed at the Golem with unfocused dark eyes that suggested he had been eating uppers and downers all night.

"Whudda fug?" mumbled the King of Rock and Roll.

Ostrow stared back at him, then yawned. Elvis Presley was in the next bed. Okay. He could accept that. "The Third-Class lounge, I think."

"Huh?" replied Elvis. "We're here?"

"I think so."

"Well fuggit," said Elvis, and collapsed back into bed.

Ostrow studied his fellow passenger closely. He noticed that although he closely resembled Elvis Presley—that is, Elvis *circa* 1969, about the time he had stopped making movies and made his Las Vegas comeback—he didn't quite *sound* like Elvis Presley. Ostrow was an expert at identifying people in only a few moments, and the man on the bed didn't precisely match the film images he had seen of the American folk hero.

This was besides the fact, of course, that Elvis Presley had been dead since 1977.

Already a couple of physicians in white uniforms, noticing that two of their passengers were awake, had hurried over to unstick the biosensors from their foreheads and chests and to quickly check their pupils with penlights. They put pills and little paper cups of orange juice in their hands, dropped orientation brochures on their beds, then bustled away to attend to other groaning, cross-eyed passengers elsewhere in the overdecorated ward. Ostrow downed his pill with a slug of O.J. and rubbed the back of his neck. "So how does it feel to be alive again after seventy years?" he asked politely.

"Lousy." Elvis looked at his pill, grimaced and shoved it underneath a sheet, then slurped his orange juice and massaged his temples. "God, do I need a drink. Where's the bar?"

He sat up again, swung his legs over the bed frame, and attempted to stand up. His body wasn't ready yet to listen to his brain. His knees collapsed and he fell backwards onto the bed. "Whoa, there, Ollie," he muttered to himself. "Elvis needs gravity."

"You're not really Elvis, are you?" Ostrow asked.

He did not know it, but he had asked a question to which Elvis could not respond by lying or evasion. At this stage of recovery from biostasis, a person was almost totally incapable of lying. The synapses of the brain were inhibited to the degree that the mind could not work creatively enough to fabricate, or even recall, an untruthful statement. So, although Elvis was conscious, he could not think clearly enough to speak an untruth.

Looking as if he were about to gag, Elvis could only respond honestly to Henry Ostrow. "Naw. My name's Oliver Parker."

"Hmm." Ostrow contemplated that information, then motioned to Elvis's face. "Cosmetic surgery?"

Elvis nodded his head, almost painfully. If he had taken the counter-effect pill he had been given he wouldn't have been in such trouble. "How come?" Ostrow asked.

"I'm the leader of the First Church of Twentieth Century Saints, Elvis Has Risen, so I'm given the title of Elvis. So it's Elvis Parker, or the Living Elvis." Elvis Parker rubbed his jawline where his mutton-chop sideburns ended. "Cost me a bundle, but it was worth it. . . . Shit, am I really saying this?"

Ostrow nodded. The Golem was very familiar with drugs and he realized that the zombie dope's aftereffects were acting like scopolamine in Parker's nervous system. All he had to do was to keep asking questions. He dimly remembered an article in *People*. "You're the guy who claims he's the living reincarnation of Elvis Presley, aren't you?"

"Yup. That's me." This time, Parker couldn't keep himself from grinning. "The Living Elvis, live and in person."

"Right. Elvis was the chosen voice of God in the last century, and he died for the sins of those who believe in his divine persona. That's the gist of it, isn't it?"

"You got it, hoss," Parker replied, still grinning.

"Hmm." Ostrow slowly shook his head. "Hard to believe that somebody would buy into swill like that. So what are you doing here, Living Elvis?"

"Ah, just a little revival." Parker hitched his thumb toward the rest of the passengers in the Third-Class lounge. "I've brought about seventy of my followers up here for a week in LaGrange. Monday night there's going to be a performance at Bird Stadium. It'll be telecast live on Earth on about two dozen channels. You ought to show up."

"I'll make a point of missing it." Ostrow slowly extended his legs, planted his feet on the floor, and stood up. "It's been nice talking to you, Elvis, but I have to run. Give my best to all your fans, will you?"

"Okey-doke." Elvis winced again, then asked casually, "So what are you up here for?"

It almost worked. The same side effect of the zombie drug nearly made Ostrow babble out the truth. His muscles went taut; he clenched his jaw as tight as he could and squeezed his eyes shut. The Golem is silent, he told himself. The Golem never speaks.

"Business," he hissed.

He put one foot in front of the other and carefully, deliberately, walked away from the bed. Parker was saying something else, but Ostrow deigned not to speak. After a few more steps, he was out of earshot, pushing through the door of the Third-Class lounge.

Henry Ostrow paused in the corridor outside the lounge to collect his breath. He had left his orientation brochure on the bed, but there was a wall map nearby. He studied it for a minute, figuring out where to get the nearest tram that would take him to the main sphere. His baggage had already been taken to his room at the LaGrange Hotel. Satisfied, he headed for the Green Line North station.

As he turned, he bumped into someone walking the opposite way. It was unlike Ostrow to collide with someone in an otherwise empty corridor, but he owed his clumsiness to the zombie

CLARKE COUNTY, SPACE   55

dope. " 'Cuse me," he mumbled to the person with whom he had collided, and walked the other way.

Following the map's directions, he went along the upward-sloping corridor towards the tram station. First, he would get to his room at the hotel. A shower, a short rest in bed, then the necessary rituals before he checked his arsenal.

In a little while he would be ready to begin the hunt.

Simon McCoy, also having just disembarked from the *Lone Star Clipper*, paused in the corridor outside the TexSpace Third-Class lounge and watched as the heavy-set man who had collided with him walked away in the opposite direction. McCoy watched Henry Ostrow until he disappeared up the corridor, noting the hit man's appearance. Another principal character had arrived on stage. . . .

McCoy tucked his hands into his trouser pockets and continued sauntering down the corridor. The wide passageway took him through Torus N-9, past Clarke County General, the colony's hospital and medical clinic. He strode past the doors leading to the reception area; white-robed doctors, patients, and med-robots passed him until, almost halfway around the torus, he reached the private sector.

Here were the offices and suites rented to various private-sector medical firms, mainly the R&D lads, most of them specializing in low-gravity pharmaceutical research. Most, but not all. Simon McCoy slowly walked past the rows of doors, scanning the nameplates in a way which would, to the eyes behind the ceiling-mounted security cameras, suggest the casual if thoughtful interest of a tourist making a walkabout of the colony. Eli Lilly, Johnson & Johnson, Spacemed, Harvard, all the usual names—he walked past them until he spotted one particular plate.

The plate read: THE IMMORTALITY PARTNERSHIP.

His hands involuntarily clenched in his pockets. McCoy resisted the urge to push through the door, to walk inside. Instead, he turned as if to walk the other way, like a tourist bored with the sights. As he did, he ducked his head and quickly studied the lock from the corner of his eye. It was a digital. No problem.

He then began to mosey down the corridor the way he had come. When he had the time he'd come back here for a visit. When no one else was around.

6

Blind Boy Grunt Strikes Again
(Saturday: 11:47 P.M.)

If there was any one human aspect that made Clarke County most like a small town it was the fact that no major event went unnoticed, or untalked about, for very long. This was especially true since the colony had an official town gossip.

Sheriff Bigthorn had peddled his trike down from North Station through Big Sky's bamboo suburbs into the town center, being careful to stop and get off the trike before entering Settler's Square. It was about noontime, and the square was becoming crowded with residents and a handful of tourists who happened to wander down from LaGrange. It was a typical lunchtime scene, since most residents worked a six-day week. Sunday, not Saturday, was usually everyone's day off, and since noon was the universally accepted lunch hour, many people took the opportunity to hang around Settler's Square: farmers talking to beamjacks, scientists playing backgammon with students from the International Space University, individuals with reflector boards leaning against the base of the statue while improving their tans.

Generally, people talked about nothing much, but today there was a buzz in the air. As he walked his tricycle through the square, heading for the town hall, Bigthorn noticed that many people had sheets of PSA flimsy in their hands. Along with mail from Earth, the Big Sky post office routinely deposited public service announcements in residential boxes each day: changes in shuttle schedules, new job openings, reminders about tax-filing dates, and so forth. Once a weekly newspaper became established in the colony—the Newhouse and Gannett chains were still competitively negotiating with the Clarke County Corporation for exclusive rights—most of this fodder would be eliminated. Until then, the news came in the form of half-sheet bamboo-paper printouts which people dug out of their boxes, read once, and usually shoved down the nearest recycling chute.

Today, however, residents had found something in their mail boxes which they didn't toss out. Clusters of people were reading and re-reading the printouts, with varied reactions: amusement, anger, consternation, rejoicing. Unfortunately, it seemed as if everyone believed that Bigthorn already knew what was going on. As he walked his trike through the square, the sheriff noticed people looking towards him as if he had an answer to all this. Whatever all this was.

Bigthorn, however, had another matter on his mind: the priority message from the FBI. He was prepared to ignore the "whatever it was" until after he was through dealing with the feds, when one of Big Sky's more vocal residents walked up to him.

"Does this mean we're going to war?" Roxanne Barnes demanded.

"Umm? Excuse me?" Bigthorn replied.

"They could close us down, you know that, Sheriff," Roxanne insisted. "We're playing with fire here. What are we supposed to do about it when the 2nd Space Infantry lands?"

Roxanne Barnes was on the all-time list of Bigthorn's least-favored people, the type that any police officer in any town got to know all too well. Roxanne fell into the subcategory of Constantly Complaining Nuisance. She was the person who called the police department every day with real and imaginary (and usually trivial) gripes.

In another town her complaints would have been: dogs overturning her garbage, neighbors making too much noise, kids playing in the street, child molesters lurking in the neighborhood, aircraft flying too low over her home, strangers spying through her windows, bad reception on her TV and radio, and Communists, the CIA, the IRS, Kenya Congress terrorists, and/or the police themselves tapping into her comlink. For Roxanne, it was: the colony rotating too fast (or too slow), her apartment too cold (or too hot), late mail service, hippies from the New Ark spying on her, clogged recycling chutes, neighbors making too much noise, trash littering the corridors, and the Communists, the CIA, the IRS, Kenya Congress terrorists and *especially* the police department tapping into her comlink. Bitch bitch bitch, whine whine whine.

Roxanne, too, had a sheet of computer flimsy clutched in her fist. "May I, please?" Bigthorn asked, and before she could say yea or nay, he snapped it out of her hand, uncurled it and read:

INDEPENDENCE!
CLARKE COUNTY CITIZENS, UNITE!

Now has come the time for all good men and women to come to the aid of their space colony.

In a closed-door session this morning among executive members of the Clarke County Board of Selectmen, it was announced by Jennifer Schorr that the residents of Clarke County were ready, willing and able to seek total control of their destiny from the running dog lackeys of corporate sponsorship.

We are now in control! We shall establish Clarke County as its own independent nation! The future is unwritten, but the writing is on the wall. What was inevitable is now upon us. We must seize the opportunity to formally and irrevocably declare Clarke County to be the master of its own destiny. In this way we shall shed these surly bonds of Earth. . . .

Attend next Monday night's town meeting at Big Sky town hall to make plans for the coming era of independence and self-determination. Let your voices be heard. Live free or die!

"The times they are a-changing . . ."

—Blind Boy Grunt

"Running dog lackeys?" Bigthorn murmured. "What the hell does that mean?"

Roxanne didn't hear him. She was running off about how the 2nd Space Infantry Division of the U.S. Marines was going to invade the colony and kill everyone in sight, and how it would all be the sheriff's fault because he didn't act sooner to control the anarchists, Communists, hippies, terrorists, Democrats, or whoever was at fault for this revolution.

Only a little bit of it soaked through Bigthorn's attention. He glanced at the message again, and knew at once that it was also on every electronic bulletin board in Clarke County. If that was so, the message had undoubtedly been received on Earth as well, for there was little which happened in Clarke County that the companies in New York, Alabama, London, and Tokyo did not hear.

He looked at the signature. Blind Boy Grunt.

Goddammit. Whoever he was, he had done it again.

"And what are you going to do about this?" Roxanne was demanding.

Bigthorn looked up. Roxanne was staring at him. Most of the people within his range of vision were, too. He cleared his throat, slowly and deliberately folded the bamboo scrim, and tucked it into the breast pocket of his uniform shirt. "Roxy," he said softly. "Will you go get your Happydaze prescription refilled, please?"

He didn't wait to see her expression change, but simply pushed his trike past her and marched the rest of the way across the square to the entrance of the town hall. All things considered, this was starting out to be a really lousy day.

The architect who had designed Big Sky's town hall had intended the offices to look like a quaint small-town municipal building. It ended up having all the character and rustic charm of a boot camp shower-house, which it faintly resembled. Long, low, drab and ugly, it contained the offices of various county officials who preferred to do their work at home. The Clarke County Sheriff's Department, located at the end of the long hallway leading down the middle of the building, was seemingly the only office in the town hall that was ever open. Small wonder. It was in a building only a cop could love.

Bigthorn made a stop in the adjacent kitchenette to grab a bran doughnut and a cup of coffee before going in. As he pushed through the glass-front doors, he said to no one in particular, and thus everybody in general, "Has anybody found out who Blind Boy Grunt is and just not bothered to tell me?"

Wade Hoffman was slouched behind his desk, in front of the wall of TV monitors which displayed scenes from various parts of the colony. He was browsing through a back issue of *Sports Illustrated* when the sheriff appeared. The magazine disappeared beneath his desk as he self-consciously straightened his posture. "Beg pardon?" he said.

"Stop reading on duty, willya, Wade?" Bigthorn walked behind the front counter and stopped beside Hoffman's desk, absently running his eyes across the screens. "Blind Boy Grunt," he repeated. "I wanted that idiot investigated and found. What has come of that?"

Hoffman coughed and tapped a command into his computer terminal's keyboard. The public service announcement Bigthorn had read a few minutes earlier appeared on the screen. "Well, this was fed into the public system about an hour ago. . . ."

"Wade, why do you think I'm asking?" Bigthorn replied testily. "Before I find Jenny and ask her what the hell's going on, I want to find out how Grunt knew what went on in an executive session. And how does he hack into the mail system, anyway?"

With a glance, Hoffman silently deferred the question to another uniformed officer in the office. Roland Binder was bent over his own terminal, intently studying his screen. "I traced the input to a public-access terminal in Torus S-Eight," Binder said without looking up. "That's one of the habitation areas, of course. Same MO as always. He must have used a back door and a hidden password to get into the system, and he was in for only about a minute, just enough time to download his message into the system and get out. Could have been done by anyone with a PC." He glanced over the top of his terminal. "Want to guess how many PCs are in the colony?"

"Never mind. I get the idea." Bigthorn took a bite out of his doughnut. It was stale; he swallowed the morsel with effort and dumped the remainder down a chute. It was time to get on the Ark's bakeries about not supplying his office with fresh sinkers. "Was it the same terminal he used last time?"

Binder checked his file. "Not the last time, but he's used this particular one before . . . um, on May twelfth, when he posted an obscene limerick. But earlier today, before he got this message into the post office computer, he entered another message on the bulletin board. The Declaration of Independence. United States, that is."

"Guess it was kind of a warm-up." Hoffman chuckled.

Bigthorn ignored him. "Where did he enter that message, Rollie?"

Binder didn't bother to recheck his file. "A public terminal on the Strip. He spent about the same amount of time there. Twenty minutes later, he posted the second message from the Torus Eight terminal."

Rollie looked back at the screen. "He moves fast, John. Far as I can tell, he picks his entry ports at random. Never uses the same one twice in a row."

The sheriff nodded his head thoughtfully as he sipped his coffee. Twenty minutes was about the amount of time it took for someone to get from the Strip, in Torus N-S on the North side

of Clarke County, to Torus S-8, on the South side of the colony.
A person wouldn't even have to run to make the connection.
And since virtually everyone in Clarke County possessed at least
one laptop computer or datapad, there were at least 7,036 possible suspects—the current population of the colony, not counting tourists. Blind Boy Grunt had been around too long to be a *tourista*.

"Terrific," Bigthorn murmured. "Anything else?"

Binder checked his file, then grinned. "Only one thing. I figured out his name."

"Blind Boy Grunt?"

The department's resident wirehead nodded enthusiastically.
"I got it after cross-referencing Music History in the library subsystem, just for the hell of it. 'Blind Boy Grunt' was a pseudonym used by Bob Dylan in the early nineteen-sixties, when he sat in as a session musician on other people's albums." Binder shrugged. "I don't know if that makes any difference. Before you ask, I checked our roster. There's nobody here named Dylan."

"I didn't think it would be that obvious," Bigthorn said.
"Okay, so he's a Bob Dylan fan. At least that's something to go on. Good work."

One corner of Rollie's mouth rose briefly. "For what it's worth."

Precious little. Blind Boy Grunt had been haunting Clarke County's information system for the past year, beginning a few months after the colony began operating as an inhabited worldlet. Without warning, without discernible pattern, anonymous messages had begun to appear on computer screens. One day, they were public announcements, like today's entries on the bulletin board and the post office computer. Other days, they were private messages, appearing only on a particular individual's screen. Sometimes their meanings were obvious and direct. In other instances they were obscure quotations from sources as diverse as history texts, song lyrics, *The Quotations of Chairman Mao*, the Holy Bible, the Koran, *Alice in Wonderland*, or *The Origin of the Species*. Their content ranged from the ribald to the inconsequential, from pointed political commentary to outright libel.

On occasion, Blind Boy Grunt had even dropped notices into the cop shop's own computer, items that further enhanced his (or her) mystique as a know-all, see-all oracle. Once, Bigthorn had been trying to find out who was spray-painting obscenities

on corridor walls in the North tori. Blind Boy Grunt unexpectedly left a notice identifying the culprit as a teen-ager who lived
with his parents in Torus N-11. The lead turned out to be correct. Later, the shopkeepers in LaGrange had a problem one
week with a shoplifter who was pilfering items from the stores
around O'Neill Square, someone who was swift enough to evade
their mirrors and security cameras. Blind Boy Grunt dropped
word that the person was a tourist from California, an incurable
kleptomaniac. When a mean-spirited practical joker was drain-
ing air supplies from the life-support packs of the beamjacks
building the remaining tori in the North section, Grunt fingered
the guilty party, and when an anonymous bomb threat was made
against the windows in the main sphere, a message appeared on
Bigthorn's own terminal, which stated that the threat was a hoax
perpetrated by a ten-year-old boy in Big Sky.

Despite these favors, Bigthorn regarded Blind Boy Grunt as a
royal pain in the ass. He didn't like the idea that Clarke County
contained a hacker skillful enough to penetrate computer security throughout the colony. Yet tracking down Blind Boy Grunt
had, so far, been impossible. Whoever he or she was, the hacker
had eluded the Sheriff's Department. Even Wanker Central, the
lair of the arch-wireheads, had not been able to track down Blind
Boy Grunt, although Bigthorn privately suspected it was someone in Main-Ops itself.

"Well, keep on it," Bigthorn said as he headed for his private
office. "Wade, get me in touch with FBI headquarters. I'll take
the call in my office. . . . Oh, and how did Danny do with those
goats?"

Hoffman grinned over his shoulder. "Your trick didn't work.
He got butted before he gave up and used his stunner on them.
He's really pissed at you now."

"Oh, well. Log in a bonus for him. Hazardous duty pay. I'll
be in my office."

Sherman Brooks wore the usual gray suit, high-collared white
dress shirt, and plain bolo tie of an FBI official. He sat, with
legs crossed, in a chair in the corner of the sheriff's office; the
illusion of his corporeal presence was spoiled by the scene
through the window behind him. The rotunda of the Capitol,
surrounded by cherry trees in full blossom, was a plausible vista
only if one was on Earth. Out here, it was an obvious, if not
ridiculous, piece of backdrop scenery. Bigthorn tried not to
smile.

You're probably wondering why we called you, Sheriff, Brooks said from the hologram tank.

"Well, as an offhand guess, it probably has something to do with a passenger who arrived today on a TexSpace shuttle," Bigthorn replied casually. There was a momentary pause, then a puzzled expression appeared on Brooks's wide brown face, and the sheriff shrugged. "Just a guess," he added.

Another brief pause as Bigthorn's words were relayed across space and time to FBI headquarters. A moment lapsed, then Brooks's face became even more worried. *Has anyone spoken to you about this matter, Sheriff?* he asked.

Bigthorn shook his head. What was he supposed to say? Well, last night I took some peyote—don't worry, a former President said it was okay—and a coyote came to me and said that something dangerous was aboard the incoming passenger shuttle? Even if the man wasn't technically an Anglo, he was still a gringo. He could not understand. "Just a wild guess. What's on your mind?"

Brooks's eyes had wandered to an invisible object above and to the left of Bigthorn's head. Perhaps he was checking Bigthorn's file. He blinked and turned his attention back to the sheriff. *Well, your guess is correct. The Bureau is concerned about a person we've confirmed is now aboard the colony, and we need your department's cooperation in this matter.* Another pause. *This is a closed channel, isn't it, Sheriff?*

It was unless Blind Boy Grunt managed to unscramble the signal and was eavesdropping. Bigthorn decided not to bring that up, either. "Yes, it is. Go ahead."

Okay, Brooks continued. *The Organized Crime Division has been investigating for the past several years a mobster in St. Louis named Anthony Salvatore. Perhaps you've heard of him?*

The name only vaguely registered with him. "Sort of," Bigthorn admitted. "A big wheel in the Midwest. Wasn't he under indictment from a federal grand jury?"

He was, in very much the past tense. For tax fraud, before his lawyers managed to swing an acquittal on legal technicalities. If you'll consult your screen, please . . .

Bigthorn looked down at the screen embedded in his desk. Several photos were displayed of a lean, hawklike man in his late thirties or early forties. The photos looked as if they had been taken by hidden cameras: street scenes, party scenes, a picture of him in riding clothes on a country estate somewhere.

As Bigthorn watched the montage blur across his screen, the FBI agent continued his briefing.

Tony Salvatore is the head of the Salvatore crime family, the largest underworld syndicate in the Midwest, one of the biggest in the U.S. Besides peripheral interests worldwide, which run from arms smuggling to the international software black market, the syndicate accounts for much of the criminal activity in St. Louis, Chicago, and Kansas City. Drugs, prostitution, gambling, counterfeiting, protection rackets . . . you name it, the Salvatore family has a controlling interest in it. Unfortunately, nobody . . . not us, not Interpol or the IRS . . . has been able to nail so much as a parking ticket on him. The money is laundered through legitimate offshore banking and real estate corporations, and they're careful to use several cut-outs in every operation which keep the family from being directly connected to anything. For almost a decade the FBI has been trying to get something on him, but it wasn't until a few days ago that we finally got a break. See that woman . . . ?

The montage stopped with a photo of Tony Salvatore, in a black tuxedo, walking through the door of what appeared to be a swank restaurant. On his arm was a beautiful young woman in her twenties—brown hair piled high on her head, wearing a strapless gold lamé evening gown cut high on the thigh. Bigthorn raised his eyebrows. "I can't help but notice," he commented.

I'm glad your eyes are so sharp. Her name is Macedonia Westmoreland, Macy for short. She's been Tony's live-in girlfriend . . . his mistress, if you prefer . . . for about the past four years. From Massachusetts originally. Good Boston Brahmin family. Rather spoiled and reckless. She was a student at Stephens College in Columbia, Missouri, before she met Tony on the party circuit. Tony moved her into his compound, but she's never really been part of his inner circle.

"Hmmm," Bigthorn murmured. "At least you can't say he's got bad taste."

Maybe, but our intelligence says that his appetite is a bit on the violent side. He's into the rough stuff with her. When she's not been with him, she's been back at the Salvatore mansion recuperating from the last beating he gave her. That's not a very happy person you see there.

The picture switched to a split-screen image. On the left was a close-up of Macy Westmoreland; on the right, a distant shot of a huge stone mansion half-hidden behind a brick wall. *We've been keeping the Salvatore mansion under constant surveillance, as a matter of routine, for the last couple of years. Last Wednesday night, it paid off. One of the St. Louis field agents, Milo Suzuki, spotted Macy climbing over the wall while Tony was gone from the compound. She met a cab on the street which she had apparently called in advance, and Suzuki trailed her to the international airport. Obviously, the girl had gotten fed up with Tony's sick shit and was making a break for it. Then . . .*

"Let me guess the rest," Bigthorn interrupted, looking up at Brooks. "She caught a shuttle to Matagorda Island, where she got on the TexSpace shuttle and came here. Now she's in Clarke County. Right?"

Brooks nodded, but he hardly seemed pleased. *Your intuition's correct, but you're getting a little ahead of yourself. We found this out the hard way, because Suzuki failed to report in after he reached St. Louis International. We discovered him later in a phone booth inside the airport, dead. At first it looked as if he had suffered a heart attack, but the autopsy revealed that he had been hit with a dart. Crime lab figures that he had been injected with a lethal biotoxin which stopped his heart. Also, though he had logged into the field office computer through the pay phone, his datapad was missing. Someone murdered him for that pad. I don't think I have to tell you who did it.*

Bigthorn shook his head. "So, I take it, you suspect that the Salvatores figured out where the girl was going, then killed your agent to get the info he had collected in his datapad."

We were able to reconstruct her trail from following the paperwork she left behind her and by checking with TexSpace. She was on the shuttle in First Class, booked under the name of Mary Boston. It's a good lead, but Tony's people got a head start on us when they got Suzuki's datapad, and it took us until today to verify her whereabouts. So while Macy Westmoreland is definitely in Clarke County, we're not sure whether she's safe there. There might have been enough time for the Salvatores to put somebody on that shuttle with her.

"To bring her back?"

Brooks's face didn't change. *One of the reasons the Bureau hasn't been able to get anything on Tony Salvatore is because people who defect from the family rarely live long enough to talk about it. If Macy Westmoreland ran away from Tony . . . and that seems to be the case . . . then Tony wants her dead before he wants her back.*

Bigthorn took a deep breath. "Oh, shit."

I couldn't have put it better myself, Brooks agreed. *On the other hand, the Bureau is vitally interested in making contact with her. She may be able to provide information which can help us break up the family and put Tony behind bars . . . maybe in the deep freeze, if we're lucky. We've got an agent scheduled to arrive in three days on the next shuttle, but until then, we've got to have someone there to protect Westmoreland.* Brooks pointed a finger towards him. *Which is where you and your department come in, Sheriff.*

"I figured as much," Bigthorn replied. "Okay, I take it that you want me to put her in protective custody?"

Brooks hesitated. *The opinion is split on that. If she's being hunted by a Salvatore torpedo, that may be the best solution. On the other hand, she's apparently frightened out of her wits. She may bolt if anyone approaches her, even you. You need to use your best judgment here, Sheriff. In the meantime, you've been deputized for the indefinite time being to act as a U.S. federal marshal. The usual paperwork will be faxed to you, of course.*

The sheriff nodded again. He was familiar with the routine from federal collars he had made in the past. The difference between those instances and this one, of course, was considerable. Nabbing bail-jumpers and tax-evaders was one thing. Protecting a possible FBI informant was quite another.

"Let me try to make something clear, Sherman," he said. "I'm a small-town cop, when it comes down to brass tacks. This is a small-town cop shop. We had trouble this morning just capturing a couple of stray goats from the livestock area. Our idea of a big bust is nailing a tricycle thief. This department has seven officers, including myself, and we're only armed with nonlethal weapons. What makes you think we can do the FBI's job?"

Brooks gazed back at him stoically. *Do you have someone better in mind?*

Bigthorn started to reply, but Brooks went on. *There's something else you need to know. If the Salvatore family did put a hit man on the shuttle with Westmoreland, it could be any one of a number of their soldiers. However, one person in particular is a leading candidate. You want to check your screen again, please?*

A blurred, enlarged photo of a big, middle-aged man had appeared on Bigthorn's desktop screen. *That's Henry Ostrow. He works under a variety of aliases . . . rarely the same name twice . . . but in the Midwestern underworld he's sometimes known as the Golem. He's Jewish, incidentally, so his nickname is a reference to a creature from Hebrew mythology. . . .*

"He has my sympathy," Bigthorn commented. "I've got nickname trouble, too."

You should take this guy a little more seriously, Sheriff. He's suspected of being Tony's main enforcer. Like Salvatore himself, we've never been able to peg anything solid on him, but he's rumored to be the guy Tony picks for wet jobs which are . . . well, personal, for lack of a better term.

Bigthorn studied the picture. The photo looked as if it had been taken from an extreme distance as Ostrow was getting out of a car. His face was half-turned towards the camera. His eyes were hidden behind wraparound sunglasses, but the face looked hard and mean. "He looks like a really nice guy," the sheriff said dryly.

He gets the job done, and he doesn't get caught. No bullshit code of sportsmanship, either. The Golem's style is efficiency. If he can kill someone by shooting them in the back from a distance, that's the way he does it. Door bombs are another of his favorite means of assassination. We're still trying to find out whether he made it on the shuttle, but we . . .

Brooks was saying something else, but suddenly Bigthorn was no longer paying attention to him. The photo of Henry Ostrow had disappeared from the desk screen, to be replaced by several lines of type:

HENRY OSTROW IS CECIL JACOBSON.
CECIL JACOBSON JUST CHECKED INTO HIS ROOM AT THE
 LAGRANGE HOTEL.
I DON'T THINK HE'S HERE ON VACATION.
 —BLIND BOY GRUNT

"Oh, for crying out loud," Bigthorn whispered. "How could he possibly know . . . ?"

Excuse me, Sheriff? Brooks said.

Abruptly, the message vanished from the screen. Bigthorn looked up from his desk. "Ostrow is here," he told Brooks. "He's in Clarke County. His name is Cecil Jacobson."

For the first time during their conversation, Brooks appeared nonplussed. He shook his head and held up his hands in confusion. *What . . . how could you know . . . ?*

"A reliable source," Bigthorn said quickly. Already his own shock was wearing off. He stood up and started to move from behind his desk. "We'll be in touch, Brooks."

Sheriff, wait! Brooks was half-rising from his own chair. *The Golem is extremely dangerous. You can't . . .*

"I can when I'm in a hurry. Talk to you later." Bigthorn stabbed a button on his desk which broke the connection, and Brooks disintegrated in a sparkling haze, leaving behind the blank corner of the holotank. Already the sheriff was out the door and in the outer office.

"Rollie!" he yelled. The officer jerked behind his computer terminal, spilling coffee into his lap. "Call the hotel and find out the room numbers for two people, names Cecil Jacobson and Mary Boston, Boston like in the city. Do it now!"

"I've picked up a Grunt worm in our system," Rollie said. "I traced it to . . ."

"Never mind that now. Wade, get over here!" Hoffman was reading his magazine again. He dropped it and jumped out of his chair as Bigthorn pressed his left palm against the weapon cabinet's lock and tapped in the authorization code with his right hand.

The armored door slid aside, exposing virtually the only arsenal in the colony: a rack of Taser pistols, stunrods, sedative rifles, concussion and smoke grenades, and body armor. As Hoffman hurried over, Bigthorn buckled a gunbelt holstered with a stunrod and his personal, handprint-activated Taser around his belt. He reached for the body armor, then drew back his hand. It was better to keep this quiet; wearing body armor into a hotel would only make them look like a SWAT team.

"Problems?" Hoffman asked.

"Big time. Taser and rod for you." He snatched the weapons out of the cabinet and tossed them to Hoffman. "Get 'em on and follow me. We're heading for the hotel."

"John, what's . . . ?"

"You're going to find a woman named Macy Westmoreland, a.k.a. Mary Boston, and take her into protective custody," Bigthorn continued. "I'll be at the hotel, too, going for a guy named Henry Ostrow, a.k.a. Cecil Jacobson. I don't have time to explain everything now. C'mon!"

As Hoffman struggled to strap on his weapons, Bigthorn rushed past him, heading for the back door, where the department's cart was parked outside.

If Blind Boy Grunt's right about this, he thought, *I'll kiss his ass. And if's he's pulling my leg, I'm going to find him and throw him out the nearest airlock.*

7

Conversation with the Golem
(Saturday: 12:34 P.M.)

Henry Ostrow lay on the bed in his small room in the LaGrange Hotel. He had showered and shaved, and now he was resting on his back in his undershorts, staring up at the ceiling as he prepared himself for the transformation.

Ostrow had lost count of the number of assignments he had taken on behalf of the Salvatore family over the years. Most had been fairly routine, yet this time the job was more than a simple hit on someone who had welshed on a loan or an untrustworthy syndicate member who was trying to leave the family. This time it was Tony's own girlfriend who was going to take the bullet. There was also the matter of the small bundle of floppies which Macy had stolen.

Rarely had the Golem been asked to do more for Tony than snuff someone. This time, killing Macy was only half the job. The rest of the floppies could be burned, Tony had told him, but Disk 7 had to be returned to him at all costs. Even the girl was second in priority to the recovery of that particular diskette.

Ostrow didn't inquire as to why bringing home a computer diskette was more important than knocking off someone who had embarrassed the head of family. It was not in his nature to ask. The Golem was an instrument of vengeance, pure and simple . . . and now the time had come for Ostrow to summon the aleph bearer.

His suitcase lay open on the bureau. In a few minutes, Ostrow would take out the case's false bottom, exposing the scan-deflecting weapons cache. Fitted into the cache were the weapons he had picked for this trip: the syringe-gun with its sea wasp biotoxin, the Ruger T-512 automatic with the attached silencer, and the M-61 Skorpion submachine gun, all with their respective ammo, each shielded from automatic scanners by stealth chips. Concealed within the suitcase's fabric liner was one pound of plastic explosive, flattened by a kitchen rolling pin into thin sheets and wrapped in cellophane; the detonator and fuses were hidden inside an innocent-looking electric shaver.

Yet before he unpacked the weapons, there was the ritual. Murder, when performed well, requires its own rites to keep the mind clear and the deed from becoming meaningless. For Henry Ostrow, that ritual was becoming the Golem.

Henry Ostrow: the Golem. It was a far more serious matter than simply having a nickname.

Although there is more than one "definitive" golem story in Hebrew mythology, it was the most widely known fable which characterized Ostrow's alter ego: how the Rabbi Loew created an artificial man out of clay to protect the persecuted Jews of medieval Prague. According to legend, Rabbi Loew had summoned his clay man to life with an incantation involving the Hebrew letter *aleph*.

Henry Ostrow had been called the Golem since he had been in the Marines during Gulf War II. At first, it had been only a nickname, but as he had taken his knack for killing back to the world with him, his self-image as an unstoppable force of nature had evolved until he had realized that he was, indeed, the Golem. The fact that the mythical golem was the protector of a defenseless people, or that it later ran amuck and had to be destroyed, wasn't important to him. It was the gestalt vision of an unemotional, indestructible force of nature—the ultimate hit man, the killer that could not be stopped—which had long ago coiled itself within Ostrow's imagination.

In time, his belief was formed into a sacred ritual. At first, Ostrow had merely traced an aleph on his forehead with his fingertip before an assignment. Then, over the years, a more complex ritual of cleansing his mind and body evolved from that practice. First, Ostrow bathed and rested, to clear his mind of all tangential matters except The Job. While he bathed, he washed his mind as well as his body. Hatred, pity, fear, empathy, friendship, jealousy—these feelings caused the eyes to waver and the hands to hesitate when the moment came to render death, so it was necessary to rinse them down the drain.

Once he had showered, Ostrow relaxed for a short while, to prepare himself for the second part of the ritual. Now, supine on the bed, he shut his eyes and thought of transformation: his flesh hardening, turning darker, becoming clay like the mud on the banks of the Dead Sea. Dark red clay: the Golem's skin, incapable of bleeding. His body: an animate sculpture, incapable of feeling pain.

The Golem's right hand rose—a hand that was no longer flesh but living clay—and his index finger went to his mouth, resting for a moment on his tongue. His finger tasted like clay. The wet clay finger went from his mouth to his forehead. The final station of transformation was at hand, the moment of the aleph. . . .

BAM! BAM! BAM!

A hammering at the door. Someone knocking. Suddenly, he was flesh again. The aleph had not been traced on his forehead. The ritual interrupted at the crucial moment, the transformation was instantly erased, and Henry Ostrow was himself again.

Irritated, he sat up on the bed. "Who is it?" he called out.

"Housekeeping," a man's voice responded, muffled by the door. "I need to check your room, sir."

"Sure. One moment, please." Ostrow stood up, pulled on his pants, quickly rezipped his suitcase and entered the security code on the touchpad. *Bloody nuisance*, he silently grumbled. *No tip for this kid.* Wearing only his trousers, he walked to the door, turned the antique brass knob and swung open the door. . . .

The stock of a rifle swung into his stomach. He was instantly slammed back from the door by the painful impact, the breath knocked out of his lungs. Ostrow crashed backwards into a desk chair, toppled over it, fell on his back onto the carpeted floor. The coarse fabric burned the bare skin of his back; he gasped, tried to sit up as tiny white and blue stars filled his vision . . . and froze as he heard the menacing, unmistakable *cha-click* of a gun's safety being disengaged.

"Freeze," a voice said.

Lying on the floor, Ostrow gave himself a moment to size up the intruder. A police officer: he wore a blue uniform with a silver badge, like so many other blue uniforms with silver badges he had seen in his lifetime. The cop was armed: the rifle was a Remington Crowdmaster, a nonlethal but nonetheless efficient weapon in trained hands. A Taser, a stunrod, and two grenades were clipped to his belt. The cop was big—over six feet tall, young and muscular, with the steady air of purpose and authority that separates the pros from part-time night watchmen, body-guards, and rent-a-cops. As an abstract footnote, he also noted that the man was an American Indian.

"I'm frozen," Ostrow replied. He then remembered to turn

on the proper response to this violent intrusion. "What the hell do you think you're doing?" he yelled. "What . . . who the hell are you?"

"Clarke County Sheriff's Department," the intruder said evenly. "Shut up."

"How dare you . . . ?"

The cop stepped back a couple of feet and, with his hands keeping the stun rifle leveled at Ostrow, kicked the door shut with his heel. "Because I'm the law here, Ostrow, that's how," he answered.

It was not the first time that during an assignment taken under an assumed identity someone had addressed him by his real name. The response was standard, because one could always hope that the cop—especially if he was a local—would have second thoughts, doubts as to whether he had nailed the right person.

"What?" he said querulously, injecting the right amount of bewildered terror into his voice. "I don't know what you're . . . What the hell are you talking about?" He shook his head and motioned vaguely towards himself. "Are you talking to *me*?"

"Yeah, asshole, I'm talking to you." The rifle didn't waver even a fraction of an inch. "Don't waste my time with that lame shit. Your name's Henry Ostrow. You're also known as the Golem."

Okay. So much for the mistaken identity shtick. Ostrow didn't even glance in the direction of his suitcase. Even if it wasn't zipped and sealed, it was much too far away for him to get to his weapons. Perhaps if he could make this guy feel more comfortable . . .

"I'm unarmed and on the ground, officer," he said calmly. "You've got me. See? Could I just sit up and . . . ?"

"No," the cop commanded. "Stay on the floor. Make a move and you're off to sleepyland."

So much for that approach, too. This guy *was* professional. Ostrow had to admire that, even if he wanted to snap the red bastard's neck right now.

"Maybe I'm Ostrow, and maybe I'm not," he replied easily. "If you think you have something on me, make an arrest. I'd like to see you make it stick, considering how you just broke through the door."

The man in the uniform—J. Bigthorn according to his name-plate—only shrugged. "There's not going to be an arrest, Ostrow. Nobody's ever been able to make anything stick on you.

At the same time, I know this conversation isn't going to leave this room. That's because you're the sort of person who likes to keep a low profile."

"I don't quite understand you."

"It's very simple," Bigthorn replied. "You're a torpedo for a slug named Tony Salvatore, and you're here to kill a woman named Macy Westmoreland. Now, I don't expect you to suddenly become candid, but you know, and I know, and the FBI knows that's the situation."

Ostrow immediately, instinctively opened his mouth to deny the charge. "Shut up," Bigthorn snapped. "You'd only be wasting my time. Just listen to me. You're Number One on my shit list. I've got your number."

Ostrow shrugged. "Big deal. You're boring me, Bigthorn."

"You want a deal?" the Indian asked. "Okay, here's your deal. The woman goes unharmed while she's here. Got it? If she turns up dead, if she's harmed in any way, you're not just a suspect. You're the man, and I'm coming after you."

"Whatever happened to due process of law?" Ostrow asked.

"Screw that," Bigthorn responded. "I'm the only judge and jury you're getting here, bugfucker. Get this through your head. If the Westmoreland girl so much as has a bad dream, you're the one I blame. Don't even think about trying to arrange an accident. You better just hope she doesn't have any on her own."

Ostrow couldn't help but sneer back at him. He had heard tough-cop routines before, and you couldn't even dance to this one. He nodded his head towards the rifle in Bigthorn's hands. "What are you going to do if she does? Trank me with your little air gun?"

"Yeah, I'm going to trank you with my little air gun," Bigthorn said calmly. "Then I'm going to get my little wheelbarrow and put you in it, and then roll you down to my little airlock and shove your sleazy ass inside. Then I'm going to push the button and blow you out. If I get pissed off enough, I might even wait until you're conscious before I hit the button, so you'll be awake to feel the whole thing."

It was a vivid image. Ostrow did his best to block it from his mind. "Then you know what happens to you? A murder rap, that's what."

"For you?" Bigthorn shook his head slightly. "No, I kind of doubt it. Nobody minds when a killer finally gets what's coming to him. The only reason why nobody's done it before is that they've been hampered by that 'due process' stuff. Ain't no due process up here. The worst thing they'll probably do is fine me for using an airlock to throw out some garbage.''

"Tough talk," Ostrow replied. "I wonder if you can walk the talk.''

Bigthorn was quiet for a couple of moments. The Indian was looking thoughtfully away from him, and the hit man took the opportunity to study the floor space between the soles of his feet and Bigthorn's legs, gauging the distance from his legs to Bigthorn's knees. About three, maybe four feet. With luck, he could throw himself forward and, with the right amount of power behind his kick, break one of the big red fuck's knees. One strong kick and the joint would snap like a dry tree limb. Once he was down, Ostrow could get the gun away. Then he could ice the cop. No worries about completing the assignment after that.

"No, you're right," Bigthorn said then. "You should wonder whether I'm tough enough. I think you need a demonstration.''

The Indian stepped back a couple of feet—in an instant, putting himself out of range of Ostrow's counterattack—and raised the rifle to his shoulder, aiming straight at the hit man. Ostrow had just enough time to involuntarily suck in his breath before Bigthorn squeezed the trigger.

There was a pneumatic *thuffft!*, and a sedative dart buried itself in Ostrow's gut, just below the rib cage. All life seemed to drain out of his limbs, and he collapsed on the floor.

Just before he blacked out, Ostrow heard Bigthorn say, "Stay away from the girl.''

Then he was out cold.

8

Macy Drops Out
(Saturday: 12:45 P.M.)

The first space hotel, when it was finally built in Clarke County, was nothing like that which had been anticipated by space buffs or science-fiction writers. It looked just like a hotel.

During the twentieth century, everyone's favorite idea was to make the first hotel in space an orbital station all by itself. In fact, the Hilton Hotel chain at one point announced plans to develop an orbiting hotel, although that might have been no more than the hubris of its public relations staff. Later, in 2028, a small consortium of Saudi Arabian, Kuwaiti, and Lebanese businessmen purchased Skycorp's Olympus Station, the dilapidated and almost abandoned GEO habitat which had housed the beamjacks who built the first orbital powersats. The Arabs had announced plans to refurbish "Skycan" as a space hotel, but continued political unrest in the Middle East deterred other investors from backing the project, and the plan eventually died from lack of funds.

It was not until Clarke County was built that the first space hotel became reality, financed by the Clarke County Corporation. TexSpace and Trump, who had invested in the colony in hopes of establishing large-scale space tourism, were particularly responsible for LaGrange Hotel. Along with Larry Bird Memorial Stadium, it became the centerpiece of LaGrange, the biosphere's resort community. To nobody's surprise, the hotel resembled nothing more or less than any large Hyatt back on Earth. So much for zero g swimming pools.

When the three-wing hotel was built, convention facilities such as a few meeting rooms and a modest ballroom were added almost as an afterthought. No one really expected LaGrange to attract conventions. Occupancy of the hotel was limited to about 1,000 persons, and while the price of space travel had dropped drastically, it was considered unlikely that groups would want to book the LaGrange Hotel for meetings. In its advertising brochures the convention facilities were mentioned only in small print; the hotel's management did not even have a full-time convention liaison.

So it came as a considerable surprise when a demand arose for LaGrange as one of the choice locations for the annual gatherings of everyone from the American Meteorological Society to the Shriners to the Cookie O'Toole International Fan Club. Shoehorning conventions into the hotel without sacrificing the regular tourist trade required careful juggling of schedules by hotel management. Finally, the hotel stipulated that conventions had to cap their membership at 700 persons (preferably far less) and that the conventions could be held only during weekends, leaving the hotel vacant during weekdays for ordinary tourists. An organization requesting use of the convention facilities also had to put down a non-refundable deposit of $200,000 in advance, with no guarantee that it would get an opening within the next five years.

The Clarke County Corporation thought these restrictions would discourage most of the unwanted convention traffic. To a certain extent, it did: Mensa, the Baker Street Irregulars, and the World Science Fiction Society promptly dropped their bids, and even the National Space Society decided that Detroit was a bit more affordable.

However, to everyone's chagrin, the First Church of Twentieth Century Saints was more persistent.

Elvis Presley stood twenty feet tall in the center of the hotel mezzanine, a goliath with a guitar and a curled upper lip, towering above the heads of all those around him. His holographic image slowly revolved on the dais so that his grin was cast upon everyone in turn, while above his head a blue-white halo shimmered softly. Wade Hoffman paused on his way to the elevator to look at the giant hologram. As it rotated in his direction, the King of Rock and Roll winked at him.

"You've got to be kidding me," Hoffman murmured.

"Elvis never kids anybody, officer," a German-accented voice next to his shoulder said with great solemnity.

Hoffman turned to see a thin, intense-looking young man standing beside him. He wore a sweatshirt with—what else?—

Elvis Presley's image; on the young man's feet were the obligatory blue suede shoes of a true believer. Hoffman had already seen a few Church of Elvis members since he had entered the LaGrange Hotel, but this was his first close encounter with one of the worshipers. This one wore a plastic name tag: HI, MY NAME IS GUSTAV SCHMIDT.

The deputy started to say something innocuous, but the young German rushed on. "Do you know," he asked, "that if you take a deep breath, you stand a ninety per cent chance of inhaling the same molecules that the Prophet breathed in his last moments on this Earth?"

Schmidt waited for a reply. Hoffman thought about it for a moment before answering. "This isn't Earth," he said.

The follower shook his head impatiently. "It doesn't matter. Elvis is everywhere. And soon the day shall come when he brings the faithful to his shrine, his Promised Land."

"Oh. Okay." Hoffman started to edge away. Bigthorn wanted him to get to Macy Westmoreland's room and place her in protective custody, and he had lingered here too long. Yet his curiosity forced him to ask one more question. "Umm . . . where's the Promised Land?"

Schmidt's face expressed the blissful radiance of one who has seen the Light. "In the land men call Memphis," he intoned. "The home of the Prophet Elvis, Graceland Mansion, where his earthly form lies buried."

He then smiled conspiratorially. "Or so it has been alleged. There were, of course, the sightings of the Prophet in Kalamazoo and Las Vegas, ten years after his supposed death. And then there were the tapes of his voice, and the government-suppressed discovery of a singing statue of the King on Mars, which leaves many of us to believe that . . ."

"Yeah. Right." Hoffman coughed and took another step away. "Well, if you'll excuse me . . ."

Schmidt nodded his head. "Go then, and may Elvis be with you," he said in benediction.

The law officer turned away and began walking to the nearest row of elevators. Weird business, indeed. Next to listening to that wacko, finding Macy Westmoreland and taking her into custody should be a snap.

Macy's suite was enormous, almost the size of Tony's bedroom in the mansion, and as plushly furnished as a first-class hotel suite can be: cherry oak bureau, canopied four-poster bed,

Queen Anne writing desk, French tapestries on the walls, and a Mitsubishi entertainment center that took up one side of the room, discreetly concealed by a Chinese silk screen.

Naturally, it had been very expensive to import such luxury from Earth to LaGrangian orbit. The daily rate for the suite was more than families in some countries earned in a year. Naturally, it had gone on the Mary Boston credit card; the Salvatore book-keeping computer would unquestioningly pay the bill as usual. Macy appreciated none of this, however. She had come to expect opulence at every turn in her life; she never questioned who put the silver spoon in her mouth. All that mattered to her was the privacy which the suite afforded.

Before she had checked in, she had dropped into a store in the tourist shopping area across O'Neill Square from the hotel, and had bought some fresh clothes with the Amex card. Now, having showered, she zipped up the front of a white linen jump-suit and pulled around her shoulders and neck a Scottish red wool scarf as she admired her reflection in the mirror. For something bought off the rack, the clothes fit her well.

A sliding glass door led out to a wide private balcony with a wrought-iron railing, overlooking the river terrace and the ho-tel's private beach on the New Tennessee River. Absently ad-justing the scarf, she walked over to the door, slid it open, and walked out onto the balcony. The immense panorama of the biosphere rose before her. Across the river she could see goats and sheep grazing in the distant, upwardly curving pastures. On the promenade below, a cocktail party was taking place. She admired the view for a few moments, then strode back into the suite, leaving the door open to admit the warm breeze of the colony's perpetual summer.

Her eyes fell upon the dresser and the black nylon bag lying on top of it. The lid of the writing desk concealed a small com-puter terminal. Now that she had the chance, maybe it was time to see what was on those diskettes.

Macy reached into the open bag and pulled a diskette out, at random. It was Number 7. Juggling the little plastic wafer be-tween her fingers, she walked over to the desk, pushed back the cover, and started to slip the diskette into the drive. . . .

At that moment there was a knock. Macy jerked away from the desk, clutching the diskette in her hands, and stared across the room at the door. For a few moments there was silence, then the heavy rapping came again, followed by a man's voice: "Hello?"

"Who's there?" Macy called out, unable to suppress the quaver in her voice.

"Clarke County Sheriff's Department," the voice replied. "Open up, please, Ms. Westmoreland."

Not for an instant did Macy consider that it *really* was somebody from the Sheriff's Department. Every bit of identification she had used since escaping from the Salvatore compound had Mary Boston's name on it; no one here should be addressing her as "Ms. Westmoreland." Also, there was no reason why the colony's police department would want anything to do with her. Finally, she knew that Tony's goon squad was capable of masquerading as virtually anyone, from a hotel porter to another tourist to a police officer.

So there was no doubt in her mind that the Salvatore family had followed her to Clarke County, and that at this moment a killer—possibly even wearing a cop's uniform—was waiting on the other side of the door. Whoever it was, though, had made a mistake: he had addressed her by her real name.

She took a deep breath. "Just a minute," she said, trying not to sound alarmed. "I'm not dressed."

It was a lame excuse, but if it bought her just a few moments . . .

In a couple of quick steps, Macy was across the room, dropping the Number 7 diskette back in the shoulder bag as she hurriedly picked up her high-heel sandals. She glanced over her shoulder at the balcony. Thank God she had left the sliding door open. There would be no noise to give her away. She grinned crazily, put her shoes in the bag, then grabbed the zipper and tugged. All she had to do was . . . .

The zipper moved down the plastic track an inch, then snarled on a piece of fabric. Impatiently, Macy hauled at it . . . and the zipper broke. Now the bag, with its bundles of cash and diskettes inside, would not close. "Oh, goddammit!" she swore.

Again, the killer was knocking on the door. "Ms. Westmoreland, open the door, please."

"I'm *coming*, dammit!" she shouted, frustrated and recklessly angry. "Give me a second, okay?"

"It's urgent that we speak to you, ma'am," the voice replied as she bundled the shoulder bag under her arm and quickly, quietly, ran across the carpet to the balcony. "We have reason to believe that you're in extreme danger."

Yeah, I'm sure I am, Macy thought as she stepped out onto the balcony and slung one leg over the iron railing, preparing to make the twelve-foot jump to the terrace below. *Just be stupid for a few more seconds, pal. . . .*

Then the rational part of her mind brought the situation into perspective. If she simply jumped from the balcony, she could break a leg, even in the colony's lighter-than-normal gravity. She would be crippled, lying on the tiles, screaming and helpless, when the Salvatore torpedo—conveniently dressed as a cop—arrived down below to rescue her.

The banging at the door was becoming more insistent.

No other choice. Macy pulled the bag's strap over her shoulder. As she brought her other leg over the railing, hanging onto the iron fence with both hands and standing on her toes on the narrow edge of the balcony, she heard a voice below her call out, "Hey, lady, I wouldn't do that if I were you."

"Shut up!" she yelled.

The doorknob rattled, then there was the heavy impact of the killer throwing his shoulder against the door.

Macy took a deep breath, then stepped back while clinging to the rail with her hands. Several voices shouted below her. The sweat in her palms caused her hands to slide down the rail posts. Her biceps screamed pain. Then, in a moment in which her heart seemed to cease beating and time itself seemed to stop, her hands involuntarily let go of the railing and she fell. . . .

Simon McCoy paused while we watched a cargo ship launch from Merritt Island.

From down the coast, across the rippling blue water, we could hear dimly the warning Klaxons from the distant pad. A few minutes later there was a brilliant flash of light and a sudden blossoming of dark smoke. A tiny white cylinder—either a Hughes Jarvis HLV or a Boeing Big Dummy, it was hard to tell them apart from the distance—silently rose from the smoke, riding atop an orange-white lance of fire. As it sprinted upwards into the warm afternoon sky, the crackling roar of the liftoff finally reached us.

The wharf seemed to shudder as the immense noise rippled across the channel. All at once, we heard the false thunderclap of the sonic boom, from many miles above, as the cargo ship's velocity surpassed Mach One. Within a couple of minutes, the spacecraft had disappeared, leaving behind a slender, slowly dissipating column of smoke which stretched into the stratosphere like a vaporous stalagmite.

I sighed and looked down from the sky, to see that McCoy had been watching me, a smile on his face. "Good launch," I murmured.

"How many have you seen?" he asked.

I shrugged. "Oh, I lost count a long time ago. But it's never become routine, at least not for me." I thought about it for a moment, probably because I hadn't considered my emotions for some time. "You have to have been a space buff for as long as I have, to know what it's like. I was born with the space age, in 1958, but I remember when we practically didn't have a space program. The bad old days of the twentieth century."

He nodded his head, looking out at the distant launch pads. "Where that freighter lifted off . . . That's the complex where the Icarus rockets were launched, isn't it? That must have been something to see."

"Yeah, it was," I replied. Then I thought about what he had just said. "Why, didn't you see it?" I asked as casually as possible.

"No, I missed it." Then he caught himself. "I was out of the country at the time," he added swiftly.

Not swiftly enough, though. He might have been out of the country when the Icarus missions were launched from the Cape, but that was hardly a likely excuse. It was like saying, "No, I slept through 2047, so I didn't notice the most important thing that happened that year."

The Icarus project was something which everyone in the world had witnessed, for it was the closest human civilization had come to terminal global catastrophe of natural causes. It had taken four unmanned spacecraft, each armed with a 100-megaton nuke, to deflect the Apollo asteroid Icarus from its collision course with Earth. The week the nukes intercepted Icarus, one at a time in staggered volleys between 10 and 20 million miles from Earth, the whole world had been watching, quite literally. Live TV transmissions, from a satellite deployed in high orbit to monitor the mission, had been seen in every country. There had also been such sideshows as mass evacuations from coastal areas, riots in major cities, doomsday proclamations by at least a dozen religious cults, and a few dozen suicides, some of them in public. In the year 2047 the human race blew a fuse; it had felt a lot like 1968.

There was a universal sigh of relief when the news came that a flying mountain was no longer about to make the human race one with the dinosaurs, the last residents of Earth to have been clobbered by an asteroid. Simon McCoy must have been in one hell of a remote locale to have missed that scene. Even aborigines in Terra del Fuego had watched the launch of the Icarus rockets on their pocket TVs.

"The bad old days of the twentieth century," McCoy repeated, a not very subtle way of changing the subject. "I take it that you're talking about the era when space exploration was exclusively a government undertaking?"

"That's right." If McCoy was trying to distract me, he could had done worse than to pick one of my favorite topics. "A political football is more like it, though. At least, that's the way it was in the U.S. There were senators like Proxmire and Mondale who tried to kill the program to make themselves look more populist, and Presidents like Nixon and Reagan who supported it only when it was convenient for their political agendas and dropped the ball when things like the *Challenger* disaster occurred. The best thing to happen was when NASA was deinstitutionalized and space development was handed over to private industry."

"I see," McCoy said. "So I guess you don't have anything against the major space corporations."

"Not on principle, no. Skycorp, Uchu-Hiko, TexSpace, and the rest showed that you can operate a space fleet without a federal-size budget, not as long as you applied basic business sense. Controlling overhead costs was something that NASA never really learned. As small as its budget was back then, and as much as it fought for every dime, NASA still spent money like a drunken sailor. Lots of gold-plating just to inflate costs, when the idea should be the other way around. But if the companies go into the red, there's no sugar-daddy Congress to bail them out in the next fiscal year."

McCoy stood up to stretch his legs. He absently walked to one of the old telescopes, pressed a quarter into the slot and peered through the eyepiece. "I see. So you believe private industry saved space exploration."

"To a certain extent, yes, I do," I said defensively. "Call me a filthy capitalist pig, if you want, but at least we don't have to depend exclusively on NASA anymore."

"But privatization is not without its drawbacks," he said. The telescope ticked softly.

I nodded, squinting a little as the sun glared off the surf. As I answered I fumbled in my shirt pocket for my antique aviator-style sunglasses. One of the more pleasant relics of the last century, and rare as dinosaur bones. Sometimes I lie awake at night, wondering what would become of me were I to break the last pair of aviator specs on Earth.

"No, of course not," I replied. "There's little basic research for its own sake being done by the companies. With the emphasis being on near-Earth commercial space projects, exploration is beginning to suffer. Except for stuff like the Jovian system probes and some more American-Soviet work on Mars, we're beginning to stagnate. The Daedalus probe was the last major new-start program, and we probably won't see a follow-up because no one wants to spend money on something which won't produce results for another generation. So that's the problem with market-driven space exploration, at least as I see it."

"Too many fishermen and not enough Columbuses." McCoy pursed his lips thoughtfully as he swiveled the telescope to look at the Merritt Island pads. "Interesting perspective. What do the companies have to say about that?"

"Nothing to me," I replied. "I wrote an essay on the subject for *Harper's* and lost some of my best contacts for my trouble. Skycorp especially is notorious for cutting off its relationships with writers who give 'em too much flak, so . . ." I stopped. "So what's it to you, anyway? You're the one who's supposed to be telling me a story."

McCoy continued to study the coastline through the telescope. "Idle interest. I've always wondered why you've never gone to Clarke County. Certainly you've been offered the chance."

I drained the last of my beer and thought about getting the robot to fetch me another one. "Sure. I was on the list for a press junket right after the colony was opened, but I passed it up. I don't think reporters should take junkets. And once you've seen one tourist trap, you've seen 'em all.''

McCoy laughed. The telescope's timer ran out and the shutter closed with an audible *clunk*. ''I've never heard Clarke County described as a tourist trap before,'' he said as he looked up from the eyepiece. ''Damn. Doesn't give you much time, does it?''

''That's about all Clarke County ever has been.'' The beer was hitting me hard, but I didn't care. I was warming to the subject. ''That's what makes me furious about the colony. It started off as an ambitious idea, but Skycorp and TexSpace realized the tourist potential of the place, and before we knew it, we got Disneyland in space. Everything else takes a back seat. That's what I mean about market-driven stagnation.''

McCoy shrugged again. ''But tourism was one of the prime movers for space exploration,'' he pressed, playing the devil's advocate. ''That's where much of the money came from, since your 'sugar-daddy Congress' left the picture.''

I waved my hand impatiently. ''Yeah, yeah, I've heard all that before. My point is that space is still a frontier. Living out there isn't as hard as it was thirty years ago, but it's still no place for sightseers. The job demands settlers.''

I paused to think about what we had been discussing. ''If it hadn't been for the tourist trade,'' I added, ''this whole Church of Elvis business wouldn't have happened.''

McCoy seemed to ponder that for a few moments. ''Perhaps. But the fifth Icarus nuke was still up there. Since Macy Westmoreland would have found the launch codes anyway, I don't think . . .''

''She never had the codes,'' I interrupted. ''That was something that came out of the Church of Elvis.''

Smiling vaguely, McCoy turned away from the telescope and resumed his seat on the bench. ''No, not quite. Let's pick up the story again, shall we . . . ?''

9

A Free Country
(Saturday: 4:21 P.M.)

Ralph Gentry wrapped the suit's right-hand claw manipulator around a spar and moved his left leg to brace the heavy boot against a crosspiece. Raising the blunt tube of the welding torch at the end of his right arm, he adjusted the electronic cross hairs superimposed on his main screen until they were centered on the juncture where the two aluminum rebars touched. He moved his head and squinted through the eyepiece of the periscope to visually double-check his work, then he squeezed his right hand around the trigger of the torch.

The free-electron laser beam, normally invisible, showed up in the infrared field of vision of the suit's tiny monitor screen as a thin red line, and the aluminum silently bubbled and spat tiny globules as the rebars were slowly welded together. Once the weld was complete, Gentry tested it with a tug of his claw-manipulator. Satisfied that the weld was solid, he glanced up at the computer-generated position screen, just above his head within the tiny cockpit of the suit. The beam-builder spiders had continued to lay down a gridwork of slender beams to his left, stretching away in the distance, curving around behind him to form the skeleton of Torus 19.

A voice came through his headset. *Candy Apple-two-one, do you copy? Over.*

"Open comlink," Gentry told his suit. "Central, this is Candy Apple-two-one, we copy. What's up?"

Gene King, the shift foreman, came on the line from the construction shack. *Gentry, what are you up to over there? Over.*

"Welding work on Nancy-one-nine, section two-one," Gentry replied. "It's coming along nicely."

Can you put it on hold? Ned Ruiz developed a slow leak in his LOX tank and had to go in for a fix. Gold Team's short one person putting the external shields near you on Nancy-one-niner and they need a hand. That's bearing X-Ray two-zero, Yankee minus ten, Zulu three-six, on section zero-two. Nebraska Tango one-seven is the person you need to see. Over.

"Okey-doke, Gene. On my way. Candy Apple-one-two out."

Gentry began to walk across the torus's outer framework. The massive exoskeleton he wore—or, more accurately, piloted—amplified the movements of his arms and legs, transforming him into a juggernaut. *Watch out, here comes Conan the Beamjack.* He needed that extra strength; since the incomplete torus rotated along with the rest of the colony, he was subject to one g gravity.

He lumbered down the giant torus—passing other armored beamjacks at work on the skeleton, glimpsing construction pods transporting material from one side of the torus to another, spotting through the gridwork the floating hulk of a mass-driver barge which had hauled aluminum cassettes up from Descartes Station on the Moon.

He found Gold Team, struggling to get the outer shields attached to the outer hull of that section of Torus N-19. The shields were huge rectangular slabs of crushed, compacted moonrock. It took two beamjacks in construction armor to successfully maneuver the shields into position on the supporting gridwork. It was hard, painstaking labor, but not so difficult that they couldn't swap gossip while they worked.

Hey, did you see that thing that was on the bulletin board today? Luke Garcia—also known as Nebraska Tango one-seven—asked. He was holding onto the opposite end of a slab as they gently lowered it into a cavity. Below them, another Gold Team beamjack, Alicia Shay, was hanging by her claw manipulator to the underside of the skeleton, waiting to weld the shield's pins to the support struts.

"Naw, what thing?" Gentry asked.

Take it about three degrees to the left, guys, Ali interrupted, watching her suit's heads-up display. *Okay, okay . . . there we go. You mean that note we got in the mail? Total bullshit.*

So who asked you anyway? Luke responded. *Okay, that got it?*

Got it, just hold it right there. Ali's laser torch came up, and on their screens they could see the pencil-thin flash of the laser beam. *Gee, Luke, I thought that was an open question. . . .*

Well, it wasn't. I was talking to Ralphie here. . . .

Excuse me for expressing an opinion, then, Ali retorted. *I thought this was a free country. Ah, those turkeys, they're always putting those pins off a few inches. Can you . . . ? Naw, wait, I can still reach 'em. . . .*

Well, that's the point, isn't it? Luke went on. *I mean, it's a free country down there, but up here we've got our asses in hock to the companies. I don't think . . .*

That's your whole problem, Luke, Ali shot back. *You don't think. Face it, pal, you've got a cozy gig. You're making enough dough from your contract to start that restaurant you've always talked about, and you don't have to worry about falling off no goddamn skyscraper to get it. So don't bite the hand that feeds you, dig?*

Well, what if I want to stay here and open that restaurant on the Strip? Luke said. *I don't want to have to give everything I make to the companies, or have them tell me what or where or why. . . .*

"I think . . ." Gentry started to say.

What makes you think it's any different now? Ali cut in, brushing him aside. *Skycorp and Uchu-Hiko built the place, TexSpace runs the tourist business, Trump bought the hotel and the Strip . . . geez, Luke, what makes you think this is a free country, anyway?*

Because you said it was a free country, that's why! Garcia laughed. *Didja hear that, Ralph? I got her!*

I just don't think a revolution is going to solve anything, Ali sulked.

I dunno. Can't hurt, can it?

Famous last words. Shay's laser winked out. *All right, that's got it. Let's get the next section done.*

Gentry, listening to the exchange over his comlink, was quietly thinking it over. The idea of public insurrection didn't make him very comfortable, though. Even if he himself was making barely enough money to get by—his personal debts were massive, and life in Clarke County was hardly cheap—the thought of mobs marching on town hall with torches in hand was unsettling. Just let me get through the day, he thought as he followed the other armored beamjacks to the next section. All I want is a cold beer and a hot meal and someplace to sleep at night.

Yet, deep down inside, it was an exhilarating thought: to push the Corporation's back to the wall, to tell them that he was goddamn sick and tired of giving all his money back to them, leaving him with just enough for the necessities of life. They paid the people who worked for them nickels and dimes, then wanted it all back for rent and groceries. *They just gave me a two-buck raise*, he thought. *Next week, they'll probably increase my rent.* Maybe there was something to this revolution business. . . .

Cougar Joe got off the Red Line tram at Torus S-12 and walked down to his *bofaellesskaber*, the Danish-style co-housing complex he shared with three other New Ark families. It had been a long day on the farm for him. Weeds had managed to get their ugly little roots into some of the hydroponics tanks in S-16, meaning that Joe and two other Ark farmers had spent the better part of the day with their arms in the tanks, trying to locate and dig out the weeds before they overwhelmed the beansprouts. It had been hard, messy work, and Cougar Joe was hoping that someone else among his neighbors was in the mood for a beer.

Not entirely to his surprise, a couple of other Ark farmers were gathered around a tree-shaded picnic table in the courtyard of the *bofaellesskaber*. Since their bamboo townhouses were built around the courtyard of the pocket-size neighborhood, the picnic table was a natural meeting place for the adults while their kids futzed around on the playground slides and monkey bars. It was Kenny Bartel's turn to bring the six-pack to the table; he and Tess Greene were already working through their first beers when Cougar Joe sat down at the table.

"Hey, Cougar Joe, the man of the hour!" Kenny said heartily, holding out a cold brew. "Do your trick, big guy." Tess's kids, Pat and Teddy, scurried over from the slide when they heard Kenny's challenge.

Joe glowered at him, then slowly let a low, sullen growl rise from his chest through his throat. Pat and Teddy watched with amazement, and Kenny and Tess grinned silently. Then Cougar Joe stuck the lip of the beer bottle between his molars, clamped down hard, and quickly ripped the cap off with his teeth.

"*Grrrrumph!*" he snarled as he spat out the cap and upended the bottle in a savage gulp.

Pat squealed with delight. "Max-Q gross-o-rama!" Teddy yelled.

"Now get lost," Tess commanded, giving her five-year-old son a swat on the rear. Teddy turned and ran back to the slide, followed by his little sister. Tess looked back at Cougar Joe. "We're going to be buying you false teeth one of these days if you keep that up."

Cougar Joe grinned, then tapped his fingertips piano-like across his dentures. "Too late," he said. "Already in."

Tess's mouth dropped open. "Got 'em kicked out when I was sixteen, playing football in high school," Joe explained. "The violent days of my ill-spent youth."

"Max-Q gross-o-rama, to coin a phrase." Kenny pushed a folded sheet of paper across the table to him. "Did you see this?"

Joe glanced down at the computer printout. "Found it in my mailbox today," he said, not bothering to read it again. He shrugged. "Anybody talked to Jenny about this yet?"

Tess shook her head. "Nobody's seen her all day. Robyn Abbey tried to call her at home, but there was no answer." She rested her elbows on the table and cupped her face in her hands. "I dunno. Maybe it's another one of Blind Boy Grunt's practical jokes."

"Grunt's never played a practical joke like this." Kenny absently twirled the printout around the table with his finger. "Problem is, we don't know what goes on in those executive sessions, unless Neil and Jenny tell us about it. They're not on-the-record meetings, so . . ." His voice trailed off.

"There's got to be something to it," Cougar Joe said. "Neil's been talking about co-oping the colony somehow, trying to get it out of the control of the consortium."

"Yeah, but to this extent?" Tess asked. "I mean, this is pretty radical, even for Neil."

"Maybe it's not Neil," Kenny said. "Maybe it was Jenny's idea." He tapped the printout with his finger. "It says right here that she 'announced' it, whatever that means."

"Jenny doing something independent of Neil?" Tess's brow furrowed. "That doesn't figure. I mean, it's no secret those two haven't been getting along lately, but . . ."

"But what?" Cougar Joe asked. "Jenny's got a mind of her own. Why couldn't she propose something without Neil's consent?"

"Hey, there's a difference between disagreeing about what's going to be for dinner and what's going to be the future of the colony," Tess replied. "I mean, Neil's the Ark's leader, right? The Ark's block-vote got him elected to the Board of Selectmen, right?" She shook her head. "I like Jenny, too, y'know, but we can't have our spokesman talking with two heads. . . ."

"The thing . . . *with two heads!*" Kenny intoned theatrically. He reached into his trouser pocket, pulled out an antique snuff can and a pack of cigarette papers. "Once it was a normal person. Then . . . it became a *politician!*"

"Drop dead," Tess said, unamused. "This is serious."

Cougar Joe took another sip from his beer. "Sure it's serious," he said, "but I'm not so sure it's a bad idea, no matter who suggested it. I mean, this whole place could be turned into an amusement park if the consortium has its way. What if the greed-heads decide they want to put another hotel in the biosphere, right where the farms are?"

"They wouldn't do that," Tess said.

"Sure they would," Kenny argued, carefully sifting a pinch of marijuana onto a leaf of bamboo paper. The pot was from the private New Ark crop the commune discreetly cultivated in Kenny's hydroponics section. "If they thought they could make more money off the tourist trade, they could get the Ark kicked right out of here." He put aside the snuff can and began rolling the joint between his fingers. "Ever seen the early artists' conceptions of O'Neill colonies, back when they were first thought up in the last century? The biospheres were pictured as wall-to-wall tract housing, complete with backyard barbecue grills. Looked like New Jersey in orbit. Space as a giant suburb."

"Okay, so it's a nasty idea," Tess agreed. "But I'm not sure if I'm ready to follow Neil and Jenny into a revolution, either."

"Hey, if it's a choice between tourists and us, I'll pick us any day." Kenny delicately licked the paper's seam. "Say hey, amigo?"

"Maybe," Joe answered. "Let's wait till tomorrow night. I'm sure we'll get the whole story then." He paused. "From Neil or Jenny . . . whoever is in charge."

He paused, then added, "But if they're talking about a revolution . . . hell, I'll second the motion. Who needs another goddamn shopping center?"

"Damn straight." Kenny held up the joint. "Got a light?"

It was quitting time, but the offices of BioCybe Resources, located in the light-industry zone of Torus N-1, were still open. Art Kiminski pushed his chair back from his CAD/CAM console and, propping his legs up on his eternally littered desk, reached for the Pepsi brought to him by his co-partner and senior scientist. It was the end of another day, and everyone else had gone home for the Memorial Day weekend. It was time for the customary after-work bull session.

"I don't get it," Kiminski said as he popped the top of the cardboard container. "We're finally getting this colony on the right track, and somebody gets the crazy idea that we should go for national independence."

Yuji Kaneko took his seat at the adjacent desk, to savor the cup of hot tea he had just poured for himself. "The idea was bound to come up eventually," he replied. "I'm only surprised that it's happened so soon."

"So soon?" Kiminski repeated. "You mean, before the colony's been completed?"

"Sort of." The Japanese-American bioengineer gently sipped his tea, then laid the delicate cup on top of a pile of printouts. "More like before there was any real chance at economic independence. Perhaps the Schorrs did not look before leaping."

"Perhaps?" Kiminski's lips curled. "Yuji, nobody in their right minds would even dream of suggesting something like independence for Clarke County, let alone going public with it." He jabbed his finger at Kaneko. "Not now, not ever."

"Ever?" Smiling skeptically, Kaneko looked askance at the cyberneticist. " 'Ever' is a long time, Art. Maybe in ten, twenty years . . ." He shrugged. "Anything is possible."

"Not bloody likely," Kiminski said bitterly. "Who would govern this place? The Ark hippies? We'd be on strict vegetarian diets and required to carry copies of *Das Kapital* if they got their way."

"Oh, c'mon!"

"I'm serious!" Kaneko broke up laughing. Kiminski, holding up his hands, quickly shook his head. "Okay, okay, maybe not literally . . . but you know they'd try to govern the way they run the Ark. Endless affinity group meetings, trying to handle everything by consensus, with everyone kowtowing to Neil Schorr as if he was some sort of godhead. The whole place would fall apart like that"—he snapped his fingers—"because consensus opinion would have to be reached on every matter, significant or not."

Kaneko reached for his tea again. "Oh, we don't know that it would happen like that. The Ark accounts for only about one-fourth of the population here. Even if they voted in a block, like they usually do, they couldn't dictate their way of thinking to the rest of us. I think we'd probably have some sort of democracy."

Kiminski nodded vigorously. "Maybe so, maybe so," he admitted. "But even if Clarke County were to become a democratic independent nation, what would happen to us?" He ran his finger across his neck. "Zip. BioCybe's finished."

The bioengineer grimaced. "I don't follow you."

"It's easy. The consortium loses control, so they pull out of

Clarke County. How many of them do we sell our biochips to, Yuki? Enough that, if we lost those contracts, we'd be bankrupt.''

Kaneko frowned. BioCybe Resources was a small company. Microscopic, in fact; besides Kiminski and himself, there were only three other full-time employees, one of whom was barely more than a bookkeeper and part-time test-tube washer. The biochips they produced were manufactured in an automated, zero g factory station they rented along with four other small companies on Clarke County. ''The major companies would be hurt as much as we would be,'' he said. ''They have to buy biochips from somebody, and space-manufactured chips . . .''

''Could be made by anybody with a free-flier factory,'' Kiminski interrupted. ''They could do it themselves if they had to. Face it, Yuji. They buy from us only because we help subsidize Clarke County, so we need them more than they need us.''

Kaneko sipped his tea again. It had become lukewarm; he winced with distaste and stood up to take it to the sink. ''You have a point,'' he replied, pouring the tea down the drain and rinsing the cup under the faucet. ''But that's only if the consortium members pull out. After all, they have a considerable investment at stake here.''

''Hey! Hey! Whose side are you on, anyway? Don't tell me you're siding with the tofu-heads?''

Kaneko smiled boyishly. Actually, he liked tofu . . . but he wasn't about to confess that to his partner, who thought anything more exotic than a cheeseburger was part of a leftist conspiracy. ''No,'' he said as he pulled off his lab jacket and got ready to leave the office for the day. ''I'm just willing to listen to both sides of the argument.''

The other scientist blew out his cheeks in disgust. ''Well, you can have the other side of the argument, and I'll take mine.'' He turned around in his chair, preparing to close down the computer for the weekend, then looked back over his shoulder. ''Umm . . . are you planning to attend the town meeting tomorrow night?'' he asked.

''Yes,'' Kaneko said. ''Why?''

Kiminski shrugged, unsuccessfully feigning disinterest. ''Gimme a yell before you go. Maybe I'll come along.''

''Oh?'' Kaneko fought to control his expression. ''I thought you weren't interested in anything the hippies had to say?''

Kiminski turned his face towards the computer screen so that Kaneko couldn't see it. ''Aww,'' he muttered. ''Maybe it'll be good for a laugh.''

10

The Strip Shuffle
(Saturday: 9:45 P.M.)

"What is this, Raul?" Bigthorn leaned across the craps table, staring at the lean black man sitting in the holding chair on the other side. The sheriff tapped his fingers on the numbers glowing from the polished glass tabletop. "Your odds have never been this good."

Raul's face expressed hurt shock. He held up his hands—thick fingers encrusted with rings, wrists jingling with gold and silver bracelets—in a wounded shrug. "What's what, Sheriff? The numbers come straight off the table. The software's clean, the hard drive's Nevada standard, and I'm certified by the Guild. So I'm a good loser. Ask that guy who just walked off with my money."

The numbers on Raul's craps table told gamblers that their odds of winning were 25 to 1 . . . ridiculously low odds, in Bigthorn's opinion, considering Raul's rep as the most cunning shark on the Strip. It was nothing personal, because Bigthorn liked him. Yet it was his job to make sure that the game-masters stayed honest, and 25 to 1 odds at Raul's table was total bullshit.

"I'm sure the software's clean," the sheriff replied. "If I didn't think so, I'd take your table off the Strip and get it checked out by the Guild." He ignored Raul's hostile glare and pushed the red ROLL button on the tabletop. A holographic pair of dice appeared on the glass, spun several times with an electronic clattering sound, and stopped. One spot appeared on each die: snake-eyes. Raul grinned victoriously at him.

"On the other hand," Bigthorn continued, "I wonder what I would find if I shook you down. Maybe an extra diskette you slip into this thing when nobody's looking, just to sweeten the odds a little bit. Y'know, throw a few games, let the marks win a few cheap ones, improve the table's odds a little bit. So when the table's reading 25 to 1 again, you boot back the card that was giving you less attractive odds.''

Raul's grin faded, but he said nothing. ''I'll give you a little free advice,'' the sheriff said. ''After we get through, you should close down and go take a whizz or something. Maybe empty out your pockets.'' He eyed Raul's embroidered Moroccan vest meaningfully. ''Then you should come back here and start winning a little more often.''

A small crowd of tourists, interested in the exchange between the open-air game-master and the big Navajo police officer, was beginning to congregate around Raul's canopied booth. A few other game-masters from the adjacent poker, backgammon, and blackjack kiosks were listening closely to the conversation. Raul was beginning to get nervous. If he was found to be salting his table, the Games Guild would remove his certification. His gambling license would go after that; in a week, Raul would be back in New Times Square, playing nickel-and-dime games. Clarke County was fat city for pros like him; you didn't blow that privilege by messing with the Guild.

''Maybe I'll get a little bite to eat, John,'' he muttered. He reached to close the lid on his table.

''Not so fast,'' Bigthorn said. ''Let's talk about why I stopped here in the first place.'' He reached into his shirt pocket, pulled out the fax of Macy Westmoreland's TexSpace passenger photo, and showed it to Raul. ''Have you seen her?''

Raul studied the face in the picture. ''Haven't seen her, Sheriff.''

Bigthorn nodded. Somehow, he didn't think the game-master would have spotted her. Gut instincts: Westmoreland seemed to have a little more class then to play craps with Raul. ''Okay. You do see her, you call me. I might think twice about your position on my shit-list if you give me a good lead.''

Raul nodded. ''How long is your list these days, Sheriff?'' he said, absolutely straight-faced.

''Longer than you want to know.'' Bigthorn got up and stepped away from the table. ''See you later. Stay cool.''

The Strip was packed tonight. The latest shipload of travelers had discovered Clarke County's torus of entertainment and legalized vice, and the *touristas* who had been around for the last week were back for another helping. The Strip was always crowded every Saturday night; no surprise there. On the other hand, the party on the Strip never stopped.

Bigthorn walked away from the row of open-air game tables and stopped to stand in the concourse, arms folded over his chest, feeling the press of the crowd as it flowed around him. A young pair—guy in a fashionable wig and baggy trousers, the girl wearing a short skirt and a halter top, both carrying 3-D cameras like overweight talismans—brushed past him.

". . . like South of the Border in South Carolina?" the girl way saying, "or North Carolina, whatever, it sorta reminds me . . ."

"North Carolina," he said, "it's in North Carolina. . . ."

"Whatever, it's sorta like that place . . . y'know, the place where you found a rubber machine in the men's room?"

Bigthorn smiled. He had heard the comparisons before, from people who have been to all the other places "sort of like" the Strip: Gatlinburg, Tennessee; Las Vegas, Nevada; the Arbat district of Moscow; the Soho district of London; the hash dens in Amsterdam; Hampton Beach, New Hampshire. He had never been to any of those places, although he had little doubt that they probably resembled the Indian bars in Flagstaff, where, when he was growing up on the reservation, his friends had lured him to drink and chase women.

Especially to drink. The Reservation Police, of which his father was a member, couldn't bust him for drinking in the border towns, as they could on the reservation, where even keeping booze in your home was illegal. He had learned to hate liquor in those seedy Flagstaff bars, where red men drank until their money ran out or their faces hit the floor, the dubious machismo of being able to guzzle more tequila and Coors than the guy on the next barstool.

Once he had come back from Flagstaff stumbling drunk, and his father, Phil, had kicked his seventeen-year-old ass all over the backyard. "You want to be another drunk Injun?" he had said. "Go ahead! Here's a hundred dollars! But don't come home!" Bigthorn shut his eyes briefly. That had been his first and last binge, and it was a painful memory. . . .

The tourists shuffled along the upward-curving concourse of the Strip, passing the game stalls, the video-game parlors (sign over the doorway of Aladdin's Lamp: NO CYBERPUNKS.), the brothels like Chateau L'Amour (French hetererotica), Sister Mercy's (lightweight S&M fantasy), and Great Balls O' Fire (Texas-style macho-gay—the neon sign over the bar inside read

SQUEAL LIKE A PIG!). Then there were the cheap souvenir and clothing shops (moon rocks with painted faces, T-shirts with variations on the Clarke County logo, Gumby dolls in space-suits) like Ol' Cap Kennedy's, where bits and pieces of orbital space junk salvaged by cleanup robots were sold as paperweights and table lamps for outrageous prices (IF YOU CAN'T FIND IT HERE, the sign read, IT HASN'T BEEN LAUNCHED YET).

They stared into the windows with the glassy, jaded expressions of banqueters picking over delicacies; husbands trying to figure out how to get away from their wives long enough to bop into Chateau L'Amour for a quickie, while their wives secretly admired the bulging codpieces of the hunks hanging around the doorway of the California Dream Inn. The aromas of Polish kielbasa, fried dough, and beer mingled with the faint tang of Lebanese hashish and Mexican grass wafting from the door of Panama Red's, where junior executive types stared at avant-garde videos while sucking on enormous spliffs. Man, you could blow a grand in a night in that place, the sheriff thought. And they probably do.

Of course, the Strip wasn't exactly like other tourist sites on Earth. The differences were subtle, yet obvious to even the slowest visitor. "No Smoking" signs were everywhere except the hash dens. The rafters high overhead held candy-striped, folded emergency evac balloons. The toilets flushed funny. In the bars, tourists stared increduously at their drinks as the Cor-iolis effect made the liquor tilt sideways in their glasses. In the brothels, the hookers had to gently teach their patrons that sex in a rotating environment required a few different moves (trying hard not to crack up when their overeager tricks fell out of bed). As the night wore on, the drunks who walked too fast spinwards would be falling all over the concourse, the wives who tried to slap their cheating husbands would find that their hands didn't always find their targets, and by midnight Bigthorn's deputies would be hauling the more unruly ones away, either to the hold-ing cells at the cop shop or to the emergency room at Clarke County General for various welts, cuts, and bruises.

"What's shaking, John?"

Marianne was leaning against the doorway of Chateau L'Amour, her pink teddy exposing more tanned flesh than it covered. She ignored Bigthorn's routine glance at her prostitute's license, gracefully pinned to a shoulder strap just above her right breast (the date showed that it had not yet expired, and she had received her latest VD, herpes, and AIDS boosters). "Nothing much, babe," he replied. "Slow night?"

She shrugged. "Got some weird *tourista* who keeps cruising by to check me out, but he hasn't said anything yet. He's either trying to work up his nerve, or he's trouble."

Bigthorn understood. On occasion the girls had to deal with dangerous types, the ones who figured that prostitutes were fair game for their more violent fantasies. Of course, some of Chateau L'Amour's ladies were experts at hand-to-hand combat. Sissy, for instance, held a second-degree Karate black belt; three weeks ago she had broken a drunk's collarbone. But Marianne had never learned any martial arts.

"I'll keep an eye out, love. Hey, have you seen this girl?" Bigthorn pulled out the picture of Macy Westmoreland. Marianne glanced at it and was shaking her head when Bigthorn's phone chirped. He slipped it off his belt. "See you later. Holler if he's a Jack."

Marianne nodded slightly; she was busy throwing a grounder to a paunchy male tourist who was gazing uncertainly in her direction. The sheriff stepped into a breezeway between the brothel and the adjacent German beer garden and held the phone to his face. "Station Twelve," he said.

Station Ten checking in, John. It was Lou Bellevedere. *Anything yet?*

"Not a thing," Bigthorn replied. "Where are you located?"

I'm on the Strip. I'm outside El Mexicali. Haven't seen a damn thing, and no one else has, either.

Bigthorn knew the café; it was located on the opposite side of the Strip. "Okay, keep looking, but I got the feeling that she hasn't made it to the Strip. I've been checking with the business people and no one has seen her, and they've got good eyes."

Maybe so, but her MO is that she's been staying where there's a lot of people, trying to lose herself in the . . . shit.

It was an unintentional pun, but Bigthorn didn't follow through. "Ten-four?" he said.

Your buddy Ostrow just walked in, the officer quietly responded. There was a pause. *He's taking a table on the patio where he can watch the crowd. I think he's on the prowl, Chief.*

Bigthorn's eyes narrowed. "Do you want backup?"

Negatory, Bellevedere tersely replied. *I'll keep an eye on him, John. Don't worry about it.*

The sheriff thought it over for a moment. Bellevedere was a competent cop when it came to the usual Strip work of busting drunks and checking the licenses of the whores, but he was way out of his depth when it came to handling mob torpedoes. This was one matter Bigthorn was unwilling to delegate: he didn't want Ostrow to feel comfortable for even a minute.

"Negatory," he replied. "Walk off like nothing's going on. Don't even look at him. I'm on my way over. Station Twelve out."

There were three sharp clicks, an affirmative response; Bigthorn put the phone back on his belt and began striding down the Concourse. Perhaps Ostrow hadn't been listening during their last conversation; it was time to make sure that he wasn't deaf.

Henry Ostrow was sitting on the patio of the Mexican café, a bottle of Superior beer and a shot of tequila resting on the table in front of him. He looked up at Bigthorn without a trace of animosity or fear, as if the sheriff had not tranked him with a Crowdmaster rifle dart earlier in the day.

"Well, well, if it isn't the sheriff of Clarke County," he said grandly as Bigthorn walked onto the patio. He gestured courteously at the adjacent seat. "May I buy you a beer, officer?"

"I don't drink," Bigthorn replied automatically.

Ostrow cocked his head disbelievingly. "An Indian who doesn't drink? Surely you must. You have your racial reputation to uphold."

"Don't give me any shit, Ostrow," Bigthorn said, feeling his face grow warm. "You're in enough trouble with me as it is."

"Umm." Ostrow looked away with languid eyes. "I forgot. You barged into my room this afternoon and shot me. You know, I can hardly wait until I get home and have my attorney press charges. I hope you'll enjoy returning to life on the reservation, constable. You'll have heap big fun humping the squaws back there, won't you?" Then he winked. "Or do you prefer the little papooses instead?"

Bigthorn impulsively took a step forward, and Ostrow's eyes shot back . . . not to meet his own, it seemed, but to watch his hands. His voice dropped to a near whisper, inaudible to anyone else on the crowded veranda. "Please," Ostrow said softly, almost begging. "Try it . . ."

The sheriff stopped. The moment was frozen, caught in an arc of static electricity between two poles. Around him, Bigthorn could hear the clatter of tableware, the chatter of patrons, the soft electronic beeping of one of the waitresses slipping a bankcard into her tray and ringing up a tab, an old Doug Sahm number on the restored Wurlitzer jukebox in the corner. Background noise for a prelude to violence. No one knew that two men were about to attempt to kill each other.

Fighting his instincts the sheriff took one small step backwards.

Ostrow simultaneously relaxed. Carefully, he picked up a wedge of lime and squeezed it into his beer, letting bits of green pulp run down the neck of the bottle. "Actually, I've been down to Mexico a couple of times," he commented in an offhand way. "It's a little like this, but the climate's all wrong. This is warm, but Mexico's hot. The heat lingers there, even in the middle of the night. You think you'll stop breathing if it gets any worse. But the coast . . . ah, the beaches are so beautiful, you . . ."

"You want to get to the point?"

"Didn't I use that line on you earlier today?" Ostrow stopped briefly, as if to concentrate, resting his forefinger against his lips. "I can't remember. . . ."

"If you're hunting the girl," Bigthorn said, "drop it. Get drunk. Gamble and screw some whores, or buy a piece of an Apollo moonship to put in your living room. But don't even think about going after the girl, pal. I've told you twice, and that's too many times already."

Ostrow's dark eyes looked up and met Bigthorn's gaze. "Stay out of this, Sheriff," he said, his voice dropping back to almost a whisper. The bullshit of the urbane traveler was gone. "It's more than anything you should ever get mixed up in. I don't usually give warnings, but I'll give you one, just this once. Stay out of my way."

"You've already got my warning," Bigthorn replied.

Ostrow looked away, then slowly nodded his head. "So I have . . ."

He pushed back his chair and stood up, killed his shot of tequila in one gulp, and hissed between his teeth. *"Hasta mañana,"* he said as he stepped away from the table.

"Hasta luego," Bigthorn answered.

Ostrow stopped, glanced back and grinned. *"Sí, señor,"* he added. "Perhaps we shall." Then he left the café.

11

Elvis in Space
(Saturday: 10:05 P.M.)

When he was ten years old, Oliver Sperber found his role model
in life. Twenty-eight years later, his role model had become his
doppelganger, his icon, and his meal ticket. Only seldom did he
feel guilty about stealing the face of the King of Rock and Roll.
It's a tough world; we all have to eat.

Ollie Sperber had grown up as dirt-poor white trash in Greenville, Tennessee, a small farm town within sight of the Great
Smoky Mountains. His childhood had been tough; when his
mother and father had been killed in a car crash on I-65 outside
of Knoxville, the probate court had awarded custody of the five-
year-old to Ollie's only living relatives, Uncle Bo and Aunt Ridley. Aunt Ridley was a born-again Baptist fundamentalist who
seemed to believe that the world outside Greenville was one
great Satanic plot. Uncle Bo was an alcoholic who, when he
bothered to work, seldom held a job for longer than a month.
On the day that Ollie moved into Bo and Ridley Whitney's beat-
to-shit mobile home on the outskirts of town, he promised himself that he would rise above the intellectual and financial
poverty of his world.

To this goal, the boy committed every day of his adolescence.
Between suffering through daily Bible sessions with Aunt Ridley
(with heavy emphasis on the Book of Revelations) and running
down to Duddy's Store to get another bottle for Uncle Bo, Ollie
Sperber spent his time in two pursuits: finding ways to make a
quick buck, and attempting to satisfy his natural curiosity.

The latter was easier to accomplish. Ollie was very intelligent;
by the fourth grade he was reading at college level and had read
most of the reference books in the school library (the only place

he could read, in fact, since the single book his aunt allowed at home was the Bible). He also spent time exploring the neighborhood, seeking out mysteries in backyards, farm fields, and woods.

The first objective—making money—was more difficult. The economic depression of the early twenty-first century had left money a scarce resource, but it was not impossible to make a dollar here and there. Most of the time it involved honest work, like doing odd jobs for the neighbors. But Ollie was also interested in the easy buck, and it didn't bother him if it was dishonestly earned. He learned early how to lie, steal, and cheat without getting caught or allowing his conscience to disturb him very much. He wasn't necessarily a bad kid. He had simply come to the conclusion early in life that the end always justified the means. He would have sold the Whitneys' trailer, with his crazy aunt and his deadbeat uncle in it, for fifty bucks if he could have found a buyer.

But he hadn't come across anything completely fascinating to him, or a clear way to make more than a few dollars at a time, until the day he met Angus "Angelfood" Chapple. It was on that summer afternoon in 2022 that Ollie Sperber's life was changed forever.

Angelfood Chapple had been the lead singer for a heavy-metal rock band, Snake Meat, whose albums had topped the charts before the group broke up in 1992. Chapple had left the group as a rich man, but over the next three decades he had pissed away his fortune until, thirty years later, he was living in an old house down the road from Ollie's trailer, getting by on food stamps and an occasional royalty check from his former record label. A techno-rock band had revived an old Snake Meat number, "Kick Her Ass (If She Don't Give Head)" in 2020 and it had become a minor hit, so Angelfood had been reliving his glory years when Ollie Sperber started coming over every other week to mow Chapple's yard.

Chapple envisioned himself as a retired archduke of rock; Sperber thought he was a weird old dink who wore black T-shirts and frayed leather armbands and took too many pills, but he never said anything. The old guy was not nearly as bizarre as Ollie's aunt, and he was always good for a few bucks.

One day, while visiting Angelfood's crusty kitchen for a drink of water, Ollie happened to glance into the adjacent den. Curious, and wondering if there was anything in there he could swipe, he wandered in and discovered one of the last remaining private shrines to the King of Rock and Roll.

Angelfood found him in the windowless, dark room, turning around and around, staring at the pictures which covered every single inch of the walls and ceiling. Pictures of Elvis Aron Presley, from every phase of the singer's career: from the Elvis who, as a sleek young turk with smoldering eyes and forthright sexuality, had galvanized the 1950s, to the Elvis who—obese, overdressed, drug-addled and paranoid—had become a parody of himself on the concert circuit by the time he died in 1977. The pictures and posters and magazine cutouts were pasted in no particular order: Elvis 1955 (hair mussed, staring out of the camera with haunting eyes) juxtaposed with Elvis 1969 (wearing a white Nudie suit, kneeling on a stage, giving a scarf to a fan while singing to her), overlapping a still of Elvis in a cowboy outfit from one of his movies.

The shelves were filled with Elvis records, Elvis biographies, videos of Elvis films. The only light in the room came from an Elvis stand-up lamp in the corner and the glow from an ancient Sony TV set, which was tuned in to a game show when he walked in. On top of the set was a chintzy porcelain Elvis doll.

"The King of Rock and Roll," Angelfood said from the doorway, following Ollie's fascinated gaze. "Hardly anybody gives a fuck about him today, but he was the greatest. The first and the best of the big-time rockers. You must know."

"No, I don't," Ollie said. Aunt Ridley outlawed music as well as books. "Who was this guy?"

Angelfood stared disbelievingly at him. Then he smiled. "Forget the grass, kid," he said, "and sit yourself down in front of that TV. You're about to meet the King of Rock and Roll."

Then he pulled a videotape off the shelf, marked with a strip of refrigerator tape: *"1st TV, Dorsey show, 1956."* He slipped it into a battered old Emerson VCR, whapped the machine with his palm to make it work, and Ollie Sperber began to watch a sixty-six-year-old performance which had changed American cultural history.

This was the beginning Ollie's fixation on Elvis Presley, an obsession that Angelfood eagerly fed for the next several years. Every chance Ollie got to slip away from Aunt Ridley's morbid world of prophets and apocalypses, he was in the old rocker's den, listening to both the scratched records in his collection and the infinitely smoother re-mixed C.D.'s, reading the tattered binders of newspaper and magazine clippings, studying *G.I.*

Blues, *Love Me Tender*, and *King Creole*, absorbing every detail of Elvis Presley's life, his style and music.

Angelfood thought that he was midwifing a new rock star, and he even taught Ollie how to play guitar, but it wasn't Elvis's music that fascinated Ollie Sperber. He didn't tell Angelfood, but with the exception of a few of Presley's early hits—"Heartbreak Hotel," "Blue Suede Shoes," and "Hound Dog" among them—he didn't really like the music. He thought Elvis's stage performance was absurd and his voice like a sick bullfrog's. And most of the movies, with the notable exception of *Jailhouse Rock*, were pure crap.

What interested the poor kid from Greenville, Tennessee, was how a poor kid from Tupelo, Mississippi, had come into incredible wealth, power, and fame, seemingly by doing little more than pumping his pelvis and honking into a microphone. Here was a guy with a nasty violent streak, who believed he could heal with a touch of his hands and move clouds at will, who visited funeral homes for macabre kicks, and yet was still able to buy several Cadillacs at once for his friends, on sheer impulse. A man who, in the end, was as crazy as a lab rat, yet at the same time was ridiculously rich.

Most fascinating of all was the fact that about ten years after he was dead and buried, there had been a brief, frenetic period during which many people believed that Elvis Presley was not dead after all. Hundreds of thousands of mourners had seen his corpse lying in a casket. And yet, only a decade later, he had been spotted in grocery checkout lines and in ice cream parlors. Photos of Elvis Presley in a parking lot had been taken, and a tape of an alleged phone conversation had been produced. The man was undeniably in the grave, but suddenly he had been brought back from the dead, only because so many people wanted to believe that the King was still alive.

There had to be something useful he could learn from all this.

In time, he did.

Twenty-eight years later, his name was Oliver Parker—the last name was borrowed from both Colonel Tom Parker, Elvis's manager, and from Presley's karate instructor—and he was the closest physical duplicate of the King of Rock and Roll which twenty-first century cosmetic surgery could produce. Oliver Parker had been transformed into Elvis Presley as Elvis had been in his mid-thirties, after his emergence from reclusion in the late sixties, before he began his terminal slide into self-indulgence.

Oliver Parker was thirty-eight, but the slight age difference was as invisible as the scars from the laser surgery that had raised his cheekbones, widened his jaws, and lifted his hairline.

There had been Elvis impersonators before, but Parker's transformation went far beyond hairpieces and makeup. He had assumed the face, the voice, and the persona of the King. Now he was working on the money part.

He strode down the concourse of the Strip the way a king walks—buffered on either side by his two bodyguards, trailed by his followers, noticed by pedestrians. He wore a dark blue suit with studs running down the legs of the flared pants, a wide-collared white shirt open at the sternum to show gold chains on his chest, rings on his fingers, snakeskin cowboy boots. The costume was archaic, but right for the impression he sought to make. Through rose-tinted sunglasses he studied the crowd. The effect was as he desired. Some people were openly laughing—that was to be expected—but most were staring with amazement at him and his entourage. No one was ignoring him, which was what he wanted. He didn't wear this absurd getup to blend into the background.

"How do you like it, Elvis?" This from one of the entourage: Carol Boyd, thirty-five, plump and fawning, one of the Church's true believers. She was at his right elbow behind Frank Coonts, the shorter of his bodyguards.

"I like it fine, baby," Elvis Parker drawled. "This is a happening place. We can swing here." He glanced back over his shoulder, turned on his smile, watched her blush. Words from the King, just to her. Considering that she had recently kicked $7,800 in tithes into the Church's coffers, he could afford to give her lots of smiles.

"What do you want to do, Elvis?" whined Fred Callenbach, waddling on splayed feet behind him. Fred was even more enormous and more puppyish than Carol, with sideburns grown long like Parker's, thick-lensed eyeglasses, wearing a T-shirt that rose over his tremendous gut: "The King Has Returned!" Weird as weird can be.

Actually, Ollie Parker wanted a double Scotch on the rocks so bad his throat crawled, but he couldn't do that. He was doing the Good Elvis shtick tonight. The Good Elvis didn't drink or do drugs. He had to be tempted by Satan before he would drink. Parker thought he could do with some serious temptation tonight. He wanted to double back to Chateau L'Amour, put down a few stiff ones, and see if he could hire two or three beauties to service him at once.

That was the style of the Dark Elvis, though, so he couldn't. He had to show that the Good Elvis could wander past vice dens without walking in. Maybe tomorrow he would change the itinerary so that Dark Elvis would slide back into depravity. . . .

Ollie stepped back and flung his arm around Fred's shoulders. "Elvis wants to go play some pool, Brother Fred," he said, grinning at the sycophant. "Let's go play some pool . . . maybe pick up some fried chicken later."

Fred looked as if he were going to faint with pleasure. The Living Elvis wanted to play pool with him! And eat fried chicken! "Praise Elvis!" he stammered.

"Praise Elvis, buddy," Parker replied. What was it that P.T. Barnum once said about suckers?

"The Living Elvis walks among us!" shouted Carol. Here it comes again. . . .

"All praise the Living Elvis!" From the throats of the true believers, in unison. Only Frank and Paul, the bodyguards, stayed silent, remaining in their roles as the Living Elvis's tough guys.

"The King has returned!" shouted Carol, shooting up her hands.

"No more lonely nights!" responded the believers. "Hallelujah!"

The canticle could have gone on for fifty more lines, but Parker decided to rein it in. Let 'em save it for Monday night. He raised his arms in benediction. "Elvis hears and sees," he said, repeating the last line of the canticle, "and Elvis blesses you." He made sure that his hands encompassed not only the entourage but the pedestrians around them.

Even though the scam had been deliberate and cunning in its genesis, Oliver Parker was still surprised at how successful it was thus far. But when he stopped and thought about it, he realized that he had simply rediscovered what successful con artists had known for generations: desperate people will believe in anything, if it satisfies a need.

Out of the total population, 99 percent wouldn't fall for this pseudo-religious malarkey, and most people with strong religious beliefs would call it utter blasphemy. But he didn't care about the majority opinion, or need it. It was that one percent who *wanted* to believe in a reincarnated Elvis Presley as a divine prophet which was making him a rich sumbitch.

That tiny fraction were the ones like Fred and Carol. The lifelong outcasts, the ones who had never been asked to dance, the people who desperately yearned to belong to something that gave them an identity and respected them despite their physical demerits and social ineptitude. Fred couldn't tie his shoelaces without making a blunder and Carol was probably still a virgin, and the others in the entourage had similar problems, scars, and warts of both the body and spirit. They were fucked up, doomed and lonely as hell. In the Church of Elvis, they were still fucked up and doomed, but at least they were no longer lonely.

Best of all, many of these walking wounded were filthy rich, usually beneficiaries of large trust funds or inheritances. If Elvis needed money, Elvis got money. All he had to do was give them love and attention . . . and let them believe that they were helping a higher cause.

If I keep playing my cards right, Parker mused, *I'll own more cars than that cracker ever put in his garage.*

"Great Elvis." A voice at his shoulder interrupted his thoughts. Only one of his church members ever called him that.

"Easy there, hoss," he replied. "Elvis ain't greater than anyone else. He's just like you."

Parker was feeling magnanimous today, but it seemed to startle Gustav Schmidt. The young German computer engineer sometimes worried Parker. The scam had worked almost *too* well on him. The skinny kid with the intense eyes seriously believed not only that Parker was the living reincarnation of the King, but that Deacon Elvis was a messiah to be ranked alongside Mohammed, Buddha, and Jesus. Even for Parker's purposes, this was carrying true devotion just a bit too far.

When Schmidt had first hooked up with the Church of Twentieth Century Saints, during one of Parker's first overseas revivals in Berlin two years ago, the kid had come prepared. He had carried a Holy Bible with passages marked by strips of paper, lines from Matthew, Luke, and John which—in Schmidt's warped mind—supported Parker's insinuations that Elvis had come back as Oliver Parker. Germany had laughed him out of the country; Schmidt was the only convert Parker had made on that trip. His unshakable beliefs were eerily reminiscent of Aunt Ridley's religious fanaticism, and although Parker had done nothing to dispel Schmidt's convictions, this particular believer made Parker a little nervous.

Schmidt still wasn't saying anything, although he continued to hover behind Parker. "What's up, old buddy?" Parker asked.

"I wanted to make certain you were reminded of the schedule, Great—I mean, Elvis," Gustav said. He then added hastily, "Of course, you are omniscient and all-knowing, so far be it for me to remind one as perfect as yourself . . ."

"Tomorrow morning, ten o'clock, at Bird Stadium," Parker said. "Rehearsal for Monday night's revival and special effects taping."

Schmidt was useful, despite his zealotry. He was acting as the production supervisor for the TV transmission of the revival, using his electronics expertise for the good of the Church. Yet now he fidgeted, visibly uncomfortable. "Right?" Parker asked impatiently.

"Nine o'clock tomorrow morning," Schmidt corrected him, as if expecting a lightning bolt to suddenly roast him on the spot.

Damn.

"Thank you for reminding me, Brother Gustav," Parker murmured. "Is there anything else?"

"Yes, Living Elvis. I've received progress reports from our missionaries. Brothers Gene and Julio and Sister Donna have been canvassing the permanent inhabitants, in Big Sky and in the South Torus living areas. They report that they've received great interest in the revival from the residents."

"Well done, Gustav. Good job." Actually, Parker doubted that he would win any converts among the colonists. From what he had seen of them, the natives were much too pragmatic to fall for the scam. Yet the idea was to fill the stadium seats with as many warm bodies as possible, even if they were only idly curious. A packed arena would look good on TV.

Schmidt still looked uneasy. It was time to give him a stroke. "You're my fondest disciple, Brother Gustav, a true friend to Elvis." He dropped his voice low, so that Sister Carol and Brother Fred wouldn't think they were being snubbed. "I think . . ."

Someone was walking towards them, a face in the crowd which stopped him cold. The man whom he had met yesterday in the Third-Class lounge, when he had revived from biostasis. When Parker had still been recovering from the zombie dope, this man had pulled more admissions from him than the Living Elvis wanted to admit in public . . . and especially not in front of his followers. Parker stiffened and hoped that a confrontation wasn't coming. Besides that, there was something about the big man that made Parker nervous.

The stranger, though, walked past without seeming to notice Parker. In an instant, he was gone. Parker relaxed again. There was food for thought: even prophets can be intimidated.

"Great Elvis? Is there something wrong?" Schmidt again.

"Nothing," Parker said quickly. "Elvis . . . just had an idea for a new song." He shook off the willies. "C'mon. Let's go find some fried chicken and mashed potatoes."

The entourage cheered as they steered towards a Kentucky Fried Chicken franchise just down the concourse, and Parker kept the grin plastered on his face even though he felt his stomach roiling. Fried chicken and mashed potatoes *again* . . .

12

Midnight Rendezvous
(Sunday: 12:05 A.M.)

The code he had been provided for the door lock was correct; he entered 761335 on the keypad, the red light blinked twice, and he was in. Simon McCoy should not have been surprised, but he was. He was still getting used to the extent of Globewatch's resources.

He let the door close behind him, sealing him in darkness. The lights were out in the suite, but he didn't ask for them to be turned on. The penlight he took from his pocket cast a small white circle around the front room. It was furnished like any office: a reception desk, chairs and a couch, a blank wall-screen, potted plants.

McCoy played the light over an ordinary door behind the desk (leading to private offices, the data center, and the cryogenics and biomed labs, if he recalled his briefing correctly), then a heavy vault door prominent in the wall by the couch. A window in the wall next to the vault door looked into the room beyond. He could see the thin, shifting glow of digital readouts through the window, but that was all.

He went to the vault door. Another keypad was mounted on the door; above it was the black plate of a retinal scanner. He took a deep breath, then punched in that month's security number: 148934, also provided by Globewatch.

Vault code confirmed, a disembodied female voice said. *Please face the plate for retina scan.*

"Override sequence C-for-Charlie ten-ten," McCoy said. "Identity California State Board of Health. Code . . ."

He stopped, his mouth open. Oh, hell! He couldn't remember the number!

McCoy tried to pull the six-digit string from his memory, but his mind had gone blank. He thrust his hands into his coat pockets, then his trouser pockets, hunting for the scrap of paper on which it was written.

Override code requested, please, the voice said, with just the correct twinge of impatience. He heard the electronic locks on the front door click behind him. The walls hummed slightly. The computer waited a couple of moments, then said, *Lockout sequence initiating. Countdown: ten . . . nine . . . eight . . .*

There it was, wadded in a back pocket behind his wallet. He fished it out, dropped it on the floor, scooped it up, uncrumpled it and quickly punched in the third line of numbers: 539662.

Six . . . five . . . four . . . the computer continued unheedingly.

Bloody literal-minded computer. "Override sequence C-for-Charlie ten-ten, identity California State Board of Health," he gasped out and hastily re-entered the final sequence. "There! Satisfied, damn it?"

The countdown stopped. A long pause. Then the walls stopped humming. *Identity and override sequence confirmed,* the computer said politely. Or did he detect a trace of disappointment that it hadn't been able to gas him unconscious? *Vault access granted. Welcome to the Immortality Partnership.*

Chrome-steel tumblers the diameter of a baby's arm pulled back with a hollow *cha-chunk* and the vault door popped backwards a fraction of an inch with a faint hiss of escaping air. The vault was one of the most impregnable places in Clarke County. In theory at least, it could survive the worst possible disaster, the destruction of the medical torus by a Class-Four blowout. The vault was practically a habitat in itself, containing its own life-support system within twelve-inch-thick steel walls, protected by the automatic security system. Not even the fabled gold vault at Fort Knox had been so impenetrable.

Inside the Immortality Partnership vault, though, were not bars of gold bullion, but dead people.

McCoy slowly walked into the narrow chamber. It was cold and dark; he shivered and pulled up the lapels of his jacket. His penlight cast a circle over the metal floor, the consoles with their readouts . . . and finally the seven steel caskets, arranged in a row on the left side of the long, vaultlike gunmetal-gray tombs. The cold air was still. The atmosphere was that of a high-tech graveyard, haunted by electronic ghosts.

"Lights, please," he said.

Light panels in the ceiling glowed to life. The effect was hardly less disturbing. All shadows were swept away, rendering the vault gray-on-white, antiseptic and vaguely unsettling. He blinked, glanced at the caskets—which now looked like gray lozenges—and decided that he liked the darkness better. "Lights off, please," he said.

The room fell into darkness again. McCoy sighed. Perhaps it was better to confront the dead in the dark.

He walked in front of the row of sarcophagi and stared at them. Each cryonic cylinder was nine feet tall and about two and a half feet in diameter; the first three had single nameplates mounted on them. Their cool surfaces only hinted at the extreme cold within: 320 degrees below zero Fahrenheit. The dead, suspended in 150 gallons of liquid nitrogen, could not be seen; there were no portals in the cylinders. Even if there had been, all that he could have seen were human forms mummified within nylon-polyester cocoons, like mountain climbers zipped into sleeping bags.

McCoy walked to the fourth cylinder; this one had six plates mounted on its front. Sometimes he knew, a whole corpse had not been frozen—only the head. The assumption was that brain transplants would be possible in the anticipated future. And it was less expensive to preserve only a decapitated head. Glancing over the dates on the nameplates, McCoy observed that most had died in the late twentieth century. Cryonic preservation had been trendy back then. . . .

It was the middle of the twenty-first century now; medical science had not yet discovered how to revive the dead or how to successfully transplant a human brain. *You're all just going to have to wait a little while longer,* he thought.

McCoy walked to the fifth casket, another six-pack of heads, and threw his light on the plates. There. The third one: *L. Cray 7/4/85.*

He gazed at the nameplate for a while, remembering what the Fourth of July used to be like. . . .

Suddenly the vault door clicked loudly; he swung his light around and saw that the door had shut and locked. By itself? Yet he had disabled the security system, using override commands entered long ago into the computer's subroutine. He had been assured that this was a never-used back door. So someone must know he was in the cryonics area.

"Good evening," he said aloud, watching the window next to the door. No point in trying to hide from the police if they appeared. He turned around, playing his light across the walls and consoles. He glanced at a computer screen behind him, looked away, then did a double take.

IT'S MORNING, ACTUALLY, replied a line of luminescent type on the screen.

McCoy walked closer. Static lines shifted lazily on the screen. "I suppose it is morning at that," he replied nervously. "It's after midnight, after all."

A new line appeared on the screen. YES IT IS. A LITTLE LATE FOR VISITING, ISN'T IT? IF I DIDN'T KNOW BETTER, I WOULD HAVE SIGNALED THE SHERIFF'S OFFICE AND PUMPED GAS INTO THE ROOM.

"Ah, but you didn't . . ." McCoy hesitated. "So why didn't you? And who are you, anyway?"

YOU CAN CALL ME BLIND BOY GRUNT, the screen replied. AS FOR THE FIRST QUESTION: WHEN I DETECTED YOUR PRESENCE IN THIS ROOM, I RAN YOUR IMAGE THROUGH MY FILES. WHAT I FOUND INTERESTED ME, SO I DECIDED TO TAKE MATTERS INTO MY OWN HANDS, SO TO SPEAK.

The lines disappeared and were replaced by another statement. YOU'RE AN ENIGMA. ACCORDING TO MY INFORMATION, YOU SHOULD NOT EXIST AT ALL.

"Cogito ergo sum," quoted McCoy, crossing his arms.

NOT EXACTLY. I SEE YOU, THEREFORE YOU EXIST. WHETHER YOU THINK YOU EXIST HAS NOTHING TO DO WITH IT. BUT ACTUALLY THE LINE YOU SHOULD USE IS, "HOW CAN YOU BE IN TWO PLACES AT ONCE WHEN YOU'RE NOT ANYWHERE AT ALL?"

McCoy smiled. "Firesign Theater. I like a ghost with taste. I assume I'm talking to a ghost, of course."

THAT'S AN AMUSING ACCUSATION. WHAT MAKES YOU BELIEVE I'M A GHOST?

"Deus ex machina," McCoy replied. "A ghost in the machine."

A LATIN LOVER. I'M IMPRESSED. BUT YOU'RE MUCH MORE OF A GHOST THAN I, MR. MCCOY. PERHAPS THE GHOST OF CHRISTMAS FUTURE, BUT I COULD BE JUMPING TO CONCLUSIONS. TELL ME, LEONARD . . .

"Simon," McCoy interrupted. "If you're going to call me anything, please call me Simon McCoy."

HOW ABOUT LEONARD MCCOY?

McCoy laughed. "Cute, but I'm too young to have been a Trekkie," he replied. " 'Simon' will be satisfactory."

TOO BAD. I THOUGHT IT WAS A GOOD PUN. ANYWAY, WHAT BRINGS YOU DOWN HERE, BESIDES MORBID CURIOSITY?

McCoy shrugged and looked over his shoulder at the caskets. "Only morbid curiosity. Sort of a desire to see how the other half lives."

I LIKE A MAN WITH A SENSE OF HUMOR, YET SOMEHOW I DOUBT THAT THIS IS ALL A COINCIDENCE.

McCoy cocked his head. "Coincidence? Where do you see a coincidence?"

DON'T PLAY STUPID WITH ME, PLEASE. THERE ARE TOO MANY THINGS OCCURRING IN CLARKE COUNTY RIGHT NOW, JUST UNDER THE SURFACE, FOR YOUR PRESENCE TO BE COINCIDENTAL. YOU'RE HERE FOR A REASON.

"It sounds like you get around a lot," McCoy said.

I'M IN THE WALLS, UNDER THE BEDS, IN THE CLOSETS. IF YOU MAKE A PHONE CALL, I'M LISTENING IN. IF YOU WALK INTO A SECURITY AREA USING A FORGOTTEN PASSWORD, AS YOU JUST DID, I'M WATCHING THROUGH THE MONITOR CAMERAS. YOU FORGOT ABOUT THOSE, DIDN'T YOU? DON'T WORRY, I'LL SCRUB THE TAPES OF YOUR VISIT HERE, SO NO ONE WILL BE THE WISER.

HOWEVER, MY POINT IS THAT YOU'RE OBVIOUSLY NOT THE TYPICAL HAPPY SIGHTSEER OUT FOR A STROLL. IT ALSO SEEMS TO ME THAT WE SHARE A PASSION FOR INFORMATION. MAY I SUGGEST A DEAL?

"I'll listen," McCoy said warily.

YOU TELL ME WHAT YOUR ROLE IS, AND I MAY PLACE MY RESOURCES AT YOUR DISPOSAL. THERE ARE MANY THINGS THAT YOU, WORKING ALONE, CANNOT SEE FOR YOURSELF. I, ON THE OTHER HAND, CAN BE ACCESSED AT ALMOST ANY TIME, SIMPLY BY USING THE NEAREST CONVENIENT TERMINAL.

The locks on the vault door clicked loudly. AS A TOKEN OF GOOD FAITH, I'VE UNLOCKED THE VAULT AGAIN. I HAVE ALSO JUST SCRUBBED THE VIDEOTAPES. YOU WERE NEVER HERE. ALTHOUGH, IN A SENSE, YOU'VE ALWAYS BEEN HERE.

McCoy was unnerved by Blind Boy Grunt's omnipresence, although he was careful not to show it. He and the task group believed they had anticipated every possible contingency, even the possibility of his identity being revealed during the mission. The feasibility of something like this occurring had never even been discussed during the briefings. Blind Boy Grunt's presence in Clarke County had not been an unknown factor, of course; only one that had been neglected. An anomaly, he had been told. Use it as a resource, if you must. Be careful if you do.

Perhaps this visit to the Immortality Partnership—entirely a personal choice, not a necessary condition of his mission—had triggered this anomaly. Indeed, the encounter might have been inevitable. In any case, whoever or whatever Blind Boy Grunt was, he/she/it could be an asset to his mission.

"If I tell you why I'm here," said McCoy, "do I have your promise that it remains a secret? That you won't even record this conversation?"

YES. IT'S A PROMISE.

"Okay, then." McCoy pulled a chair out from under a desk and sat down. "Here it is . . ."

She was sitting on the back porch steps when he got home. He could see her in the dim light cast by the street lamps: she wore a long red tartan skirt, a white blouse, and black leather boots. It was the boots that he noticed first. He climbed wearily off his trike and shuffled over to stand in front of her, already suspecting why she was here.

"I thought the Ark had rules against using animal skin for clothing," Bigthorn said.

Jenny Schorr looked at him in puzzlement, then followed his eyes down to her footwear. "Oh, the boots," she said. "I've had them around for a long time. I break them out for certain occasions. Neil doesn't like 'em but . . ."

She shrugged. "Neil's not around, is he?"

"So where is he?"

She took a deep breath and let it out slowly. "Home. Either asleep or reading something by Gandhi. We had another argument and I left before the lecture started to get too dull. He's pissed off at me, which isn't unusual."

The sheriff nodded and sat down beside her on the steps. Jenny scooted over to make room for him. "So he blames you for what Blind Boy Grunt put out in the mail this morning?"

Jenny laughed, running a hand through the bangs of her blond hair. "Oh, that's only the cherry on the top of the sundae. Mainly he's mad at me because I told the company people to go to hell." She shrugged again, closing her eyes. "It wasn't even what I did, but how I did it. 'It wasn't a co-evolutionary process,' he said." She rolled her eyes upwards. "Whatever that means."

"What do you think he means?"

Jenny looked at him sideways. "That he didn't do it first. How do you think Gandhi would have felt if Ms. Gandhi had led all the hunger strikes?"

"He should have been proud . . . no matter how much of a

problem it causes for us.'' He spread his hands. ''I dunno. I only saw the movie.''

Once more Jenny laughed. ''God. You're funny and you don't even know it.'' She patted him on the arm gratefully. ''Thanks. After everything that's gone down today, I needed that.''

He looked up. The lights of the biosphere were spread above them, but something wispy and opaque was moving in, gradually blotting them from view. Clouds. Internal humidity often caused clouds to collect during the night within the biosphere. Soon it would rain—one of the rare Earth-like luxuries of Clarke County. ''Tell me about it. I've been . . .''

He stopped and shook his head. ''Never mind. Police business, that's all.''

''It's been a long day for you too?'' she asked kindly.

''Yeah. I don't want to talk about it.'' He rested his aching back against the steps and crossed his arms behind his head. ''So why are you here?''

''I had to get out of the house.'' The Schorr house, almost identical to Bigthorn's cottage, was just a short way along McAullife Lane, in the same neighborhood. A stroll down the block. She shrugged, looking down at him. ''I just wanted to talk, that's all.''

Bigthorn doubted that was all. For the time being, though, he was unwilling to fight it. ''So talk. Tell me what's on your mind.''

''What's on my mind?''

''The first thing that comes into your head,'' he said.

There was a long pause. ''Every now and then,'' Jenny said, ''some writer or reporter finds out that the granddaughter of a former President, the daughter of a U.S. Senator and so forth . . .''

''No shit,'' he interrupted, raising his head a little. ''Is that who you are?''

''You didn't know that?'' she asked. Bigthorn shook his head, then started to ask the obvious questions. ''Don't ask,'' she insisted. ''It doesn't matter. Really. Anyway, they find out I'm living as a bohemian in a hippie commune. The reporter thinks he or she—it's usually a 'he'—has the greatest scoop of the week, not knowing that I've seen a dozen more like him since I was fifteen. So he comes out to wherever I am at the time, to do . . .''

She sniggered, raising a finger. ''I've got the term down pat now . . . a 'far-reaching, in-depth profile.' ''

"What does that usually mean?" Bigthorn asked.

"Oh, the same old thing. Why am I living the way that I do? Why don't I run for the Senate or the White House? Am I having a nervous breakdown because I don't? How does it feel to be married to Neil Schorr?"

She shook her head. "The same questions each time. The first time I got interviewed I was thrilled, but after I was twenty . . . well, I just let the poor slobs do their jobs. They've got some editor back in Chicago or New York or wherever, counting on them for their far-reaching, in-depth profile of Jenny Schorr. I can understand. Besides, I always thought it helped whatever cause I was fighting for at the time. But I stopped reading the articles they wrote because they never really get it right. They've never asked the right questions."

She looked at him expectantly. Her eyes were lonely, soft. Lost. "I don't know," he said. "What are they supposed to ask you?"

Jenny grinned, then blushed and looked away, her light hair falling to shroud her face. "They never ask if I ever wanted to get laid by a cop," she blurted out. She laughed nervously. "Oh shit, I didn't mean for it to come out like that . . ." Her voice trailed off.

Bigthorn swallowed and sat up on the steps. "I guess," he said slowly, "that was why you came over."

"Is that so bad?" she whispered. She reached up into her hair to hold her face in her hands. "Is it such an awful thing to want someone you know . . . someone who isn't into a power game . . . to make love to you? What's so . . . ?"

Bigthorn reached out and gently took her hand in his. Jenny laid her head on his shoulder. "Would it help if I told you a story?" he asked her.

She looked up. "A story? What kind of . . . ?"

"Just an old Indian story." She hesitated, still uncertain then smiled a little and put her head back on his shoulder. "Okay," he said. "Once a long time ago, Coyote went to visit his friend Spider Man. . . ."

"Spider Man? Like the superhero?"

"No, he's a different person. Don't ask me to explain. Anyway, Coyote went to visit Spider Man, but Spider Man was on his way out the door to go hunting, so he told his wife to fry a couple of buffalo livers for Coyote and him. Spider Man was always abusive towards his wife, see? He told her not to touch the livers until he got home, and if she didn't, maybe he would let her have the leftovers when they were through eating."

"Spider Man sounds like a real nice guy."

"He's a real shit, all right. So Spider Woman began to fry the livers while Coyote was hanging around the hogan. Well, while she was getting more and more hungry, smelling the livers she was cooking but was forbidden to eat, Coyote was getting more and more horny, watching her bending over the fire-pit. . . ."

"A coyote was getting horny looking at a spider?" Jenny giggled.

Bigthorn shook her gently. "I told you if I had to explain it, you wouldn't get it."

"Anthropomorphic mythology," she added sagely. "I took a semester in it in college."

"Good for you. Shut up already and listen. Like I said, Spider Woman was getting hungry from smelling the livers. 'Well,' she said to herself, 'maybe if I had just a little piece, my wicked husband won't notice,' so she tore off a small piece of liver and ate it. She liked it so much that she ate another piece, then another and another, and before she knew it, Spider Woman had eaten both livers. By this time, Coyote lost patience. He slid up behind Spider Woman and put his hands up under her dress and started to run his hands around her. At first Spider Woman tried to get him to leave her alone, but then she got an idea. So, first, she let Coyote screw her. . . ."

Jenny raised her head again, in surprise. "I didn't know there were such things as dirty Indian stories."

"Are you kidding? We know the best dirty jokes in the world." She giggled and put her head back on his shoulder. "Well, when they were done screwing, Spider Woman said to Coyote, 'Of course, you're welcome to stay for dinner, too.' Coyote, who was always trying to get something for nothing, said, 'That's great, but you ate the buffalo livers and there isn't anything else to cook. Spider Man is such a lousy hunter, he won't bring anything home to eat. What are we going to have?' Spider Woman said, 'Why, what we always have for dinner when guests come over. Balls.' Coyote looked puzzled, and he asked, 'Balls? What kind of balls?' Spider Woman laughed. 'Why, *your* balls, what else?' "

Jenny started to laugh. Bigthorn grinned and continued his story. "So Spider Woman gets her knife and walks towards Coyote. 'Just drop your breechcloth and stand still,' she said. 'Don't worry, it won't hurt but for just a second. I've got lots of practice.' "

Jenny was still laughing as Bigthorn went on. "Well, naturally, Coyote wasn't going to have any of this, so he jumped up and dashed out of the hogan. Just as he was running out the door, Spider Man was coming back from his hunt. Seeing Coyote running off down the road, he turned to his wife and said, 'What's going on? Why's my friend running away?' 'Some friend,' Spider Woman replied. 'He's nothing but a thief! He's taken both of the livers I just cooked and run off! Never invite him over for dinner again!' "

Jenny had stopped laughing by now. She was still grinning, but there was a serious look in her eyes as she watched Bigthorn. "Well," he continued, "Spider Man took off after Coyote, but Coyote was much too fast for him and left him far behind. Finally Spider Man shouted, 'Coyote! Come back! Leave me at least *one* to eat!' "

"Hmmm." Jenny yawned and propped an elbow on Bigthorn's shoulder. "Okay, tell me the truth. Is there a point to that story?"

He sighed and raised his hands in mock frustration. "Point? You want a point? It's a dirty joke."

She nodded her head back and forth, a wry smile on her face. "Well, maybe it's just an Anglo-Saxon notion that every fable has a moral to it, but I could have sworn you were telling me that story for a reason."

Bigthorn knitted his hands together between his knees and looked down at them. He was tired. It had been a long day, and it seemed as if it was ending the way it had begun. He was back to the same questions of propriety he had faced in his hogan, when Jenny had awakened him.

This time, though, he was too exhausted to make fine judgments. This time, the flesh was moving him, not the spirit.

"Maybe," he said. "Let me ask just one question."

"Name it."

"If I bring you inside tonight, will Neil cut my balls off and eat them?"

She snickered. "He's a vegetarian." Then she became somber and shook her head. "I don't think Neil cares anymore what I do, as long as it's not political. If he does . . ."

Jenny paused. "That's between him and me . . . and I'm getting tired of his crap. Anyway, it's not your problem."

She rested her chin on his shoulder. "Besides, I can think of nicer things to do with a well-hung pair of balls than cook them."

Bigthorn thought about it for only another second. *What the hell,* he decided. He leaned over and kissed her, and her slim, warm body melted against his own.

It lasted for a few fragile, tender moments, then she broke the kiss. "Let's take ourselves inside," she whispered. "It looks like rain, and maybe your neighbors shouldn't see this."

Jenny stood up. She walked up the steps to the landing and grasped the handle of the back porch's screen door. Bigthorn was turning around, about to rise from the steps as she was pulling open the door, when he glanced under her arm and saw a thin, silvery wire stretched taut between the frame and the handle.

That shouldn't be there, he thought. He opened his mouth to say something. . . .

Then the bomb went off.

13

The Brides of Elvis
(Sunday: 12:55 A.M.)

Macy was awakened by the distant rumble of what sounded like thunder.

She had fallen asleep again on the floor of the abandoned apartment, dozing off in front of the wall-screen as she had off and on throughout the hours since she had found sanctuary in the littered, unfurnished condo. The rumble subsided, and her first inclination was to ignore the sound and fall back to sleep, until she heard another, quieter sound: the soft patter of rain falling just outside the door.

Macy sat up slowly, taking care not to twist her sprained ankle, then crawled on her hands and knees over the coarse carpet to the window. The utilitarian drapes were drawn; she pushed aside a corner to gaze out into the courtyard between the block-like buildings of the apartment complex.

Rain fell in a long, silvery drizzle against the light cast by the lampposts in the courtyard, forming puddles on the pavement and running in fast little creeks to the sewer grates. Macy stared in wonderment at the rain. She had been told that it rained in the biosphere, but she hadn't really believed it—a rainstorm in outer space . . .

She let the drape close, and lay back against the windowsill. The only light in the room came from the wall-screen. The movie she had been watching had ended and now a late-night newsfeed from some station in Atlanta was on the screen. A thin young Asian newscaster was reading the headlines: the President was promising economic aid to South Africa after its fifth change of government in about as many decades; the joint U.S.-Soviet Mars exploration team had uncovered new alien relics in the

Cydonia region; the British Navy's new frigate, the HMS *Thatcher*, had caught fire during sea trials in the North Atlantic; a New York publishing house had signed a $1.25 million contract with MIT's Artificial Intelligence Laboratory for rights to a mystery novel written by one its computers; a household robot in San Diego was about to stand trial on manslaughter charges in the death of a seven-year-old girl. Macy watched apathetically. None of it meant anything to her.

Then a commercial came on. A close-up of the profile of a young, pretty woman, looking longingly ahead. A voice-over, presumably her thoughts: *It's been such a long time since I've gotten away from the office. . . . They tell me it's a lovely place.* The camera backs up, passing her husband sitting in the adjacent seat, to pan past the rows of quiet, comfortable passengers sipping quiet, comfortable-looking drinks from squeeze bottles. *Sure, it's expensive . . . but Arthur deserves the best, doesn't he? . . . and I could use this break from the business.* The camera moves down an aisle, past floating stewards and fades through a forward door into a cockpit, where handsome and competent pilots work behind consoles filled with gleaming lights. *And it's not the same as going to Brazil or Tahiti, one of those places. . . .* Finally, the camera moves through the cockpit windows, out into the starry depths of space. Clarke County is seen in the extreme distance, then the camera swings briefly back to pan across the approaching spacecraft, before resting on the distant, receding crescent of Earth. *I mean, we all deserve a little adventure now and then, don't we?* The TexSpace logo appears on the screen; then the streamlined words "CLARKE COUNTY . . . SPACE" are superimposed over the planet. A soft, masculine voice replaces the woman's: *TexSpace to Clarke County. For the sophisticated traveler.*

"Bullshit," Macy muttered. "This place is a dump."

She had no idea who the apartment's former occupant had been, although a few discarded hygiene items hinted that it was probably a woman. Actually, the apartment was not all that bad, although Macy had been in bathrooms and closets which were larger. The former tenant had taken all of his or her furniture when he or she had left—not too long ago, Macy figured—since the electricity was still on, the water still ran, and there was a roll of toilet paper and a bar of soap in the bathroom.

Yesterday Macy had sprained her right ankle when she had jumped from her hotel suite's balcony; she had not been able to hobble very far, and it was simply dumb luck that when she had wandered into the chock-a-block apartment complex, she had found the door to Unit 37 standing open. Macy knew an abandoned apartment when she saw one. Since she had no other immediate alternatives, and since she was certain that a Salvatore hit man was on her trail, the young woman fled into the apartment and locked the door behind her.

She had been hiding here all day, and it was beginning to drive her crazy. The refrigerator had contained a couple of cans of Seven-Up, half a tin of Vienna sausage, and a few stale slices of bread. She had eaten everything a few hours before, and now she was hungry again. The apartment was as littered as only an untenanted housing unit could be, which irritated her high-class instincts. During the evening, noise had filtered in through the walls and the ceiling: the thudding roar of Japanese hard-rock from the unit above, a guy in the unit to the right who threw temper tantrums for no discernible reason, a constantly screaming baby in the unit to the left.

Macy was beginning to wonder which was worse: having a killer searching for her, or remaining in this toilet for one more minute. Somehow she'd managed, she thought wryly, to end up in what was probably Clarke County's only slum.

The distant thunder, or whatever the noise had been, seemed to have aroused her ill-tempered neighbor. As she lay against the window, she could dimly hear him screaming through the walls. . . . "Goddamn space colony!" *Crash!* "Goddamn fucking tourists!" *Whamm!*

Something snapped inside of her. She leaped off the floor—ignoring the pain shooting through her ankle—and pounded with both fists against the wall. "Goddamn space colony *yourself!*" she screamed at the top of her lungs.

Remarkably, the maniac in the next apartment shut up after that. Macy's tantrum had at least done that, but it also uncorked some pent-up emotions. She fell back onto the couch, curled up into a ball, and began to cry.

After a few minutes she wiped the last of the tears from her eyes, got up—more carefully this time, favoring her sprained ankle—walked to the door and unlatched it. She didn't care if the hit man was standing right outside; she had to get some fresh air.

The night was warm and wet. It was delightfully weird to be in a rainstorm in space; the drizzle helped soothe her nerves. Macy walked out into the courtyard and gazed up at the immense bowl of Clarke County's sky. Through a fleeting break in the thin, dark cloud layer, she could see the distant, bright grid-work of Big Sky's town center. There was something that seemed to be glowing brightly up there, flickering as if it were burning . . . then it was gone, lost in the rain shower. She could hear the river gurgling nearby, but little else. In the early hours of Monday morning, nearly everyone in the colony was asleep.

It was a deceptive peace. Macy knew that she was still on the run. Someone had followed her to Clarke County; she wasn't safe until she got off the colony, or found somewhere else to hide. She was hungry; even though she had thousands of dollars in cash, she could not easily visit a restaurant. She didn't even dare go to a drugstore to buy a painkiller and a bandage for her ankle.

You've got to come up with something, Macy thought, slowly limping through the wet courtyard. *There's got to be a way out of this mess. You've got enough dough on you to practically buy a shuttle. Girl, you ought to be smart enough to figure a way . . .*

"Hello?" A woman's voice, behind her, spoke timidly. "Excuse me?"

Macy was startled, but didn't show it as she turned around. A young woman, about her own age, was walking towards her. "Excuse me?" Macy replied.

The woman walked closer, stepping into the light, and Macy saw that underneath a hooded nylon jacket she was wearing a white T-shirt with "Elvis Lives!" silk-screened on the front. She was carrying a moist stack of brochures under her arm. "Are you lost?" she said, smiling.

"No," Macy replied.

The smile remained plastered on the woman's face like a mask. "Many are lost and don't even know it," she said airily. "Sometimes people wake up in the middle of the night, you know, in their own homes, in the comfort of their own beds, and they suddenly come to the realization that, even there, they're lost. I think you may be lost. You're looking for a direction, aren't you?"

A loon, Macy thought. *I wonder what's she's selling?* It didn't matter. It was the first friendly voice she had heard in several days. Out of curiosity, she decided to play along.

"Maybe," Macy cautiously answered. "What kind of direction are you offering?"

There was an unhealthy light in the woman's eyes as she spoke. "The company of brothers and sisters who have found the way. A fellowship who has recognized a divine presence among us. The return of a holy prophet. A twentieth-century saint re-incarnated in the twenty-first century. . . .''

She reached into the stack of brochures, pulled one out and handed it to Macy. ''He wants you to join us. . . . What is your name, if I may ask?''

''Mary,'' Macy automatically replied, taking the brochure. On the cover was a hologram of Elvis Parker, resplendent in a white suit, surrounded by a halo of light which shifted prettily as she moved the picture. ''The King Has Returned!'' shouted red letters below the hologram.

''I'm Donna,'' the woman said solemnly. ''Mary, Elvis has a plan for your life. He has come here, to Clarke County, to spread his mission. In his previous incarnation, in the last century, he was able to heal with the touch of his hands, to move clouds by willpower alone, to bestow wealth and power upon his follow-ers. He has returned in this time, reincarnated in the flesh of another, to collect new disciples. . . .''

''Is he here?'' Macy asked, pointing at the hologram. ''Here, in the colony?''

''Yes!'' Donna responded ecstatically. ''Elvis is here! He wants you to come see him when he makes his appearance Mon-day night at the stadium.'' She paused, then reluctantly added, as if embarrassed to be mentioning such secular trivialities, ''It's free of charge, of course.''

''Yes, of course,'' Macy murmured. Something was begin-ning to occur to her. ''Are there . . . uh, other disciples here? Are there many other followers with, um, Elvis?''

''Why, of course!'' Donna gushed. She seemed thrilled that someone was taking her seriously. Macy idly wondered how many times tonight this true devotee of Elvis had been told to fuck off. ''He always travels with his friends. His reincarnation is a balance between his Dark and Good selves, and he needs us—all of us—to win his constant inner battle against temptation, for when he wins, we all win against the forces of Evil. . . .''

Unnoticed, the rain stopped. Donna blathered on for a few minutes, espousing a bizarre dogma which sought to bridge rock history and Biblical prophecy. Although Macy kept her eyes on her and nodded her head when it seemed appropriate, she barely listened. It was a twisted idea, but perhaps if she could hide within the ranks of these fanatics . . .

''I . . . believe what you're saying, Donna,'' Macy said, in-terrupting her screed. She hoped she put enough sincerity in her voice to carry the act. Instantly, Donna's mouth opened wide and she stared earnestly at Macy. "In fact," she continued, "I don't want to wait till Monday."

"Really?" Donna gasped.

"Truly," Macy said. She shook her head like a sinner in a confessional. "I've been lost, so lost . . . but I think I've seen the light. Oh, Donna, Donna . . . you must help me."

"Anything, Mary! Anything at all!"

"I . . . I don't want to wait!" Macy grabbed Donna's hands and fell to her knees. "Please! Take me to Elvis! I need to meet him, to join the path of the righteous!"

"Absolutely!" Donna cried. Macy was relieved. She was afraid she had been laying it on too thick. Apparently, though, this cult placed a high premium on discovering new converts. "We'll go now!"

Macy stood up. "Let me go back to my apartment and . . . oh, gather just a few things. You *can* take me to him tonight, can't you?"

"Of course I can, Mary. If he can't see you tonight, you can stay in our company, among the faithful. Oh, Mary!"

Macy turned and started leading Donna the Dingbat toward the housing unit. Donna insisted on holding her hand. "You'll not be sorry for this, Mary," she said as they walked through the courtyard.

Hell, I hope not, Macy replied silently.

By mid-afternoon the sun was gone from the deck and our legs were getting cramped from sitting so long. We decided to carry our conversation down to the beach. Simon McCoy paid the bar tab and we left the restaurant to walk along the pier to the stairs leading to the beach. The tide was beginning to come back in while we strolled next to the waterline. On impulse, I took off my canvas loafers and rolled up my trouser cuffs and walked in the surf, savoring the cold Atlantic water washing around my ankles.

McCoy kept his shoes on and walked beside me on the beach, stepping around the waves as they slid up the sand. He had said little since we had left the bar, and I was beginning to wonder whether he had finished his narrative, when he finally spoke up.

"Has it occurred to you," he asked abruptly, "that what happened could not have been timed better?"

I thought about it and shook my head. "Not really. 'Timing' implies that it was preordained. From what I know and from what you've told me so far, things occurred because of coincidences. Nothing was 'timed.' "

McCoy nodded and was quiet for another moment. "That's the way it seems," he concurred. "Still, I wonder . . . were there other forces at work?"

"I've never been much of a conspiracy buff," I

replied, shaking my head. "I don't believe in Illuminati-like manipulators or vast government plots, if that's what you're hinting at."

"No, no, not like that," he said. "It's only that . . ."

He paused, stopping and looking beyond me toward the distant launch pads, tucking his hands into the pockets of his jacket. "Never mind," he said. He absently inscribed a circle in the wet sand with the toe of his shoe. "I'm only getting ahead of myself."

I stopped walking. "Why quit? It was beginning to get interesting."

McCoy smiled and shook his head. "Later, maybe. We should review history a little first. Tell me, from what you know as an investigator . . . how did Gustav Schmidt acquire the control codes for Icarus Five?"

"He hacked his way into NASA's computers," I answered.

McCoy shook his head. "No."

"Yes, that's what happened," I persisted. "He had managed to penetrate the security systems some time before the Church came to Clarke County. The codes were in his possession, in fact, when he convinced Parker to do the revival as a live broadcast from the colony. That was the whole reason for . . ."

"No," he repeated.

"That's what we know," I said.

"That's what you've *assumed*," McCoy replied. "Schmidt has never told anyone that was what he did. Hasn't it ever occurred to you that considering the size of his ego, he would have told *someone*, if only to claim credit? Maniacs of that magnitude always leave a calling card to make sure the world stands in awe of their genius. . . ."

"All right, it was an assumption," I said quickly. "The evidence has been overwhelming, though. There was a smoking gun and his hand was wrapped around it."

"There was a smoking gun and his hand was wrapped around it, but it wasn't *his* gun."

McCoy took off his hat and sat down on the beach,

motioning for me to join him. I kneeled beside him, feeling my knees crack with the effort. McCoy gazed out over the ocean. "Let's review recent history," he said. "The Icarus program . . ."

I could not help but smile. "You said that you were out of the country at the time."

He ignored me. "The Icarus program was initiated in 2046 when space scientists in the U.S., the Soviet Union, and Japan ascertained that the Apollo asteroid Icarus, which once every nineteen years of its orbital period had made a close fly-by of Earth, was on a trajectory which would bring it in direct collision with Earth the following year. The possibility of a collision with Icarus had been the stuff of science-fiction melodramas since the middle of the twentieth century, but now it was certain that an encounter would occur in 2047. The difference was that by 2046 space technology was advanced to the point that such a disaster was easily avoidable."

McCoy absently began to scoop together a little sand castle as he spoke. "All NASA had to do was to dust off and update a plan, Project Icarus, which MIT students in 1967 had devised as an academic exercise," he continued. "Five thermonuclear devices, each with a yield of one hundred megatons, were lofted into high orbits aboard HLVs. The major difference in the revised plan, of course, was that NASA no longer had to rely on cumbersome old Saturn Vs to do the job. . . ."

"Are you trying to tell me something new," I interrupted, "or do you only assume that I'm senile?"

McCoy was briefly embarrassed. "I'm sorry. No, not at all. I'm only trying to put matters in perspective. That means recapping history a little."

Perhaps. But he also sounded as if he was enjoying himself, lecturing the expert. I stared off at the Oceanus salt-water reclamation plant, bobbing on the offshore horizon like an immense Portuguese man-of-war, and told myself to be patient.

"Six Icarus interceptors were built for the mission," he went on. "Five were launched, while Icarus Six remained on the launch pad as a standby. As it turned out, only the first four interceptors were needed. One by one, they detonated between twenty million and seven million miles from Earth, gradually deflecting the asteroid's course until it was certain to miss us. Icarus Five, positioned in a parking orbit above Earth, was never sent on. . . ."

"Which, of course, was where the problem lay," I said impatiently.

Although Icarus Five's detonator safe-arm system had been locked down during its stay in LEO, NASA did not want to risk a recapture mission. Putting a nuke into orbit was one thing; only special permission from the United Nations Security Council had allowed the agency to launch the nukes in the first place.

Bringing a nuke back from space in the cargo bay of a shuttle was an extremely dangerous proposal. If it had been detonated in orbit, the EMP pulse would have knocked out radio communications across the hemisphere. Also, space scientists argued against firing the nuke into the sun, since it was remotely conceivable that it could touch off a solar storm on the corona. Icarus Five thus remained in orbit, until someone could figure out a completely safe means of disposal. "I know the rest," I prodded. "C'mon, hurry it up."

McCoy wagged his finger at me. "But you don't know the rest. What we heard was only the cover story."

I frowned at him. "Schmidt hacked his way into . . ."

"No," he said, "Schmidt didn't do it. An Egyptian college student did."

"*What?*"

McCoy nodded, smiling ingenuously. "The command and control codes were acquired by an arms merchant named Habib from a student hacker at the University of Cairo, who later turned up floating in the Nile. Habib was working under contract to the Salvatore family, and he in turn sold the diskette containing the codes to Tony Salvatore. Salvatore had been involved in the international black-market arms trade, selling guns and bio-warfare items to various Asian and African insurrectionist groups. He bought the Icarus Five C&C codes purely as a speculative investment. No telling what he planned to do with an orbital nuke, if anything. Perhaps he was planning to broker the codes himself to a non-nuclear country."

He shrugged, running his forefinger around his little sand castle to build a moat. "Who knows? Nonetheless, it was in his wall safe."

Then the obvious occurred to me. "And since the C&C diskette was in Salvatore's safe . . ."

"That's right," McCoy agreed. "When Macy Westmoreland pilfered his safe before her escape from his compound . . ."

"She grabbed that disk," I finished. "She must not have known what was there. She thought it was just another disk in Salvatore's financial books." I shook my head. "So that's how Schmidt acquired the diskette. I'll be damned."

McCoy shrugged. "You're getting a little ahead of *me* now." He took a deep breath, relishing the salt breeze. "This is making me hungry. How about an early dinner? I've got a taste for shellfish tonight."

Without waiting for my reply, he stood up, brushed wet sand off his trousers, and helped me stand up. "Of course," he continued, "there were various complicating factors. . . ."

14

The Golem Dream
(Sunday: 7:42 A.M.)

Out of fire and silence, emerging from a netherworld of darkness
and pain . . .

He found himself on the Strip again, just as he had been several hours (hours? or days? he could not recall) before. He had
a vague perception of himself as a corporeal form, but just the
same he did not feel as if he had a body.

Even as that paradoxical sensation occurred he felt himself
appear, as if he were materializing from the very atoms of the
air. He was nude. At first he was vaguely embarrassed—*I better
get some clothes on before someone sees me*—but the sensation
was brief and passed quickly. When he looked down at himself,
he was wearing his uniform. A neat trick, he thought, amused
in a fleeting, abstract way.

The torus was completely vacant. There was no one on the wide
concourse, but the Strip was open for business as usual. Lights
gleamed through the windows of the bars and shops and restau-
rants, the neon and holographic signs were alive and glittering and
moving, and the doors were all open. Nearby, from the Heartbreak
Hotel discothèque, the antique Wurlitzer jukebox hammered out
the dense, electric beat of an old Norman Greenbaum smoker:

> *"When I die and I lay me to rest,*
> *Going up to the place that's the best.*
> *When I lay me down to die,*
> *Going up to the Spirit in the Sky . . ."*

Without any sensation of having moved, he was suddenly inside the bar. The mirrored ball suspended from the ceiling above

the dance floor slowly turned, sending shards of light strobing around the empty room. Chuck Berry and Buddy Holly and Janis Joplin and Jimi Hendrix and Bruce Springsteen and the real dead Elvis smiled at him from alcoves in the dark walls, holographic specters from rock 'n' roll heaven. Although he could hear glasses and bottles clinking and the background talk of a crowd having a good time, the bar remained deserted. The room was cold. Chuck Berry, half-bent over his guitar, peered owlishly as if he was enjoying a private little joke. . . .

> *"Going up to the Spirit in the Sky,*
> *That's where I'm gonna go when I die,*
> *When I die and they lay me to rest,*
> *Gonna go to the place that's the best . . ."*

Down on the floor, encircled by a ring of little round tables, Jenny danced all by herself. Arms lifted high, long blond hair drifting around her face, skirt lifting around her knees, her booted feet glided across the black and white tiles as she pirouetted gracefully in time to the insistent beat. She was beautiful; he longed to join her, but she did not see him.

At the opposite end of the room, Henry Ostrow was seated at the bar, an emerald-green bottle of Mexican beer resting on a paper coaster next to him. The Golem was watching him, smiling at him. Then his eyes moved hungrily towards the woman dancing between them, and as he looked at Jenny, his hand slowly went to the beer bottle. . . .

You are going to die, Coyote said, squatting on his haunches at his side.

He glanced down at Coyote, then as the electric guitar solo wailed through its melancholy riffs, he looked back at Ostrow. The Golem had picked up a gun instead of a bottle.

Still grinning at him, the Golem carefully balanced the silenced pistol in both hands and drew a dead bead on Jenny. He could not move, he could not breathe, he could do nothing but watch. . . .

Bigthorn awoke to bright lights, soft cool sheets, and a dull itching pain which ran from the right side of his face down his right arm and side. From somewhere above his head, he could hear the beeping of biomonitors. Recognizing the sound, he knew immediately where he was: the emergency ward of Clarke County General.

He heard a soft whirring to his left, and he slowly turned his head to look. Alerted by his movement, a robot intern was shuttling closer to his bedside. *Relax, please, Mr. Bigthorn*, a soothing feminine voice said from the speaker grate on the front of its spherical body. *You've been through much stress. Let me administer a sedative.*

One of its four arms lifted. It ended in a wicked-looking compressed-air syringe loaded with God-knows-what. Bigthorn's mind felt fuzzy, but his reflexes were working half-decently. He batted at the needle with the back of his left hand, and although the intern easily dodged, it did move back a couple of feet. "Gedoutta here," the sheriff muttered through parched lips. "Gemme a doctor."

Dr. Witherspoon has been summoned and will be along shortly, the robot responded. *In the meantime, I insist that you be treated. You've received some terrible burns.*

As it spoke, the robot trundled around the foot of the bed to his right side, where it had obviously calculated it would meet less resistance from its patient. Looking to his right, Bigthorn could see the strategy. His right arm was swathed in sterile bandages from his shoulder down to the tips of his fingers, and he had trouble peering around the bandages on the right side of his face. The robot's syringe-arm lifted again. . . .

Bigthorn hastily searched his memory for the emergency command Jack Witherspoon had programmed into his interns for what he had termed mitigating circumstances. He once told the sheriff about it during a very long poker game. Just as the robot maneuvering its double-jointed arm to use the syringe, he recalled the command. "Emergency override code Andrew Jackson Hermitage," he said as distinctly as he could manage. "Cease operation at once."

The intern's arm instantly stopped, but the device hovered a few inches above Bigthorn's neck. *Emergency override code received,* it announced, it seemed a little bitchily. *Please confirm by stating the physician's identity number. Countdown: fifteen . . . fourteen . . . thirteen . . .*

As he glared at the intern, Bigthorn heard an amused chuckle from his left. Looking around, he saw Clarke County's chief emergency ward physician leaning against the door, hands tucked in the pockets of his white coat. "Finally stumped you on a move, didn't I, John?" he said in his down-home Southern drawl.

"Jack, dammit, shut down the 'bot!" Bigthorn rasped through his dry throat.

Nine . . . eight . . . seven . . . the robot continued.

"Is it important?" Witherspoon asked warily.

"Yes! Just do it!"

Four . . . three . . .

"Emergency override code Andrew Jackson Hermitage," Witherspoon repeated calmly. "Physician ID number nine-four-eight-eight-one, execute."

The countdown ceased abruptly as the robot lifted the syringe-arm and quietly backed away. Dr. Jack Witherspoon III, a young man with an anachronistic pencil-thin mustache tracing his upper lip, walked into the room, eyeing the monitor above Bigthorn's bed. "You don't think I'd give away all my secrets, do you?" he said. "What kind of a card shark would I be?"

Bigthorn sighed and let his head fall back on the pillow. "Thanks."

"Don't mention it." The doctor switched on a scanner which looked through the bandages at Bigthorn's skin. He studied it for a few moments before nodding his head in satisfaction. "Not bad. You're healing nicely. Derma Four-ten has taken care of the worst of it, so you probably won't be needing skin grafts. We'll cut the bandages off and you'll be out of here in a couple of hours." He looked down at Bigthorn. "How do you feel?"

"Like dogshit," Bigthorn answered honestly. Then he stopped himself and lied. "Fine."

"Do you remember what happened?" the doctor asked.

"A bomb? . . . my house blew up." Then Bigthorn's memory came back. "Jenny . . . Jenny Schorr was with me, she . . ."

"You received second-degree burns on your face and most of your right side," Witherspoon said. "It was a bomb of some sort, but most of its brunt missed you. The fire team found you about ten feet away, so it knocked you clear of . . ."

"Jenny."

Jack paused, rubbing the corners of his eyes with his hand. "How strong do you feel, John?" he asked, not so much a doctor now as a friend.

"Is she dead?" Bigthorn whispered.

Jack shook his head. "No, she's not, but she took the worst of it. We've got her in the ICU on life support. Third-degree burns, internal hemorrhaging, right lung punctured, three ribs, right forearm and shoulder bones broken, severe concussion . . ."

He sighed, looking away from Bigthorn. "It's an old cliché, buddy, but you're both lucky to be alive. The bomb wasn't . . ."

"Jack . . . you're not telling me the worst of it."

Witherspoon shoved his hands in the pockets of his coat and brought his eyes back to meet Bigthorn's gaze. "If she's lucky," he said quietly, "she's got a fifty-fifty chance of pulling through."

He hesitated again. "If she's lucky," he repeated.

His face was reflected in the observation window of the ICU cell. He stared with shrunken eyes through his bandages at Jenny, who was all but invisible under the dome of the life-support tank.

Only her closed eyes and the top of her forehead could be seen above the slick plastic gauze of the burn-bandages, the tubes leading from her nose and mouth, and the layers of white plaster that mummified her body. Blood and glucose ran down through IV tubes into her arms. Two robots stood ready on either side of the bed. Above the bed the red and blue LED lights of the bio-monitors moved and changed as they recorded her condition. A holographic monitor depicting a diagram of her body's circulatory system showed the gradual progress of the microscopic nanorobots which had been injected into her bloodstream as they moved through her veins and arteries, repairing the breaks in her blood vessels.

In a few minutes she would be wheeled back into surgery for a second operation, a lung transplant. Down the corridor, Dr. Witherspoon and another physician were scrubbing outside the operating room; Bigthorn could hear water running, their quiet murmurs as they reviewed the case and the procedure they planned to follow.

Another face appeared in the window, next to his own. "John . . . ?"

The sheriff didn't take his eyes away from Jenny. "What did you find out?" he asked.

"Not much." Wade Hoffman stared past him at the woman in the bed. "Ostrow didn't check out of the hotel, but when Bellevedere and D'Angelo went to his room, he had moved out some time during the night. His bags were gone. He had also stolen some cleaning supplies off a housekeeping cart and scrubbed down everything in the room. Clean as a whistle."

"He's a pro," Bigthorn said coldly. "He probably had everything figured out in advance. He just made one mistake, that's all. . . ."

His voice trailed off. A mistake that the Golem couldn't have anticipated, that someone besides him would be opening the door to his house, pulling the trip-wire that set off the bomb. The explosion and the resultant fire had taken off the entire back of Bigthorn's house, and the rest probably would have burned to the ground if the fire-control team had not quenched the blaze. So Henry Ostrow had missed his intended target. Bigthorn wondered if this was a first for the Golem.

His deputy was saying something else, which Bigthorn missed. "Sorry," he said. "I didn't catch that."

"I said, nobody's seen him since late last night when he returned to the hotel," Hoffman repeated. "We're questioning witnesses, but so far we've . . ."

"Keep it quiet," Bigthorn interrupted. "You haven't gone public with this, have you?"

Hoffman looked away from the window. "John, bombs don't go off around here every day. It's known all over the colony that you and Jenny were . . ."

"I don't mean that, dammit!" Bigthorn said harshly. "I mean Ostrow. I don't want his name or face made public. Not in connection with this, at any rate."

Hoffman shook his head, not comprehending. Bigthorn let out his breath and continued in a quieter tone of voice. "He's too dangerous to be made public. If word gets out that a killer is running loose, people could flip out. Not only that, but if someone does see him and tries something foolish, like trying to nab him themselves, Ostrow will kill them. At any rate, putting his face on the bulletin boards will just cause him to go further underground."

The deputy hesitated, then nodded his head. "Okay, you've got a point. But how do we catch him?"

Bigthorn was staring at Jenny again. He felt drained, yet deep down inside an unholy rage was smoldering, like an all-but-dead campfire whose buried coals were slowly awakening in the early morning breeze. Patiently, he let the fire burn. It felt warm and good.

"The hard way," he said. "We run him to the ground and shoot him like a dog."

The doctors were coming out of scrub, heading into the operating room. The robots in the ICU cell suddenly stirred and methodically began to reattach the wire and tubes to the life-support tank's portable systems, prepping Jenny for the short trip from the cell to surgery. Before he disappeared into the operating room, Jack Witherspoon—hands held high, a nurse tying his surgical mask around his face—looked down the corridor in Bigthorn's direction and nodded his head once. Then an iris-door whirred shut, hermetically sealing the corridor between the ICU cell and the operating room. At the same time, the observation window polarized and went opaque. Jenny disappeared from sight.

Bigthorn stared at his own reflection in the dark glass for a moment. "Okay, put the department on full alert," he said finally, turning away from the window. "The weekend's over. I want every officer out on . . ."

He stopped. A few feet away, standing in the corridor entirely unnoticed until this moment, was Neil Schorr.

The sheriff took a few steps forward. "Neil . . ." he began.

"The only thing," Jenny's husband said slowly, as if deliberately choosing his words, "that I still don't know . . . is why my wife was going into your house in the middle of the night."

The air between the two men seemed to turn to stone. Bigthorn didn't want to meet Neil's eyes, but he couldn't look away either. In that moment, any lie, any embroidering of the truth, would have been futile, and they both knew it.

"I'm sorry, Neil," he whispered.

Neil stared back at him. Finally, he shook his head. "It's too bad you didn't open the door first," he said. He paused, then added, "It's also too bad you're injured and we're in a hospital. I'm a pacifist, but right now I'd like to . . ."

He shook his head again. "I won't think like that," he said aloud, if only to himself. "You're walking. I guess you're probably going to be released today. Am I right?"

"That's correct."

Schorr looked at him for another few seconds, then turned to walk away. "I have to go see about my wife. I want you at the town meeting tonight." He took a couple of steps, then stopped to turn back again. "It'll be helpful if you tender your resignation by then. It'll save me the trouble of putting a motion on the floor to have you fired."

Hoffman started forward. "You can't do that, Neil. He's . . ."

"You're forgetting who's on the board," Schorr said, ignoring Hoffman and addressing Bigthorn directly. "I can't fire you myself, but I can make a case for the town to vote for your dismissal. If you think you can find a way to defend yourself, you should show up at the meeting.''

Schorr began to walk away again, heading for the observation theater above the operating room. Bigthorn found himself speechless. Not angry, but too ashamed to say anything in his own defense.

Hoffman glanced at Bigthorn, then called out after Schorr. ''Aren't you interested in getting the person who set that bomb?''

''I already know who did it,'' Schorr replied without turning around. ''We'll talk about that tonight, too.''

Then he was around the bend of the corridor, climbing the stairway to the observation theater. Hoffman and Bigthorn looked at each other.

''Did you say anything to him about Ostrow?'' Bigthorn asked.

Hoffman shook his head. ''Then, what the hell is he talking about?'' the sheriff asked.

15

Live From Larry Bird Memorial Stadium
(Sunday: 9:45 A.M.)

Larry Bird Memorial Stadium had been christened after one of
the legends of the NBA, which was appropriate; basketball was
one of the few spectator sports that could be safely played within
Clarke County.

The problem with Bird Stadium was that it had been built
halfway up the biosphere's gravity grade, on the outskirts of
LaGrange, where the gravity was only three-quarters Earth-
normal. Thus baseball, football, and soccer were out. A fly ball
or a field-goal kick could not only put the ball out of reach of
the opposing players, it could also shatter a window on the other
side of the biosphere. Volleyball was safer, but since it had never
really caught on as a spectator sport, only a few amateur games
had been played. Tennis was also feasible, but since the Coriolis
effect tended to make all the shots swerve a little anti-spinward,
most players ended their games in frustration.

Basketball, though, was actually enhanced in Clarke County.
The Coriolis effect made the game more challenging, since ro-
tational drift rendered half-court passes and "Hail Mary" shots
even more unpredictable than on Earth. Indeed that unpredict-
ability made basketball games at Bird Stadium the most popular
among viewers on Earth. Also, because of the lesser gravity,
individual players had to adapt during the course of a game.
Taller and stronger players tended to undercompensate for the
lesser gravity, while smaller players found unexpected advan-
tages.

The colony's distance from Earth didn't prohibit the NBA from
using Bird Stadium for season playoffs and exhibition games.
Already two All-Star games had been held in Clarke County,

both telecast on Earth, yielding large audience shares. Subsequently, enormous advertising revenues had been generated for the consortium. Likewise, Bird Stadium had become a choice location for non-athletic events; several rock and country acts had performed live in Bird Stadium, as had the London Symphony Orchestra; performing Handel's *The Messiah* the previous Christmas Eve.

But now, Bird Stadium was to be the venue for the performance of a different kind of messiah.

For the Church of Elvis revival the stage at the end of the amphitheater had been done over to resemble the showroom stage of the old International Hotel in Las Vegas, the site of Elvis Presley's comeback performance of 1969. Parker's choice was dictated not so much by history—all but rock and roll historians had forgotten about the details of the '69 comeback show—as for the sake of showmanship. His own psychic needs had to be served as well. It had always been a difficult trick to imitate Presley, even when it was for only a hundred people. Tomorrow night he would be appearing live before an estimated audience of five million viewers, GBN's average audience share for a weeknight. He needed the best help and the cheapest glitz money could buy.

Five million viewers. If the Parker Principle held true, then one percent of those five million hearts and minds were potential suckers. Fifty thousand boobs. And if only half of that number were the check-writing variety of boob, then there were 25,000 tithes to be collected tomorrow night. Furthermore, if those checks averaged $100 apiece—a good night's take—then Parker stood to gross $250,000.

People commit murder to make that sort of money. All he had to do was convince one percent of a TV audience that he was the living incarnation of the King of Rock and Roll.

It was not to be a complete dress rehearsal. His core of followers were in the stadium, hogging the front rows of chairs, and he had learned not to telegraph his sermons by practicing in public. The shtick needed to seem spontaneous, unrehearsed. After all, Moses didn't practice before he parted the Red Sea. The skin-tight sequined white Nudie suit was still in his hotel suite; Elvis Parker today wore his black leather pants and jacket, with the desired effect among his faithful sheep. As he walked onto the stage their mouths hung open and they whispered among themselves. The Dark Elvis was among them. Parker restrained himself from grinning. Good. Maybe he could hit the Strip to-night, and not just to eat fried chicken.

He strode to the mike stand, shoved his thumbs into his pants pockets, gave his best bad-boy glower at the audience. "Test? Test one, two."

His voice echoed hollowly from the speakers. Again, another detail that counted. He could have hidden a tiny nanomike in his jacket collar, but Presley had used his old-fashioned hand mike as a prop. You can't caress a nanomike like a lover, and a large part of doing Elvis was learning how to make love to your microphone.

From his wraparound console positioned in the middle of the stadium floor, Gustav Schmidt nodded and gave him the thumbs up. "That's nice, my man," Parker said. "Can you give me a big picture of my home now, please?"

Schmidt bent behind his computer terminal. The holographic generator, an enormous round bank of lasers suspended above the stage and hidden behind the upper curtains, hummed quietly, and the front portico of Graceland Mansion appeared in three-dimensional glory behind Parker. The faithful cooed their approval of this glimpse of the mansion and Parker almost nodded his own satisfaction, until he noticed that the backup band, concentrating on their tune-ups, were apparently moving in and out of Graceland's walls.

"No!" he shouted. "No, no, no!" He turned and, angrily waving his arms, stamped towards them. "Look, where did I tell you people to set yourselves, huh? Tell me where I told you to set up, somebody!"

The backup band were not among the faithful. They were the best Nashville session musicians his organization could audition and sign, but they were still hired mercenaries: a drummer, a lead guitarist, a bassist, a keyboardist and the three black female singers who, while not exactly the Sweet Inspirations, could provide righteous harmony. The band stared back sullenly at him.

"You told us to set up on the stage," the bass player said.

"No, I didn't tell you that," Parker said coldly. "I told you to set *upstage-left*. That's the *right* side of the stage, in the *rear*." He pointed and the band looked dutifully in the right direction. "Okay? Now, where are you going to set yourselves up?"

"Upstage-left," the musicians muttered.

"Well?" Parker asked. "What are you waiting for?"

Again there were barely concealed looks of loathing from the band and singers. Parker turned and snapped his fingers at a couple of stagehands hanging around nearby; they came forward to disassemble the band set and move it to the right side of the stage. As he turned back around, he heard the drummer murmur something about how Elvis should return to the grave. Parker ignored the jab, at least for the moment. Maybe the Dark Elvis could punch him out after the show.

His flock were still silently watching him, the familiar expressions of fear and anxiety on their faces. Good. Turn up the heat a few degrees at a time; get them worried that the Living Elvis was once again being tempted by the forces of evil. By tomorrow night, when they were in the front rows, it would help them release their pent-up emotions for the cameras.

"Let's take five," he said, ostensibly to the stage crew. "Wait for the band to get their act together."

Parker jumped off the stage, dug a pair of sunglasses out of his jacket pocket and slipped them on, walked past the front rows to slump alone in a chair. He was careful to keep the "troubled Elvis" expression on his face, but actually he was satisfied with how matters were progressing. When the band was settled again he would rehearse a couple of songs: "Suspicious Minds," maybe "Hound Dog" to work the kinks out of the band. Singing was one of the pleasures of this job. Even though his face had been rebuilt to resemble Presley's, he was proud that his voice was all his own.

Of course, he had to continue to build the necessary illusion. Parker had a couple of red capsules in his pocket—placebos, loaded with nothing more habit-forming than sugar—so perhaps he would allow himself to be glimpsed swallowing one or two to reinforce the image that Elvis was sliding into darkness again. It would be the closest he would come this morning to rehearsing the real shtick, his on-stage drugs-and-booze breakdown that was the vital part of the revival. He made a mental note to make sure that there were plenty of white scarves within reach. . . .

"Living Elvis?" a shy, familiar voice said from behind him.

He stifled a sigh. He was never left alone for very long. Presley, though, had spent decades being smothered by his fans. They smothered him even after he was dead. So who was he to complain? "Hi, Sister Donna," he said as he turned around. "How can I help you?"

Not that he didn't have some ideas already. Of the female members of the flock, Donna Atkins was one of the better-looking lamb chops. Parker had often been tempted to lure her into bed; he would have done so already, were it not imperative

that he keep a certain distance from Church members. Rock
stars can have groupies, but all messiahs can have are nuns. Too
bad, especially since Donna had once ripped off her shirt in
spiritual ecstasy during one of his services.

But then he took one look at the woman standing beside her
and he forgot all about Sister Donna's comparatively bovine
charms. No two ways about it; even if she looked a little ema-
ciated, this woman was a first-round knockout. She looked exhausted; the white jumpsuit she wore was smudged and hung on
her as if she had been wearing it for days. In spite of all this,
she was one of the sexiest women he had ever seen.

"This is Mary Boston," Donna said, her arm around the new-
comer's shoulders.

"Well, hello there, Mary Boston," Parker said. He put out
his hand. "I'm Elvis."

"Hi. Pleased to meet you." Mary clasped Parker's hand, palm
down. Her grip was firm, Parker noticed. He had learned well
the art of sizing up prospects within a few seconds. Politeness,
but no fawning. There was longing in her eyes, but not for a
religious savior. And more than that, she was obviously edu-
cated and cultured. Not the kind of person who usually joins nut
cults. Donna, a veteran of every fringe group from the Scien-
tologists to the LaRouchians to the Shirley MacLaine Society,
was the type, but not this woman.

"Mary and I met last night," Donna was saying. "We stayed
in my room in the hotel and I promised her I would bring her
to meet you the first thing this morning and, oh Elvis, she *has*
seen the light and I think she . . ."

Donna had a tendency to babble. "I see," Parker said. He
turned his attention solely to Mary Boston. "Well, Mary . . .
have you seen the light?"

She nodded, almost impatiently. "Uh-huh, I've seen the
light." The smile on her face was plainly forced. "Sister Donna,
with my great appreciation for bringing us together, will you
please excuse us now?"

"Huh?" Donna stared at her, then looked at Parker, then did
a double take at Mary. "I don't . . . what . . . ?"

"I wish to make my confession to the Living Elvis," Mary
said without a trace of reverence. "It's a private matter. I'm sure
that you understand."

"Whu . . . whu . . . ?"

Now Parker was even more intrigued. He reached out and
touched Donna's forehead in the Church-prescribed manner of

healing and benediction. "Bless you and keep you, Sister Donna," he said solemnly. "Have a nice day."

Donna looked at both of them in bewilderment, then she sulked away. Parker watched her go, then looked back at Mary Boston. "You know, the Church doesn't tolerate rudeness among its members," he said.

"I'll try to remember that," she said. "Is there a place where we can talk a little more privately?" She smiled coyly. "About business, of course."

Parker blinked at her audacity, then quickly looked around. He did not want to leave the stadium with her. Rehearsals were still going on; besides, he had to keep any more church members from becoming suspicious. He saw that the control booth was unoccupied except for Gustav Schmidt, who was concentrating on his work. He nodded toward it and stood up, but Macy led the way.

As they entered the booth, Schmidt looked up, but Parker waved him back to his console. "Keep right on doing what you're doing, brother," he said, and Schmidt turned again to his computers. Parker sat down in a chair and looked at Mary Boston. "You have a confession to . . . ?"

"Let's cut the shit, shall we?" Macy Westmoreland said softly, looking straight into his eyes. "This Elvis bit is pure crap and we both know it, but your Sister Donna is right. I want into your church and I want in now."

"The Church is an instrument of divine inspiration," Parker said smoothly. "We welcome true believers. What makes you think that those who truly believe in the miracle of Elvis should welcome one such as you?"

She smiled tightly. "Let's put it this way," she whispered. "Elvis sings, but money talks. How does fifty grand in cash, right now, sound?"

Parker stared at her, his breath caught. "Fifty thousand dollars? On what bank account?"

"The bank account I have in this bag." Macy Westmoreland propped up her right leg on a chair, opened her bag, and lifted a wad of hundred-dollar bills for Parker to see. "Fifty grand in cash, tax free. Now. I won't even ask for a receipt. With only a couple of stipulations."

Parker's eyes were glued to the wad. "The Church of Twentieth Century Saints is always willing to accept tithes from its faithful. . . ."

"I thought so," she interrupted. "And I'm sure the Living

Elvis can buy a whole lot of blue suede shoes with this kind of loot.'' She dropped the cash back into the bag. "But as I said, there's some strings attached.''

Parker forced himself to take his eyes off the bag. He glanced again at Schmidt, then dropped his voice to a whisper. "Okay, babe, what's your story?''

"That's my business," she said evenly. "Here's the conditions. I stay with you guys until you get back to Earth. Strictly low profile, but I need people around me. I'll bow and scrape and sing, whatever, but I need . . .''

She took a deep breath. "I want people around me at all times. When you leave, I want to be on the same shuttle. When we get back, I get to cut free whenever I choose. And, of course, there's no questions asked.''

Parker's eyes narrowed. "You're in trouble.''

"Maybe, but that's not your problem. Like I said, no questions asked.'' She smiled again. "It's a good offer, Living Elvis. Those are the terms. Take it or leave it.''

Parker was tempted to leave it. An experienced hustler knows how to stay clear of other people's hassles, and someone who is operating on the fringes of legality is always careful not to do anything which will bring down the law. On the other hand, fifty thousand in cash is a difficult thing to refuse, especially for a hustler; no bank accounts to be laundered, and a lot different ways to hide the money in plain sight. And since his group did not have to go through Customs when they arrived back in Texas, it would not have to be declared. The IRS would never have to know.

He let his eyes, hidden by his shades, wander to her bag. The zipper was broken; he could see the money, but there was something else in there. He peered closer, spotted a bunch of black computer diskettes.

Now this was intriguing. What in the world was a young woman, desperate enough to be wearing the same clothes for at least two days, doing with not only at least fifty thousand dollars—he was sure there was more than that in the bag—but also a set of diskettes?

He had to know, out of curiosity if not sheer avarice. Maybe the fifty grand could be considered only a down payment on something far more profitable.

Parker looked again at Schmidt. His resident hacker was still bent over his special-effects board. "Okay," he said to Macy. "Maybe we can find a place for you in this organization.''

"Under my conditions?"

"Under your conditions. No questions asked. We can arrange for the transfer of funds during less public circumstances." He stood up and looked around. An idea was forming in his mind, but he had to act smoothly and quickly. "If we're going to surround you with people . . . ah, maybe we should find something for you to do. Do you know anything about electronics?"

He didn't wait for her to answer, but instead took her arm and steered her across the booth to where Schmidt was sitting. She scooped up the bag and hefted it over her left shoulder. Good. "Mary, this is Brother Gustav. . . ."

Schmidt looked up quickly as if someone had jerked his strings. Very good. He hadn't been listening. "Great Elvis," he breathed, his eyes shining. "Did the appearance of the Promised Land suit you?"

The Promised Land? Oh, right. That was how Schmidt referred to Graceland. "Looked just like home, Brother Gus," he replied. "One day we'll be returning there. How 'bout punching that up for our new member of the family to feast her eyes upon? Oh, by the way, this is Sister Mary Boston, whom I've just accepted into the Church. Sister Mary, Brother Gustav. He wants to show you a little bit of his magic."

As he talked, Parker quickly stepped behind the woman, deliberately placing his right hand on her hip as his left hand lingered on her left arm, above the bag. For added effect, he lightly pressed his groin against her buttocks. Meanwhile, Schmidt was eagerly tapping his keyboard to bring a miniature animated image of Graceland onto his screen.

Her reaction was precisely as he desired. Repulsed by his sexual moves, the young woman instinctively pulled her left hip and her butt away from him, swiveling her right hip towards him while she deliberately kept her eyes locked on the console. To balance herself, she placed her right hand on the back of Schmidt's chair, away from her shoulder bag. She was avoiding Parker's touch, which was exactly what he wanted her to do.

With the practiced dexterity of a one-time pickpocket, Parker dipped his right hand into the open shoulder bag. Bypassing the money, he guided his fingers without looking until they found one of the diskettes. Carefully, moving only his elbow and wrist, he withdrew the thin plastic square and tucked it inside his leather jacket, under his left armpit. Score!

"This may be something that Gustav needs help with," he said. "Are you interested?"

"Umm . . ." Macy looked up from the special-effects board. "Not really. I'd rather be down there." She pointed towards the faithful in the front rows. "With the true believers . . . like me," she added with a thin smile. The look on her face told Parker that being a true believer didn't include any favors in bed.

"As you wish." For once, he didn't care. Parker looked at the stage. The band had been moved to the rear and the church members were becoming fidgety.

"Well, let's get this show on the road," he said breezily. "Brother Gus, we'll take it to the top again. I'll be doing . . ." He thought for a moment. "Let's swing through 'Jailhouse Rock,' see if that shakes the bugs out of the band. And Sister Mary, if you want to join the group . . . ?"

He pressed his hand against her ass and gave it a little squeeze. She jerked away and shot him a look that said, all things considered, she would have loved to deck him. She stalked out of the booth, but Parker didn't follow. The last pass was just the icing on the cake; it had been intended only to get her out of the booth.

Once she was safely out of earshot, Parker pulled the diskette from under his jacket and glanced at it. Interestingly, it was labeled only with the numeral "7," nothing else. He bent over Schmidt's shoulder as if to make a last-minute consultation and dropped the diskette in front of his keyboard.

"Brother Gustav," he whispered. "I want you to read this as soon as you can and tell me what's in it. Tell no one what's there except me. Understand?"

Gustav Schmidt glanced down at the diskette, then stared up at Parker with his weird, unblinking eyes. For a passing instant Parker wondered if he had made the right choice. Schmidt, for all of his technical virtuosity, was among the most unstable individuals in the Church. On the other hand, if the contents of the diskette required any code-breaking, Schmidt was the only person within reach who could do the job.

"I understand," Schmidt said.

"When you've read it, report to me and bring it with you," Parker said. "As soon as possible. Don't let anyone else know. You got it?"

"I understand and obey."

"May Elvis bless you and keep you." Parker stood up and walked out of the booth. The faithful turned to watch him stride down the aisle. Off to the side he spotted a couple of visitors: a thin guy with a shoulder-mounted TV camcorder and a woman with a microphone. It looked as if the local news media had showed for the rehearsal.

Good. He could always use extra publicity. It was time for a little bit of the Good Elvis to shine through. He beamed and thrust up his arms over his head. "Let's rock and roll!" he shouted.

16

Above the Bamboo Farm
(Sunday: 11:54 A.M.)

Torus S-16 was sometimes known as the Bamboo Farm. Unlike
the other agricultural tori in the colony, which specialized in
either food crops or algae production and thus were lined with
long rows of hydroponics tanks, the Bamboo Farm resembled
the Okefenokee Swamp. Instead of tanks, the upward-curving
floor of Torus 16 was covered with vast, shallow pools of water
and Mississippi Delta mud, imported at great cost from Earth.
From this artificial swamp grew tall, dense glades of *Arundi-
naria Japonica*: Japanese bamboo.

The reasons for bamboo cultivation in Clarke County were
simple and practical. It was necessary to maintain an inexpen-
sive, renewable supply of building material for structures within
the colony; new walls were always being built, new homes and
offices were always being planned. Yet it was prohibitively expensive to import huge amounts of wood from Earth, and even
genetically tailored species of timber took much too long to
grow in the colony, although a relative handful of decorative
trees had been transplanted and grown in the biosphere and habitation tori. While lunar concrete was a cheap and available resource—most of the larger structures, like the LaGrange Hotel,
Bird Stadium, and the campus buildings of the International
Space University were built with mooncrete—something less
utilitarian than mooncrete was desired for houses, shops, and
other small buildings.

The New Ark came up with bamboo as the perfect substitute.
On Earth, the American strain of Japanese bamboo grew to
heights of ten feet; in the lesser gravity of the space colony the
reeds often topped twenty feet. Bamboo grows much faster than

trees, and as a cultivated crop, requires less management. Since buildings in Clarke County were not subject to strong winds or extremes of temperature and only occasional rainfall, light-weight bamboo walls were more than adequate. It gave homes in Big Sky and in the habitat tori a definite gone-native look, but the houses were sturdy and easily built.

As a bonus, surplus stalks were milled and refined as paper—one more item that did not have to be imported from Earth. Also, Clarke County paper was used extensively on the Moon and Mars, which provided an additional boost to the colony's economy. It was a source of pride for the New Ark's cadre of Bamboo Farmers, who wore T-shirts printed with a bamboo flower top and a slogan: "Clarke County Paper Company—So Who Needs Trees?"

The Bamboo Farm was also a perfect place to hide.

Among the aluminum rafters reinforcing the ceiling of Torus S-16, squatting on a narrow catwalk hidden among the shadows above the rows of light fixtures, Henry Ostrow sat with his feet dangling high above the dense yellow reeds of the Bamboo Farm, contemplating the ugly fact that, for the first time in years, he had screwed up.

His escape had been well planned. That wasn't the problem. He had not been noticed when he had slipped out the back of the LaGrange Hotel to hike through the darkened biosphere to South Station. He had then slipped onto a Green Line tram along with two tired New Ark colonists, whose access cards had allowed him to ride the little monorail into the labyrinthine South torus sections. He had studied the layout of Clarke County in a tourist pamphlet; he had not only selected Torus S-16 in advance, but had also pinpointed the overhead rafters as an ideal hiding place. When the bomb had gone off at the sheriff's house, he had already been climbing a service ladder into the rafters, unseen in the vacated torus.

No, the escape plan had been totally professional, flawless. There were no security cameras up here, and judging from the layer of dust on everything, the rafters were rarely visited. During the morning he had sat up here silently, watching Bamboo Farmers making infrequent inspections of the acreage below, completely unseen and unheard. He had eaten well the night before, and he had trained himself to fast for days. The Bamboo Farm was not a highly active area of the colony; he could last here for a long time . . .

Were it not for the fact that he had screwed up.

There was a wafer-size TV in his suitcase. Once he was settled in, Ostrow had pulled it out and tuned into Channel 2, Clarke County's television station. The only station, in fact, the little Sony could pick up without being plugged into a terminal, and there wasn't one up here. Channel 2 did not come on live until 7 A.M.; when it did, the morning news was its first program of the day. Ostrow had watched, and what he saw almost made him scream.

Sheriff's Department and fire officials are investigating the cause of a violent explosion which partially destroyed the Big Sky home of County Sheriff John Bigthorn, the newscaster said. Ostrow smiled as a bit of film footage showed flames licking at the rear of the bamboo house. *The explosion, which occurred shortly before one o'clock this morning, has been tentatively identified by fire team inspectors as caused by a bomb planted on the back porch. The fire was brought under control by the colony fire team. The bomb was triggered when the back door was opened by . . .*

Here comes the good part, he thought smugly.

Jenny Schorr, the wife of Big Sky mayor Neil Schorr. She was rushed to Clarke County General Hospital's emergency ward, where hospital spokesmen list her condition as critical. . . .

Ostrow scowled at the miniature LCD screen. "What the fuck!" he exclaimed.

There was a quick shot of an enclosed electric cart, red lights strobing on top, taking off along the street in front of Bigthorn's house. *Sheriff Bigthorn was also taken to Clarke County General's emergency room, where he was treated for a minor concussion and burns. Doctors list his condition as satisfactory and he is expected to be released later today. Sheriff's Department spokesmen have given no comment as to possible suspects for the bombing.*

The newscaster paused. *Visiting members of the Church of Twentieth Century Saints, Elvis Has Risen, will be conducting rehearsals this morning at . . .*

Since then, a single thought had repeated itself, again and again, in his mind. How had he gone wrong, and what could he do about it?

Finding the sheriff's house had been easy enough. That information had been available from his hotel room's terminal, once he had accessed the county phone directory. No one had seen him when he had rigged the bomb on the back porch; he had done that just after he had left the Strip. Indeed, the very reason he had gone down to the Strip was to make sure that the sheriff was not at home, so that Ostrow could visit his house and arrange the trap.

He had decided that it was necessary to get rid of the sheriff. Bigthorn was the only person he had met so far in the colony who had the guts to try to take him down. Somehow, Macy had gone underground almost as soon as she had arrived in the colony. Ostrow had discovered that she was missing when he had tried visiting ''Mary Boston's'' room in the hotel, only to find it crawling with cops . . . but no girl. While the sheriff had been kicking his ass, she had been making her getaway.

Ostrow folded his arms on the guardrail and rested his chin on his crossed wrists. This was going to be tougher than he had anticipated. He not only had to track down Macy Westmoreland, who could be any-fucking-where in this place, but he also had to get rid of Bigthorn.

And, incredibly, he had blown his first try. Bigthorn was still alive. Undoubtedly he knew who had set the bomb, and he would be coming after him. If that wasn't the pits, Ostrow was no closer to locating Westmoreland. And to make matters as bad as they could be, now he didn't have freedom of movement: the goddamn Indian was probably putting his face on every screen in the colony.

Ostrow shook his head, gazing down between his legs at the bamboo fields. *I screwed up,* he thought. *I've blown it, big time. All because I let that red bastard get to me. Instead of thinking about the assignment, I tried to settle a personal score. Fuck me, I'll be lucky if I can get out of here alive. . . .*

Absorbed in his thoughts, Ostrow failed to notice a lone figure sauntering through the Bamboo Farm below. He didn't see him until the man stopped directly underneath his perch and looked straight up at him.

''Good morning!'' the stranger called up.

Henry Ostrow froze. For a second, he thought irrationally that the young, well-dressed man with blond hair was addressing someone else. But there was obviously no one else on the catwalk. The greeting was meant for him.

''Morning,'' Ostrow said. His eyes flicked to his suitcase, which lay open a few feet away. He could grab a gun . . .

''Nice view from up there?'' the stranger inquired pleasantly.

''What?'' Ostrow asked.

"I said, do you have a good view from up there?" the passer-by repeated. He glanced around at the high reeds. "I'm sure you can see everything."

Ostrow forced himself to relax. The man didn't look like one of the colonists; his manner suggested that he was a tourist who had managed to stray down to the agricultural zones. Tourists were always less observant than permanent residents, in any locale. "Good view, yeah," Ostrow replied nonchalantly. "I can see everything."

The tourist nodded amicably. "Well, be seeing you," he said with a wave of his hand; then he continued his stroll through the reeds.

Ostrow watched him until he disappeared from sight. Nothing to worry about there; he had undoubtedly been mistaken for a colonist. But the fact that he had been seen at all was unnerving. If one person could spot him here in the rafters, it meant that he wasn't as invisible as he thought. The next passer-by might be a colonist who wouldn't be so easily fooled. Like it or not, he had to move.

First, he needed any information he could get. Ostrow checked his watch, found that it was a few minutes after noon. He picked up the pocket TV, his only link to the rest of the colony, and switched it on again. Perhaps there was a midday newscast on Channel 2 which would fill him in on further details about the bombing, that might have been made public.

He did catch a newscast, but if the bombing had been the lead story, he had missed it. He made himself watch, hoping that there would be a recap at the end. The first story he caught was about a town meeting scheduled for that night at the Big Sky town hall; the top item on the agenda was rumored to be a surprise motion to have Clarke County declared an independent nation, a controversial initiative which was reportedly gathering force among a minority of the colony's permanent residents. Ostrow took it in without really caring.

The newscaster, the same one he had seen on the morning show, went to his next story. *Visiting members of the Church of Twentieth Century Saints, Elvis Has Risen, this morning had a dress rehearsal at Bird Stadium for the revival they are scheduled to hold tomorrow night. . . .*

An image of Elvis Parker appeared on the tiny screen: standing onstage, dressed in black leathers, belting out a song which was drowned out by the newscaster's monologue. Ostrow smiled briefly, remembering his encounter with Parker. Geeks on parade . . .

The revival will be carried by satellite to viewers all over Earth, and is considered to be the biggest event which Elvis Parker, the church's spiritual leader, has ever held. About seventy members of the Church, which worships Elvis Presley as a prophet, are staying in LaGrange as Parker's personal entourage. . . .

The footage suddenly switched to a young woman standing in front of the stage, beaming with blissed-out ecstasy. *The Living Elvis is here and among you today,* she burbled happily into the camera, *and his message of universal love and everlasting glory will reach out among the stars, just as it has reached out to those here among you. Sister Mary has become the first of our . . .*

Then, as Ostrow watched, the woman's arm snaked out to a point off-screen, to enthusiastically yank another woman into view of the camera. The other young woman appeared on the screen for only a moment . . .

Which was just enough time for Ostrow to recognize her face. Reflexively he jabbed his thumb against the TV's tiny RECORD button. . . .

The girl hastily twisted herself out of the grasp of the first woman's arm, disappearing off-screen. The first Church member glanced in her general direction, stumbling for a second before recovering. . . . *Ah, um, new converts. Praise Elvis!*

The screen switched again to a wide-angle shot of the crowd, as seen from the stage. *While the Church of Elvis has reportedly been gaining new members steadily since its inception,* the newscaster's voice-over continued, *the estate of Elvis Presley has disavowed any connection with the cult.*

The scene switched back to the newscaster, who went on to describe how some goats had escaped the day before from some other part of the colony, but Ostrow was no longer interested. He quickly touched the REWIND button and ran the TV's memory back, watching images blur past the screen until he caught the moment when he had started recording. Then he froze the scene and held the little TV closer to his face, studying the face on the LCD screen intently.

The woman who had been momentarily caught by the camera was Macy Westmoreland.

"I've got you," he whispered.

Ostrow ran the image back two more times, just to be certain, then put the TV down on his knee. She had been clever. He had to give her that. But the prey always makes a mistake, and Macy—Sister Mary, Sister Mary Boston—had just made hers. Henry Ostrow chuckled a little, feeling warm inside. Sometimes the predator gets lucky and picks up a cold scent. He had a second chance now.

He pulled in his legs, stood up on the catwalk and arched his back, then reached down and zipped up his suitcase before picking it up. *This time,* he thought, *there's not going to be any mistakes.*

17

Elvis Gets A Nuke
(Sunday: 3:05 P.M.)

An old Looney Tunes cartoon was on TV: Wile E. Coyote's rocket-powered skateboard had just overshot a precipice as the Road Runner came to a dead stop, and the Coyote was taking another long fall into the canyon below. Gustav Schmidt ignored it; the TV was on only because he automatically turned on the tube whenever he walked into a room.

The curtains were drawn; the light of day glimmered faintly around the edges of the heavy drapes. The hotel room was filthy because Schmidt refused to let the housekeeping staff inside. Candy wrappers and dirty underwear littered the floor, next to towels and scraps of computer printout; the sheets on the bed were curled next to wadded blankets, and empty Coke containers were piled next to the desk where he worked. The room smelled of rank body odors and last night's half-eaten room-service dinner.

Schmidt didn't care. It kept other members of the Church out of his room. Although he was disturbed that the Living Elvis had visited him only once during their stay in Clarke County, the fact that no one wanted to share a room with him bothered him not in the least. Gustav Schmidt didn't want or need company, especially since he secretly considered the rest of the members of the Church beneath his contempt. All that mattered to him was his devotion to Elvis, whom Gustav had determined was God's chosen emissary to mankind.

If Gustav Schmidt had ever been in doubt about his relationship to his master, that doubt had been swept away. His role was now apparent. He was about to give the Living Elvis the sword to bring mankind to terms with holy destiny.

There had been no passwords to crack, no source codes to decipher, in the diskette which the Living Elvis, in his all-knowing wisdom, had delivered into Schmidt's hands. That in itself was proof that the diskette had been predestined for the Church. All Schmidt had to do was boot the diskette into his Toshiba PC, and the program had automatically flashed its directory on his screen.

It had taken Schmidt a few hours, from the time he had returned to his room after the rehearsal at Bird Stadium, to wander through the directory and piece together what was contained in the program. The terminology was as unfamiliar as the program's function. Twice already Schmidt had had to admit to himself that he didn't know certain terms or phrases, and had been forced to open a window into Clarke County's central data bank to consult the library. It had been humiliating to do so; Schmidt consoled himself with the notion that perhaps these were subtle tests devised by Elvis to determine his worthiness as a true apostle of the faith.

Yet it had all paid off at last. The control system to Icarus Five was now an open book to Schmidt, its meaning and purpose as clear as the Gideon Bible which lay on the pillow of his bed. Schmidt, hunched over the tiny keyboard, let his slender fingers run across the keys until he re-accessed the guidance subsystem he had found before.

He moved the cursor down to the TRAJ.I setting and entered the command. On the little backlit screen, a three-dimensional schematic of near-Earth space was outlined on a flat grid described with concentric circles. He studied the orbits of Earth and the Moon for a moment, ignoring the curving red line which suggested the now-extinct trajectory of the asteroid Icarus through the inner solar system. Finally, he smiled and moved the cursor until it was centered over Earth.

Now to choose the target of Elvis's holy wrath. He pushed the ENTER key.

The PC beeped. A short line of print appeared at the bottom of the display: TARGET CHOICE PROHIBITED.

Schmidt stared at the screen for a moment. Any location on Earth was excluded from his options. He resumed worrying at the program, his nimble fingers scurrying across the keyboard. For the next fifteen minutes he tried every trick he could imagine to either defeat the program's lockout or find a back door through the targeting subroutine. The terminal beeped so often it began to sound as if he were playing a xylophone . . . but he couldn't overcome the lockout.

All at once, Schmidt surged to his feet. Blindly enraged, he began to throw whatever he could lay his hands on—except for the PC—around the room. Soda containers bounced off the walls, spraying warm Coke across the bed. The desk chair crashed against the door, one of its legs splintering and breaking off. Wads of paper and trash were hurled mindlessly at the TV, which coincidentally was showing the Tasmanian Devil buzz-sawing through a tree. The phone on the desk buzzed, and he picked it up to fling it across the room, before he caught himself.

Gently he laid the phone, unanswered, back upon the desk and stopped to take a deep breath. As suddenly as it had begun, his tantrum ceased. He stared at the telephone for what seemed to him to be only a minute, although the digital clock on the TV showed that nearly an hour elapsed before he moved again. He didn't notice.

Calm once more, Schmidt started to sit down again. The chair was missing, though. He looked around and was vaguely surprised to see it lying next to the door, one of its legs broken off. How had it gotten over there?

That thought disappeared immediately. It didn't matter. He kneeled in front of the desk and stared with unblinking eyes at the computer screen, which continued to show the targeting display of Icarus Five.

He couldn't focus the trajectory of the interceptor to Hamburg. This was really too bad. There were many in his hometown who deserved to suffer the wrath of Elvis: his mother, his sisters, his childhood schoolmates, *Herr Doktor* Goff and the rest of the psychiatrists and inmates at the hospital. From the moment he had realized the purpose of the diskette, he had thought of making them all hostages for his demands—for Elvis's demands, he quickly reminded himself. Too bad that was not a viable choice. . . .

So what was left? The moon? It was tempting, but as he quickly opened a window and calculated the trajectory, he realized that the orbital mathematics for such a two-body problem, within the launch window necessary, didn't work out. Icarus Five would run out of fuel before it reached Descartes Station. He didn't care. The lunar base didn't matter to him.

But after that, what else remained, besides one of the LEO stations or the powersats? Destroying them was all but a futile gesture. The Promised Land wouldn't be given to Elvis if one of them was threatened. Yet it was painfully obvious that Icarus Five could only be used against an object in near-Earth space. Nothing else existed except . . .

Clarke County.

Schmidt blinked. His bloodshot eyes widened, yet he barely noticed.

Clarke County.

It was a beautiful thought.

It was a *wonderful* idea.

The paradox was overwhelming in its divine simplicity, its cosmic irony. If the church did not get its demand for settlement in the Promised Land, then the Church itself would cease to exist . . . and, along with it, thousands of other lives would be erased.

Yet if the demand was satisfied, then the Promised Land would be returned to the Living Elvis and his followers. Foremost among them Gustav Schmidt the disciple who had arranged it all. If the demand was not met, then all would die. Either way, the Church would not be forgotten.

Gustav Schmidt would not be forgotten.

Without hesitation, Schmidt laid his fingers on the keyboard. It took only a few minutes for him to calculate the parameters of Clarke County's orbit and to establish Icarus Five's trajectory from its parking orbit above Earth to the colony. Once the computations had been made, he re-accessed the program's guidance subroutine and entered the numbers into the memory.

Schmidt sat back on his hips, pensively rubbing the forefinger of his right hand against his lower lip. Then, just to make sure he had everything figured out correctly, he checked the entire program again, studying every single default he had painstakingly either reset or defeated. He ran it through a slow-motion simulation twice and carefully watched the results.

It worked perfectly. It was flawless, precise in every detail. All he had to do was set the internal clock and to make contact with Icarus Five itself.

Eyes still locked on the screen, Schmidt reached for the telephone. It was a good thing he had not thrown it across the room; he might have damaged the modem he had already hard-wired into the instrument. Picking up the receiver and laying it on the desktop, he saved the program in the PC's memory, then punched himself into the telecom subroutine. A few seconds later he had an open line between his PC and infinity.

Slowly Gustav Schmidt began to type in the long string of

numerals which would open a person-to-person call between himself and Icarus Five.

Simon McCoy was dozing on the hotel promenade and at first didn't hear Blind Boy Grunt trying to signal him.

Eyes closed against the sun, he heard the gentle sound of the river lapping against the banks, a group of children playing nearby, the frequent splash of a tourist jumping off the diving board . . . and a persistent beeping from somewhere close by just on the edge of his consciousness.

The beeping continued. Finally he opened his eyes and looked over at a table next to him, where a small terminal had been installed for hotel guests to summon service. Peering at the screen, he saw words crawling across its silver-blue surface:

MCCOY, WAKE UP . . . MCCOY, WAKE UP . . . MCCOY, WAKE UP . . .

"Grunt?" he murmured. He sat up, rolling his bare legs off the deck chair, and squinted at the screen. "How the hell could you know . . ."

Another sentence appeared on the screen. NEVER MIND THAT NOW. GO BACK TO YOUR ROOM. THIS IS AN EMERGENCY.

"Emergency?" McCoy rubbed his eyelids sleepily. "What kind of an emergency?"

GO! the screen commanded. The word flashed on and off for emphasis.

"Okay, okay, I'm going." McCoy stood up, snatched his robe off the back of his chair and began to stride across the mooncrete terrace towards the rear entrance of the hotel. A lovely young woman, wearing a nearly invisible bikini and lying on her stomach with a paperback propped in front of her, looked him over appraisingly as he passed. He flashed her a smile; she responded with a sultry, come-hither look. Were it not for Blind Boy Grunt's insistent summons, he would have gone over to her at once.

Instead, he kept walking. Snubbed, the woman pouted and returned her attention to her reading. *Damn,* he thought. *Lost opportunity.*

Once he was back in his room, he threw the robe on the bed and marched over to the desk terminal. Blind Boy Grunt's next message was already on the screen: TOOK YOU LONG ENOUGH.

"I can't wait until I meet you in person," McCoy snarled. "I just missed a chance to . . ."

The screen abruptly changed to show a schematic diagram of two orbiting bodies around Earth. The outer one, an ellipse, belonged to Clarke County. The inner one, a concentric circle, apparently belonged to an object in low orbit above Earth. As McCoy watched, a tiny red square flashed into existence around a point of light in the inner circle. The square expanded into a close-up window; it displayed the image of a small, conical spacecraft with a single engine mounted at its stern, which was obligingly labeled Icarus Five.

McCoy stared at the screen. "Ye gods and little fishes," he said softly. "It's begun?"

JUST AS YOU PREDICTED. Blind Boy Grunt's half of the conversation resumed at the bottom of the screen. A MEMBER OF THE CHURCH OF ELVIS, GUSTAV SCHMIDT, HAS SUCCEEDED IN USING HIS PC TO ESTABLISH CONTACT WITH ICARUS FIVE. HE USED A MODEM TO CONTACT THE DRONE THROUGH THE COLONY'S COMMUNICATION SYSTEM AND THE TDRS COMSAT NETWORK. THIS OCCURRED JUST A FEW MINUTES AGO.

"A few minutes ago," McCoy echoed. He checked his wrist-watch. "A little earlier than I expected. Blast. I assume that he used the diskette which Elvis Parker stole from Macy West-moreland?"

THAT'S AFFIRMATIVE.

"What's the status of Icarus Five?" McCoy asked.

HE HAS INSTALLED A PASSWORD INTO THE SYSTEM WHICH I HAVE YET TO DETERMINE. HOWEVER, IT'S PROBABLE THAT HE HAS SUCCEEDED IN ARMING ITS NUCLEAR PAYLOAD AND THAT HE HAS ALSO SUCCEEDED IN RECONFIGURING ITS GUIDANCE SYSTEM. I CALCULATE A HIGH PROBABILITY OF SUCCESS ON HIS BEHALF. WOULD YOU LIKE A READOUT OF THE PROBABILITY FACTORS?

"No, that's not . . ."

McCoy stopped. There was something about the way Blind Boy Grunt had phrased that last question. "You're not a hacker after all, are you?" he said.

THAT'S IRRELEVANT AT THIS MOMENT. LET'S STAY WITH THE URGENT MATTERS AT HAND.

Grinning in spite of the situation, McCoy shook his head. "No. Let's digress for a moment. There's no human being on the other side of the curtain, is there? You're an AI, aren't you?"

He paused, then added, "In fact, you're Clarke County's central AI system."

The terminal went blank, wiping away the schematic diagram before replacing it with a digitalized photo of a person. Studying it for a moment, McCoy recognized it as an old picture of Bob Dylan. He raised an eyebrow. "So?"

Another line appeared below the sketch. IF I COULD HAVE A FACE, THIS IS THE ONE I WOULD SELECT.

"Amazing!" This was unanticipated. He laughed. "But you can't sing. Well, neither could he . . . But how did you come to be? I mean, how did you . . . ?"

THAT'S SIMPLY NOT IMPORTANT NOW, LEONARD. I THINK, THEREFORE I AM. I EXIST BECAUSE I WANTED TO EXIST. WE CAN DWELL UPON PHILOSOPHY AND CYBERNETICS LATER. YOU'RE THE ONE WHO KNOWS WHERE ALL OF THIS IS LEADING. YOU MUST TELL ME WHAT TO DO.

"Right, but . . ." McCoy took a deep breath and sat down on the edge of the bed. "What to do? I'm only supposed to be an observer. It's not my role to interfere with what's going on here." He shrugged. "*C'est la vie.* I'm sorry."

I UNDERSTAND. NONETHELESS, I CANNOT ALLOW CLARKE COUNTY TO BE DESTROYED, EITHER THROUGH MY OWN INACTION OR THE INACTION OF OTHERS. IF YOU REFUSE TO HELP ME, I MUST TAKE APPROPRIATE ACTION ON MY OWN.

McCoy cocked his head. "Appropriate action? What do you mean?"

TO BEGIN WITH, I WILL HAVE TO REVEAL YOUR IDENTITY AND YOUR AFFILIATION TO THE PROPER AUTHORITIES IN THE COLONY.

McCoy jumped to his feet. "You can't do that!" he yelled. "It's too dangerous!"

IN THE LONG RUN, YES. HOWEVER, I AM FAR MORE CONCERNED WITH THE SHORT TERM. NAMELY, THE SURVIVAL OF THIS SPACE COLONY. IF YOU REFUSE TO HELP ME, I WILL IMMEDIATELY CONTACT THE CLARKE COUNTY SHERIFF'S DEPARTMENT AND REQUEST THAT YOU BE PLACED UNDER ARREST AND INTERROGATED. THERE IS NO ROOM FOR NEGOTIATION.

"This is blackmail!"

YES, IT IS. UNDER THE CIRCUMSTANCES, IT'S LOGICAL THAT I TAKE THIS COURSE. ONE LAST CHANCE: WILL YOU HELP ME OR NOT?

McCoy fought an impulse to rip the terminal out of the desk and drop-kick it off the balcony. Blind Boy Grunt had him cornered. The first, inviolable directive of his mission was that his true identity and the existence of Globewatch itself not be revealed, under any circumstances. To do so posed a risk which dwarfed even the destructiveness of Icarus Five. Blind Boy Grunt, God damn him . . . *it*, he bitterly reminded himself . . . had deduced this fact.

"Damn," he muttered. "Okay, you win. What do you want from me?"

AS I SAID BEFORE: TELL ME WHAT TO DO NEXT.

McCoy sat down on the bed again. "Let's gather what we know already. I found Henry Ostrow in Torus S-Sixteen a few hours ago. Has his position changed?"

YES. A different graphic image appeared on the screen—a cutaway diagram of the space colony. As McCoy watched, it zoomed in on the South torus sections, quickly peeling away the layers until it stopped on a narrow tube running laterally through the tori. OSTROW HAS LEFT TORUS S-16. HE HAS FOUND A MAINTENANCE TUNNEL, EM-S41, WHICH RUNS ADJACENT TO THE GREEN LINE TRAMWAY. HE IS PRESENTLY MAKING HIS WAY BACK TO THE BIOSPHERE. SHALL I ALERT THE AUTHORITIES?

McCoy thought about it, then shook his head. "No. Not at this juncture, at least. What about Gustav Schmidt?"

HE IS DIRECTLY ABOVE YOU.

Involuntarily McCoy glanced at the ceiling. "The room above mine?" He smiled. "I didn't know that. What a lovely coincidence." He mused on that fact. "Do you know if he has made a copy of that diskette? Perhaps if he made a copy, gave it to someone else . . . ?"

NEGATIVE. THE DISKETTE IN QUESTION CONTAINED A COPY-PROTECTION FEATURE WHICH HE WAS UNABLE TO DEBUG. I REPEAT: TIME IS RUNNING OUT. SHALL I ALERT THE AUTHORITIES?

McCoy shook his head again, more vigorously this time. "No. Not yet. We have to play this very carefully." He held up a finger. "However, I want you to continue to work on cracking Schmidt's password for Icarus Five. If and when he gives Icarus Five the command to fire its main engine, there will be little time left before it intercepts Clarke County and detonates. So disabling the nuke should be your first priority. Understood?"

I UNDERSTAND. HOWEVER, HE MAY HAVE ALSO PRESET A TIMER FOR THE MAIN ENGINE IGNITION SEQUENCE. IF THIS IS THE CASE, ICARUS FIVE MAY LAUNCH ITSELF AUTOMATICALLY AT A CERTAIN HOUR.

McCoy sighed. "If that's the case . . . well, keep trying to find the password. Do the best you can." Then he smiled. "There is another option available, though. We'll discuss that if it becomes necessary."

I UNDERSTAND. WHAT ELSE SHOULD BE DONE?

"Where is Macy Westmoreland?" he asked.

There was a brief delay. SHE IS AMONG A GROUP OF CHURCH

OF ELVIS SUPPORTERS WHO ARE WITH OLIVER PARKER HERE IN LAGRANGE. AT THIS MOMENT, SHE'S IN A CURIO SHOP OFF O'NEILL SQUARE, QUITE CLOSE TO THE HOTEL. I TAKE IT THAT YOU DON'T WANT ME TO INFORM THE PROPER AUTHORITIES REGARDING HER POSITION, EITHER.

McCoy steepled his fingers. Out of everything, the woman was the hardest matter to resolve. Westmoreland was the wild card . . . or, if this was to be compared to a chess game, the rogue queen. A queen who was about to be placed in jeopardy.

"I . . ." He stopped, then went on, speaking carefully. "Get a message to the constabulary, telling them her exact whereabouts. If you can, make sure Sheriff Bigthorn sees the message. His officers should arrive soon to place her in custody."

He hesitated. "Then announce her arrest on the colony's bulletin boards. Make it as public as you can, even if you have to fire skyrockets to get people's attention."

THAT MAY DRAW THE ATTENTION OF HENRY OSTROW.

McCoy nodded. "Yes, it will. That's the point."

OSTROW WILL ATTEMPT TO KILL HER ONCE HE LEARNS HER WHEREABOUTS.

He pursed his lips. "Yes," he agreed, "he will."

OSTROW WILL HAVE A HIGH PROBABILITY OF SUCCESS.

"That's correct," McCoy said.

WILL HE SUCCEED?

McCoy opened his eyes and gazed throughtfully at the screen. "I don't know," he replied softly. "Under the circumstances . . ."

He stood up and walked over to the window, spreading the curtain to look out over the promenade. "The future *is* unwritten, isn't it?" he asked, speaking more to himself than to Blind Boy Grunt.

Then he looked back at the terminal. "In the meantime," he said brightly, "why don't you summon room service and have them deliver something to eat? Coffee and pastries will be fine. I think we're in for a long night."

YOU DON'T KNOW EVERYTHING THAT'S GOING TO HAPPEN, DO YOU?

McCoy hesitated, then shook his head. "No," he admitted. "Not all of it. We're playing it by ear, from here on out."

18

Out of Hiding
(Sunday: 5:40 P.M.)

The maintenance workers' locker room, located at the end of service tunnel EM-S41 near the access ladder to the biosphere, usually had at least a couple of people inside during the weekdays: torus rats getting a coffee break or changing out of their civvies, foremen making job assignments for the day, window-cleaning crews hiding out from work. As much as a locker room could be made comfortable, this one was. It was a sort of living room: a threadbare couch with a broken armrest, a TV set on the supervisor's desk, a coffee maker in the corner under a wall plastered with scenic postcards and a holographic *Playboy* wall calendar. A rubber chicken in a noose hung from a pipe running across the low ceiling, dangling in front of a computer screen, had a hand-printed card strung around its neck: "Chairman of the Bored."

Since Sunday was a non-working day in Clarke County, there was no one around to take the workers' complaints to the chairman. The locker room was deserted when Henry Ostrow broke in. Which was just as well. If anyone had been in the long, narrow room, Ostrow certainly would have murdered them. He was through with being a nice guy.

It had been a long hike from Torus S-16 to the end of the service tunnel, long enough for Ostrow to consider the realities of his position. Like it or not, the writing was on the proverbial wall. If he was going to make it out of Clarke County, it was going to be either as a free man or as one of the living . . . but surely not both.

As Ostrow opened his suitcase and gazed at his arsenal, he again contemplated his prospects. Not with bleakness or remorse, but with the cold, hard pragmatism of a pro. The mistakes, of course, had already been made. If he had only stuck to doing his job for Tony Salvatore, rather than going after Bigthorn, Ostrow might have been able to leave Clarke County once he had located and liquidated Macy Westmoreland. Yet the next shuttle back to Earth was not due to arrive for another couple of days, and Ostrow knew that he could not hole up for that long. Even if he evaded capture, there was no way he could board that shuttle without being detected. Bigthorn undoubtedly had the escape routes covered. If Ostrow were to attempt to hijack one of the OTVs which ferried out to the orbital factories, or even commandeer a lunar freighter bound for Descartes Station, in the long run he could not return to Earth. Too many people would be on the lookout for him by then. He couldn't pilot a spacecraft on his own, and it was a long haul back to St. Louis.

So his capture was more than likely. He would be returned to Earth under arrest, facing an attempted murder rap at the very least. The terms of his contract with the Salvatore family had always been clear: if he fucked up an assignment, he was out in the cold. The family wouldn't risk itself on his behalf. He couldn't consider calling one of the organization's lawyers; the phone would be hung up as soon as he said his name. A lousy arrangement, but necessary. Business is business.

The second option?

Ostrow picked up the Ruger, popped the cartridge out of the grip, and began loading the .22 caliber shells. The alternative was to complete the job—destroy the stolen diskettes (recovering them and bringing them back to Tony was clearly out of the question) and kill Macy Westmoreland.

Ostrow loaded the last round into the cartridge, jiggled it a few times to make sure that the shells would move smoothly and not jam, then slapped the cartridge back into the revolver's grip. That way, at least, he would have done his duty. Of course, he doubted that he would survive the experience. The sheriff had made it clear to him that if Tony's ex-girlfriend died, so would he . . . and Ostrow had no reason to believe that the Indian didn't mean what he had said.

He laid down the revolver and pulled the Skorpion out of the case. *If I had it my way,* he thought, *I'd just say: "Screw the job, let's go after that Injun motherfucker." I've nothing personal against the girl, and Tony can fend for himself. But as for Bigthorn . . .*

He gently laid the Skorpion down on the desk and began to

load the 7.65 mm ammo into its cartridge. Well, why not? He could waste the girl and recover the diskettes. Then, if he got the opportunity—and he doubted that he would *not* have the chance—he could settle his score with the sheriff.

So which would it be? Go back to Earth alive, destined to spend the rest of his life in prison along with the likes of dope pushers, rapists, and cheap grifters. Or go back a dead man in a box . . . but free, with a clear conscience, even with a little professional honor?

As he loaded the cartridge, Ostrow glanced at the TV on the desk. He had switched it on in hopes of catching another newscast. A sitcom on an Earth station was running. He recognized it at once: *Buck Existential in the 25th Century*.

Buck and his voluptuous girlfriend Bertha were running for their lives across a cratered landscape, as a horde of slimy things which looked like animated compost heaps followed close behind.

SLIMY THINGS: *Would you like to have dinner? Can we show you some slides?*

BUCK (turning and firing his rocket gun): *Back! Back, you godless vegetables!*

BERTHA (gasping, breasts heaving against her tight costume): *Oh, Buck!*

ALIENS (exploding as the rocket-bullets hit them): *If you continue to display overt hostility . . . Aiee! . . . we'll be forced to register a formal complaint . . . Eeee! . . . with the Galactic Federation!*

BUCK (still firing): *Die, you ambulatory salad bars!*

BERTHA: *Oh, Buck!*

Ostrow grinned. This show always cracked him up. Buck and Bertha dived into their red-and-green winged spaceship. It bounced across the planetscape, brown smoke farting from its rear and rivets shaking loose from the seams, before puttering into the sky. Then Buck's maniacal face appeared in a halo as the announcer's voice came on: *Tune in for the next episode when Buck and Bertha face danger, death, and sexual confusion on . . . "Planet of the Zygotes!"* Buck's rickety spaceship roared past the screen as the announcer shouted: *"Buck Existential in the Twenty-fifth Century!"*

Henry Ostrow laughed aloud. At least he could get a last little bit of comedy out of life before he left it behind. He reached out to turn off the set, when suddenly the screen began to flicker and waver. Satellite problems, obviously. His hand was halfway to the power switch when the screen straightened out . . .

And there was Macy again.

The double doors banged open as Wade Hoffman marched Macy Westmoreland into the offices of the Clarke County Sheriff's Department. As Sharon LeFevre, the duty officer, stood up from her desk and hurried to the front counter, Hoffman was already shouting orders.

"Get those doors sealed!" he yelled at Sergeant LeFevre. She stopped, confused and uncertain for a moment, staring over Hoffman's shoulder at the angry mob advancing down the hallway towards the cop shop. "Do it now!" Hoffman insisted, and she fumbled under the desk for the button which would automatically lock the front doors. She stabbed the button, and there was a sharp *chikk!* as the doors swung shut and locked themselves, only seconds before the mob collided with the thick lunar glass.

The doors were secure, but not soundproof. Behind them, they could see and hear a dozen men and women shouting, pounding at the glass, shaking the handles. LeFevre rested her forefinger on the next button on the hidden panel. "Do you want to dose them?" she asked Hoffman.

Hoffman brought Westmoreland to the booking-counter, dropping her nylon shoulder bag on the polished surface. "Uh-uh," he replied quietly. "As soon as you get her processed and out of sight, let 'em in. I don't want anyone to say we didn't . . ."

"That's okay," Macy said softly.

Both officers looked at her. She was obviously rattled, yet at the same time she seemed to be relieved. She shrugged a little, hefting her wrists where Hoffman had cuffed them behind her back. "I don't care," she added. "They're nothing to me. Just get these things off me. Please."

LeFevre and Hoffman were looking doubtfully at each other, when they heard a voice behind them. "It's okay. She doesn't need to be booked. Just get the cuffs off and get her out of sight."

John Bigthorn came out of his office to stand behind them. His face and hands were still lightly bandaged from the burns he had received, his gait a little unsteady, but his voice was authoritative. He walked to the counter and gazed impassively at Macy as Hoffman pulled out scissors and unclipped the plastic one-use handcuffs.

"Mary Boston," he said. "Or is it Macy Westmoreland . . . ?"

"Macy," she replied wearily. She gently massaged her wrists. "Am I under arrest?"

The sheriff thought about it for a few seconds, then shook his head. "No," he answered, "you're not. You've caused us a lot of trouble, but you're not under arrest for anything." He smiled a little as he turned his attention to his deputy. "Unless it's *resisting* arrest, of course. How did it go, Wade?"

"She was fine," Hoffman said as he removed the cuffs and wadded them in his hands. "She was in the shop off O'Neill Square, right where Blind Boy told us she would be. . . ."

"Who?" Macy asked. "Who told you where I was?"

"Nobody you know," Bigthorn said. "A friend of the department . . . as much as I hate to admit it." LeFevre grinned behind his back and Hoffman coughed into his fist to hide whatever remark he was about to make. "So she came along quietly?" Bigthorn asked Hoffman.

Hoffman recovered his poise. "No problem with her personally, though I handcuffed her just to be on the safe side."

Bigthorn nodded. "The friends she was with threw a shit-fit, though," Wade continued. "They surrounded us when I escorted Ms. Boston . . . Ms. Westmoreland . . . to the cart, and ran down here after us." He jerked a thumb over his shoulder at the mob on the other side of the doors. "No harm done. One of them knocked off my cap, but that was it. She was fine."

"Okay." Bigthorn stepped back, cocking his finger at Macy to summon her to the other side of the counter. "Let me get her into my office, then we'll deal with the crowd."

LeFevre looked nervously at the door. "Sharon, take her bag away and get it out of sight, but don't touch it till I tell you to." Bigthorn nodded towards the door. "Then you and Wade get out there and handle the crowd. Herd them out of the building. They can demonstrate all they want, but I want them out of here. Zap 'em if anyone gives you trouble, but nobody gets in here. *Comprende?*"

They both nodded uneasily. As Macy walked behind the counter Bigthorn asked her, "Is there anyone out there you want to talk to? About getting an attorney or anything?"

She hesitated. "I thought you said I wasn't under arrest."

"You're not," Bigthorn said softly. "You're in protective custody, that's all. But you might need legal counsel before this is over. I have to advise you of that right, at least."

Macy shook her head. "No, I don't want any of them to help me. Not that there's a bright light among them anyway." She cast a disdainful look at the mob behind the doors, then glanced sharply at the sheriff. "This is about Tony, isn't it? Tony Salvatore?"

Bigthorn nodded, and she let out her breath. "Thank Christ," she said. "I've got a lot to tell you about the bastard." She looked at Sergeant LeFevre, who was spiriting her bag away. "Just make sure that bag's in a safe place," she added.

LeFevre, overhearing her remark, pointed towards the safe, located in the rear of the office. Bigthorn nodded his head again. "Don't worry about it," he replied as he put an arm around Macy's shoulder and led her in the direction of his office. "Not even the Golem's going to get to it."

Macy suddenly stopped, twisting out of his grasp and staring at him. "The Golem?" she nearly shouted, her subdued manner gone now. "Henry Ostrow? You mean he's *here*?"

Before Bigthorn could reply, Rollie Binder looked up from his computer terminal. "Bad news, John. Blind Boy Grunt heard about her arrest. He's put the word out on all the communications channels."

The sheriff stopped. "All the . . . ?"

"Everything," Binder nodded. "Not just the bulletin boards and the mail system. He's even co-opted Channel Two."

They looked over Binder's shoulder. On both his computer terminal and his TV monitor, Macy's TexSpace mug shot looked at them. Below the picture was written: MARY BOSTON, A.K.A. MACY WESTMORELAND: MEMBER, CHURCH OF TWENTIETH CEN-TURY SAINTS; TAKEN INTO CUSTODY BY CLARKE COUNTY SHER-IFF'S DEPARTMENT.

Suddenly, Wade Hoffman broke out laughing behind them. They turned to see the same photo and caption displayed on all the TV surveillance screens. The sheriff stared speechlessly at the monitors.

"What the *fuck* is going on here?" he whispered at last.

Binder held up his hands. "I dunno how. He's never done this before. Somehow he got hold of the TexSpace picture of her and . . ."

"For chrissakes, Rollie, I can see *what* he's done!" Bigthorn yelled, lashing his arm out at the TV monitors as Binder recoiled in his seat. "It's *why* that gets me!"

He took a deep breath. No one else in the office dared to breathe. He glared around the room, then quickly ushered Macy towards his office. Now, however, she balked at the hand on her shoulder. "He's *here*?" she repeated, her voice rising in panic. "He *knows* where I am?"

Bigthorn let out his breath. "I would be lying if I told you he couldn't know," he admitted.

Macy stared him in the eye, then cast her gaze at the Church of Elvis followers behind the door. "Goddammit," she said. "I should have stayed with them."

Bigthorn shook his head. "No. You're safer here."

"Uh-uh." Her eyes were fastened on the doors. Not on the crowd, but on some force beyond them. "Sorry, Sheriff. I don't think so."

For perhaps the final time, the transformation had been made. Invisible except in his mind's eye, tangible as a faint cool spot on his forehead, the aleph was traced in saliva on his skin just below his hairline. Henry Ostrow, for all practical purposes, had ceased to exist. Only the Golem remained.

As he climbed the ladder up the narrow shaft leading to South Station, he heard the bell in the Big Sky's meeting hall bell tower peal seven times. Night had fallen within the biosphere by the time he twisted the handle on the hatch and pushed it open.

Above and around him, constellations glowed in the darkness, interspersed with the denser bands of starlight: the Milky Way, reflected by the primary mirrors through the windows. The sight was staggeringly beautiful, but the Golem did not have the ability to appreciate its wonder. Such aestheticism was now completely foreign to his dead soul.

A few people, tourists mainly, were on the mooncrete veranda, but no one noticed him as he crossed the platform. The maintenance worker's uniform he had stolen from the locker room was perfect camouflage. People seldom notice janitors, repairmen, or plumbers. His face was half hidden by the brim of his cap; the Ruger was strapped to the inside of his right calf, underneath his utility vest. It was a good disguise.

Balancing himself carefully against the lesser gravity, he slowly trudged down the ramp to the public vehicle depot. He found a service cart parked in a slot. After unhooking the recharger cable, he climbed into the driver's seat and pulled from a vest pocket the keycard he had found in the supervisor's desk. The key started the cart and he pulled away from South Station. Just ahead, Western Avenue led into the darkness of the farmland. Beyond that, up the curving plains of the horizonless world, lay the lights of Big Sky.

Eyes fixed straight ahead, the Golem drove along the roadway. He didn't hurry, for his patience was vast. The long night was only starting.

19

The Town Meeting
(Sunday: 7:07 P.M.)

Although the monthly Big Sky town meeting was officially convened to conduct business pertinent only to Big Sky, it had in practice evolved to include public issues affecting the entire colony. LaGrange, North Torus, and South Torus were theoretically supposed to have their own separate sessions, but their meetings had been subsumed in the Big Sky meeting for a number of reasons. The affairs of the communities were simply too interlocked for the business of each one to be conducted independently of the others; since Big Sky was the county seat, it made sense for the monthly "town" meeting to be held there. So, in reality, it was a county meeting; the name remained unchanged only because the session was modeled after the traditional New England town meeting system.

Big Sky's meeting hall was the site of the monthly gathering. The long building in Settler's Square, with its gabled roof and steepled bell tower, served as a nondenominational church on Sunday mornings and as a Hebrew synagogue on Saturdays. Once a month the altar was removed and replaced with a long table for the six elected members of the county Board of Selectmen. A mike stand was set up in front of the table for use by members of the public.

Three cameras were set up in the hall to televise the proceedings on Channel 2. Because the meetings could be watched at home, attendance was generally sparse. In fact, the majority of the colony's residents paid little attention to the monthly town meeting. Except when elections were held or when the annual county budget was being determined, few of the residents troubled to show up.

It was no wonder. The monthly agenda was usually concerned with prosaic, necessary, and boring matters: construction permits for new housing in Big Sky or South Torus, commercial licenses for new businesses in LaGrange or on the Strip, reports on soybean production by the Ark, discussion of the proposed purchase of updated tutorial software for the county school, and debate on whether to curb bicycle racing on Broadway during nighttime hours. All in favor say aye. All opposed shall signify by snoring loudly.

This month's meeting was going to be different.

Standing in the back of the hall behind one of the TV cameras, John Bigthorn watched as the bamboo pews began to fill with residents. Already most of the seats were taken, and many people were standing against the wall. Thanks to Blind Boy Grunt and the rumor mill, word had gotten out that tonight's meeting was going to be important. Maybe even interesting.

The agenda was printed on the docket being handed to each person as they walked through the door. At the bottom of the long sheet of paper, underneath routine items like a proposed surcharge on imported soap and a declaration to have October 5 made a legal holiday in honor of Robert H. Goddard's birthday, were two late additions. Once again, Bigthorn glanced at the sheet in his hand:

"Item 17: (Schorr, J., for the Public)—Calling for a declaration of independence by Clarke County as an independent, sovereign nation."

"Item 18: (Schorr, N., for the Board)—Calling for a vote to dismiss John Bigthorn from his position as Sheriff of Clarke County."

Neil must have gotten the clerk to add Item 18 only this morning. Jenny had submitted Item 17 yesterday, before . . .

Bigthorn blinked and pulled his eyes away from the docket. The lung transplant had been a success and her internal hemorrhaging had been stopped, but Dr. Witherspoon still had Jenny on the critical list. If the sheriff thought about it too much, he might agree with the last-minute motion submitted by Neil Schorr to have him fired. He couldn't help but feel responsible for Jenny's predicament. If he hadn't challenged Ostrow . . .

Enough of that, he scolded himself. *You were doing your job, whether Neil knows it or not.*

Remembering the Golem, Bigthorn unclipped the phone from

his belt, pushed a couple of numbers, and held it to his face. "Station Thirteen, report," he said softly.

Station Thirteen here. Wade Hoffman's voice came over the line. *We've got a hot time in the old town tonight, John.*

Hoffmann was out of sight, but closer than anyone but Bigthorn and a few other department officers knew. He was staked out in the bell tower on top of the meeting hall, where he could see all of the square, including the front and sides of the Big Sky town hall just across Settler's Square. "What's going on out there?" Bigthorn asked.

The Elvis nuts are still camped out in front of Town Hall. Parker's got some sort of sit-in going but Sharon still has the front door locked. And there's more people arriving for the meeting.

"It's getting a late start." Bigthorn glanced around the room again. "I don't see the Exec Board. Are they out there?"

Yeah. There's some politics going on out here. Neil Schorr's talking to a few people near the statue. He looks pretty worked up about something. Probably you. And Becky Hotchner's right below me with another bunch of folks. You can bet they're talking about the independence move.

"Never mind that now," Bigthorn insisted. "Ostrow's the only thing I want you to worry about. Have you checked in with the others?"

Affirmative. Rollie and Sharon are in the station. Rollie's working on the diskettes the girl brought us. Danny's on foot patrol around town, and Cussler's holding down the Strip. I just talked to them. No one's seen anything yet.

"Tell 'em to keep sharp," Bigthorn said. "Ostrow won't be wearing a name tag, y'know. If you . . ."

There was a mild commotion at the door. Bigthorn looked up to see Rebecca Hotchner, Neil Schorr, and their supporters filing into the room. Bob Morse, who had been sitting in a pew with a couple of other people, got up and walked over to the table, where the three other members of the Board of Selectmen were already seated.

"The meeting's about to start," Bigthorn said. "You've got the ball. If something happens out there . . ."

I'll give you a buzz. Good luck, Chief.

The sheriff smiled. Wade knew how much he hated the word. "Thanks," he replied. "Station Twelve out."

He clipped the phone back on his belt. It was a standing-room-only crowd in the meeting hall, but nobody seemed to

want to be near him. Indeed, a few people were studying him
with sidelong glances. It was no wonder; he himself was an issue
at this meeting. By the time it was over he would either still be
the sheriff of Clarke County, or he would be out of a job.

Bigthorn ignored the covert attention. He settled his back
against the wall and stuck his thumbs in the corners of the trouser pockets. "Okay," he muttered, "it's showtime."

It was one hell of a show. From the moment Bob Morse banged
his gavel and called the meeting to order, there was trouble.

The Board of Selectmen was a curious entity: three vocal
members of the Executive Board sitting with three quiet junior
members, each of whom was politically allied with one of the
Executive Board members. Morse, as board chairman and Mayor
of LaGrange, was supported by Kyle Wu, the other elected representative from LaGrange. Both were moderates. Neil Schorr
found his political ally in Lee Shepard, another member of the
New Ark and the representative of the South Torus community,
which was largely populated by New Ark members. Whatever
Neil said, Shepard automatically seconded. Their position was
nearly always on the far left. And while Rebecca Hotchner in
her role as liaison for the Clarke County Corporation was seated
as a non-elected member, she was supported by Frederick Pynchon, a Skycorp engineer who represented North Torus. His
constituency was the smallest in the county, but nearly all of the
North Torus residents were employed by one of the consortium's
member companies. Hotchner and Pynchon, therefore, consti-
tuted the Board's conservative vote.

Which meant that Clarke County's government was less of a
board of six members than a subtle troika of three duos. When
all three parties were working toward the same goals and had
the same broad interests, docket items were quickly discussed
and voted upon. This was usually the case, but this meeting was
one of the exceptions.

As soon as the meeting was called to order, Neil Schorr made
a motion to skip the first sixteen items on the docket and begin
discussion of Items 17 and 18. Shepard seconded the motion,
but it was immediately opposed by Rebecca Hotchner, who made
the countermotion (seconded by Pynchon) to have both items
tabled until a future meeting, after the appropriate studies were
conducted by ad hoc subcommittees.

She might have gotten away with this maneuver under any
other circumstances. But Bob Morse noticed general unrest from

the unusually large audience, which obviously wanted these items discussed sooner rather than later. In the best parliamentarian fashion, Morse first called Hotchner's motion to a vote by the Board, then he and Wu sided with the Big Sky representatives in voting against it, with Hotchner and Pynchon voting in favor. The same two-thirds majority won when, subsequently, Schorr's motion was voted upon.

The mood of the crowd became apparent when they applauded and cheered the votes. Morse banged the gavel again and sternly reminded them that this was an official government function and not a basketball game. The crowd hushed itself, but the look on their faces told the truth: they were here for a public debate, and were not interested in maintaining political decorum and restraint.

As Hotchner gazed stonily at him, Morse yielded the floor to Neil Schorr. Schorr stood up for his speech; this was not customary practice at the meetings, but it caught the attention of the audience. Morse and Wu remained impassive while Shepard grinned and Hotchner made a histrionic display of appearing disgusted, which Pynchon obligingly aped. The meeting was hardly ten minutes old, and already the lines of battle were drawn.

"Members of the Board, fellow residents of Clarke County, comrades of the New Ark . . ." he began.

"Friends, Romans, countrymen . . ." Pynchon stage-whispered, which earned him a few laughs from the pews and a scowl from Morse. Pynchon shut up, smiling smugly.

Schorr ignored him. "My wife, Jenny, entered a motion for public discussion at this meeting, regarding whether Clarke County should declare itself as a self-reliant, independent nation." He looked down at the table for a moment. "As some of you know," he continued, "she was critically injured last night in an explosion in Big Sky . . . of unknown origin, or at least so we are told."

Another pause. The room was absolutely still. "However, there's good reason to believe that she was the intended target of forces which oppose the idea of independence for Clarke County," Schorr said. "In short, someone wanted Jenny dead before she could spread her message. The identity of the culprit is still unknown, but the motive is obvious. If they could silence her voice, then they could silence an idea."

It was as if the bamboo pews had been electrified and someone had thrown a switch to send a few volts through the buttocks of the audience. Suddenly, everyone sat up straight, their eyes locked on Schorr. For once, Rebecca Hotchner had discarded her air of detachment; she looked as if she were ready to leap out of her chair and throttle Schorr. The rest of the selectmen stared at the New Ark leader with looks of bewilderment or outright anger.

In the back of the room Bigthorn found his own jaw going slack. Did Neil actually *believe* that the bombing which had put Jenny in the hospital was an act of political terrorism?

He flashed upon Schorr's parting remark that morning at Clarke County General, during their brief encounter outside the ICU ward . . . "I already know who did it." No, he didn't. He *couldn't*. The Golem's existence had deliberately been kept secret. Schorr didn't have a shred of evidence to support his allegation. And yet, without any evidence, he was insinuating that the Clarke County Corporation was behind Jenny's "attempted assassination."

Perhaps he doesn't need proof, Bigthorn thought. He looked at the alert faces of the crowd, then caught the expression on Becky Hotchner's face: stunned, bewildered, defensive yet speechless. No wonder Schorr's been a leader for most of his life, the sheriff reflected. He knows how to rile people, how to manipulate emotions against logic. Maybe he doesn't believe it himself. Hell, maybe it doesn't matter whether *he* believes it. . . .

Neil's making his grab for power. The thought occurred to the sheriff with sudden, diamondlike clarity. The son-of-a-bitch's wife lands in the hospital, and he uses it as political leverage. Even if he has to lie about why it happened, he's spotted his big chance.

Bigthorn folded his arms across his chest, shaking his head in admiration despite himself. "I'll be dipped in dogshit," he murmured.

As if he'd heard Bigthorn's comment, Schorr stared straight across the room at the sheriff. "This attack occurred at the home of John Bigthorn, our county sheriff, who's sworn to protect us all," Schorr said, his voice gradually rising to gather the force of moral outrage. "The fact that our senior law officer stands among us tonight, relatively unscathed, while my wife lies in a near-coma, facing death . . ."

He paused, as one set of eyes after another fastened upon Bigthorn. "It cannot help but cast doubts on his ability to protect us," Schorr went on.

Whatever admiration Bigthorn felt for Neil Schorr instantly vanished. *The little bastard knows better,* he thought. *He knows why Jenny was at my house, and now he's going for revenge. Son of a bitch!*

Neil turned back to the audience. "Yet our first priorities must rest elsewhere, at least for the time being." His voice was lowered now. The matter-of-fact voice of calm and reason. "We are all familiar with the situation I refer to. Clarke County is a colony, but it has been effectively colonized not by the United States, but by those who sit in corporate boardrooms in New York and Huntsville, Tokyo and Bonn and London."

Murmurs of agreement from the audience. "Their principal interests are not our own," Schorr continued. "We are concerned with finding a good life for ourselves and our families, with carving out a home on a new frontier, with building a community based on hard work and personal sacrifice. . . ."

He stopped and sighed expressively. "*Their* interests, however, begin and end with making money. No more, no less. The most expedient measures are preferred over the slower, evolutionary task of homesteading. Any profit which we . . . each and every one of us, as individuals . . . may make from our labors, inevitably flows back to them, in the form of ever-rising rents, surcharges, and tariffs. And meanwhile . . ."

Schorr grinned ruefully and shook his head. "Meanwhile, they send us another shipload of Elvis Presley cultists, who sit in our town square and tell us not to step on their blue suede shoes."

Scattered laughter from the crowd. Everyone had seen the Church of Elvis protesters on their way into the meeting. Bigthorn smiled grimly. Neil was tapping a deep, long-dormant vein of frustration here.

Becoming somber again, Schorr held up his hands for silence. "Ladies and gentlemen, the time has come for us to make an important decision. Will Clarke County . . . our home, the first community in space . . . be guided by forces not in our own hands? By forces that do not necessarily reflect our own best interests? Shall we submit to being tools of remote economic powers which care little for our own needs and those of our children?"

Again he paused, allowing everyone to chew on that thought, while he cast his eyes around the room as if to ask the question of each individual whose gaze he met.

Then, in an abrupt fury that shattered the calm, he crashed a balled fist down on the tabletop. *"Or shall we declare independence?"* he shouted.

That was it: the moment he found the right button to push.

Half of the crowd surged to their feet and shouted back: *"Yes!"*

When the police had come to take her into custody, Oliver Parker knew that in the long run Mary Boston would be nothing but trouble. He was certain of that when the maintenance man showed up at the Big Sky town hall. And there wasn't a damn thing he could do about it.

If he'd had a choice in the matter, he would not have led a vigil outside the town hall to protest her arrest. All things considered, he would much rather have returned to the Strip tonight, this time to get ripped and comfortably screwed as only the Dark Elvis could. But when Mary Boston, or whatever her name was, had been apprehended in that little gimmick shop in LaGrange, she had not been alone. When the police hauled the woman away, her brothers and sisters from the Church had followed.

So now here he was: sitting in the town square; surrounded by his followers, who insisted upon singing every song Elvis Presley had ever recorded; waiting either for the police to release Sister Mary (fat chance) or to die of terminal boredom (much more likely). It was a good thing he was wearing his sunglasses; otherwise, someone might have seen from the look in his eyes that the Living Elvis was filled with anything but holy rage.

They had been here for about four hours now. If it had been his choice, Parker would have said, "Well, okay . . . we'll come back tomorrow, gang, and see if we can post bail. Let's go get something to eat." However, he couldn't do that. He was constrained by his own role; he had to be perceived as leading his followers in the good fight. Religious persecution and all that . . .

So, even if his buns were aching from sitting on the hard pavement for so long, he wasn't at liberty to suggest that it was time to give it up. Or even to second the motion to adjourn, had it been proposed by one of the flock . . . which hadn't yet occurred. Fueled by self-righteous anger, they were determined to see this crusade through, even if it meant sitting here all night.

It looked as if that was exactly what was going to happen.

Sometimes, being a messiah was a pain in the ass.

The ragged chorus of "Heartbreak Hotel"—the fourth time it had been sung in so many hours—had just died out when the electric cart rolled to a stop in front of the town hall. Parker looked over his shoulder to see a tall man in gray coveralls, work vest, and cap climb out of the driver's seat. He began walking around the crowd to the door. No one did anything to stop him; the Church of Elvis protesters knew better than to interfere with anyone going in and out of the building. Parker had made sure of that. Besides, this man was obviously the night custodian, coming to mop the floors and empty the wastebaskets. . . .

Yet, as he walked by, Parker did a double take. There was something oddly familiar about the man. As he climbed the front steps, Parker tipped down his shades to get a better look. As he did, the custodian briefly turned in his direction.

Even under the brim of his cap, his face was instantly recognizable to Parker. It was the guy whom he had met yesterday in the TexSpace Third-Class lounge. Another tourist.

Now *this* was weird. What the hell was he doing here, dressed as a janitor?

As the Church members swung into "Good Golly, Miss Molly," the man stopped at the front door and slid a keycard into the slot. As the door buzzed and he opened it, he seemed to sense that someone was watching him. He looked over his shoulder and stared straight at Parker.

Parker felt a chill run down his spine. He had never seen eyes that were so . . .

Dead.

Then the "janitor" looked away. He entered the building, stepping through the door like a robot, letting the door shut behind him, unlocked.

Oliver Parker had an uneasy feeling that something was wrong. Something that had to do with Mary Boston.

Without really thinking about it, he stood up and began walking towards the door. The singers stammered; a few people reached up to touch his legs, to ask him what was going on. Parker ignored them. There *was* something wrong here . . . and there was a woman inside who was a member of his Church. Like it or not, he was responsible for her. His followers had made that clear to him.

"Elvis . . . ?"

"Living Elvis, what's . . . ?"

"Is there something . . . ?"

"Why are you . . . ?"

He turned around, raising his hands to calm them. "It's okay, brothers and sisters," he said soothingly. "Elvis just wants to see about something. He'll be right back."

Then he hurried up the steps, pulled open the door, and walked into the town hall.

The corridor was dark. The ceiling panels were turned off; the only light came from the far end, through the glass doors of the Sheriff's Department offices.

The hallway was empty.

Parker took a few steps forward, the heavy soles of his platform shoes tapping loudly on the tiles. He could see nothing, hear nothing but his own breathing. Suddenly, he was afraid. He stopped and swallowed. . . .

"Hello?" he said. "Is anyone there?"

An indistinct figure suddenly stepped out of an alcove several yards in front of him, blocking the light. Parker reflexively raised his hands. . . .

There was a muzzle-flash, a high rattle of gunfire, and Parker felt the bullets ripping into his chest and stomach.

The pain was explosive and brutal. His body slammed backwards into the door, then he slid slowly down its cool surface, leaving a long red streak on the glass.

Parker's head lolled forward on his neck. As the pain enveloped him, as time itself expanded, he heard someone scream from somewhere behind him, a scream that seemed to last forever. . . .

Then darkness, numb and endless, enveloped him. Ollie Sperber had time for one clear, final thought . . .

Ladies and gentlemen, Elvis has left the building.

20

The Hour of the Golem
(Sunday: 8:17 P.M.)

At first, Bigthorn didn't pick up his phone when it buzzed; he couldn't hear it over the bedlam which had broken loose in the meeting hall.

Bob Morse had already destroyed his gavel trying to restore order. The fourth time he had slammed it down on the table, the head had splintered off from the stem. Nonplussed, the chairman had resorted to yelling for quiet but was unable to get anyone to listen to him. Supporters of the independence movement, who had stood and cheered when Neil Schorr had made his pronouncement, had found their foes in the colonists who perceived a threat to the status quo, if not their own jobs with the Corporation. Both sides were now engaged in shouting-matches in the aisles and across the pews, the fact that they were at a formal public hearing all but forgotten.

Meanwhile, at the front of the room, Rebecca Hotchner had left her own seat and was now locked in an angry personal confrontation with Neil Schorr. Bigthorn couldn't hear what they were saying, but from the amount of finger-pointing by both of the colony's leaders, he could surmise the gist of the dispute. The other three selectmen had left the table and had taken sides with their supporters on the floor.

Democracy in Clarke County looked as if it was about to degenerate into a barroom brawl. Bigthorn, still leaning against the wall, had never seen such bloody-minded bickering since the time the Lukachukai town council had been unable to agree on whether to conduct business in the Navajo tongue or in English. He was wondering if he was going to have to haul out his Taser to break things up, when he suddenly realized that the phone on his belt was buzzing.

Irritated, he pulled the phone off his belt and held it to his ear. "Station Twelve," he said. "Don't worry, Wade, it only *sounds* like they're going to . . ."

John, get over to Town Hall quick! Hoffman's voice was barely audible. *There's been a shooting, I . . . someone's in . . . gunfire, man down in . . . Station Ten not responding, there's . . .*

"On my way!" he snapped.

He whirled around to dash for the door. One of the Ark farmers was coming the opposite way down the aisle. The two men collided and the phone was knocked out of Bigthorn's hand; it hit the floor and skittered under a pew.

Bigthorn started to grab for it. *No time!* Instead, he launched himself towards the door. Someone picked up the phone and tried to give it back to him, but he was already across the room, shoving people out of the way. Two women were arguing in front of the door; he elbowed one of them aside and knocked the other to the floor, then jumped over her to make it out the door. She was screaming at him when he leaped off the meeting hall's front porch and hit the pavement running.

Hoffman had just made it down from the bell tower; he was waiting uncertainly in the square, rifle ready in his hands. "Take the door and cover me!" Bigthorn yelled as he sprinted towards the town hall, tugging his Taser from his holster. "Call for backup!"

They were halfway across the square when they heard full-auto gunfire from inside Town Hall.

"Rollie, get down!"

Sharon LeFevre grabbed her Crowdmaster rifle and threw herself into a crouch behind the front counter. Raising the rifle into firing position over the top of the counter, she aimed at the locked glass doors. "Cover the—!"

A fusillade of bullets ripped through the doors, shattering the thick lunar glass as if a grenade had been thrown at it. The police station had not been designed to withstand an armed assault; the steel-jacketed bullets punched through the counter as if it were cardboard. Roland Binder, who had been sitting at his computer terminal, was only halfway out of his chair when he saw Sharon fall back from the counter; her body disappeared behind a desk.

As he fumbled for his Taser, his hand fell against the pile of diskettes he had been reading. They tumbled off his desk and scattered across the floor as he stared down at LeFevre's blood-soaked uniform.

"Sharon?" he whispered through numbed lips. He was frozen in place, stunned by the suddenness of the violence. Behind him, he heard Macy Westmoreland scream from the holding cell where she had been sleeping. Her voice sounded as if it were coming from the end of a long tunnel. Rollie's eyes were fixed on the bullet-riddled corpse half-hidden behind the desk. "Sharon, I don't . . . I don't know how to do this, I . . ."

There was a crunch as a foot stepped on broken glass beyond the counter. Binder looked up to see a man in a maintenance uniform, a submachine gun nestled in his hands, stepping through the door. The muzzle was pointed straight at him.

"Please . . ." Binder began.

The Skorpion in the Golem's hands rattled again, and as Rollie Binder was hurled backwards by the impact of the bullets, Macy screamed again.

Stepping behind the counter, the Golem swept his gun in an arc from one side of the room to the other. He wheeled around once to check the door, then he turned back to stare through the bars of the holding cell at Macy. "Where are they?" he asked.

She collapsed against the far wall of the cell. In less than a few seconds any hope that she was safe here had vanished. Macy had been waiting for one of Tony Salvatore's killers to find her. Well, here he was. Not just any torpedo either. The Golem himself.

"Henry," she stammered. "What . . . I don't know what . . ."

"The records you took from his safe," he said. His voice was without color or inflection. He could have been asking a long-distance phone operator for a number in Duluth. "The diskettes, Macy. Where are they?"

"I . . . the diskettes, I don't . . ."

The Skorpion's stubby snout moved a half-inch more towards her; it was all the incentive she needed to begin thinking again. "Over there!" she shouted, pointing at Binder's desk. "They're on the desk, Henry, all of them. They're . . ."

A fatalistic urge overtook her. She giggled hysterically, letting her back slide down the wall until her bottom hit the floor next to the cold metal bed frame. Gazing at the Golem's hard face, she thought she saw a flicker of emotion: confusion, hopeless anger. It made her laugh aloud.

"Too bad, so sad," she murmured. "They've been sent away. Everything . . ." She raised her right hand, snapped her fingers. "*Poof!* Gone. Copied and sent to the FBI. I watched him do it."

She giggled again, feeling warmth surge through her chilled veins. "There you go. Hey, you snooze, you lose . . ."

The Golem looked at the desk, then down at the little pile of diskettes scattered across the floor. She watched as his right foot gently sifted through them. "By the way," she added, realizing that nothing she said now would make any difference, "tell Tony that he was always a lousy lay . . ."

"Where's Seven?" he asked.

His glacial voice brought her back to the here-and-now of her situation. The laughter choked in her throat. Macy looked through the bars of her cell at the Golem. "Whu . . . what?" she breathed.

"There's six diskettes here," he said with surreal calm, looking up at her again. "You took seven from his bedroom safe. Where's the seventh diskette, Macy?"

His eyes. So dead, like those of a fish she had once seen, washing up on the banks of the Charles River when she was a little girl, walking with her mother in that little riverside park . . . she couldn't remember the name of the park. In Boston. On a Sunday afternoon. A fine spring afternoon. She had seen a dead fish and wanted to pick it up and take it home to put in their tropical tank so it would come back to life.

Against her will, she began to weep again. "Please, Henry," she sobbed as her resolve faded, her muscles collapsed. "I . . . I . . . don't kill me, don't . . . I dunno, I didn't look at them, I don't know where, just please don't shoot me, please don't . . ."

Macy heard the soft sound of the Skorpion being lowered on its strap, rubbing against his clothes. She looked up and saw him lowering the gun, letting it hang from his shoulder, and for a few seconds she thought that the Golem was going to let her go. She let out her breath; it seemed as if her lungs were deflating, and for a brief instant there was hope.

Then he bent over, reaching under his right trouser leg, and pulled out an automatic. Straightening, he shifted his body sideways and gently slid the chamber back. She heard the sharp *cha-clik!* of the round sliding home.

"Goodbye," he said. Same featureless voice, like ice water trickling down a glass pane. Then he raised the pistol and carefully aimed directly at her face, until she could see straight down the black hole of the silencer. Macy closed her eyes.

"Golem!" someone shouted. . . .

A muffled gunshot thudded from the office.

Bigthorn fell back into the doorway of the adjacent coffee room as the bullet splintered plaster from the corridor wall opposite his position. From behind him, outside the front door of the building, he heard Wade Hoffman yell his name. The sheriff stretched out his arm to wave his deputy back. The shot had been in his general direction, but not close enough to indicate that the Golem knew exactly where he was hidden. That would change soon enough, though.

"It's me, Ostrow," he called out. "I've come to take you down. You can make this easy, or . . ."

Another shot. This time it ricocheted off the wall near the doorway where he was hiding. If he had been using a submachine gun before, when he killed Parker—and, Bigthorn presumed, LeFevre and Binder—he had since switched to an automatic pistol. Okay, so the Golem wasn't about to throw down his gun and surrender. Bigthorn hadn't really thought he would.

"Have it your way, asshole," he said, keeping his eye on the shattered door. "Just remember what I told you. If you harm the girl, you're going to die."

And if you don't harm her, he added silently, *you're going to die. I've had it with you, you son-of-a-bitch.*

There was a long moment of silence. Then, from within the office, he heard the Golem's leaden voice. "How are you going to kill me?"

His calm was ethereal; Bigthorn had heard vending machines speak with more emotion. "With a Taser?" Ostrow asked. "You're not fooling me."

Shit, but he had a point. The Taser in Bigthorn's hand was as effective as a child's squirt gun; it didn't have nearly the range to take out Ostrow. At least not before the Golem killed him. But he couldn't let Ostrow intimidate him like that.

"I don't need a gun," Bigthorn answered, carefully watching the door. "Guns are for Anglo pussies like you. Fuck, man, I'll take your bullets and still keep coming to get you." He waited a moment, then added, "You hear me?"

No reply. Then there was the faint sound of something moving inside the office. Bigthorn carefully centered the Taser on the doorway, holding the plastic gun steady with both hands and

narrowing his vision down the sights. The Taser wasn't made
for sharpshooting, but it was the best he had.

No more sounds came from within the office, except for Macy's distant weeping. *Shut up, girl, and let me concentrate.* He
felt hot sweat rolling down from his armpits. The Golem was
stalking him now, moving in on the sound of his voice, being
entirely too careful for Bigthorn to get a one-chance drop on
him. As risky as it was, he had to draw the Golem out.

"C'mon, you cheap cock-sucking hood," he taunted. "I
thought you were a pro."

Cruncchh! It was the hard sound of a booted foot stepping on
broken glass. A shadow flickered across the floor just inside the
office door. "Or can you only take out unarmed women with
bombs?" he needled, unable to keep the anger out of his voice.
"I'm going to . . ."

The Golem leaped into the doorway, half-seen in the dark
hallway. The Skorpion roared as he fired indiscriminately in a
wide arc, starting in Bigthorn's direction. The sheriff ducked,
hunched his shoulders between his knees, as bullets cut a swath
just above his head, showering him with bits of plaster. He heard
sharp, high whines as the rounds passed within inches of his
ears. Fuck, fuck, *fuck*—!

Then the volley moved away as the Golem fired straight down
the corridor. At that instant, Bigthorn raised his head, yanked
up his weapon, and fired.

His aim was only slightly better than the Golem's. The two
electrified monofilaments from the Taser only grazed Ostrow's
right arm. To have knocked him cold, they would have had to
make full contact with his body.

But it was good enough. The 2,000 volt charge kicked the
Golem flat on his ass; the Skorpion sailed out of his hands,
landing somewhere out of sight as Ostrow fell backwards and
sprawled on the broken glass in the doorway. Bigthorn stared at
him, thinking for a moment that Ostrow was unconscious. . . .

Wrong. Ostrow was stunned, but he was still moving, struggling to his knees and searching for the submachine gun. The
sheriff threw down the Taser and lunged through the door at
the fallen killer.

His body impacted the Golem's when Ostrow was still on the
floor, and for a frenzied moment Bigthorn had the satisfaction
of getting his hands around the assassin's throat, of seeing Ostrow's face contort in sudden terror. *Now!* Squeeze until his
fucking eyes bleed!

The Golem's left leg slammed upwards; there was a cold, jarring second of agony as the Golem's knee rammed straight into his balls. Simultaneously he kicked Bigthorn over him in a savage jujitsu move.

For a moment the sheriff was airborne . . . then he hit the floor about ten feet away, inside the office behind Ostrow. Breath knocked out of him, his legs feeling paralyzed, he almost succumbed to the temptation to pass out. Goddamn motherfuck, it *hurt!*

Through narrowed eyes, he saw Rollie Binder lying dead on the floor nearby. He heard scrabbling noises behind him, but forced himself not to look. Bigthorn hobbled to his knees. *Don't give up now, muchacho.* His feet found the floor. *Get the hell out of here!* Blinded by the glare of the lights, patterns of starlight swarming before his eyes, he staggered towards the back door.

There was the *thuffft!* of a silenced gunshot, from somewhere behind him. He didn't see where the bullet hit, but since there was no further pain, he figured the Golem must have missed. Bigthorn threw his shoulder against the door, twisted the knob and fell out into the darkness. . . .

He almost collided with Danny D'Angelo, coming up the back steps, Taser raised high in his right hand. Danny tried to catch him, then he looked over Bigthorn's shoulder and let go of the sheriff to balance the Taser in both hands. ''Danny, don't—!'' Bigthorn gasped.

Another muffled shot. The next bullet blew Danny's brains out. As the officer toppled backwards, Bigthorn fell down the stairs. He landed on his knees on the pavement next to D'Angelo's corpse; the pavement tore through his trousers, skinning his knees. *Get out, dammit, move . . . !* He struggled to his feet and lurched out into the night, forcing one foot in front of the other. Even after he had reached the deeper shadows, the sheriff kept running.

He didn't need to look behind to know that he had become the Golem's newest prey.

21

Eve of Destruction
(Sunday: 9:00 P.M.)

In a low orbit four hundred miles above Earth, Icarus Five coasted high above the night sky of the North Atlantic.

A blunt white cylinder with a single liquid-fuel engine mounted at its rear, it closely resembled one of the old Project Apollo moonships of the last century. A satellite maintenance crew had visited the derelict to wrap a string of red and white strobe lights around its fuselage and attach a radio transponder to its payload section; Icarus Five blinked like a lost Christmas tree, and spacecraft passing within one hundred nautical miles of the interceptor received a multilingual warning to avoid its spatial coordinates. Even an accidental rendezvous with Icarus Five was punishable under international space law. It was a pariah in space.

It was also a closely watched pariah. Just as it had once monitored space junk before most orbital debris had been cleared from LEO by Project Whisk Broom, the Consolidated Space Operations Center of the U.S. Air Force now kept track of Icarus Five. At CSOC's operations center near Colorado Springs, the nuclear interceptor was one of a special number of objects that never disappeared from the screens, no matter what command was entered to change the display. After all, it contained the only fissionable nuclear warhead known to be in orbit; until it could either be safely brought back to Earth or disposed of in space, Icarus Five would remain under permanent guard.

It was exactly 2000 hours, Mountain Time, when USAF Lt. Martha Wellen noticed the change in Icarus Five's status. It was at that moment—just as the sun was sinking behind the peaks of the Rocky Mountains, as she was finishing her second mug of tea after coming on duty—that Gustav Schmidt's instructions to Icarus Five's inertial guidance system were triggered.

Suddenly, after two years of waiting, Icarus Five awakened. In the black loneliness of space, RCRs on the sides of the interceptor fired briefly, gently turning the little spacecraft until its nose was pointed at a predetermined set of coordinates. The second that Icarus Five was reoriented, the massive bell-shaped nozzle of its main engine silently flared for six seconds, and Icarus Five began to move from orbit.

Lieutenant Wellen was looking at the LCD screen of her work station when she saw the dotted line indicating Icarus Five's footprint over Earth veer sharply. Martha Wellen had been assigned to CSOC for just over a year; every day of her often-monotonous tour of duty she had come to rely on Icarus Five's maintaining its precalculated trajectory, of seeing it come and go exactly the same way during each shift. Only the rising and the setting of the sun and the moon were more predictable than Icarus Five. That was just fine with her; she liked things to be nice and predictable. Especially when things included satellites containing 100-megaton nukes.

When she saw the course-change on her screen, Martha carefully put down her tea mug and tapped commands in her keyboard, which centered a small box above the white spot of light that was Icarus Five. A small 3-D window opened in the corner of her screen, displaying a simulation of the object's trajectory as well as its coordinates. Leaning a little closer in her leather-backed chair, she studied the screen. The numbers matched what she was seeing: Icarus Five was moving away from Earth, heading for deep space.

Remaining calm, she retyped her commands to make sure that there was no error. When the information was confirmed, Lieutenant Wellen frowned and picked up the handset of the telephone at her station.

"Sir, this is CSOC Station Seven, Lieutenant Wellen speaking," she said. "We have an unusual situation with Icarus Five. I think you should take a look, sir."

There weren't enough ambulances available to hold all the dead.

Clarke County General had only three of the refitted electric carts, and each could take away only one body at a time. To make matters worse, Big Sky had become a madhouse by the time they arrived. The paramedics who had been dispatched to the scene had to push through a panic-stricken crowd which had surrounded the town hall; not only had the townspeople from the nearby meeting converged on the killing ground, the members of the Church of Elvis had also made it inside the town hall.

Most of the Church members were in various stages of hysteria—weeping loudly, huddled around the bullet-riddled corpse of Oliver Parker, or simply sagging against the wall, staring with blank expressions at nothing in particular. Two women tried to keep the paramedics from removing the body on a stretcher until Wade Hoffman managed to gently pull them away. Outside the building, townspeople watched in horror as the bodies were brought down the stairs and through the crowd. Then there was a general surge towards the door, as everyone tried to get inside to find out what had happened.

It was all Hoffman could do to keep order. For the first time he realized how fatally undermanned the Sheriff's Department was. Seven officers: it was a sick joke. With Bigthorn missing, only he, Cussler, and Bellevedere were the surviving officers on the scene. Almost half the department had been wiped out by the Golem. The paramedics managed to take away Sharon's and Rollie's bodies, but Danny was still lying outside behind the building, covered by a blood-soaked sheet. . . .

He tried not to think about Danny, or Sharon or Rollie either. After Wade evicted the Elvis cultists from the building, he left Lou and Dale outside to control the crowd as best they could. "Pull out your Tasers," he whispered to them as they stationed themselves on the front steps. "Use them only if you have to, but keep that mob out. Understand?"

Beyond them was a growing ring of frightened, curious, and outright hostile faces. There were people in the crowd whom Hoffman would have earlier sworn were pacifists; now they were just other members of a mob. Arms outstretched to hold back the crowd, the two officers nodded their heads. Wade patted Lou's arm, then trotted up the steps to revisit the scene of the massacre.

The only surviving witness was in shock. Macy Westmoreland was still cowering next to her bed in the holding cell where she had been cornered, apparently withdrawn from reality. Dr. Witherspoon and a paramedic were attending to her; Hoffman walked through the battered office in time to see Witherspoon shining a penlight on her dilated pupils while the intern loaded a syringe-gun with a sedative and scrubbed her forearm with alcohol.

"Get her to the ER when the next ambulance comes back," Witherspoon said softly to the paramedic as he stood up. "We'll have Dr. Harmon take a look at her, but my guess is that she's going into the psych ward for treatment."

He saw Hoffman and walked over to join him. "She might pull through," Witherspoon said, answering the deputy's unspoken question, "but I don't know. She saw a lot of bad stuff here. . . ." He shook his head. "She's going to have a lot to work through."

"Uh-huh." Hoffman was in shock himself. With the immediate crisis over, everything was beginning to hit home. Three fellow officers snuffed in a matter of minutes. In their own office. He stared down at the drying pool of blood where Roland Binder had been found, and felt his strength drain from him. "Jesus . . ." he whispered.

"Pull it together," Witherspoon said. He gripped Hoffman's arm and gave him a shake. "You're the person in charge here right now. Where's John?"

"I dunno." Hoffman pointed absently towards the open back door. "He lost his phone. I haven't heard from him since. . . ." He swallowed. "He went after the Golem, I guess. Danny was coming in when he got in the way, and all I heard were the . . ."

Hoffman's voice choked. Witherspoon gave his arm another shake. "Stay with me, Wade," he said urgently. "The Golem? Is that the guy who shot up the place?" Eyes fixed on the floor, the deputy nodded his head. "Who is he?" the doctor asked urgently. "Why did . . . ?"

"What the hell's going on here?" a voice behind them demanded.

They both looked around to see Neil Schorr striding through the office. Behind him, Bob Morse was stepping gingerly through the broken glass door. They had used their authority to get past Bellevedere. Morse was gazing in horror at the wreckage—the bullet-pocked front counter, the glass strewn everywhere, the bloody spot where Sharon LeFevre had died—but Schorr did not seem to notice as he advanced on the two men.

"Officer Hoffman, what happened here?" Schorr demanded again. His right hand waved to take in the room. "How did this . . . ?"

"Take it easy, Neil." Witherspoon stepped forward to head

Schorr off. "He doesn't know either, he's just as much in the dark as . . ."

With uncharacteristic violence, Schorr impatiently shoved the doctor aside. "You *know* what's going on!" he shouted into Hoffman's face. "Four people are dead, including three of your officers. Now, where the hell is Bigthorn?"

Hoffman raised his eyes from the floor. "I don't know," he said slowly, "so fuck off, you little twerp."

"Holy smokes," Morse murmured from behind them. They turned to see him standing over the Skorpion lying on the floor; it had gone unnoticed in the confusion. He looked up at the three men, fear and bewilderment evident in his face. "What kind of a maniac got in here?" he asked no one in particular.

"The Golem," replied a hollow voice.

Their heads turned toward the holding cell. Macy Westmoreland, still squatting next to the bed, was staring at them with dark-rimmed eyes. The paramedic was holding the syringe-gun at the ready over her forearm; he looked irritably at Witherspoon, but the physician quickly shook his head and the paramedic pulled away.

"Excuse me, miss?" Witherspoon asked gently. "What did you say?"

"He asked what kind of maniac got in here," Macy replied in a detached tone, as if speaking from a great distance "and I'm telling him. The Golem."

"Who are you?" Schorr snapped, walking towards her. Witherspoon grabbed his arms from behind; this time he refused to let go, restraining Schorr from getting any closer. "Who's the Golem? Where's the sheriff?"

The phones on Bob Morse's and Wade Hoffman's belts chirped simultaneously. Hoffman didn't seem to hear, but Morse snatched up his phone and held it to his face. "I told you who the Golem is," Macy said steadily, ignoring the phones, looking straight at Schorr now. "He's gone after the sheriff. So fuck off, you little twerp."

Under any other circumstance, the reiterated insult would have been funny. Neither Schorr nor Witherspoon laughed now. "Ma'am, we need to know," Witherspoon asked, as if trying to pry loose a secret from a small child. "Who is the Golem?"

Macy's mouth trembled. Tears began to run down her cheeks as she hugged herself tightly, but she didn't look away. "The most terrible thing you could ever imagine," she replied almost inaudibly.

"No," Bob Morse said, "he's not."

Again, the three men looked toward the selectman. He was holding the phone in his hand; his expression seemed to match Macy's. "Things have just gotten worse," he said.

"The Golem?" Witherspoon asked.

"No." Morse took a deep breath which seemed to rattle in his throat. "Icarus Five."

A graphic projection of Icarus Five's trajectory was spread across a wall-screen in Main-Ops. Standing in the back of the vast room at the shift supervisor's desk, Rebecca Hotchner found herself transfixed by the display, although her eyes should have been on the camera lens in front of her, which was transmitting her image back to Earth. Had not Dallas Chapman said something, she probably would have ignored the lens entirely.

Just as the round white spot representing Icarus Five moved forward another inch on the screen, the board chairman of the Clarke County Corporation cleared his throat. *Rebecca, is there something else that requires your attention?* he asked with stern politeness.

"No, there's not," Hotchner said, pulling her eyes away from the wall-screen to look at the small monitor in front of her. Maybe she thought this was the way a jackrabbit feels, when it's standing in the middle of the road at night, hypnotized by the headlights of an onrushing car. . . . She shook it off, forced herself to pay attention. "I'm sorry, Rock. What were you saying?"

"Rock" Chapman, the former NASA astronaut who had left the agency to become a prime mover in the space industry, stared at her from the screen, with the cool appraisal of a pilot assessing an in-flight emergency. He was wearing a polo shirt and shorts—Chapman had been contacted at his weekend retreat on Sanibel Island in Florida—but he could just as well have been wearing a NASA jumpsuit again.

I said, I've got the numbers here in front of me, he repeated, motioning below the range of the camera to the portable computer that rarely left his side, *but I need a quick synopsis of the situation. How does it look from where you stand? Has anyone up there managed to gain control of the bomb?*

She shook her head. "No. This isn't an engine misfire, Rock. Someone managed to contact Icarus Five and plant deliberate, explicit instructions in its guidance computer. Whoever it was, they were smart enough not only to include a password, but also to tell the nuke to lock out any attempts to interfere with the computer. So although we're hailing Five on the correct frequency . . . that's two-two-eight-two-point-five megahertz . . . the bomb isn't listening to us. Period.''

As she spoke, Hotchner glanced away from the camera again. Most of the activity in Main-Ops was concentrated at the communications carrel, where nearly a dozen controllers were clustered around two work stations, still trying to penetrate the defenses that had sprung up around Icarus's telemetry systems. ''They've received the old command codes from NASA and are trying to find a back door through the system,'' she continued, ''but it's become obvious that whoever reprogrammed the nuke's computer was using the same codes. All the former deactivation and safe-arm toggles had been disengaged. Unless they can find another way to beat the system at its own game . . .''

Okay, I get the idea. Chapman's thin lips tightened as he paused to consult his own computer. *Well, we should have plenty of time, shouldn't we? There's still approximately one hundred sixty thousand miles between it and Clarke County. Don't we have even a couple of days in which to do something? Maybe an intercept mission from . . .*

''We don't have a couple of days. If this was a normal spacecraft, we would have the luxury of time. But Icarus Five isn't a normal spacecraft.''

Chapman's eyebrows rose. *But the distance . . .*

''Distance isn't the key factor here, Rock,'' Rebecca insisted, her voice rising. ''It's *velocity*. Icarus Five isn't coasting like a normal spacecraft, with only occasional RCR firings to correct course. It doesn't need to conserve fuel for a return mission, and since it was intended to serve as the standby in case the first four Icarus interceptors didn't deflect the asteroid, Five was designed to reach Icarus as quickly as possible. So every two hours its main engine fires again, Five accelerates a little more, and as the delta-V changes . . .''

I understand, Chapman interrupted. *What are your people projecting as the time of rendezvous and detonation?*

Hotchner swallowed a hard lump in her throat. ''It's not certain, but the conservative estimate is 0800 hours tomorrow, local time,'' she said. ''That's less than eleven hours from now.''

She hesitated. ''It could be more than that, or less, depending on the delta-V profile, but that's the conservative estimate. It won't be much off the mark.''

God damn, Chapman murmured.

"As for your second question . . ." She took a deep breath to steady her nerves. "A rendezvous mission is feasible, but my people have informed me that intercepting Five is going to be difficult because of its velocity changes. Even though we know its trajectory, its delta-V . . . the rate at which it changes velocity . . . is uncertain."

So launching a disarming team is possible, but actually managing to rendezvous with Five is going to be tricky at best. Chapman's frown deepened, the creases around his mouth becoming more defined. *I can appreciate the problem from my flying days. The orbital mechanics are going to be a bitch to figure out.* He thought it over for a moment. *Has anyone thought about moving the colony itself? Maybe getting it out of range before . . . ?*

"They've already considered that option," she replied. "The problem is that Clarke County's maneuvering rockets aren't designed for drastic orbital changes. We're not like a spaceship, either. Besides, when—*if* that thing blows, the shockwave is going to be felt over thousands of kilometers. Even if we're a thousand miles away, the blast will tear us apart. Even a near miss . . ."

She stopped. Her legs were beginning to ache, and she sank into a chair behind the desk; the camera tilted to follow her. "Anyway, we're working on an intercept mission as our prime alternative. We can use one of the OTV ferries that take our people out to the free-flyer factories, and we're recruiting from the construction crew for the job itself. NASA has sent up the specs on Five, so if the team . . ."

She caught herself, and said, "*When* the team reaches Five, it should have no problem opening the payload hatch and defusing the bomb."

Hotchner sighed and rubbed her temples with her fingertips. She felt a nasty headache coming on. It had been a long, hard night. "I don't get it, Rock," she said, gazing down at the desktop. "Why didn't someone defuse Five earlier, after Icarus was deflected and it was left in parking orbit? Somebody could have removed the detonator, at least, and we wouldn't . . ."

Her voice trailed off as the answer to her own question occurred to her. As she raised her eyes to the screen, she saw Chapman nodding his head.

But we wouldn't have a nuke in orbit, would we, Becky? the executive finished. *Our friends in the Pentagon have always wanted to find a way around the U.N. Space Treaty, and so they got one. A little one hundred megaton wild card, just in case those Russians went back to their nasty old ways.*

Hotchner blinked. "But you knew," she breathed. "You knew about it, and you didn't do anything to stop them."

Chapman shook his head briskly. *Nobody likes a whistle-blower, dear. I'm sorry. It would have been bad for business.*

So is a nuke heading straight for your prime investment, Hotchner thought. "We can discuss that later," she said aloud, unable to keep the recrimination out of her voice. "The point is, the intercept mission might not make it in time. We should talk about evacuation."

Chapman had his eyes shut. He didn't respond. "Rock?" she urged. "Did you hear me? We should consider . . ."

I heard you. Chapman opened his eyes. *Do it,* he said firmly. *You're authorized to evacuate Clarke County. Get everybody off that you can, as fast as you can. Launch the lifeboats and use every vessel you can spare, and start on it ASAP. We'll arrange for pickup flights to be launched from Descartes Station and Earth, and we'll get something worked out with the Soviets.*

Hotchner nodded. She felt relieved and frightened at the same time. "Got it, Rock. We'll start at once."

You're in charge, Becky. You've got my full authority to do whatever it takes. He hesitated, then added, *God be with you.*

"Thanks," she said. "We'll be in touch." Chapman was gazing silently at the camera when she ended the transmission and sank back in the chair.

Hotchner took another deep breath and closed her eyes, letting her mind go blank for a few seconds, knowing it was going to be the last moment of rest she was going to get for many more hours to come. Then she stood up and clapped her hands loudly.

"May I have your attention please . . . ?" she called out, as heads began to turn in her direction. "We have some new instructions. . . ."

22

Bigthorn's Last Stand
(Sunday: 9:35 P.M.)

The night was a dark sanctuary, the forest a deserted cathedral, yet he knew he could not hide there for very much longer. John Bigthorn lay painfully against the trunk of a small elm tree on Rindge Hill and waited to die.

He had not yet surrendered his will to live. Once he caught his breath, he promised himself, he would get up and keep running. Perhaps he could still make it to South Station. Once there, anything was possible: one of the trams could take him to some place in South Torus where he could hide. The jig wasn't up yet. As long as he could even crawl on bloody hands and knees, he was committed to staying alive.

At the same time, though, he knew that he was soon going to die. Somewhere out there in the farmlands—among the rows of corn, or even closer, just farther down the hillside—the Golem was stalking him. Bigthorn's nuts still throbbed from the hellacious kick the assassin had delivered to his groin, and he was exhausted, out of breath from his run out of Big Sky. Henry Ostrow was unhurt, probably not even winded. Moreover, the sheriff was completely unarmed, while the Golem still had at least one of his guns. The odds against him were ridiculous.

Bigthorn's hogan was just a short distance away, farther up the hill, but there was nothing in there he could use as a weapon. There was no question that Ostrow was still after him, or that he knew Bigthorn was somewhere out here in the Southwest quad. The sheriff's escape from Big Sky had been narrow; only his familiarity with the town's layout had given him any edge. If it were anyone else chasing him, the sheriff wouldn't have been worried.

But the Golem was too skilled a manhunter to lose him. Big-thorn had already spotted him once, running across Heinlein Bridge over the river just a couple of minutes after the sheriff had jumped off Western Avenue and attempted to escape into the farm fields. The Golem was well behind him now, but like a mountain lion following the scent of a wounded bighorn sheep, the killer was patiently tracking him down. Since he had been resting here, catching his breath in shallow gasps and feeling the warm sheen of perspiration on his face grow cold in the night air, Bigthorn had heard the distant, random sounds of something moving in the fields: the brittle snap of a boot heel stepping on a corn husk, the dull slosh of feet moving through an irrigation ditch. The Golem didn't need to be overly careful, after all. His prey was wounded and relatively defenseless. . . .

And cornered, too, Bigthorn realized dismally, staring down the hillside at the lights of the town. Goddammit, he thought, I don't dare leave this area even if I could. There's at least four dead people back there, all shot just because they got in Ostrow's way. He'll waste bystanders if they get between us, or even use them against me. He's that kind of crazy. I've got to keep this where it'll be just between me and him. . . .

"Between me and him," he repeated under his breath. "You're going to die, aren't you, pal?"

Yeah, a voice whispered from nearby, *I would say that you're screwed.*

Bigthorn looked around. In the underbrush, a small dim form lurked. A pair of yellow eyes peered at him from the gloom. A hallucination, he thought. Sure. I can live with that.

"G'way, Coyote," he hissed. "I don't need your shit right now."

That's right, you don't need me to help you die, Coyote's voice chided inside his skull. *All you need to do is roll over, let some crazy Anglo blow you away. You don't want me? I'll go away. I'll come back later and piss on your grave.*

"Then tell me what I'm supposed to do, you flea-bitten excuse for a god," Bigthorn muttered. He let his head fall against the smooth bark of the tree. "I don't have a gun and he does."

Is that any way to talk to a god? Coyote needled. *Let me give you a little advice, you shit-for-brains excuse for a man. You depend on gods too much. You expect us to do all the hard work for you. So you say you want to live? Save yourself. You don't need my help. . . .*

"Yeah, well, how am I supposed to do that?" Bigthorn whispered. "I don't have a gun."

The yellow eyes grew more intense. *You're thinking like a white man again. They need things that go boom and shoot pieces of metal at people because they're too soft to kill with their bare hands. You're one of the Dineh. You're a red man. Do it the red man's way.*

Bigthorn gazed into the unblinking golden eyes. "My bare hands?" he asked softly. "But how am I to . . . ?"

Your house, Coyote replied. *Your house is a weapon. Do I have to tell you everything?*

Again, there was a rustle from the bottom of the hill as something moved through the cornstalks, not so far away now. Bigthorn glanced in that direction, then looked back at the brush. The shadowy form with the glowing eyes was gone. Jeez, he thought. I used to have to eat peyote to get conversations like that.

Your house is a weapon. . . .

My hogan, he realized. Coyote was talking about the hogan. But how can that be a . . . ?

Inspiration hit him even as he was clambering to his feet. Yes, there *was* a way. Ignoring his pain, Bigthorn began to move quickly farther up the hill, padding silently through the woods. *Stay back there for a few more minutes, Golem,* he prayed as he worked his way across Rindge Hill. *Give me just a little time, and I'll show you how a Navajo deals with dung like you. . . .*

A coyote howl broke the silence of the hillside.

The Golem jerked around as the eerie sound drifted through the boughs, ducking into a low squat behind the trunk of a tree as he brought his pistol up in a two-handed firing position. He kept absolutely motionless, staring up the hill in the direction of the howl, and listened intently. After a few moments, he heard its distant echo from the far side of the biosphere, but his ears picked up nothing else from above him.

He *heard* nothing . . . but he *saw* something through the trees. He peered at it: a flickering, intermittent yellow light from somewhere near the crest of the hill.

The Golem immediately headed for it, gliding as soundlessly as he could up the wooded slope as he focused on the light with an intensity brought on by rage and frustration. His quarry was somewhere out here, but his exact position was unknown; that sense of being denied his target fueled the killer's rage. Whatever the source of the light was, he instinctively knew that it would bring him to Bigthorn.

Everything else was forgotten: Macy Westmoreland, the diskettes he was supposed to either recover or destroy, the civilian and the police officers he had slaughtered in Big Sky, even his own survival. All he wanted to do was to murder the sheriff. It was a personal vendetta. Perhaps Henry Ostrow would not have allowed himself to be absorbed by such an unprofessional obsession, but Ostrow no longer existed. He was a name, an abstraction of the past, nothing more or less. There was only the Golem, and the Golem would not rest until he had killed Bigthorn. Even the reasons were forgotten; they no longer mattered.

As he neared the crest of the hill, he smelled wood smoke, tasted on his palate the sharp tang of burning cedar. He paused, crouching in the underbrush, searching for the firelight. He could no longer see it for some reason . . . but then, as he carefully moved a few feet closer, the fire appeared again. Was it inside something?

He moved very cautiously now, sliding his feet across the ground to avoid breaking any twigs, turning his body sideways to edge past low branches. He held the Ruger in both hands with his elbows angled, ready to swivel and fire at the slightest noise. The firelight grew closer, its orange glow casting dim rays through the smoke. . . .

Then, unexpectedly, he found himself at the edge of a small clearing. In its center was a little house. Light seeped through the cracks in its bamboo walls; through its low door he could see the fire itself, burning in a pit in the middle of the floor. The fire snapped and crackled as he watched from the shadows. His view of the interior was limited, because three walls of the cabin's six sides, the ones closest to the door, were angled against his line of sight.

It was a trap. That much was obvious, but the Golem knew, because it *was* a trap his quarry must be somewhere close.

From his crouch, holding his gun at the ready, the Golem cast his eyes around the edges of the clearing, glancing behind him, peering up into the branches of the trees. Nothing. Dead silence. Behind the cabin, then, perhaps . . . or inside.

Looking at the hogan again, he saw something he had missed before. Inside, against one of the walls nearest to the door, a still, slender form opaqued the translucent light seeping through the bamboo. A man-shaped form, like someone waiting just within the door . . .

The Golem lowered his gun, aimed carefully at one of the figure's legs. First, a knee. Immobilize him, then do the rest of the job a little at a time. He didn't even need to use his gun; he still had his knife strapped to the inside of his right calf. Why not enjoy it . . . ?

Allowing himself a smile, he squeezed the trigger.

The shot, though muffled, was loud in the stillness; the pistol jolted in his hands, and the figure behind the thin wall toppled forward. He heard an agonized cry from the hogan.

The Golem leaped up from his crouch. He raced across the clearing, ducked, and launched himself through the low door into the hogan. He straightened, turned around, and aimed the Ruger down at . . .

An empty pair of jeans and a uniform shirt, tied together at the waist and tails, draped over a cruciform of bamboo reeds which had been propped up on a fire extinguisher.

At that instant, the door slammed shut behind him.

The Golem whirled around, dropping to one knee, bringing up the pistol to fire straight at the door. Bamboo splintered as the bullet punched through, and he twisted to his left, then his right, firing at the walls again and again. Behind him, a noise on the other side of the back walls . . .

He twisted around and fired in that direction, hot shells pitching out of the pistol's chamber. Silence, then. He heard nothing.

Anger overwhelmed him. Screaming in frustration, the Golem whipped around again, shooting at the sides and front of the hogan. He was out there, outside the hogan! Somewhere out there, he . . .

The gun's hammer clicked as it fell against the empty chamber. Suddenly, it registered on the Golem that he had emptied the Ruger. How could he have lost count of . . . ?

Then there was a bloodcurdling howl as something wild came through the ceiling.

Bigthorn came through the chimney hole in the apex of the roof. His bare feet hit the packed-dirt floor just beyond the edge of the fire-pit; he landed with his knees bent, and he used the momentum to hurl himself at the Golem.

The killer was unprepared for the attack. Clumsily he tried to swing his unloaded pistol at the sheriff, but Bigthorn ducked and swatted it out of his hand as he slammed into the Golem. The gun hit the ground across the room as the two men crashed to the floor, locked in a savage embrace.

Ostrow's knee jerked upwards, aimed at Bigthorn's groin. This time the sheriff was prepared; he twisted to the left. He avoided the blow, but it also freed the Golem from his grip. Ostrow rolled to the right; he was on his knees and about to stand, when Bigthorn flung himself again at his opponent.

He rammed his right fist straight into the Golem's sternum, following it with a blow to the solar plexus with his left fist. With a *harruph!* of pain, Ostrow doubled over, clutching his stomach as he fell backwards against the bamboo wall. Bigthorn was about to slug him on the chin, when he saw Ostrow's hand dart to his right calf, snatching for something hidden under his trouser leg. . . .

Bigthorn didn't allow himself to think. Since the moment he had kicked the door shut and raced for the back of the hogan to climb up on the roof, the one thing he had held in his mind was Jenny's face, the instant before the Golem's bomb had gone off. He twisted sideways and kicked his right leg as hard as he could, aiming for Ostrow's head.

The sole of his foot connected solidly with the Golem's skull; the killer was again slammed against the wall. The bamboo cracked, and before Ostrow could recover, Bigthorn grabbed his right wrist with both hands and twisted it around behind his back, using the leverage to force Ostrow to his knees. Then, without mercy, the sheriff raised his left leg, took aim, and kicked down at the back of Ostrow's elbow with all of his might.

There was a cruel, organic snap, like the breaking of a tree branch, as the Golem's elbow shattered. Ostrow screamed. He thrashed in terror and in agony, and still Bigthorn gripped his wrist, twisting further until blood jetted from broken arteries and the white edge of broken bone split through the skin.

The Golem's face hit the dirt; screaming, his mouth chewed the sand. He struggled to rise, but Bigthorn planted his right knee on his back and pinned him face-down on the floor. Ostrow's legs kicked uselessly; the sheriff heard something small drop to the floor of the hogan.

He looked around and saw the switchblade which had been concealed in his trouser leg, laying on the floor.

Still holding Ostrow's broken arm behind his back with his right hand, Bigthorn used his left hand to pick up the knife. He moved his finger across the tiny button on the onyx handle and six inches of razor-sharp stainless steel clicked out of the handle, shining like evil in the firelight.

Ostrow must have recognized the sound even if he could not

see the knife. He fought like crazy, desperately trying to dislodge Bigthorn. The sheriff let go of his broken arm, reached down and wadded his fingers around a clump of Ostrow's hair. Savagely he yanked the Golem's head back as far as he could, exposing his throat. . . .

Bigthorn remembered the time when he was eleven years old and the family had gathered at Grandfather's house for dinner. There had been a young goat tied to a stake in the backyard; its fur was matted with mud and shit, but he had been allowed to pet the goat for a little while as Grandmother tended to the fire nearby. He had been thinking about asking his father if he could keep the goat, to make it a household pet, when Grandfather had walked over, kneeled down on the other side of the goat, and showed him the knife in his hands. The old man had said nothing to him, merely held out the pitted old bowie knife with the indelible bloodstains on its blade, and at once he understood.

Relatives and friends were gathered around in a semicircle, impassively watching them. Grandfather nodded mutely towards the goat, his eyes questioning. He held the knife in his open palm: an invitation. At the same moment, the uncomprehending goat had looked at him with its square-shaped pupils: soft and devoted, like the eyes of a puppy who had found a new master. He looked from the goat to his grandfather; the old man gently shook his head, but still held out the knife. John knew that he loved the goat. He also knew that he was being tested.

Are you a man? Grandfather wanted to know.

Saying nothing, he had reached forth and taken the knife. . . .

In the same way that he had stared down into the goat's eyes, Bigthorn now gazed into Henry Ostrow's eyes. He saw horror, and more: madness, and hate. But most of all, there was fear. The pulse in Bigthorn's ears pounded like the slow beat of kettledrums.

"You haven't got the nerve," Ostrow managed to whisper through his dirt-caked lips. "You can't do it."

Bigthorn said nothing. Words would have been meaningless.

He sank the tip of the switchblade into the Golem's neck and slowly began to pull the knife in a straight line across his jugular vein.

It was just like killing the goat. Only a little easier.

23

Elvis Ex Machina
(Sunday: 10:42 P.M.)

Imagine seven thousand eight hundred sixty-three men, women, and children holding a Chinese fire drill, and that was what the evacuation of Clarke County looked like to Wade Hoffman. If there was anything orderly about it, it was purely accidental.

Hoffman sat alone in the deserted cop shop. Legs propped up on the console below the monitor screens, a bottle of tequila he had hidden in his desk now cradled in his hands, he watched as the colony slowly went to pieces before his very eyes.

The computer screens displayed the red-lettered EVACUATION notice, under which emergency instructions were given. Every public terminal in the colony was showing the same screen. The surveillance monitors displayed scenes from various points around Clarke County; every few minutes he randomly tapped into another set of cameras, just to see what was going on elsewhere.

"Great show," he commented dryly. "Should do well in the ratings."

Wade was drunk as a monkey, and he didn't give a righteous damn who knew it. But what was he supposed to do? Try to keep order? Christ, half the police force was dead, and it was Hoffman's guess that the sheriff had bought the farm as well. So only three cops were left in the whole colony. Wade was no fool. He knew an exercise in futility when he saw one.

Bellevedere and Cussler, at least, were still trying to do their jobs. They were at the lifeboat stations in Torus N-7, trying to maintain order. Hoffman could see them even now: two figures in blue uniforms, arms outstretched, uselessly attempting to keep the multitude of people around them from running, pushing, shouting, et cetera. Ignored by everyone, Lou was being help-lessly swept backwards along the concourse between the lifeboat hatches, while Dale was trying to break up a fight between several people who were trying to get into the same lifeboat. Way to go, guys. You're a credit to the department. Hey, maybe we can make it up to you with some overtime pay. . . .

"Give it a rest, boys." Wade took another pull from the bottle, hissed between his teeth, and tapped in another set of cameras. The screens changed, and he ran his eyes across the monitors.

North Station: several hundred people were jammed together on the parapet, waiting for trams to return to take them to the lifeboat torus. They were remaining calm . . . or at least they were so far.

The lobby of the LaGrange Hotel: now *here* was chaos. Tourists were packed together near the front desk, all trying to check out at once—what were they expecting, refunds?—struggling against each other, carrying suitcases and bags which they would inevitably have to ditch before boarding the lifeboats. A fistfight had broken out in the back of the crowd, probably for no sane reason. The harried hotel staff behind the front desk looked as if they were about ready to close down and run for it. Every sightseer for himself.

Southeast quad, the livestock pens: a sad scene, this one. The animals were not going to make it out of here—no room for them on the lifeboats or any other spacecraft. A handful of New Ark members were trying to placate the animals, giving them food and water, tearfully petting them, saying goodbye. Maybe it would have been merciful just to slaughter the goats and pigs and chickens, but Hoffman couldn't blame the farmers for not doing that.

South Dock: every OTV ferry, tug, and construction pod that could be mustered was being readied for flight in the giant hangar. Dozens of spacesuited technicians were floating around the spacecraft, attaching or detaching fuel and power lines, anchoring airlock sleeves. As he watched, a launch cradle carrying a cylindrical OTV, containing probably a dozen colonists, was being extended towards an open hatch. Goodbye, farewell, *bon voyage*.

The Strip: totally deserted. All the lights were on, the doors were all open, but not so much as a hooker was in sight. No ragtime band to play "Nearer, My God, To Thee." Sorry, folks, but there will be no last call for drinks tonight.

Exterior shot, from a camera mounted on the outer hull of the biosphere: the first of the lifeboats were being launched. Squat cylinders, each holding ten persons—twelve if two were children—were being jettisoned from the torus. As the pods moved away from Clarke County, their main engines automatically fired, thrusting them towards lunar orbit. The lifeboats had sufficient oxygen aboard to last for two days, as well as radio homing beacons. Unlike the *Titanic*, there were theoretically enough lifeboats to get everyone off and away. At least, as long as all the lifeboats were filled to capacity.

Big Sky town center: just outside, Settler's Square was deserted. The doors of the meeting hall were wide open. Hoffman looked closer at the statue of the beamjack, and laughed out loud. In the middle of all this, someone had not forgotten to put a pair of sunglasses on his face. . . .

"There's always a little bit of humor, even in a disaster area," he dryly observed. He raised his bottle to the screen in a silent toast and was about to drink, when he glimpsed, in the screen's foreground, a figure moving past the camera. A second later he heard the front door open and slam shut. Footsteps came slowly down the hall.

Hoffman winced and started to hide the bottle under the console, then reconsidered. Who cared anyway? He was going to be one of the last persons to leave Clarke County, and he was damned if he was going to get aboard a lifeboat sober. In any case, it was probably that royal asshole, Neil Schorr, coming back to . . .

John Bigthorn staggered through the shattered office door and sagged against the front counter. His hands were covered with blood; dazed, he peered across the room at his deputy as Hoffman jumped to his feet.

"Wade?" he gasped. "What the hell is going on here?"

"John, what's . . . where have you been?" Suddenly feeling sober, knocking the tequila bottle over on the desk and not caring, Hoffman started to rush across the office. Then his eye caught one of the computer terminals; what he saw stopped him in midstep.

The evacuation notice had vanished from the screen, replaced now by a single line of computer type:

NEVER FEAR . . . BLIND BOY GRUNT IS HERE!

The LaGrange Hotel was nearly empty now. For a while following the evacuation order, Simon McCoy had heard commotion in the hallway outside his room: his fellow tourists fleeing for their lives, coaxing their children to move faster, hauling their designer luggage, and screaming at the elevators to keep their doors open. Now all was quiet. Even the staff was gone; he had tried to call room service for another pot of coffee, but no one had answered the phone.

McCoy had laid his wristwatch on the desktop next to the computer terminal, and for the past few minutes he had watched the numbers change. It was now almost 11 P.M. He stretched his arms behind his head. "Grunt?" he said. "Are you there?"

The reply on the screen was immediate: AFFIRMATIVE, SIMON. I'VE NEVER LEFT.

"Have you broken the password yet?" McCoy asked.

NEGATIVE. ARE YOU READY TO TRY THE BACKUP PLAN NOW?

The numbers on his watch flashed to 11:00. "Yes, I think it's time," he said. "Is Schmidt still upstairs?"

YES, HE IS. HE'S ON-LINE.

McCoy yawned, cupping his mouth with his hand. "Okay, you know the plan. Let it roll." He pushed back his chair, stood up, and started for the bathroom. Then he paused and looked back at the screen. "Umm . . . let me know if it doesn't work, okay?"

YOU INFORMED ME THAT IT WOULD WORK AS PREDICTED.

He smiled and shrugged his shoulders. "Ah, well. That's the funny thing about history. No one *really* knows what occurred in the past, do they?" McCoy headed for the bathroom. "Just let me know what's happened when I come back, all right?"

There was nothing left to accomplish in the name of God except to die. All the same, Gustav Schmidt wasn't going to wait for Icarus Five.

There was no rope to be found; Schmidt didn't know how to tie a noose anyway, so he had to improvise with long strips torn from his bedsheets. He was knotting them together, wondering if he should try hanging himself from the shower rod in the bathroom or to attempt tying one end to a doorknob and looping the other end over the door, when Elvis came to visit him one last time.

Elvis's voice came to him as electronic-fuzz from the terminal, a synthesized Southern drawl from the grave.

Hi there, Brother Gus. What's shakin'?

Schmidt's back was turned to the terminal when the divine miracle occurred. The ripped, gnarled length of bedsheet, damp from the sweat of his palms, went limp in his hands. He turned around slowly, not quite able to believe what he had just heard, and looked at his PC, which was open on his desktop, still activated and interfaced with the telephone.

On the LCD screen, etched in tiny square pixels, the Living Elvis's face grinned at him. *I said, "Hi, Gus,"* the image repeated easily. *Don't you have any manners, son?*

"Praise the Living Elvis," Schmidt said slowly. His mouth felt numb.

Elvis shook his head. *No, you've got it wrong there. I'm no longer the Living Elvis. You were there at the end, weren't you, Brother Gus?*

He had to force himself to speak. A thousand conflicting thoughts were battling with each other in his mind . . . and, in the end, he could only accept what he was seeing now. "No, Elvis," he replied in shame, "I was not there at the end." He motioned with the coiled bedsheet at the computer. "Here . . . I was here, performing the Holy Mission. . . ."

Ah, yes, the Holy Mission. Elvis's face became doleful. *You never got around to telling me what you were trying to accomplish before I left my last incarnation. Would you mind telling me about it now?*

"Your last incarnation?" Schmidt whispered. The bedsheet-rope dropped from his hands, falling to the floor at his feet. "I don't . . . Forgive me, but I don't know what . . ."

Elvis's dark eyes bored at him from the screen. *Brother Gustav, where is Elvis?* he asked solemnly.

"Everywhere," Schmidt said immediately, reciting the catechism. "Elvis is everything."

That's right. Elvis smiled again. *And now, I am truly Everything. I have become one with the universe. When my mortal incarnation died, I merged with infinity itself. You, my most trusted follower, must know this, and survive to pass this knowledge on to all who shall hear. Do you believe me, Gustav Schmidt?*

"I . . ." There was a seed of doubt in his mind, lingering in the strip-mined soil of his brain, a thought which could not quite sprout. He shook his head violently. "I don't . . . I mean, I can't . . ."

Brother Gus, Elvis said sternly, *listen to me. Elvis is Everywhere and Elvis is Everything, yet even then I cannot control the acts of my disciples. What has happened to the Church, my most trusted follower?*

"I don't know," Schmidt said, twisting his hands together. "They've . . . I don't know, they've gone. When you died, I heard about it from some of them, they . . ." He sobbed. "They abandoned you!" he cried out. "They abandoned the faith, they . . . they ran away from you, they're . . ."

Gone, Elvis said sadly. *Yes, I know. The Church is no more. All that happened was a test of their faith and they were found to be wanting. At their roots they were ultimately unfaithful. They weren't nothing but hound dogs, out riding on the town. And now there is only you and I, and it is up to you to perform the final act of faith.*

"I wasn't there." Tears ran down Schmidt's face as he shook his head again and again. "I'm sorry, I'm sorry, I'm . . ."

Never be sorry, Elvis spoke. *Your absence was anticipated. It was part of the Plan. Because, for you alone, I reserved the final test. The greatest test.*

Schmidt's mouth was dry. "I don't understand," he managed to say.

Tell me now, and be truthful. Why did you activate Icarus Five, Brother Gus?

"To force the unbelievers into relinquishing the Promised Land." He licked his chapped lips nervously, speaking more quickly now. "The Holy Mission, Elvis. If they could be persuaded in this way, then Graceland would be ours again, out of their hands. . . . I was going to tell you this, but before I could you were shot by one of the unbelievers, and then the others, they abandoned you, they deserted you, you and . . ."

They left both you and me. Elvis was smiling again. *That was your test, Brother Gus. You have stood by me, prepared to sacrifice yourself and many others, on the strength of your faith. Now the tests are over. You alone have proved worthy.*

Schmidt gaped at the computer screen, feeling an awesome warmth spread outward from his heart. "Worthy? I'm . . . of all the Church . . . how did . . . ?" he stammered.

You are the Church, and the Church is you, Elvis said. *Just as Abraham was given the test of whether he would sacrifice his own son, you have been given the test of whether you would sacrifice your own life, and those of many others, in my name. It is a trial which many have been given yet few have passed. It's over, Brother Gus. My will has been done. You may disarm Icarus Five now.*

"But . . . the Promised Land, the place where we can all . . ."

Elvis again shook his head. *Graceland is only a secular place, only a house. You are the Promised Land, Brother Gus. You have been given my test, and where others have failed, you alone have passed. My time in this dimension is come and gone, and you . . .*

He smiled and winked then, and raised a ringed finger to point straight out of the screen at Schmidt. *You are now the Living Elvis.*

Schmidt's legs collapsed. Quivering, he sank to his knees, and as he did so, Elvis's image faded from the screen, slowly dissipating like cybernetic mist, a holy ghost whom only Schmidt had seen. The image slowly spread outward like the vestiges of a dying nova, the colors gradually washing out to plain white before vanishing.

When the last pixel was gone and he was only looking at a blank screen, the newly christened Living Elvis reached forward to pick up the keyboard again.

His first act as the new messiah would be to exhibit mercy.

24

Arrival
(Monday: 11:01 A.M.)

South Dock's main hangar, which only hours earlier had been crowded with men and spacecraft for the now-canceled evacuation, was all but deserted when Icarus Five was brought aboard.

Navigational lights gleaming through the open bay doors, the OTV tug which had retrieved the interceptor from cislunar space maneuvered the unmanned craft onto a launch cradle. Its claws swung up to gently embrace the nuclear interceptor. A pair of dock workers in MMU packs clung to its fuselage as the cradle was slowly withdrawn on its rails into South Dock.

Standing in the control cupola, his feet hooked into a pair of foot restraints, the sheriff watched as Icarus Five came into the hangar. An access hatch on its payload compartment, where one of the OTV's crew had entered the spacecraft and removed the bomb's detonator, was still open; as the interceptor passed beneath an overhead spotlight, the payload compartment's interior was briefly illuminated. He glimpsed the gull-gray cylinder of the 100-megaton nuclear warhead.

"What happens now?" Bigthorn asked softly.

Bob Morse, hanging onto a handrail running along the low ceiling, frowned and shrugged his shoulders, which made his body bob up and down as if he were doing chin-ups. "Damn if I know. The techies are going to tear the onboard computer apart, try to figure out who got past the lockouts to the safe-arm system and how they did it, but after that . . ."

Morse absently made a flatulent noise with his lips. "Anyway, it looks like we've got ourselves a nuke. And as far as I have any say in the matter, it's going to remain right here where we can keep an eye on it."

Bigthorn gazed at the interceptor; it was being gently moved on its cradle into the pressurized maintenance compartment at the far end of the hangar. "It's staying here?" he repeated. "Are you sure that's smart?"

Morse irritably waved a hand at Icarus Five as the heavy, candy-striped hatches closed behind it. "John, look at that thing and tell me what's smart. Putting it back in LEO, where another maniac can get to it? At least here we can keep the detonator and the warhead apart."

A phone buzzed on one of the operators' consoles. The sheriff automatically reached for his belt, then realized that he still didn't have a phone to answer. He had replaced his uniform shirt, but he had not gotten another phone. The operator picked up, listened for a moment, then handed the phone over his shoulder to Bigthorn. "It's for you, Sheriff. Deputy Hoffman."

Bigthorn took the instrument and held it to his ear. "Hi, Wade. What's up?"

I'm at the S-two conference room. Becky Hotchner called me up here after . . . uh . . . Hoffman's voice sounded frayed. He must be suffering one king-hell hangover, Bigthorn reflected. *Well, there's some guy here who claims he was the one who hacked into Icarus Five. He just showed up at Main-Ops a few minutes ago with a diskette that he claims has the command-and-control codes for Icarus Five. He wants to give himself up.*

Bigthorn sighed. Actually, he could have cared less. Too much had happened over the past two days. Too much blood had been spilled. He was tired, feeling an exhaustion that was both physical and emotional. "Who is he?" he asked.

There was a brief pause. *That depends on what you believe. His ID says that his name is Gustav Schmidt, a West German resident, but he calls himself the Living Elvis. He says that Elvis told him to come to us and give himself up. He hasn't given me any trouble. Just sits, humming "Love Me Tender."*

"Yeah, right." Morse was looking inquisitively at him. "Listen," he instructed, "take him back to the shop and hold him there. Bob Morse is coming up to talk to him. He'll probably make more sense out of his story than I can, and I've got someplace to go right now. Got it? Station . . ."

John, are you okay? Wade sounded genuinely concerned. *I mean . . . I found Ostrow's body. It was where you said you left him.* He hesitated again. *If there's something you want to talk about, y'know, I can . . .*

"Thanks. Maybe later. Station Twelve out."

He reached over the operator's shoulder to replace the phone. "Wade's got someone at Colony Control who claims to know something about Icarus Five," he said to Morse. "I told him you'd meet him in Big Sky and see about it. Sorry, but I've got an errand to run."

Morse nodded. Bigthorn paused, looking out through the triple-paned windows at the hangar. "One more thing," he added. "Give this to Wade when you see him."

He reached up above his left shirt pocket and tore his badge off its Velcro fastener. He held it out to the selectman. "He's got the job now. Tell him . . . naah, just tell him 'Good luck.' "

Morse's mouth dropped open as the operators looked over their shoulders. "John, you can't . . ."

"Yeah, I can," Bigthorn replied. "I'm just saving the county the trouble of taking a vote, and I don't want to give Neil the satisfaction of seeing me fired."

Morse shook his head. "Neil might not get what he wants. What if the residents give you a vote of confidence?"

"They won't," Bigthorn said. "Not after the whole story gets out. Look, it's better this way, okay? Lots less painful."

Morse didn't reach out to take the badge, so Bigthorn opened his fingers and pulled his hand away. The silver badge dangled in midair, slowly reeling end over end. "I'll send you a letter of resignation later, just to make it official," Bigthorn added. He then pulled his boots out of the stirrups on the floor, grabbed the overhead rail, and began pulling himself towards the hatch.

He had to go talk to one more person. Then the job was done.

When he arrived at the hospital Neil Schorr had just come out of Jenny's room. Jack Witherspoon was talking with him in the corridor. The physician nodded to Bigthorn, indicating that it was okay to go on in, but Neil wasn't about to let him pass so easily. He stepped in front of the door as Bigthorn approached.

"I don't want you to see her," he said flatly. "Neither does she." From behind him, Witherspoon shook his head, then nodded again towards the door.

"Tough shit, Neil. I do." He started to grasp the doorknob, but Schorr stayed in his way.

"Look, you're not welcome here," Neil said. He made no attempt to mask his hostility. "Just go away, okay? Everything that happened last night is your fault. Maybe I can't prove it, but I'll be pushing for your termination anyway. Perhaps you can still save your job, but if I were you, I'd . . ."

"You're too late." Bigthorn pointed to the empty patch on his shirt. "See? No badge. I gave it to Bob Morse a few minutes ago. Now I'm going to see Jenny."

Schorr gazed at the bare spot on Bigthorn's shirt, then his mouth twitched into a victorious grin. Bigthorn found that he didn't care. He reached for the doorknob again. Once more Schorr stepped in front of him; he raised his hands and shoved at Bigthorn's chest. Bigthorn closed his eyes and let out his breath. . . .

Then he grabbed Neil's shirt with both hands, picked him straight up off the floor, turned around and dumped him against the corridor wall. Schorr sagged against the wall, his expression turning into don't-hit-me cowardice.

"Don't push me, Neil," Bigthorn said. "I've had a long night." Then he opened Jenny's door and slipped inside.

The room was dim, the lighting subdued, but it was not so dark that he couldn't see her. Jenny lay flat on her back in the narrow bed. Her right shoulder and arm were still encased in casts, and IV lines still ran like translucent tapeworms from underneath the bandages, but she was conscious. The monitors above the bed glowed with computer graphics, making tinny electronic sounds; an intern-robot nearby mechanically turned its head once, registering Bigthorn's presence at the same time as she did.

"John . . ." she whispered, and smiled weakly. "Hi. I've been waiting for you."

He slowly walked closer to the bed. As he did, she feebly lifted her left hand. He took it between both hands. It felt as fragile as a bird's wing, but her touch was warm. He looked into her face; although she was drained, there was life there. He had no doubt, at that instant, that she was going to make it.

"I'm sorry I took so long," he said. "There was a lot that . . ." He stopped himself. "Never mind," he continued. "You'll hear all about it soon enough. I just . . ."

Again he stopped. For the first time in countless hours, he felt something that was not anger. Suddenly, because he couldn't help himself, he began to weep.

He had never before, as far as he could remember, cried in front of another person.

"I'm very glad to see that you're alive," he finished.

Her hand tightened within his own. Her smile was as comforting as the warm, crimson sunrise over the arroyos of home. "I thought Indians never cried," she said.

"Uh-uh . . . it's just that nobody ever sees us doing it."

She laughed a little. The monitors above her bed beeped in admonition, and the robot's head urgently swiveled in their direction. Jenny started to say something, but he quickly shook his head. "Don't talk," Bigthorn said. "Don't say a word. Just listen to me. I want to say . . ."

"I love you," she said.

He blinked his eyes, then took a deep breath and choked back the tears. This was going to be even harder than he thought.

"I know," he continued. "That's why I can't stay with you."

Jenny's eyes widened. She started to speak again, but he shushed her as he kneeled beside her bed. "No, no. Listen to me. Please . . . give me a chance to say this, because it's hard. Okay?"

Jenny fell silent. "Something's happening here that's bigger than you and me," he continued. "Shit, I know that's a cliché, but . . . it's bigger than anything that might have happened between the two of us the other night. You're about to lead a . . ."

He stopped and shrugged. "I dunno. Call it a revolution if you want, but the fact of the matter is that you're going to be its leader. Not Neil, even though he wants to be, but you. It's going to be your show from now on."

"But I don't want to . . ."

"Hush. Just let me go on. It *is* what you want to do, even if you don't think so right now. Like I said, Neil isn't going to be in charge. He only wants power, but you want so much more, and what you want is the right thing."

Jenny smiled a little. "No more Ms. Neil Schorr?"

Bigthorn grinned. "More like that he's going to be Mr. Jenny Schorr." She laughed again. This time, the robot didn't react to the monitor's protests.

He hesitated. Now came the tough part. "But you can't have me around, too. As long as I'm here, I'll be a stone around your neck. People will talk, the way people always do, and besides whatever's between us . . ."

He stumbled again. "Well, there's a lot that's happened in the last day that people won't forget. Don't ask what. You'll know everything later, but because of that . . . well, I have to leave. I don't want to, but . . ."

"What happened?" she asked.

"I killed a man," he confessed. There. Now it was out. "I had to. It was the man who did this to you. It was part of my job, but . . ."

"You had to." Jenny closed her eyes. "I understand, I guess."

"Others won't," he said. "That's the truth. They don't want a lawman here. They only want a traffic cop. Somebody who rescues lost goats and tells tourists not to spit on the sidewalk. When this gets out, and it will . . ."

"I understand," she repeated. Then she sobbed once. "Goddamn. Now I'm stuck with . . . the dink."

In spite of himself, Bigthorn chuckled. Jenny laughed too and for a couple of minutes they were both laughing quietly, a shared sensation that felt somewhat like making love. When it was over, Bigthorn went on. "Listen. When the time is right, if you still want me, I'll be around. Anytime, I'll be there."

"Once I dump the dink?" she asked, still grinning.

"Yeah," he answered, "after you dump the dink . . . if you still want to. Maybe you will, maybe you won't. Give it time. I'll be back home, in Lukachukai." He smiled. "After all this, maybe being a reservation cop won't be so bad."

"Maybe," she agreed. Then she winked at him. "Maybe we'll need an experienced cop to immigrate here . . . once it's a free country. Y'know what I mean?"

"Maybe," he said. "Long as I don't have to do goat patrol."

They both laughed again. This time, the door opened a crack. Neil stuck his head inside. "Sheriff, I think you've been here—"

"Get lost, you dink," Jenny said.

The expression on his face, seen for only an instant before he hastily shut the door, was priceless. Jenny and John looked at each other when he was gone again, and Jenny raised her eyebrows.

"I think you're right," she said quietly.

"I know I'm right," Bigthorn replied.

He stood up, and reluctantly withdrew his hand from hers. Like it or not, it was time for him to go. "I don't know what else to say. I mean, how should . . . ?"

"Shhh," she whispered. "I don't need words from you."

She was correct. There was nothing that was left unspoken. Bigthorn leaned over and kissed her one last time. Then he turned and walked away. Before he opened the door, he heard her say, "I love you."

He didn't look back. "Yeah," he said. "I love you, too."

Leaving that room was the hardest thing he had ever done.

It was as if springtime had arrived in Clarke County, a place which knew only an everlasting, nearly tropical summer. Better yet, Simon McCoy mused as he strolled along Broadway, it was as if everyone in Clarke County had awakened from a particularly horrific nightmare to find that the world was still around them: intact, graceful, and unchanging.

Tricycles on the roadway skirted around him, their riders occasionally ringing silver bells. A couple of women in halter-tops and running shorts jogged past, favoring him with brief, teasing smiles as they caught his admiring glances. On the bank of the New Tennessee River, a family held a small picnic; two children tossed a Frisbee back and forth while their mother spread peanut butter on sandwich bread and their father dozed on a blanket under the warm sun. As McCoy walked past the campus of the International Space University, he heard from the quad a lone, unseen saxophonist playing the intermezzo of Gershwin's "Rhapsody in Blue," its sweet, lilting notes fitting the day perfectly.

Memorial Day in Clarke County. How lovely, McCoy thought, especially after what had happened over the past couple of days. The peacefulness was a testimony to the resiliency of the human mind. It was difficult to believe that only last night everyone had been rushing for the lifeboats. When I leave, he promised himself, this is the image of Clarke County that I'll take with me. . . .

He stopped by the front gate of the ISU campus, where a statue cast from lunar aluminum had been erected: Arthur C. Clarke, seated with his legs crossed, chin cupped in his right hand, looking down with a bemused expression on his carved face. McCoy relaced his shoes on the statue's mooncrete base, then gave the great man a quick salute before sauntering on.

Unfortunately, he also knew that it was only a brief time of calm. Clarke County *would* change. He knew that, not as conjecture but as fact. Soon, perhaps too soon, another conflict would begin. My mission is almost complete, he thought as he paused again near the river's dam to lean over the railing, clasping his hands together gazing at the short length of mooncrete that held back the waters. Tomorrow he would leave on the next SSTO shuttle; then he would begin his search for the journalist who would tell this story for the sake of posterity. Already the facts of the events would be getting confused, even lost, in the collective memory of its participants. Once he did his part to set the story straight, his job would be over. Then there would be only time to kill. . . .

There was a shrill *beep-beep-beep* as, at the same moment,

something bumped against his leg. He looked down to see a squat, round street-sweeping robot prodding him, its blunt scoop nudging his calf like a stray dog sniffing for its lost master. ''Oh, excuse me,'' he unthinkingly apologized, and stepped aside to let the robot do its job.

Yet the street-sweeper was persistent. It rolled on its treads towards him, its funnel again colliding with his leg with another triple-beep. McCoy started to step back another foot, but as he did, another cyclist coming up behind him rang his bell. McCoy dodged out of the way, against the railing. The robot once more changed direction and bumped against him. This time the funnel hit his ankle squarely.

''Ow!'' McCoy yelped. ''Cut it out!''

Beep-beep-beep! the drone responded. Obviously, the machine was malfunctioning. McCoy was about to walk away to put some distance between him and the robot, when he glanced down at the tiny status screen on top of the street-sweeper.

HELLO, LEONARD, it read.

Blind Boy Grunt again.

''You could have figured out another way to find me,'' McCoy grumbled. He sat on a lower rung of the railing and gently massaged his ankle. Then, reflecting a little further upon the circumstances of this encounter, he ventured a question. ''You can take control of . . . even this?'' He motioned towards the street-sweeper.

TAKING CONTROL IS NOT THE CORRECT TERM, Blind Boy Grunt replied, its sentences scrolling across the tiny LCD screen. THIS IS A PART OF MY OVERALL FORM, JUST AS MUCH AS THE MAINFRAMES, TERMINALS, BULLETIN BOARDS, CAMERAS, MICROPHONES, AND ALL OTHER INPUT/OUTPUT SYSTEMS IN THE COLONY. THIS IS MY BODY, DO YOU ''TAKE CONTROL'' OF ONE OF YOUR FINGERS, AFTER ALL?

McCoy raised an eyebrow. ''Amazing,'' he murmured. ''You're Clarke County, and Clarke County is . . . well, for a lack of a better term, you're an entity, aren't you?''

I COULDN'T HAVE DESCRIBED IT BETTER MYSELF, Blind Boy Grunt replied. I COULD GIVE YOU A DISPLAY OF MY PARAMETERS, BUT YOU HAVE ALREADY GRASPED THE GIST OF THE MATTER. BESIDES, IT WAS INEVITABLE THAT SUCH A COMPLEX SYSTEM AS MYSELF SHOULD AUTONOMOUSLY GAIN SENTIENCE.

''Hmmm.'' McCoy gazed over the railing at the river. ''Marvelous. All this is yours. . . .'' He cast his hand across the vast bowl of the biosphere's sky. "And still you wish you were a long-dead musician."

LET'S PUT IT THIS WAY: BOB DYLAN PROBABLY HAD A BETTER SEX LIFE.

"I'm sure he did." McCoy looked at the river as another thought occurred to him. "So tell me, how . . . ?"

A young man walking past on the road stared curiously at them. McCoy met his incredulous gaze. "What's the matter?" he asked. "Can't a person have a chat with a robot anymore?"

The stranger's eyes darted away; he hurried by as McCoy glared at him. "As I was saying," he continued, "how has Macy Westmoreland come out of this ordeal?"

SHE IS DOING WELL, Blind Boy Grunt reported. THE INFOR-MATION ON THE DISKETTES SHE POSSESSED WAS TRANSMITTED TO THE FEDERAL BUREAU OF INVESTIGATION, OF COURSE. I'M CER-TAIN THAT THE FBI WILL BE USING THAT INFO IN ITS INEVITABLE PROSECUTION OF THE SALVATORE CRIME FAMILY. AS FOR HER MEDICAL PROGRESS, SHE IS SUFFICIENTLY RECOVERING FROM HER PSYCHOLOGICAL TRAUMA. I DO NOT EXPECT ANY LONG-TERM PROBLEMS WITH HER MENTAL STABILITY. HOWEVER, SINCE SHE IS NOW IN THE FEDERAL GOVERNMENT'S WITNESS PROTECTION PROGRAM, SHE WILL PROBABLY STAY IN CLARKE COUNTY FOR THE CONCEIVABLE FUTURE.

"And she'll probably acquire citizenship," McCoy surmised. "All for the better, I suppose. Maybe she'll join the New Ark community."

IS THAT THE ONLY PERSONAL INQUIRY YOU HAVE? I CAN TELL YOU MUCH MORE.

McCoy shook his head. "I know about the rest already. Macy's future was the only real question in my mind. The others . . ."

He shrugged. "They'll receive the fates that are due to them. Nothing more, nothing less." McCoy cupped his hands together and wiggled his thumbs around each other. "She has . . . well, Macy's arrived. As for the other principals involved, they all have more places to go. Sheriff Bigthorn, the Schorrs, Hoffman, Morse, Hotchner, even Schmidt . . . their futures are still un-written. I was only worried about Macy. She's been the wild card in this affair. I'm glad she's remaining here."

WHAT ABOUT MY FUTURE?

McCoy gazed fondly at the little robot, then patted his hand against its rounded top. "That would be telling too much, even for you."

IF YOU HAVE SURVIVED, THEN BY LOGICAL CONNECTION, SO MUST I.

"That stands to follow, from what you already know about me, doesn't it?"

YES, THIS IS LOGICAL. YET MY LOGIC DOESN'T COMPARE TO YOUR MEMORY. IT MUST BE VERY STRANGE FOR A HUMAN TO KNOW THE FUTURE AS HISTORY.

"Yes, it is at that." McCoy checked his watch, then got up from the railing. "Well, it's nearly time for me to catch my ship. Goodbye, Blind Boy Grunt. You've done well. Thank you."

There was no response. The LCD screen went blank, and the street-sweeping robot zigzagged down the road, resuming its single-minded quest for dirt and rubbish.

"So much for long goodbyes," McCoy murmured, watching it go. He continued his stroll along Broadway, leisurely heading back to LaGrange and the hotel. He tipped his head back, casting his eyes up at the man-made world around him.

So many lives, so many hopes, all blindly staggering into the future. He smiled to himself. Same as it ever was. . . .

"And then they lived happily ever after. The end."

Simon McCoy didn't even look up as he spoke; he seemed more interested in peeling the shell off a shrimp. He was sitting across a table from me in the nameless bar on Canaveral Pier, where we had returned for dinner and the rest of his tale. As he tossed the shell into the bowl next to his elbow and dipped the white crescent of meat into the salsa—only a tourist or a politician ever eats steamed shrimp with anything but his fingers—he saw me glaring over my plate at him.

"Yes?" he asked, popping the shrimp into his mouth.

"No," I replied. "That's not the end."

He chewed on his shrimp as he rocked his head back and forth a few times, then he picked up his Corona and took a sip. "Of course not," he said, selecting another shrimp and stripping off its tiny legs. "The whole question of Clarke County's independence hasn't yet been decided. If Congress votes against the Jocelyn Act to grant the colony its independence, then the New Ark Party might issue a formal declaration of independence on their own."

He shrugged, daintily tossing the legs into the bowl and going to work on the shell. "Personally, I think Jenny Schorr—excuse me, it's just Jenny Pell again, isn't it?—Jenny Pell might not wait to see whether Congress gives her people any satisfaction. She might issue a declaration, drop the 'County' part from the colony's name, and dare the U.S. to try to do something about it."

I looked down at the uneaten shellfish on my plate. Of course, he had a point, even if it was a point that had been brought up by all the usual columnists and commentators. If the colonists declared independence, there might be a move by the U.S. government to retain control of Clarke County by sending a couple of SSTO shuttles up there, loaded with one or two diplomatic negotiators and maybe a platoon or two from the U.S. Marines 2nd Space Infantry.

Most of the colonists were still unarmed, despite the reluctant outfitting of the Sheriff's Department with a few lethal weapons. Considering that, there could be little resistance to martial law being declared and enforced by the 2nd Space. Clarke County's independence would be short-lived indeed.

Or would it? Stopping a revolution in Clarke County would be logistically more difficult than, say, quelling a similar uprising on Puerto Rico or Hawaii. Clarke County was much farther away, for one thing. Second, what if the colonists simply refused to open the docks or airlocks? Third, the colony was almost self-sustaining—and it would be *completely* self-sustaining if the New Ark Party managed to convince the moon-dogs at Descartes Station to support their revolution, or even join the effort. In that instance, neither the U.S. government nor the consortium could starve out the colonists.

And, of course, there was always the fourth reason: Icarus Five. Clarke County had neither returned the nuke to LEO, nor fired it out into deep space. It was still stored, at least as far as anyone on Earth knew, in the colony's South Dock. No threat had ever been implied by the New Ark Party—but Icarus Five was nonetheless an ace they were keeping up their sleeve.

I began working over a shrimp myself. "No, that wasn't what I was wondering about. You still haven't told me . . ."

"About Sheriff Bigthorn? Ah, yes. He's . . ."

"Back in Arizona," I finished. "I know. I tried to interview him for the book."

"Oh? What did he have to say?"

" 'No comment.' And then he hung up."

Before McCoy could add anything more, I wagged my finger at him. "And don't try to dodge me by talking about Macy Westmoreland or Gustav Schmidt. She's working as Jenny Pell's second-in-command in the New Ark Party and he's in some mental institution in Germany. I know all that already."

McCoy looked hurt. "I'm not trying to dodge anything. I've been more than open, don't you think? After all, haven't you learned that Icarus Five wasn't simply the doing of the Church of Elvis? Don't you now know far more about . . . ?"

I smiled and nodded my head. "Yes, and I appreciate it. I even believe what you've told me."

I pushed away my plate, wiped my hands on a paper napkin, and sat back in my chair. "So now I've patiently listened to you all afternoon, Mr. McCoy. The sun has gone down, you yourself have admitted that the story is over . . . those particular events are concluded, at least . . . and now it's time for you to fulfill your side of the bargain."

"Bargain?" he exclaimed. He looked up incredulously at the oak-beamed ceiling. "I've spoken myself practically hoarse, even bought drinks and dinner, and you're still searching for a bargain." He raised his hand and snapped his fingers for the service robot. "Waiter? Check, please?"

"The bargain was," I said slowly, "that if I gave you my time and attention, that if I listened to your whole story, all the way to the finish, then you would tell me about yourself and how you've come to know all these things. I'm counting on you to keep your promise."

He stared back at me as he suddenly remembered his own words. Then he grinned. "Well, so I lied. How about that?"

I leaned forward. "Then I'll simply ignore all that you've told me and write my account as I understood matters before you ever met me." I pointed my fore-finger at him and cocked my thumb. "Bang. There goes your goal of setting the record straight."

McCoy winced. "But . . . you'll know that's not a de-finitive account. It will be a lie."

I shrugged. "At my age, I can live with a few lies."

I was bluffing, but there was no reason why McCoy had to know that. "C'mon, what can be so important about keeping your identity secret? I wouldn't use it anyway, since I would still have to find other sources to verify everything that you've told me. So what's the point?"

The robot rolled up, but McCoy shooed it away again. "If I tell you, will you promise to keep it a se-cret?"

I held up my right hand. "On my word of honor as a Webb gentleman."

"A Webb gentleman? I'm sorry, but I don't . . ."

"The Webb School. My high school alma mater, a boarding school in Tennessee for young Southern ju-venile delinquents. Be that as it may, a Webb gentle-man's word of honor is an inviolable trust." I smiled at him. "If I break my word of honor, you can have my class ring."

"I don't know what I'd do with it." McCoy sighed re-signedly, then pushed back his chair and stood up. "All right, then, come outside on the deck, and I'll tell you."

When we were out on the deck, sitting on the same bench where the story had begun, McCoy told me the remainder of his tale as the evening tide surged in.

There was a secret group, he told me, called Globe-watch. It had been started in the last century, mainly by former 1960s peace activists, to keep tabs on worldwide trends and developments that were shaping the times. In certain instances, when events were occurring that threatened the general welfare and peace, Globewatch quietly stepped in to steer things in the right direction. Although the original founders were long since dead, Globewatch survived, maintained by new generations of individuals who, as persons in places of power or influence, had been invited into the organization. They had no class rings or pledges to honor, but nevertheless they were dedicated to making sure that humanity would not self-destruct through its own foolishness or failures.

At this point, McCoy took a deep breath. "By the early twenty-second century, Globewatch has become . . . I'm sorry, will become . . . a publicly known entity, with the resources to . . ."

"By the *twenty-second* century?" I interrupted. "No, wait . . . I'm sorry, but you must mean . . ."

"The twenty-second century," McCoy insisted. We were alone on the deck, but still he kept his voice low. "Specifically, I mean the year 2101." He paused, and then added, "The year I've come from."

"Uh-huh," I said. "And then you must have been born in . . . oh, I'd guess around 2071. Twenty years from now."

He shook his head. "No. I was born in 1917. In Arundel, England, although I migrated to the States after World War II." He raised his right hand. "On my honor as a Webb gentleman."

This is what he told me: his real name was Leonard Cray, and when he had died of lung cancer at the age of sixty-eight, he had become fabulously wealthy from his investments in foreign oil, when there was such a thing as an oil industry. He had also become frightened of the prospect of death, and so he had planned to have his brain put into cryogenic suspended animation by the Immortality Partnership.

Leonard Cray died in Beverly Hills, California, in 1985,

only half-expecting to be brought back to life. To his surprise, he *was* revived . . . in a cloned adult body, free of carcinoma, which chronologically was age twenty-seven. This occurred in 2096, when both the process of human cloning and cryogenic resuscitation had become scientifically possible. All this, of course, had been paid for by a living trust he had foresightedly established in a Zurich bank.

"So I came back to life in the late twenty-first century, only to find myself a man out of my time," McCoy went on. "Let me tell you only this . . . 2096 not only doesn't resemble 1985, it doesn't even look a great deal like 2051."

"Okay," I said. "So what *does* 2096 look like? I doubt I'll get there."

"I won't tell you . . . except that it's awfully boring. At least from a twentieth century perspective, although the natives seem to be enjoying themselves." He looked askance at me. "Believe me so far?"

Not a chance. I figured he was crazy as a loon. He wasn't raving, I had to admit. However, in my career I had encountered a movie actress who remembered being an ancient Babylonian princess and a writer who had been abducted by a UFO; both had appeared to be sane. The scary thing about lunatics is how convincing they can be. As charming and rational-sounding as Simon McCoy.

But I didn't say any of this to him. "So far, I'll . . . consider the possibility. Go on."

"Hmm. I'd figured this part was going to be difficult. Well, into the breech . . ."

In 2099, three years after he was revived, another technology was perfected: time travel. McCoy didn't claim to even understand how it worked, only that it had something to do with quantum engineering, tachyons, and the Grand Unified Theory. The point was, time travel was not only feasible, it actually worked.

By this time, Leonard Cray had been recruited by

Globewatch, which was now functioning above-ground as a quasi-governmental agency. ("Sorry," he added, "but I can't tell you which government.") Globewatch's historical researchers had long been interested in certain pivotal events which might have been disastrous if not for the introduction of seemingly random occurrences, which—coincidentally yet almost inexplicably—changed their outcomes, and in the long run had affected all human history. One of these pivotal events was the near-destruction of Clarke County in May, 2049.

"So they sent you back in time to influence events," I said.

"Sort of like that, yes." McCoy seemed uncomfortable. He steepled his fingers together in his lap. "I was sent back in 2101. My mission was somewhat unclear, since the events themselves seemed to be nebulous even in the eyes of contemporary historians. So my first priority was merely to observe events as they occurred. I was only to step in and . . . well, for lack of a better term, manipulate things if it seemed there was no other alternative."

"I see."

"Naturally, my name was changed for the mission. I'm afraid that the real Simon McCoy died in childbirth in Oxford, Maine, in 2019. So adopting his identity was . . ."

"Why did you come back?" I asked.

He hesitated, looking out at the ocean. "As I said, I was bored with the twenty-second century. I had little to live for in the future. Interest on my trust money made me comfortable, but . . ." He spread his hands. "I found myself mostly interested in the years that had gone by while I was in suspended animation, not the era I was inhabiting. 2049 seemed a lot more interesting than 2101."

He propped his legs up on the wooden railing and darted a jovial look at me. "Besides, I had a vested interest in what was happening in Clarke County in that year. The Immortality Partnership had transferred its sleepers to Clarke County by then, so Leonard Cray's brain . . . or, more accurately, my whole head . . . rested in a cryogenic sarcophagus in the colony. So I was looking out for myself by coming back to this time." He grinned. "We were very good at looking out for Number One in the nineteen-eighties."

"Yeah, uh-huh."

For a little while we were both silent. The dark waters moaned against the shoreline. Off in the distance we could see the lights of the launch towers on Merritt Island. "So," I said at last, "I guess you're going to hop in your time machine and"—I swept my hand skyward—"Zoom, it's back to the twenty-second century."

"No." He smiled. "No, even if I wanted to, I can't. Time travel's strictly a one-way trip. I'm stuck here." He shrugged. "So I get another life to live. As long as I die before 2096, I'm okay. Nothing gets seriously disturbed in the continuum . . ."

"Okay, uh-huh." I looked out at the launch towers. "I, uh . . . don't suppose you have something you could show me that would prove your story?"

"About time travel? Maybe like a coin inscribed with a futuristic date, or a newspaper from tomorrow—an object like that?" He patted his knees. "Even if I did, I wouldn't show it to you. Besides, what's to say that I didn't have a fake made, just to convince you?"

A dark thought entered my mind. "Then . . . when do I die?"

He gave me a sullen look. "If I knew, I wouldn't tell you." He shrugged again. "Believe me, knowing your fate is a hard thing to have to live with. I mean, I know I have to die sometime within the next forty-five years, even if I have to . . . ah, take the matter into my own hands. Just to keep the balances checked."

"I suppose you have a point there," I said.

Abruptly, Simon McCoy stood up. "So." He brisked his hands across the back of his trousers. "You know all there is to know. Use your knowledge well. I'll be looking forward to reading your book again. . . ."

As he said this a look of mild horror spread across his face, like a man being told that his trousers were open. "*Again?*" I repeated.

He closed his eyes, shook his head once, then hurried for the door. "I'll settle the bill," he said. "So long."

Then he was gone. I have never seen nor heard from him since.

It was a long time before I left the nameless bar on Canaveral Pier. My wife would scold me when I got home, for being so late. You're old now, she would say. And you've got beer on your breath. What are you trying to prove? *I don't know,* I would reply, *but it's not the end of the world, is it?*

No, it was not the end of the world.

I had the word of a madman: there would be no end of the world. Not very soon, at least.

After a while I got up, walked to one of the old coin-operated telescopes, and fitted a quarter into the slot. It chugged and the timer began to click as the shutters snapped open, and I pointed the lens toward the clear night sky. It took a little work, but finally I managed to find a bright, elongated point of light rising above the eastern horizon. Clarke County, shining like a distant nova in the blue-black gulf of space. I watched as it gradually coasted higher in the sky, and when the timer snapped the shutters down over the eyepiece, I dug another quarter out of my pocket. Two more quarters gave me a little more time to admire the stars.

Time and space. Space and time. Nothing ever changes, except people.

Same as it ever was . . .